Cold Water and Stone

P Nolan

* CHAPTER ONE *

The Lighthouse

'Just keep the fire burning, but stay away,' pounded young Ralph Devereux's thoughts, when he ate his supper of fish, milk and bread.

'Just keep the fire burning, but stay away,' rang in his ears, when he practised his sword skills.

'Just keep the fire burning, but stay away,' seeped through his head, when he studied his Latin text of ancient Rome.

A boy's day is busy, and many thoughts pull at his mind. Later, as Ralph sat at his table examining the faded lines and smudged text of an ancient map of DunFaythe peninsula, he pushed his fingers through his thick curly brown hair and suddenly noticed the reddening stains of sunburn on his stretched thin arms. Red ... hot ...burn ...FIRE! He jumped up from the table, leaving behind the wrinkled parchment.

'The fire! ...The fire! ... Pádraig Bocht will be waiting ... Father will be -'

Ralph raced down the stone steps of the tower, on the north side of the courtyard. His tightly fitted linen breeches reached to his knees, hampering his stride. Beads and bubbles and snail trails of sweat dripped from his forehead and down his neck. When he reached the door at the fifty-second step, he shoved it open, trying not to slow down. Finding it difficult to sprint on the shiny, polished floor, he lost balance and almost bear-hugged old Alesia, who was collecting the remains of a meal from a wide wooden table.

'Someday that fire will go out,' she muttered, through her two teeth, 'and look at you, thin as a stick. How will you ever become a Lord Devereux?'

'Not today,' shouted Ralph, crashing through a curtain onto a stone-floored corridor overlooking the courtyard of DunFaythe castle 'The fire will not go out today.'

Passing a tall window he glanced down into the castle courtyard and saw the local Irish selling their farm produce of eggs, chickens, barley, wheat and calves or goats to anyone who would buy them. It was mid August and DunFaythe Castle in fourteenth century Ireland was the centre of commerce for the locality.

He found Meave, his twin sister, seated on a low bench, wearing a full-length dress, vertically divided into stripes of blue and yellow, playing with a black bundle of a tomcat, a present she had received from Old Alesia for her fourteenth birthday, two weeks previously. An embroidered silk girdle encircled her waist.

'C'mon Meave,' he shouted, as he sped past her. 'Let's keep the fire burning.'

Meave, who was enjoying the spectacle of the market through a window of the castle, stood up and unhitched the tomcat from her dress. She was as tall as Ralph was, same dark hair combed in plaits to her shoulders, like the Irish. Her nose, which she was very aware of, was quite long. She smiled when she heard Ralph, and the whiteness of her teeth matched the pool of ivory surrounding her deep charcoal eyes. Her lips although not as full as Ralph's were slightly raised and coupled with high cheekbones and a strong chin, marked her as royalty.

Most times when Ralph came running with an urgent mission, she ignored him and let him swish past her. Ralph ran and talked, so Meave usually understood the first part of the message and heard the last few words as an echo or a low whisper. This time however, she heard the words "fire" and "burning" as Ralph whizzed past her, and she knew she had to go and help him. Keeping the fire burning was very important so she followed him down the long corridor, skipping between shadows, columns and shafts of sunlight, past wide framed paintings of her ancestors – horrible people with silly hats, crooked noses and black glazed eyes, who never smile and who stare, keeping their secrets and looking angry. Nonetheless, this was her favourite place, her castle within a castle.

Meave and Ralph arrived at the animal stockade below the castle walls.

'Hurry up,' urged Ralph, untying a donkey from one of the columns, supporting the terrace that surrounded the enclosure, as he cast his eyes over the contents of the cart fettered to the animal.

'Let's go Nell,' he shouted at the donkey, and he jumped on the cart, grabbing the reins, followed by Meave.

Meave struggled to make herself comfortable among the sacks on the cart. Nell turned her head towards the children. She was enjoying the sun, and the last thing she wanted to do was pull a cart, two children and heavy sacks to the beach. The donkey struggled to draw her load towards the castle gate, her hooves making a slipping, scraping sound on the cobbled corral.

'I would be quicker carrying them myself,' moaned Ralph, looking up at the sun and feeling sticky sweat drip down his back.

'C'mon, you silly donkey, we have to keep the fire burning,' he urged.

4

Meave smiled, slipped one of her long arms into a sack, moved it about, jumped out of the cart and ran her hand along Nell's wiry coat and then cuddled the donkey's ear in her hand.

'There you are old girl,' she whispered, holding two carrots in front of Nell.

She then looked at Ralph, twitched her nose and jumped back onto the cart beside him.

'Let's go Nell,' she said.

Nell, chewing the carrots moved briskly, pulling her cart toward the castle gate. As they moved through the castle gate, Meave kept a wary eye on a group of soldiers standing in battle formation, dressed in their full armour. Ralph saw only their flowing cloaks and shiny weapons and wished he was a soldier himself.

When they reached the track to the beach, Ralph shivered, feeling the chill breeze of the sea against his sweaty tunic. Meave, however, enjoyed the cool draught.

The party rumbled and rattled along the track towards the beach. Meave knew that the nearby DunFaythe Lighthouse, balancing on a mound of perfectly square rocks, had an important influence on her father's life. The eight-hundred-year-old lighthouse overlooked the Celtic Sea, the white beach of Trá Bán stretching for miles on either side of it. Just as they reached the beach the cart slowed down, as Nell found it difficult to pull her passengers and load through the sand of Trá Bán, covering the track. Ralph's heart beat faster, and to his left he could clearly see the huge weather battered tower balancing on the cut rocks. He wondered where the rocks had come from – who cut them? – who carved them?

Out to sea white foam sprayed and splashed on jagged reefs, jutting out to defy any ship to approach land. Several boats slept on the beach, their nets spread out on the sand, resting before their toil began. Despite the bright sun, a flame could be seen spitting from the top of the lighthouse. The gentle hands of the sea wind shaped the black smoke surging from the lighthouse into a long curling snake. Meave could smell the dry stench blowing along the beach.

'The lighthouse fire is burning hot,' she said, covering her mouth with her long fingers.

'Tis,' replied Ralph, not concerned with the smoke, but wishing that one-day he could climb to the top. He tried to focus his eyes on the dark figure, standing at the lighthouse door.

'We'll walk from here and try to drag the sacks along the sand. Nell will never pull the cart. The sand is too soft,' he said, jumping from the cart.

'Will Pádraig Bocht help us?' asked Meave, squinting to try and see him.

'You know he doesn't stray from the rocks or the lighthouse,' answered Ralph.

They pulled a sack from the cart and dragged it along the sand towards the lighthouse. Ralph's nostrils widened with the familiar smell of fish – the aroma was always there, even in winter. Meave also wondered about the odour that was always in the air at the rocks, even though Pádraig Bocht never fished. She knew that the sacks contained small pieces of wood or kindling to restart the lighthouse fire in the event of a sudden rain shower, but she could never figure out why Pádraig Bocht needed so many supplies of cheese, chicken, carrots, buttermilk and bread. Vessels of oil, wrapped in goatskins, to keep the torches alight in the lighthouse were placed in the neck of each sack. Pádraig Bocht also needed rolls of parchment and writing quills. These were carried in a small linen bag and were usually the first items that he looked for. He spent all his days tending the lighthouse and writing. Meave loved to study, but she never read or even saw anything that Pádraig Bocht had written.

As they struggled closer with the sack towards the lighthouse, Meave spotted the figure at the top of the stone stairway that lead to the lighthouse door.

'Wouldn't you think he would help us,' she moaned.

'Never leaves the rocks,' repeated Ralph, coughing and feeling a bit dizzy, as he tasted the smell of fish and inhaled the swirling smoke. 'He is The Guardian of DunFaythe Lighthouse, father would punish him if he left. Do you know he calls father Colclough the Red? They say he and father fought many wars together years ago.'

'I don't care how many wars he has fought. I have heard so many different stories. They are all just silly tales. Anyway, he should help us with the sacks,' replied Meave, pulling her plaited hair across her sullen face and feeling her eyes burn hot.

Ralph could now plainly see the tall, thin figure, his green eyes pasted into socket holes stared at the children. His hawk nose dropped over his thin twisted dry lips and his yellow brown skin stretched along his bony face like a two-day-old corpse. A thin strip of black hair covered his pointed chin. Bronze buttons fastened his grey tunic from foot to neck. He wore a green hooded cloak, hiding an enormous broad sword balanced around his midriff.

6

He was barefooted. They groaned and moaned about Pádraig Bocht, as they struggled with the sack towards the lighthouse rocks.

'Can you help us Pádraig Bocht?' Ralph shouted. It was the same ritual each day when they came with the sacks.

'*Fan Noiméad.* Wait a moment,' roared Pádraig Bocht, skipping down the stairway from the lighthouse.

He often spoke in Irish and then repeated himself in English and the twins weren't sure why.

'*Táim ag teacht.* I'm coming.'

He took five giant steps and then towered over Meave and Ralph. While opening and closing his thin dirty fingers, he reached down and effortlessly picked up the sack. Ralph looked for the medallion that always hung from the chain on his sword belt. The medallion had four circles cut into it, each circle inside the other. Pádraig Bocht saw him staring at it. A flicker of a grin crossed his lips

'We are thirsty and hot … need a drink. Meave is not feeling well ... smoke is making her weak,' said Ralph, studying the medallion.

Meave wondered what Ralph was up to as a sore cough rose in her chest.

The last thing she wanted to do was stay in the smoke. They never stayed; they never went into the lighthouse. Her father's words echoed in her ears too. ''Just keep the fire burning, but stay away.''

Pádraig Bocht's eyes narrowed and a hint of a smile exposed his yellow teeth.

'*Tar liom.* Follow me,' and he adjusted the sack on his shoulder and swaggered up the steps to the door of the lighthouse.

'Let's go,' cried Ralph, bursting to see inside the lighthouse, the fire, the tower and the view from the top. Slow burning oak trees fuelled the lighthouse fire. They arrived by wagon every two weeks and were stacked in mounds at the far side of the lighthouse rocks. He remembered his father had once said: ''On a fine day you can see Wales from the top.''

Meave stood still, her arms hanging limp, her mouth open, smoky tears running down her cheeks.

'I'm not coming,' she whispered, staring at the sand.

'It's our chance,' urged Ralph, his bright eyes widening.

She knew his mind was racing, and she was waiting for his legs to start running. She often wondered how Ralph, with his thin frame and long arms, could have so much stamina. She thought of her father Lord Colclough Devereux and could see the similarity in Ralph's features, an elongated face with full royal lips and a high intelligent brow. Yet his eyes, unlike his fathers were always dancing in their sockets as if trying to scrutinise every feature or colour or shape of rocks or animals. Often he walked around in his bare feet to cool down. He slept only when he was exhausted. One day, she guessed he would get himself into serious trouble.

Pádraig Bocht reached the rusty door of the lighthouse then turned and faced the children. A huge yellow-toothed grin formed on his face. His nose receded into his forehead like a yawning lion.

'*An bhfuil sibh ag teacht?* Are ye coming?' he teased.

Ralph needed no urging. He skipped up the stone stairway and stood beside Pádraig Bocht. Meave reluctantly followed. Ralph soaked in the lighthouse, the door, the fire and Pádraig's medallion, as he stood gaping up at his host.

Meave's face tightened; she saw evil in the lighthouse and malice and pain in Pádraig Bocht's yellow smile. She wished that she was back in her safe castle, with her tomcat and her noisy Irish market. This was a sinister world, a cold world. Meave edged her way up the steps towards Pádraig Bocht. Pádraig Bocht's long fingers pushed against the rusty orange door. Ralph spotted markings etched on the metal, similar to those on Pádraig Bocht's medallion. He also noticed shapes that looked like different phases of the moon. The door opened with a groan, a creak and a blast of stale foul air, inviting them into the world of DunFaythe Lighthouse. Pádraig Bocht's long frame filled the entrance.

'*An bhealach seo.* This way,' he growled, stepping inside the lighthouse.

Ralph could almost taste the smell of fish , he followed Pádraig Bocht into a circular chamber.

Spotting a staircase to his left, climbing in the direction of the lighthouse fire, he hoped that he would get a chance to climb to the top of the lighthouse. To his surprise he also saw steps under a large map on the wall, tunnelling into the ground. He was curious about what could be under the lighthouse, and wished he could explore the stairwell. Quivering with excitement and anticipation he guessed it might lead to stolen treasure. Pádraig Bocht pointed to a wooden table in the centre of the room, chock-full with plates and pots filled with bread and cheese.

'*Suígí ansin.* Sit there,' he snapped, pulling over two small stools.

Meave, despite her nervous state, was fascinated by the drawings on the rough wall of the lighthouse. The drawings looked like a large map of the earth and planets with lines connecting them and numbers and letters linking them. There were images of a full moon, first quarter, last quarter, stars and the sun. The blue hue of the walls changed to white then yellow and finally red, as she followed the images. Below the paintings on the wall were shelves, presses and containers of maps, documents and pictures of strange ships or carts. Some of the documents were open where they rested, others were neatly coiled and many were worn and torn from usage and study. Her attention was drawn to a small drawing of the full moon on the lighthouse wall, with dates and times scrawled across it. She noticed a window opening to the sea and was amazed at how thick the walls of the lighthouse were. She saw that the floor was covered with dry seaweed.

They sat on small uncomfortable stools whilst Pádraig Bocht opened a cupboard and clattered and banged for a few moments.

'*Sea, seo iad*. Yes, here they are,' he said, taking out two small cylindrical shaped earthen vessels and placing them on the table in front of the children.

'Your destiny is here Young Red. Drink to your destiny,' he said, pointing to the vessels.

Meave placed her trembling fingers around a vessel.

'Your sister is afraid, she thinks I'm the devil incarnate. But you want to know more. You have your father's eyes, your father's questions. Drink! Drink!' urged Pádraig Bocht, leaning against the table.

Ralph picked up the vessel and placed it to his lips, closed his eyes and let the liquid drop onto his tongue then waited for a bitter taste. The sweet flavour washed around his mouth, down his throat, through his tired arms and weary legs. He opened his eyes.

'Yes!' said Pádraig Bocht. 'Every cloud has a window to the sun.'

Meave turned to Ralph, who was sitting upright and alert.

'I … will not … drink it!' she said, shaking her head.

'Drink it, Meave,' cried Ralph then gulped down another mouthful. 'It's a magical refreshing drink.'

He was not afraid. His father was lord of the castle. No one would dare harm him. Pádraig Bocht turned and stepped over to the window, cradling his medallion in his hand.

'Your time is soon Young Red,' he said, looking out of the window at the mounds of oak trees piled below the lighthouse. 'And you Madam may someday know another world.'

'What do you mean?' asked Meave. 'What world? … Where? … What are all these images? … What are all these drawings? … Who painted them? …Who created the maps? … What is the - '

'Just a moment young lady. I see you also have many questions.' answered Pádraig Bocht. 'I'm The Guardian of the lighthouse. Future generations will continue searching until the knowledge is found.'

'What knowledge?' gulped Ralph.

'Do ye want to see the fire?' whispered Pádraig Bocht, ignoring the question, his eyes darkening. 'I know Ralph does.'

Ralph nodded his head.

'Of course.'

'*Tar liom.* Follow me,' grunted Pádraig Bocht and then disappeared up the winding stone steps of the lighthouse. Ralph jumped up, knocked over his stool and followed the Guardian. Meave was now feeling a little more confident after bravely asking her questions.

'*Another world ... Where? ...When?*' she asked herself, standing up from her stool and glancing around at the drawings on the wall before hurrying towards the stairway. Meave often listened to the locals telling stories about sea people but could never understand all of them; she loved their tales of heroes and heroines and savoured their language. *Bó* for cow and *bainne* for milk often limped off her tongue as, she tried to master the accent and dialect.

Steps worn from thousands of footfalls forced themselves up through the ancient walls, turning, turning until they reached the summit of the lighthouse; steps stained with dust and grains of yellow seaweed. As he climbed the winding staircase Ralph noticed to his right solid wooden doors with more moon shapes carved into them. He followed Pádraig Bocht through the open door at the top of the stairs and strained his neck to look up at the spitting flames of the lighthouse fire, belching out black clouds of burning smoke. The flaming oak timbers nested in an iron basket, supported by four tall black marble legs that Ralph guessed were three times his height. A low wall surrounded the legs of the furnace. Ralph walked along a narrow passage between the marble legs and the sea wall of the lighthouse that reached to his chest and had several vertical openings, allowing him to view the expanse of the Celtic Sea.

'*Be curamach.* Be careful,' warned Pádraig Bocht, touching the cold stone of the sea wall. 'It's a long drop to the sea.'

Ralph's eyes focused on the angry rocks out to sea and imagined ships crashing and breaking up on them. Meave reached the top of the stone stairway and walked around the narrow passageway, feeling the heat of the fire above her. Looking through one of the vertical openings in the lighthouse wall she saw DunFaythe peninsula stretched out before her with the blue rolling sea on either side.

'Look!' she said, raising her arm. 'There is DunFaythe Castle.'

Her eyes scanned the green brown earth with its winding road north. Looking down on the proud castle surrounded by tilled rectangular fields, she saw toy people in a toy market. The roaring lighthouse fire and Pádraig Bocht were behind her, a magical world in front of her. Ralph hopped over to her side.

'The market is still on,' he gasped, gulping in every detail of the view.

His eyes followed every little lane and track on the green map before him. His attention was drawn to a narrow string of dark earth drawn on the terrain below him that started at the castle, stopped at a hedgerow and continued at the far side, crossing three fields and making a sharp turn south. He guessed it was an old path, as it curled and twisted through several meadows and then stopped suddenly at the beach directly in front of the lighthouse. Pádraig Bocht sauntered up beside Meave and placed his bony, stained fingers on her shoulder. She shivered, feeling a cold dampness through her light dress.

'Devereux land as far as the eye can see,' he said, pointing north, in the direction of the peninsula. Pointing to mountains to the west, he said, 'Radford land.'

Meave felt a tingle of pride. Pádraig Bocht was her father's man, her father's soldier, her father's lighthouse guardian. But she feared him. He was Irish and had knowledge and secrets that could endanger them all. She was of Norman descent and believed that the Irish had a mystical view of the world, that they knew magic, and their stories had a strange sense of truth about them.

The sun blazed; the fire blazed. Ralph's mind was bursting with questions. He was thinking about the steps leading down from Pádraig Bocht's room and was wondering about the markings on the doors that he had seen on his way up the stairs.

'May we go down below the lighthouse?' he asked

'You're not ready. Time to go,' answered Pádraig Bocht, moving his medallion from finger to finger.

Meave relaxed. She did not want to enter another world of mystery and heat. Not today anyway. It was time to go back to her tomcat. Ralph turned to walk down the steps and return to the beach.

'Your time will come soon,' whispered Pádraig Bocht, as he moved past Ralph and ghosted down the stone stairway.

Ralph looked at Meave, his face white, his lips dry. Then he followed Pádraig Bocht, as if a rope was pulling him.

'Wait for me,' she cried, running after him.

Ralph reached the bottom of the stairway, but Pádraig Bocht was nowhere to be seen. Meave rushed down the stairway, not wanting to be left alone with the lighthouse fire, slipped on the last step and crashed into Ralph. He reached out and prevented her from falling, remained silent and walked out of the lighthouse and down the steps to the beach. She ran and caught up with him.

'What ... did he whisper to you?' she asked, panting.

'He said my time will come soon,' answered Ralph, without slowing his pace or looking at her. 'The maps, the drawings, the moon shapes, the fire, something is going to happen soon. Have you seen how worried father has been lately?'

'He often stares at the lighthouse for hours at night time,' replied Meave, trying to keep up with Ralph's quick steps.

'Is he waiting for something or somebody to arrive?' asked Ralph, stopping and looking back at the lighthouse.

Ralph remembered his father telling him several years ago that their mother had died from the plague on a visit to Wales. Since then his father, of the huge hairy face with his curly red beard and the once clear blue eyes and wide shovel hands had turned into an unhappy, slow moving, stooped giant. Ralph often heard him whispering to himself, standing on the castle battlements in the moonlight and staring at the lighthouse fire. Many times Lord Devereux had said to Ralph,

"If the fire goes out, ships will be wrecked on the rocks; we will lose our trade, our wine, our horses and they will come. The horror will begin!"

Ralph always remembered why he had to keep the lighthouse fire burning. He often asked who would come. His father always refused to answer that question

* CHAPTER TWO *

Meave and Ralph

When Meave and Ralph returned from the lighthouse they decided not tell their father about their encounter with Pádraig Bocht. But as the days passed, Ralph was filled with a gripping unease. Eventually he related their tale to Lord Devereux, who roared with fury,

'You are both forbidden to enter the lighthouse again! Soldiers will bring what is needed to Pádraig Bocht from this day forward.' His eyes swelled, and his arms shook.

'The captain of the cavalry will take responsibility for keeping the fire burning,' beads of perspiration glistened on his brow. He paused for a few moments stroking his beard and then placed his hand on Ralph's shoulder.

'Do not disobey me, Ralph. It's for your own safety and the future of the Devereux line.'

Ralph was disappointed and tried to explain.

'But Father! - '

'Enough!' replied Lord Devereux, and he left Ralph standing alone in the Great Hall of DunFaythe Castle.

Ralph knew his father's word was law. He had dominion over vast lands. Many Irish chieftains and Norman dukes paid homage to him. He never demanded taxes or tributes. Each of his vassals had sworn to keep five thousand soldiers ready to defend their lord. Often when Lord Devereux had drunk too much wine he would roar, 'I can raise an army of sixty thousand to drive them back!'

August passed, a beautiful season of plentiful harvest and happy days of horse riding, sailing and outdoor banquets. Each evening Ralph stood on the battlements and looked out at the lighthouse, wondering about Pádraig Bocht and the drawings on the walls of his lighthouse chamber. Often he imagined that the crows, the swallows and the grazing cattle were watching and waiting. Other times when he was on Trá Bán, he saw fishermen staring at Pádraig Bocht standing on the rocks and then turning their nodding heads towards the sea.

Summer's death began with a cold north breeze gently blowing over DunFaythe peninsula and winter crept up on DunFaythe Castle like a dark silent stranger. The castle never slept; the forges burned, churning out swords, spears, arrows and armour, born from the raw iron ore imported from the midland kingdoms. The blacksmiths never spoke about using their creations, hoping that the day would never come.

One winter's evening Ralph stood on the castle ramparts watching the cold moonlit sea reflecting the lighthouse fire. The raw granite tiles numbed his feet, as he listened to the echo of the waves dying on Trá Bán. Frosty diamonds of moonlight sparkled on the castle walls. He felt a deep sense of unease and neither torches of oil and wicker, mounted on the battlement nor his thick warm cloak offered solace to his discomfort. Each time he moved or blinked a chill ran through him. He thought of his mother and images of a pale flawless face framed by threads of golden hair drifted into his mind. Every time he tried to focus on the image it faded away.

'Ah! There you are Ralph,' a voice bellowed from the darkness.

Ralph turned and saw his father. Meave was standing by him, enveloped from head to toe in a cloak of green wool trimmed with gold fur. Lord Devereux whom Ralph thought never felt cold was dressed in leather tunic and knee length breeches. His loose hanging cloak revealed his broad sword in its scabbard. His hair and his beard had been trimmed, and he looked younger, taller and stronger.

'Father!' said Ralph, raising his voice, trying to sound cheerful.

'A frosty night Ralph, you should be warming yourself inside,' replied Lord Devereux, they approached him.

Looking into his father's eyes and shivering he said,

'Father! Tell me about the fire … Tell me about mother … Tell me about Pádraig Bocht. I am old enough to know these secrets'

Lord Devereux placed his large hands on the children's shoulders and pulled them both close. They could feel the safe warmth of his cloak. Meave looked into his kind eyes and felt happy and loved.

'My children,' he began, 'this land is full of danger. Events happened many years ago that will determine our future.'

'What events?' asked Ralph, with a curious look on his face.

Lord Devereux remained silent. He knew that the cruelty of the world would touch his children soon. He wanted to protect them forever.

'Your mother Iascmna,' he continued, 'was a princess. She was beautiful and fair. Kindness and wisdom were her virtues. She came from a people far away, and she had a deep insight into the power of nature, especially the sea and the wind. Iascmna always needed to be able to see and smell the sea and view the storm clouds of the ocean. Fishermen often sought her advice about squalls and the locations of fish. They say her predications were always correct.'

He paused and then turned and looked at the fire burning in DunFaythe Lighthouse. His eyes moistened.

'Children! Many years ago before you were born, when I was a young captain in my father's army -'

'My Lord!' a young soldier approached. 'A messenger has arrived with urgent news and awaits your audience.'

'Tell us more father,' pleaded Meave.

Deep furrows appeared on his brow, he hugged the children.

'Later,' he said and followed the young soldier through the torch-light; his leather soled boots scraping on the frost, until he disappeared into a doorway of one of the towers of DunFaythe Castle. The children stood silent and still.

'Some day Ralph, it will all be revealed. We must be patient,' said Meave, frowning.

'I can't,' he whispered, exhaling a soft sigh.

She placed her cheek on his shoulder.

'Please Ralph. Don't do anything to endanger yourself or upset father.'

Ralph grasped Meave's shoulders.

'Meave! My head, my dreams are filled with mother's face and the fire. Sometimes, when I am on Trá Bán and the wind and the gulls are screaming, and the waves are deafening, I think I hear a soft voice whispering, "Ralph! Ralph! My son Ralph!"'

Meave stepped from his embrace, her hands dropped to her side. The hood of her cloak crumpled to her shoulders. She nodded.

'I've also heard voices,' she said, looking at the lighthouse fire sparking against the black sky.

'It is you Queen Meave … It is you Queen Meave,' she recited.

'Queen Meave!' exclaimed Ralph.

'Yes, When I was examining the sketches on the wall in Pádraig Bocht's chamber, I heard it,' said Meave, stammering a little.

'You would make a great Queen,' exclaimed Ralph, bowing low in front of her.

'Don't make fun! There … is more.'

'More!' cried Ralph. 'I think we are both going mad. But you are the sensible one. If you are hearing voices, then someone is talking.'

She continued, 'Sometimes, when I am on the beach and the lighthouse fire is smoky and black, my skin begins to harden and stretch and feels like leather to touch. My eyes get sore and heavy and I'm able to see great distances out to sea. Once I saw a galley in full sail on the horizon. I was certain that it was not there before my eyes changed. When the feeling passed I could no longer see the galley. Later in the day I saw the same ship coming ashore further up the coast. This only happens to me when I am near the sea and never happens when I am in the castle or riding my pony.'

Ralph stood dumbfounded. It was one of the few times that Meave saw him lost for words.

'Don't believe ... you!' he stuttered. 'Are you sure that I have not a witch for a sister?'

'I'm not a witch. Well! I don't think I am. It's as if the voice I hear is trying to warn or protect me.'

They remained silent for a while each trying to make sense of what the other had said. Meave felt better after sharing her thoughts with Ralph.

'Let's go inside,' said Ralph, breaking the silence and trying to move his almost numbed toes.

The two children walked along the cold stone parapets.

'In here,' suggested Ralph, pointing to a narrow arched doorway.

They entered a small fire-filled room in one of the towers that was often used by the castle tutors. The walls were adorned with tapestries of wild wintry seascapes. They stood in front of a roaring fire, shivering from the touch of heat and the excitement of the conversation. The fire shadows dancing on the stone walls added to the mystery and magic, filling their senses. For a few moments they stood side by side, searching the blazing logs for answers.

'How is mother speaking to us?' asked Ralph, feeling the warmth on his face.

Meave did not reply, she continued to look into the fire, her shapely face transfixed in the gloaming, against the jumping darkness of the room; a golden firelight danced in the torc adorning her neck. Ralph stood looking at her and felt for that precious moment that he was standing in the presence of a queen. She turned and looked through him, and he detected a sparkle of knowledge in her eyes.

'Her spirit is here with us,' she proclaimed.

Ralph could not answer. The warmth of the fire and Meave's change of stature added to his weariness and confusion.

'We must retire now,' she said, lifting her chin.

To Ralph it sounded like a royal command.

'Yes of course,' he answered.

They left the room through a wooden-panelled door adjacent to the fire and ambled down a stone stairwell to the castle courtyard. The familiar chatter of the guards lightened their spirits. Meave's tomcat came running to her, purring with expectation.

'Ah!' she cried, 'my little hairy friend, no worries for you tonight.'

'Maybe your cat knows more than we do. They say that a cat has nine lives. Does that mean that he has lived for nine lifetimes?' asked Ralph, raising his eyebrows.

Meave giggled.

'Only you could view nine lives like that.'

* CHAPTER THREE *

The Messenger

Lord Devereux strode towards the Great Hall, his steps echoing around the tiled, torch-lit corridor. Hugh LaMitchel, his chief adviser, a bald little stump of a man, followed directly behind him, wearing a long white gown with black high collars, supporting his fat flabby jowls; a wide leather belt restrained his extended midriff and his hand confidently grasped his scabbarded sword. Bringing up the rear and in order of seniority was General Fredrick Sinnolt, Commander of DunFaythe Castle, dressed in full armour. His long, grey beard hung low on his chest, like the sad disposition of his spirits. He was Lord Colclough Devereux's most trusted soldier. News of a messenger had interrupted his evening meal of chicken and roast duck and he did not like to hear of urgent dispatches.

Firelight and torch-light reflected from the polished timber and bronze fittings of the open doors of the Great Hall. Guards froze to attention, as the party approached the gathered crowd of captains and soldiers; each one dressed in chain mail, knee length breeches and leather leggings with hair tied back in a single tail. Tapestries hanging from the walls and paintings of past Lord Devereuxs seemed to shudder from talk of war, pillage and death. The stamp of Lord Devereux's boots on the mahogany floor announced his arrival amongst his troops. His orange beard and thick hair glistened with dampness from the night air.

As he raised himself up to his full impressive height and pushed back his shoulders he remembered his father Lord Ely the Great telling him that a time comes in every man's life when he has to stand alone – he knew this was his time.

Silence descended on the gathering, each man waiting and watching. Slowly the soldiers melted back to the corners of the Great Hall, leaving a passage of bodies, directing Lord Devereux to a figure, sitting stooped in a wooden chair. Clenching his fists, Lord Devereux walked towards the visitor and saw a young man wrapped in a grey cloak. He had a thin grey face with black frightened eyes, frozen in an empty stare; his shaking hands grasped a vessel of hot wine. Lord Devereux stood before him. The young man didn't move or acknowledge his presence.

'Lord Devereux is before you. Know your place!' shouted one of the captains, a young, nervous man.

'Silence!' commanded Lord Devereux. 'Our visitor is in no fit condition to observe pleasantries,' noticing that the young man's short, dark hair was stained with dried blood. He saw that the brooch supporting his cloak had the familiar insignia of the Radford line, an anchor balanced on the tips of two diagonal swords. Towering over the trembling messenger, his attention was drawn to a deep sword wound in his upper arm that had been treated with a poultice of berries and lichens, beginning to bleed and stain the timber floor of the Great Hall.

'Drink my young friend. Then we will hear your news,' he urged, and he reached out and held the shaking wine vessel, guiding it to the young man's lips.

The young man gulped a mouthful of wine, spilling it down his fingers, his legs and onto the floor. Wine and blood mingled on the timbers of DunFaythe Castle, forming a little river that reached Lord Devereux's boot.

'Your blood and my wine,' said Lord Devereux.

A whispering murmur drifted through the massed ranks, now surrounding Lord Devereux and the messenger.

'A good or bad omen, I don't know,' he continued. 'What's your name?'

The young man's gaze turned to Lord Devereux. Forcing his hands to stop shaking, he placed the vessel by his feet and moved his body forward as if to stand up.

'My Lord ... I have urgent ... news,' he gasped.

Hugh LaMitchel met the staring green eyes of General Fredrick Sinnolt. Both men felt the icy wind of fear press through their thoughts. LaMitchel's grip on his sword weakened, his hand fell to his side. Sinnolt's eyes closed, and he ran his wrinkled fingers through his loose grey hair. Both men knew that this young man was bringing horror and death to their peninsula.

Lord Devereux knelt down on one knee, scooped up the young man and carried him over to a low, fur-covered cot beside a blazing fire. The soldiers remained in an arc-shaped cluster around him and his young charge. The beech and cedar ceiling reflected the dancing flames of the fire. The heat of waiting soldiers warmed the great columns of the hall that had witnessed many strange events during their long history. They were about to witness the beginning of another. Old Alesia, who had been watching the young visitor, gave him bread and bacon to eat and refilled his drinking vessel. An ornate bronze chair with purple and gold padded armrests was carried forward and placed beside the resting messenger. Lord Devereux sat on the chair, placing his thick muscular limbs on the armrests.

'What's your name boy?' he asked again, softening his voice.

Eight hundred eyes waited for the answer; heads strained to view and listen.

'I am Arthur Furston from the land of the Radfords,' he cried, raising his head and looking directly at Lord Devereux. My foster father Cedric Radford sent me. GuaireDun has fallen! ... An army of cruel savages from the sea invaded Radford lands, one month ago.'

Lord Devereux's face paled; his fingers gripped the armrests.

'Each one wore armour of mail underneath their black monk's habit,' continued Arthur.

'From the sea you say,' interjected Lord Devereux.

'Yes ... from the sea. They came ashore in many boats with black and yellow-striped sails. My foster father said there are about thirty thousand of them.'

The soldiers of DunFaythe Castle remained silent. Not a shuffle or whisper was heard. Each one thinking about his family and imagining the future.

Arthur continued his tale, 'These invaders murdered everybody before them. Their black and yellow painted faces was the last view of this world that many of my kinsmen saw.'

He paused for a painful moment and stared into the blazing fire then gulped down two mouthfuls of wine.

'Citbeag is their leader. Some say he is a dwarf. He also wears a black monk's habit, but never removes the hood. No one has ever seen his face. He carries a long staff inserted into an eagle's head carved in ivory. They conquered the lands and castles of Ros na Mara and CarraigDubh, before they arrived at GuaireDun. My foster father, his family and one thousand loyal warriors are in FiordWex, waiting for the hordes to arrive. I have come to warn you. I did not desert my comrades. I would have gladly stayed to fight and die with my kinsmen. Lord Cedric sent me to warn you and to plead for your assistance. Many died so I could journey here. I came through The Devil's Belly.'

'GuaireDun ... The Devil's Belly,' repeated Lord Devereux, his eyes closing, his chin dropping to his chest. He remembered, after a long and tiring journey on horseback, with his father Ely the Great, through forests and limestone escarpments, devoid of plant life or water, arriving at the stony beach of Trá na gCarraig.

High up on cliffs of limestone criss-crossed with scars of grey granite sat the fortress of GuaireDun. He remembered GuaireDun; the seat of learning whose three towers catered for the study of literature, music and drama. He remembered entering the Devil's Belly, a vast cavern cut into the cliffs that could only be accessed from a concealed tunnel on the beach and being greeted by Lord Cedric of GuaireDun. Lord Cedric provided musicians, and his father and escort sang songs of past heroes until the setting sun closed the day.

'My Lord! My Lord!'

General Fredrick gripped Lord Devereux's shoulder, and he returned his focus to the young messenger.

'We … must … prepare,' stammered General Fredrick. 'There's no time to lose. I will send messengers to the castles of Ryanside and Hayesdorf in the Northwest and Murphan and Nolcrean in the Northeast.'

Lord Devereux remained silent. The Great Hall was as hot as a cauldron, fuelled by the roaring fire and the beating worried hearts of the soldiers.

'We'll defeat these fiends,' cried a soldier holding his sword above his head.

'We'll go tonight,' answered another, his fury feeding his courage. Lord Devereux stood up and looked around at the expectant angry faces of his soldiers.

'This is a time for clear thinking first and then valour,' he announced.

A wave of mumbling chatter drifted through the gathering. Each man agreeing with his master and feeling some solace from his determined statement. Silence descended on the group once more. Lord Devereux looked down at Arthur, who had his face buried in his hands.

'Tell me about GuaireDun,' he said and a tense, worried look cramped his face.

Arthur lifted his head from his cupped hands and raised his eyes in an anguished stare at Lord Devereux.

'All those died so I could live. I do not deserve to live!' he moaned, wine dripping down his chin.

'As I was stumbling along Trá na gCarraig that evening, I looked back and saw two black pillars of smoke rising in the sunset. I then knew that GuaireDun was taken.'

Arthur covered his face with his wine and blood-stained hands. Nobody spoke in the Great Hall of DunFaythe Castle. They looked to Lord Devereux, waiting for guidance, waiting for soothing words. He stood up, drew his broadsword and looked around at the flushed, fevered faces.

'They will not take DunFaythe,' he roared, brandishing his broadsword.

The soldiers cheered.

'Now we must prepare. Send for Pádraig Bocht!'

* CHAPTER FOUR *

Pádraig Bocht's Story

Ralph awoke at the sixth hour. His first thoughts were of the messenger. Then he became aware of the silence of the castle, no servants running around doing chores, no footsteps of guards patrolling along his corridor. His chamber was dark and cold; his fire was dead. This surprised him since it was usually kept burning by the night watch. The blackness of the fire and the silence made him nervous. He jumped out of his cot, shivering, as he put on his tunic, breeches and cloak. As he closed his chamber door behind him he thought that it was very strange that there were no torches lighting the corridor. An uneasy feeling washed across him. Then a light escaping from under his father's door at the end of the corridor attracted his attention. He relaxed slightly, knowing that he was not completely alone. Using a long shadow born from the escaping light as a guide, he made his way towards his father's door. As he edged towards the light, he felt something hit his chest. It happened too quickly for him to feel fear or anger. He stopped immediately and reached out with his hand, catching a softball of hair in his grip.

'Bad cess to you, young fella,' moaned old Alesia, falling to the ground. 'One of these days you will be the death of me.'

Ralph bent down and helped her to her feet. He had often collided with Old Alesia, but never in the darkness, this early in the morning.

'Why are the torches not lighting? Where are the guards? Where is Father?' he asked, holding her arm.

Old Alesia lifted her wrinkled worn face and stared up at Ralph, her wet hanging eyes wide with fear.

'It's war! They've come. We'll all die screaming in our cots,' she cried, tightening her bony-fingered grip on his arm.

Ralph tried to speak, but his tongue locked.

'What's wrong with you boy?' she asked, releasing her grip on his arm.

'What war? Who's coming?' he blurted.

'Ask your father,' returned Old Alesia, and she turned away and shuffled down the corridor.

Ralph approached his father's door and stopped for a moment, his hand ready to push.

'Have they come?' asked his father, from behind the door.

23

'Don't know … Don't think so … I still don't understand the prophecy,' returned another voice.

It was Pádraig Bocht!

'I have searched all the great books in the castle library and studied the Book of Time, The Book of Draíocht and the Book of Truth. I have spent many long nights in the lighthouse reading, sketching and calculating. The answer will not reveal itself,' he cried in a despairing voice.

'Who … are these devils?' asked his father, his voice shaking with anger.

'Must be part of the prophecy,' answered Pádraig Bocht.

'Whether they are or not, they will be defeated,' shouted his father, and Ralph heard the clink of a sword on stone.

'She must have the key,' Pádraig Bocht replied, his voice fading, as he walked to the far end of the room. Lord Devereux's voice also weakened. Ralph found it difficult to hear the conversation.

'… is still young … all were,' muttered his father.

Ralph guessed it would be better if he went to Meave's chamber, as he did not feel good about listening to his father's conversations. He wondered what was in the library. He knew that Meave spent a lot of time there. Making his way towards Meave's chamber, he was relieved to meet several soldiers, lighting torches along the corridors and bringing fires back to life in various chambers of the castle.

'You're up early Master Ralph,' one soldier said, as he passed him in a passageway. Ralph didn't answer, he was too busy thinking, worrying and questioning and needed to talk to Meave. He opened her chamber door and a waft of warmth from a blazing fire touched his face. Meave was sitting on her bed wrapped in her woollen cloak, reading a large volume, bound in goatskin and lavishly decorated with leaves of gold.

'You are early,' she said, keeping her eyes fixed on the page.

'Something terrible has happened,' said Ralph, shivering, as he warmed his hands at the fire, trying to control his excitement.

'I know,' answered Meave, continuing to read. 'The Radford lands have been invaded by an army from the sea.'

Ralph looked at her, his mouth open, his eyes blinking with surprise, trying to figure out how she would know about the invaders.

'Who told you?' he demanded.

'One of the servants,' she answered, turning a page of the volume. 'She said that we have to prepare for war.'

Ralph was bursting with questions, as he walked around Meave's chamber, clenching his fists.

'What will we do? Will we fight? Are the soldiers ready? Meave! Will you talk to me? How can you read a volume at a time like this?'

'Ralph!' replied Meave.

Ralph stopped walking and talking and looked at her. He could not remember the last time that he had heard her shouting.

'Father will know what to do,' she said and looked back at her volume.

'But that's the problem,' answered Ralph, walking around the room again. 'He doesn't know what to do. I heard him talking with Pádraig Bocht. They mentioned a prophecy, and Pádraig Bocht said something about three great books in the library.'

Meave stopped reading, jumped from her cot, walked over to the fire and reached out to warm her hands. Ralph watched her, waiting for her to speak and was glad that he had finally got her attention. She pulled her cloak tighter around her shoulders, as if Ralph's news had caused her to feel a cold draught. The chill she felt was not from the cold, it was a chill of fear drifting across her thoughts.

'What books?' she asked, looking into the fire and sighing deeply.

Ralph watched the flames of the fire dancing in her eyes. She looked like a queen again.

'The Book of Time, The Book of Draíocht and The Book of Truth,' answered Ralph.

The blaze of the fire reflected off her eyes, narrowing her pupils, as if she was viewing something in the flames. She turned to Ralph, her face flushed and drawn.

'They are locked in a large wooden chest in the library and contain knowledge about ancient history, magic and the future. The Book of Time was written in Ogham, a secret, ritualistic language, difficult to read and even more difficult to write.'

She looked back to the fire, as if she was searching for something.

'… The letters consist of five perpendicular or angled strokes, meeting a centre line. The main fifteen letters were also the names of fifteen trees sacred to the druids. The Book of Draíocht is written using symbols and sketches. Nobody knows who wrote this book. An ancient Irish prophet, Luaig O Faoleain, wrote the Book of Truth in the language of Greece.

Old Alesia once told me, ''Keep those books locked in the chest. When they are taken out, a time of woe and despair will descend on us all.''

She swayed on her feet for a few moments then swivelled her body and faced Ralph. She looked past him for a few moments, as if she was in deep thought.

'Let's go to the library now,' she said, looking worried.

Ralph could not believe what he was hearing. He did not expect Meave to show an interest in a story about ancient books.

'Yes of course' he replied. 'So you do know about these books?'

'Do you want to look at them?' she asked in a low whisper.

'Of course I do,' gulped Ralph.

Meave did not reply as she left her chamber followed by Ralph. They walked to the library, along corridors filled with soldiers, down a stately oak stairway, covered with a purple and gold carpet, across the polished floor of the Great Hall and then to a narrow high door into the library. Meave opened the door. She had been here many times, studying Latin and Greek plays and prose. Ralph had only visited it when he was searching for her, and it was always the first place that he looked.

The library was a vast chamber, panelled from ceiling to floor with ornate oak, engraved with swords and coats of arms on one wall and animals running and roaring on the opposite wall. Wolves frozen in wood and galloping horses were carved in the timber beside deer with huge antlers of oak standing guard.

Six rows of shelving reaching to the ceiling ran the length of the room. Each row was divided into six racks, containing shelves of volumes, bound with red, blue and yellow dyed animal skin. Several shelves were buckled and warped from the weight of their load. Large books, small books, fat books, thin books, old and new books lived in DunFaythe library.

They stood in the doorway, inhaling the musty dry smell of leather hide and stained timber. The low light of the flickering torches blinking around the walls changed the colours and textures of the sleeping books, as shadows danced over them. The two children made their way down the centre aisle towards a large wooden chest mounted on a dark metal frame. Ralph was surprised that a chest, containing such important books, could look so plain with no panelling, no gold, no leather or lettering to highlight its importance. A metal lock lay on the floor beside it

'It must be open. The lock has been removed!' he cried.

He wanted to open it immediately. Meave was pondering on the books inside the chest. She had often seen the chest, but had been warned by her tutors never to open or read the ancient texts.

'Will I open it?' asked Ralph, his eyes pleading, hoping that Meave would agree with him.

'I don't know what to do,' answered Meave, 'But I do know that The Book of Time recalls the history of Ireland, back to ancient times, when settlers arrived here from Egypt. There are references to Moses and the great flood in it. If you read this book you will grow old quickly and die slowly.'

She paused for a few moments, reached out, as if she was going to open the chest and withdrew her hand.

'The Book of Draíocht contains secrets about life, about how to change the direction of the wind. How to talk to animals. How to make potions that will cure any ailment. It is said that if you read the Book of Draíocht, you will gain all this knowledge, but you will be so shocked with what you discover that you will not be able to tell anyone or use any of the knowledge. You will also live alone and be despised.'

She paused for a while puckered her lips and then took a step closer to the chest.

'The Book of Truth tells us about the future, when major events are going to happen. This book has riddles in it. You must solve the riddle to find the knowledge. If you read the Book of Truth you will never die, but you will always be tormented by the wish that you had never read it.'

She then took a deep breath, as if she had been relieved of a great burden and eyed Ralph.

'I think Pádraig Bocht has read the books,' whispered Ralph. He was wondering how the books could affect the war and the invaders.

'Maybe we should open it,' she said, with a glazed look in her eyes.

They stepped forward together and grasped the lid of the chest. It opened with a low whistle like a draught wafting up a chimney and rested back on its metal hinges. They both stood over the chest looking into it.

They saw green velvet lining indented with the shapes of three large heavy volumes like the hollows in a pillow after sleep.

'Its empty!' moaned Ralph.

'I'm glad it's empty. Those books are cursed,' cried Meave, grasping Ralph's arm.

'Yes! It's empty,' boomed a voice behind them. 'It's been empty for a long time.'

The two children jumped. Meave let out a little cry and turned around. Ralph lost his balance, stumbled and nearly fell into the chest. They both searched through the flickering shadows for the source of the voice. A tall lean figure dressed in a green hooded cloak appeared from behind one of the racks of books. It was Pádraig Bocht. His face under the dimmed light of the torches reminded Ralph of a closed fist waiting to strike. A shimmer of dread passed down his spine. Pádraig Bocht was his father's man and this was his father's library. Yet he could never be sure about Pádraig Bocht's loyalty.

Meave didn't see a closed fist; she saw an empty wooden chest and a man, who was angry and cruel.

Pádraig Bocht approached the children. His seeping, red eyes, his stained face, his protruding yellow teeth, struck terror into Meave. She leaned against Ralph, who was standing tall. He looked at her reassuringly.

'Don't worry I have been in worse situations than this,' his eyes told her.

'Pádraig Bocht,' he said, trying to sound brave. 'The DunFaythe Books are missing from the chest.'

Meave felt proud of Ralph, who saw no danger anywhere, he lived to explore and learn and had the determination and strength of will of her father. She wished sometimes that she could be like him. She felt her heart slow, her knees and fingers stopped shaking.

Pádraig Bocht moved his piercing red eyes away from the children and looked at the empty wooden chest.

'Do you have the books Pádraig Bocht?' she asked, feeling braver now that Ralph had set the mood.

'*Sea*. I do,' hissed Pádraig Bocht, 'and I regret the day I set eyes on them. I will never die and I will never live because of those wretched books. They should be tied with rocks and cast into the sea and never seen again by the world of man.'

Meave felt a tinge of sorrow for him. His pitiful appearance and his mournful cry touched her, as he walked over to a chair in the corner of the library, a chair Meave often used. He sat down and placed his elbows on the adjoining table and buried his tormented face in his long bony hands. Not knowing what to do, the children looked at each other for guidance. Meave indicated to Ralph with a movement of her eyes that he should follow Pádraig Bocht. Ralph went to the table and looked down at the sorrowful wretch. Meave approached him. They were close enough to smell the odour of fish and smoke from his cloak. He did not say a word; his long fingers stroked his crooked nose and wet smoky eyes. Meave nudged Ralph hoping that he would break the tense silence. Ralph took a deep breath and opened his mouth to speak, but words would not come. Meave nudged him again. He tried to imagine his mother's face which calmed his rushing mind, allowing him to form a question.

'Why did you take the books Pádraig Bocht?' he blurted out.

Pádraig Bocht raised his head and let his hands slide down his face. He looked up at the children, his face twisted with cracks of despair and terror, like an infant, who awakes alone in the darkness of the night.

'*Suígí an bheirt agaibh.* Sit down both of you,' he said, without a hint of menace or anger. 'Do you know why I am called Pádraig Bocht?'

Before the children could answer he said,

'Because I read those cursed books. Reading the Book of Truth has made me grow old. Reading the Book of Draíocht frightened me so much that my appearance changed. It would be difficult for both of you to imagine that I was once strong and handsome with the strength of four men. Because I read the Book of Truth I will never die. I shall remain an ugly beast forever. Now! Before you ask any questions there is something you should know.'

He took a small earthenware vessel from a pocket in his cloak, put it to his mouth and took two gulps.

'A little potion I have to help me forget who and what I am,' he said, examining the vessel.

His features began to change, his face softened. The deep wrinkles on his face thawed out and a soft shadow of a smile blossomed across his thin lips. Meave tried to imagine what he was like, when he was a young man and a close friend of her father. Ralph wanted to ask him for a taste of the potion, to try it out on his old dog Bones, who was almost blind.

Pádraig Bocht viewed the children, sitting opposite him, their eyes beaming with wonder and expectation. He had to tell them about their ancestors, their history and their destiny and had always hoped that the day would never come when the prophecy would be fulfilled. But now invaders were threatening DunFaythe Castle, and he had lost control of events.

The children waited.

Pádraig Bocht began,

'About four hundred years ago your ancestor, Maolmheasa Devereux lived in this castle, with his father and two sisters. There is an image of him on the wall in the corridor overlooking the southern courtyard.

'I've seen that sketch,' said Meave. 'a handsome man except for his long nose.'

Pádraig Bocht ignored Meave's comment.

He continued,

'DunFaythe Castle was similar to what it is today. The lighthouse also burned brightly in those days as a warning to seafarers. When Maolmheasa was a young man his father, Lord Duncan, hoped that he would marry the daughter of Marcus Barrett from the midland kingdom, thus forming an alliance with the Barrett line. Maolmheasa however, was more interested in fishing, hunting, horse riding and swordplay. When he reached the age of twenty-three years he was considered old, not to have found a wife. His father was getting concerned and would often say to him, "I suppose I will never have Devereux grandchildren to entertain me in my old age."

Maolmheasa never answered this observation. He just carried on busying himself with his entertaining lifestyle.

However, one summer morning he was walking along Trá Bán towards the lighthouse. The sharp bright sun bounced off the calm sea and the carpet of white sand, forcing him to avert his eyes from the glaring expanse. After walking for a short time he raised his eyes to look at the lighthouse and saw an object in the sand before him. From a distance it looked like a bundle of colourful garments. Many objects and clothing were washed up on the sand over the years, so he did not pay much attention to it. He decided he would leave it for the fishermen, who often combed the beach for debris. As he approached the colourful bundle, he saw that part of the material was green with gold circles. Another piece was red with yellow diamonds. Blue cloth with yellow stripes also formed a section of the pile. This was strange; he had never seen such rich colours combined before. As he passed the colourful load he glanced down again to avert his eyes from the sun. To his surprise and horror he saw a hand fall from under the green and gold material onto the sand. The arms and face of a female form followed. He looked away, rubbed his eyes with his fingers, closed them and then opened them and looked again.

The female form raised herself off the sand and wrapped the red and yellow material around her shoulders. Maolmheasa realised this was a colourful silk cloak. No! It was not an apparition caused by the amount of wine he had drunk the evening before. Beneath the cloak he saw that her legs and arms were covered with burnished ringlets of new mail armour. He never saw armour fitting so comfortably like this before. She was the most beautiful woman he had ever seen. The sun's rays on her back highlighted the colours of her cloak. He found it difficult to hold his gaze at this dazzling vision. She looked like a goddess surrounded by a halo of sunlight.

"I am Farraingrá," she said. "I come from Tír na Leasa. I lost my way, and I came here to rest."

Maolmheasa found it difficult to speak. He had never seen such a vision of beauty in his life. Stepping closer to her, he realised to his amazement that it wasn't a coat of mail she was wearing; her arms and legs were covered with fish scales! The silver scales with their cast of blue and gold nested perfectly into each other. She was not wearing a coat of fish scales; they were part of her body like the feathers of a peacock! Her face was flawless; she had short golden hair with tiny ringlets stained with wafts of sea salt. Her eyes were deep blue and had tiny fins at the edges of them; her fingers also had a coating of scales like the down of a new-born chick. As he stepped even closer he detected a slight odour of seaweed tinted with a fragrance of almonds.

"I am … Maolmheasa Devereux" he stuttered. "May ... I … help … you."

Farraingrá spoke a mixture of Irish, Norman and a language that he could not understand, and he discovered to his astonishment and disbelief that she lived in a world beneath the ocean, Tír na Leasa, a world of rebellion, betrayal and grief. Her father was king and his jealous half brother was about to rebel against him. Maolmheasa first thought he was under the spell of a witch. However, as her story continued, the melodious soft tone of her voice relaxed him, and he believed that Farraingrá was a real person. He offered her food and shelter in the castle. Farraingrá was hesitant at first, but then she wrapped herself in her colourful garments and walked with him to the castle. As they entered the castle, soldiers and servants stood and stared at this lady dressed in polished white mail, wearing a colourful cloak.

"Perhaps," they said, "Maolmheasa has a visitor from Wales or France."

She remained in the castle for several weeks. However, his father Lord Duncan was not happy with him befriending this strange creature, so she had to stay in her chambers during the day and only came out at night, when soldiers and servants would not see her.

As the weeks passed she adjusted to the world of man and learned the language, the customs and social behaviour of DunFaythe Castle. Every night she visited Trá Bán, wondering if she should stay or go back to her sea world.

Farraingrá began to lose the scales from her legs and hands. The more she changed the more she wanted to remain in the castle. But she was always aware that some day in the future her people would come for their princess. She eventually changed into a beautiful young woman. Maolmheasa and Farraingrá fell in love and married exactly one year from the day they met on Trá Bán.

But that is not the end of the story. Maolmheasa and Farraingrá had one daughter and two sons. Their daughter's name was Mairlan and she was tall and fair like her mother. One day she came screaming into the castle, her face stained with sand, her clothes dripping wet.

"They tried to take me away," she cried. "Fish men from the sea! They told me to come with them."

Mairlan then fainted and remained in a deep sleep for days. She never awoke and died two weeks later. Maolmheasa and Farraingrá were heartbroken. Farraingrá knew that her father had sent soldiers to take Mairlan back to Tír na Leasa. Since Farraingrá was living in the world of man, she could never become queen. But Mairlan was your age Meave and was still young enough to begin preparations for her crowning. One of Farringra's sons became Lord Devereux, who married and had two daughters and a son. It was always said that the daughters of the Devereux line were blessed with gifts and unusual powers. There are many stories and tales about these Devereux women, who had the blood of sea people running in their veins. The sea people have not yet come back to claim their queen. We are waiting for the day.'

Pádraig Bocht sat back in his chair exhausted. The two children remained silent, their thoughts flooded with the story they had just heard. Pádraig Bocht fell into a deep sleep, his arms resting across his chest.

Ralph was the first to speak.

'Do you have the sea in your blood? I know you have gifts,' he said, turning to Meave.

Meave did not reply. She felt a gush of excitement rise in her breast and was overcome with a peaceful happiness.

'I did hear voices,' she thought. 'They want me to go back to Tír na Leasa.'

'Meave!' cried Ralph. 'What about the prophecy?'

'We will hear about the prophecy another day,' she answered and she walked around the table to Pádraig Bocht, who was sleeping soundly, his face almost at peace. She laid her hand on his shoulder.

'Won't we Pádraig Bocht,' she whispered and then turned and walked down the length of the library, mixing with the shadows and the dancing torch-light. Ralph followed her.

* CHAPTER FIVE *

Run of the Lances

Two cold, cloudy weeks passed at DunFaythe Castle while Lord Devereux anxiously waited for his scouts to return with reports of Citbeag's advance. However, his scouts encountered no monks. They often arrived at a deserted monk's camp or burned village and many times they saw plumes of smoke on the horizon, as the monks ravaged the countryside.

Lord Devereux was preparing for war, placing detachments of cavalry in increasing circles of one mile each, around the castle, to give an early warning of an imminent attack. Ralph and Meave had not encountered Padraig Bocht since their meeting in the library. He had returned to the lighthouse and remained locked in his chamber. Meave heard no more voices nor experienced any strange feelings in her eyes or arms. The lighthouse fire burned, but nobody watched it. Winter deepened. Short, dark frosty days followed by long chill nights framed their world.

'Bring me Arthur Furston,' said Lord Devereux to General Fredrick Sinnolt one dark grey morning, as they studied a large map of his kingdom. Arthur was in the forge, a noisy, smoky, hell fire of a den, overseeing the creations of the blacksmiths. Sixty sweaty blacksmiths attended their iron anvils, bending, twisting and shaping molten metal into swords, maces, arrowheads and spearheads. Their eyes red from smoke and their wide barrelled hairy chests peppered with scars from flying cinders and droplets of molten metal; bald bearded drones, the life force of Lord Devereux's army.

Arthur's recovery was slow and painful. His wounds had healed, but his mind and soul still suffered. Terrifying images of screaming monks and dying soldiers during the siege of GuaireDun filled his waking dreams. But now with his strength restored, he was full of vengeance and was ready to fight. His every waking moment was consumed with thoughts of revenge, thoughts of recapturing GuaireDun and watching Citbeag burn. He never smiled and was prepared to die to achieve these goals. Two strips of leather tied back his hair. His young face, often mistaken as a sign of weakness, concealed an iron will. This strength of soul had sustained him during his long walk from GuaireDun, living on berries and the odd rabbit or pheasant he had trapped, as he avoided the marauding hordes of Citbeag. Each day he waited for Lord Devereux's summons. That day had arrived at last.

He entered Lord Devereux's chamber and was surprised to see that no rugs or carpets covered the flagstone floor which was furnished with one old worn table, three chairs and a cot in a corner. The bare stone walls had no tapestries or paintings to warm them. Lord Devereux, wearing a sleeveless tunic, sat at a table drinking wine and eating bread and cheese. Arthur could see old scars criss-crossing his muscled arms. Red cinders glowed in a fire opposite him.

'Sit down boy,' he said. 'I need you to take a message to Cedric in Fiordwex.'

'Sire?' replied Arthur, trying to remain calm.

'I want you to tell him that we have not forgotten him. Tell him to prepare the remains of his army to leave. Tell him that we have sent messengers to Ryanside and Hayesdorf. They will send reinforcements, and we will retake GuaireDun.'

Arthur felt a ripple of excitement pass through his body – at last, they were going to drive these devils back to the sea.

The following day an icy wind blew from the east and the sun hung low in the sky. Grey clouds speckled with dark rain stains, watched, as Arthur led twenty lightly armed cavalry through the northern gate of the castle. Each man carried a sword in a scabbard and a long bow strapped across his back. Heavy cloaks lined with thick linen protected them from the biting cold.

They travelled north-east for two days, through wet and soggy meadows, through bare branched woods, past farms and villages. Their travels brought them further than any of Lord Devereux's scouts had ventured.

A watery pale orange orb of a sun was setting in the west, when they reached the hill of Annaske. Travel weary bodies slumped off their horses and prepared to set up camp in the old ruined fort of Keycor. To the south lay the low lands of DunFaythe Peninsula. To the north was the Sarabande River and beyond was the castle of Fiordwex. Sleep came slowly to Arthur and his band. What little rest they enjoyed was interrupted by every sound of the night. Each slight whistle of the wind or shuffle of their horses, and every cough or sleepy yawn caused them to grip their swords. Arthur fell into a deep sleep, his head in his cloak and his body resting between the surface roots of a weeping cherry tree.

A bright cold sun awoke them They struggled onto their horses; their cloaks and weapons coated with glistening frosty stars. The warmth of their animals gave them some comfort, and they continued their journey. After several hours on horseback, Arthur halted the procession of exhausted men. Pointing to a green hill in the distance he said,

'Fiordwex is beyond that hill, but first we must cross the Sarabande River. Be careful it is fast and furious!'

A gentle rocky slope adorned with heather and ferns led them to the river. They stopped and watched it roar and churn past them, spitting foam and froth, crashing over jagged jutting rocks, shaped by a thousand years of its cold current. Beyond the river and sloping to the sky was a hillside, thick with pine trees. They approached the gushing torrent.

'We will find...a shallow area...to cross down river,' said Arthur, between yawns as his gaze drifted up the hillside beyond the river.

'Rest here first and eat, then I'll take two of you with me down river to find a crossing. '

They were glad to rest and ate what was left of their rations of bread and pork. Arthur and two of his comrades followed the river downstream.

Arthur knew that the river was the last hurdle before they reached the safety of Fiordwex castle. They followed a stony path along the riverbank and admired the bright sun recoiling off the gushing torrent, forming tiny rainbows, as droplets of moisture rose to meet it.

Feeling at ease in the cold morning sun Arthur dreamed of being behind secure battlements. His dream was interrupted by a dull rumbling sound, increasing in intensity.

'There must be rapids or a waterfall ahead,' he shouted and urged his horse forward.

The trio continued their trek towards the sound of the deluge, hoping to find a crossing. The waterfall they found was slow and majestic, dropping down a steep cliff like a silver curtain draped down a stone wall. A gentle breeze moved it from side to side, and the sharp rays of the sun painted it with hues of differing colours. The rainbow red flowed into yellow, mixed with green which changed to blue, spraying the shore. For a peaceful moment, Arthur and the two soldiers watched the myriad of colours, dancing beneath them, along the hem of the cascading silver curtain. Then Arthur noticed that the river flowed shallow before it disappeared over the edge of the cliff.

'We will cross here,' he said, coaxing his mount to cross the summit of the waterfall.

One of the soldiers made his way back to the others. The remaining soldier followed him across the flowing river, along the roof of the waterfall, towards the pine trees on the opposite bank.

Long thin trunks of the pine forest protruded from the hillside, casting narrow dark intersecting shadows and inviting Arthur to climb to the top and perhaps view Fiordwex. The two riders bent low on their horses, avoiding the hanging branches of the pine trees, forcing their tired mounts to climb the steep hill. Arthur looked back towards the racing river below him and hoped that the pine forest would give him some protection for the last leg of his journey.

His tranquil thoughts were shattered by a hissing sound behind him, followed by a soft moan. Turning he saw three black arrows protruding from the upper back. He saw the face frozen with shock. The eyes staring at a spot on the ground. His comrade lurched forward, dead before his head reached his horse's neck and fell to the ground without ever knowing how he died. Arthur drew his sword and searched the pine forest for monks, waiting for his arrows of death to arrive. Nothing happened. The river roared. His heart pounded. He guessed that he would be the next to die

He dismounted and crouched behind the narrow trunk of a pine tree. The dull grating sound of metal on stone behind him triggered in him a vision of monks. He turned around to see three spears, pointing directly at his throat.

'You're coming with us,' growled one of the monks, a low sized squat of a man. His thick neck supported a round bald head and his button nose reminded Arthur of a mountain hare. Two vertical strips of yellow dye, bubbling with sweat, streaked down his face; his black eyes showed no fear. The foul stench from his breath and monk's habit forced Arthur to turn away.

'Why do you come to the land of the Devereux's,' asked Arthur.

The monk parted his lips to reveal his stained teeth and a cruel shadow of a smile.

'It's the will of Citbeag,' he said.

Arthur was surprised that the monk spoke his language. He was about to answer when his attention was distracted by a small thimble like phial attached to the sleeve of the monk's habit. The monk saw Arthur looking at the phial. He grabbed Arthur's wrist and held it tight, moving his face close to Arthur's.

'The Deoch of Citbeag,' he hissed, spit dribbling down his chin. 'It's what will defeat you. You drink the Deoch … Show no mercy … you kill.'

He threw back his large round head, looked at the sky and guffawed loudly. Arthur stood speechless studying the lines on the monk's face.

'Let me kill him now,' said another monk, reaching for his sword.

'No!' replied the first pointing to the brooch, securing Arthur's cloak.

'This one is important! See! The insignia of rank he wears.'

Arthur looked at the spearheads and then at the monks, with their dripping mouths and wide eyes, like a pair of jackals waiting to devour a wounded deer.

'Blindfold him,' said the first monk.

They placed a wet sack over his head, tied his wrists together with strips of leather and led him up the hill of pine trees like a goat to the market.

'Where are you taking me?' croaked Arthur, from beneath the wet sack.

'We have a few questions to ask you,' replied one of the monks, pulling on the leather strips.

'You'll never defeat us,' choked Arthur, his wrists stinging with pain.

The monks stopped pulling him. He felt the point of a sword pricking his throat.

'We don't want to defeat you. We want you to join us,' said one of them, and Arthur felt the sharp sting of a sword piercing his neck.

'We could never become like you,' he cried, from the beneath the sack.

'You're like us, but you don't know it yet,' answered the monk. 'Enough talking.'

Arthur stumbled and tripped, they dragged him up the hill. The leather strips cut deep into his wrists. He screamed. They jeered. He cried. They shouted, showing him no mercy. Blood dripped from his throbbing wrists and the drying sack was tightening around his head and neck. A choking dizziness numbed him; he slumped to his knees.

'Need water,' he pleaded.

A rough hand pulled the sack from his head, and he felt the gush of air mixed with the clean scent of pine rushing up his nostrils. His chest expanded painfully, as he gulped in the cold air, and he found himself at the summit of the pine-covered hill. He was surprised to see that he was facing the entrance of a tent village, consisting of four rows of black flat-topped tents, each with a yellow pennant placed above the entrance. At the end of the centre row facing him was a larger tent with a conical shaped roof. Hundreds of black cloaked monks walked between the tents, some were sharpening swords and others were cooking or drinking. At the edge of the camp there was a pen made of felled pine trees, filled with horses, saddled and ready for battle.

'I know what your are thinking,' said one of the monks. 'We will take Fiordwex, and then DunFaythe will fall.'

Arthur realised that he had to survive to warn Lord Cedric in Fiordwex, no matter what he had to endure. He was certain the monks had a weakness. He was determined to find it.

Monks cheered and hooted, as they watched Arthur being dragged down the passageway between the tents.

'DunFaythe will be next!' shouted one of them.

'Lord Colclough Devereux will be our next prisoner,' shouted another, and they all roared with laughter, raising their swords and spears.

He noticed that they all looked strong and fit and were eager to fight and kill.

'Why do you come to the land of the Devereux,' he screamed.

They continued to jeer and taunt him and push him to the entrance of a small tent at the end of the aisle.

His wrists burned, his feet stung, his legs numbed.

'This is your new home,' said one of them, shoving him through the flaps of the tent.

He fell exhausted to the ground. A freshly cut pole of pine protruded from the soil in the centre of the tent. They tied him to the pole and left, leaving him on the cold ground shaking and aching. He could hear the monks all around him, arguing amongst themselves, swearing and cursing. For several hours he sat there whilst daylight faded.

Through the thin walls of the tent he could distinguish the glow of fires and the shadows of monks patrolling the camp; dark shapes moving through the stillness, watching, listening and waiting.

He fell into a light sleep, but was soon awakened by a tug of his tunic. Opening his eyes he saw a giant of a monk standing over him, his large frame reaching to the ceiling of the tent. Looking up at the monk's face he saw that his neck was as thick as a young oak tree. His large ears were pinned against his skull, and his tiny nose was like a pimple on the vastness of his wide gargoyle face. The giant monk's soft eyes examined Arthur for a few moments, and then he handed him a bowl of water and a metal plate filled with several slices of cold chicken. Arthur gorged the food and drank the water. The monk remained silent, but continued to stare at him.

Arthur, looking into the gentle blue eyes of his visitor, felt no hatred. He realised that this one was not like the others The giant then removed a linen cloth from a pocket in his habit. A shadow of kindness crossed his face for a moment. He untied Arthur's wrist and wiped the blood from them with the linen cloth.

'All of us are not evil,' he said, turning his massive frame towards the exit 'My name is Azaromel.'

'Follow me,' and he walked through the exit flaps of the tent. 'He wants to   see you now.'

'Who wants to see me?' asked Arthur.

The giant did not answer. Outside the tent, the camp was now silent. The enemy slept under a dark cloudless sky, fires glowing, a monk standing at each tent. Arthur knew that it was impossible to escape and followed the giant Azaromel to the entrance of a tent with a spherical roof. He had not seen this tent when he was dragged through the camp. Draped across the entrance flap was a bright yellow pennant. Two large muscular monk wearing a white sash across their midriffs, stood guard. Arthur followed Azaromel through the entrance flaps. The giant monk stopped several paces inside the tent, blocking Arthur's view. Arthur could not see anything except a warm light that filled the interior of the tent.

The idea that his comrades waiting at the river would now know that there were monks hiding in the pine forest heartened him. He was determined to show no fear and perhaps an opportunity to escape might arise.

'Is he here?' echoed a voice from the far end of the tent, interrupting Arthur's thoughts.

'He is, Master' replied Azaromel, standing aside.

Arthur felt the skin on his face tighten. All thoughts left his mind. Images of ghost stories he had heard, when he was a child flashed through his mind. Skulls! Devils! Fire! The room was lit by a semicircle of large wooden candelabras. Each one held a dull metal skull with three lights burning in it. The flickering dancing flames of the lights bounced off at least fifty monks, standing in a semicircle in front of the candelabras, their faces lost in the shadows of the cowls of their habits. Each one wore a long vertical white sash, reaching from their chins to their feet. A blood red carpet covered the ground. In the centre of this half circle of monks stood a figure dressed in a white habit and cowl, his face in shadow.

Arthur was convinced that he was going to die. The white monk lifted his gaze.

'Come forward,' he ordered.

Arthur moved towards him. The others watched from beneath their cowls.

'You may stand now,' said the white monk in a low threatening voice.

The monks encircled him. The flickering skulls in the candelabras above their heads created giant moving shadows on the walls and ceiling of the tent, dancing and mocking him.

The white monk moved three steps toward Arthur, raised his head and removed his cowl. His face had unblemished clear skin and wide blank eyes. A mane of grey loose hair fell to his shoulders; a deep dry scar bore into his right cheek. Arthur realised that he was looking at the young face of an old man.

'You have come a long journey,' said the white monk, touching his bottom lip with a pink nailed finger. 'We've been watching you.'

Arthur did not reply. The scar on the white monk's cheek fascinated him, changing shape, as he spoke.

'You've a decision to make. I hope you make the correct choice.'

'Why do you come to the land of the Devereux?' asked Arthur, trying not to be afraid.

The white monk frowned at him, and then his wide bright eyes darkened, and his thin grey lips attempted to create a smile.

'It's our destiny that we should come,' he replied, rubbing his fingers together. 'Padraig Bocht of DunFaythe knows that it is written.'

'Padraig Bocht is the Guardian of DunFaythe Lighthouse, a mystic and loyal servant of Lord Colclough Devereux,' answered Arthur, trembling with fear and excitement.

'Who are you?' he asked, not expecting an answer.

'My name is Zilamar. I am Citbeag's Grandmaster and Citbeag is Lord,' replied the monk, moving closer to Arthur.

'What is the Deoch of Citbeag?' asked Arthur, trying to calm himself by talking.

'Enough!' roared Zilamar. 'No more questions.'

The monks in the circle around him raised their faces and stared at him. Vacant eyes, closed cruel lips and grey sickly skin, peered out from beneath the cowls. Arthur saw that Zilamar's face was covered with thin intersecting lines, like the web of a spider, highlighted by the lights in the candelabras. He noticed that his eyes were changing colour and shape from button blue to a narrow grey to an oval green. Finding it difficult to avert his gaze from Zilamar's shifting eyes, penetrating into his mind, Arthur was certain that he was using magic on him. He tried to turn his back to Zilamar.

'Look at me,' whispered Zilamar.

The circle of black monks closed on him; he could smell their stale stench. Zilamar's eyes continued to alter their shape and colour from blue to grey to green.

'I want the Book of Freagra,' he said, clenching his fists.

41

'There's no such book,' answered Arthur, trying to stop his knees shaking.

'Meave Devereux is the one,' continued the white monk, raising his voice.

Arthur was finding it difficult to breathe. A terrible weight pressed on his chest. He could not move his arms.

'Meave is the daughter of Lord Devereux. She is a young girl,' he gasped, shocked that Zilamar should mention Meave's name

'We need her with us. Meave has more knowledge than you can imagine,' replied Zilamar, continuing to stare at Arthur.

'What do you want of me?' asked Arthur, hoping that the white monk would release him from his haunting stare.

'To join us and bring Meave Devereux to me'

Arthur's stomach felt weak and vomit rose in his throat. He tried to speak. His tongue would not move in his mouth. The circle of monks moved closer. Zilamar placed his hand on Arthur's shoulder.

'You look unwell young man. But you can have a future with us,' he said, pausing for a moment. Images of Lord Devereux and Meave passed through Arthur's conscious thoughts, a strong brave lord and a happy, carefree, innocent girl – how could she have knowledge that they want? It would better to die than be a traitor. He couldn't be responsible for their deaths. His mind filled with a visions of smoking pits of burning bodies, a dead young girl, the broken body of Lord Devereux, and Citbeag standing on the battlements of DunFaythe. Zilamar's voice brought him back to his horrible reality.

'You've a choice to make. If you decide to join us we will give you the Deoch of Citbeag to aid you. If you decline our offer you will be put through the ordeal of the lances. It is a test we give to those who we consider are disloyal to us.'

'I must have time to consider your proposal,' answered Arthur.

'One hour. Take him away!' hissed Zilamar.

Azaromel stepped forward.

'I will take him now my Lord Grandmaster,' he said, indicating to Arthur with a nod of his huge head.

Zilamar nodded, turned and left the arc of glowing skulls, followed by a procession of the monks. Arthur watched them fade into the darkness of the tent beyond the arc of light. He looked up at Azaromel's massive sculptured head.

'Is...Citbeag here?' he asked.

'Follow me.'

Azaromel led him from the tent, down an aisle of closed tents and guarding monks.

'Where are you bringing me?' asked Arthur.

The giant remained silent, walking in front of Arthur. His giant steps and upright stance suggested that he was a commander in the monk's army. They stopped at a wooden door cut into a wall of standing pine logs. Azaromel pushed open the door and indicated with a slight nod of his huge head that Arthur should enter. A single torch attached to a wall lighted the cell. The floor was covered with withered pine leaves.

'Wait here,' said Azaromel.

He left and closed the door behind him. The rattle of a key in a lock told Arthur that he could not escape. Looking around his cell his eyes adjusted to the orange flickering light of the torch. His attention was drawn to items of clothing scattered on the floor, an old tunic, a leather belt and a damp torn cloak. He knew that he was not the first visitor to this cell.

On the wall below the torch the name Malachy was carved into the pine logs. As he walked over to examine the carved name he felt an object under his feet. Removing the withered pine leaves he found a small dagger. Its wooden handle felt damp; its blade had spots of yellow rust. He wondered what had happened to its owner, and he hid the dagger in his tunic.

He sat on the floor, his back resting against the rough wall, waiting for his summons. At the far end of the cell he noticed another door, he knew it was locked. Arthur's heavy eyelids closed, as the trials of the day forced sleep on his weary limbs. His hands fell limp and his head moved to the right and rested on his chest. Down he drifted towards the blankness and peace of sleep. However, he never reached that quiet place of rest. Sensing the presence of someone, Arthur reluctantly returned from his journey to sleep. He struggled to his feet, angry that he was awoken, just when sleep was removing the horrors of his world from his mind for a brief moment. He leaned against the rough pines of the wall and looked into Azaromel's gentle eyes, set in his granite like hewn features.

'It's time' said Azaromel, placing a clenched fist in front of Arthur's chest. 'Time to go.'

He knew that he could stab him in the heart right then and escape, but he couldn't kill this man.

Azaromel opened his fist. Arthur looked down at the expanse of his palm and the withered lined skin of his thick fingers. Resting in the middle of this desert of flesh was a circular shaped fragment of purple linen. Azaromel carefully peeled the fragment from his hand using his bulbous thumb and forefinger. Arthur was surprised that two bulging fingers could manipulate such a small fragment of linen. He reached out and grasped Arthur's hand opened his fingers and holding the linen by one corner, he placed it in the centre of Arthur's palm. Arthur could feel it sticking to his skin.

'There is a venomous serum in the centre of the cloth,' said the giant. 'If it touches skin the victim dies painfully within seconds. You are protected by the glue that is holding it to your palm. The other side contains the poison. Be warned! Do not close your fist, or you will die immediately. This may help you when your ordeal begins.'

Examining the purple spot stuck to the palm of his hand, it struck Arthur that he had the power to kill glued to his hand.

'Why are you helping me?' he asked, looking suspiciously at Azaromel.

'He murdered my family,' answered Azaromel, closing his eyes.

'Who killed your family?' asked Arthur, feeling sorry for the kind giant.

Azaromel opened his eyes and looked down at Arthur.

'You must follow me now. Remember! Do not look into Zilamar's eyes,' and he moved towards the other cell door and opened it. A chill breeze watered Arthur's weary eyes, as he walked over and stood in the open doorway. The vision he saw reminded him of ancient Roman texts he had read, when he was a student, studying the lives of the Roman emperors. It reminded him of the descriptions and stories of ancient Roman gladiatorial arenas where victims were massacred to amuse the Roman masses. He looked into an oval shaped arena that could have been lifted from the ancient poems of Livy or Horace. Burning torches standing on pine stakes flanked the perimeter. Above the smoking torches and seated on rows of wooden steps were hundreds of monks, waiting, whispering and watching. Waiting for the spectacle to begin – whispering about his chances of survival – watching every move he made. Facing Arthur at the opposite end of the oval arena, on a raised platform, stood Zilamar, his arms folded in the sleeves of his habit, his cowl pulled low over his face. Behind Zilamar stood ten fully armed monks. Beside Zilamar, sitting on a cushioned chair sat a small monk. Arthur could not see his face. Ten flag poles bearing yellow and black pennants flapped in the cool breeze behind the armed monks.

As he stepped into the arena, the whispering mob of monks fell silent. Each one watched like a vulture waiting to devour a carcass. Zilamar glided down the steps from the platform to the arena and walked towards the centre of the areana.

'Your fate will be decided shortly,' he boomed, beckoning Arthur to enter the arena.

Arthur took a deep breath and reluctantly stepped into the arena towards Zilamar.

'Have you made your decision?' Zilamar asked.

Arthur looked into his inky black eyes. Then he remembered Azaromel's words and looked away.

'I will not betray my kinsmen,' he answered, feeling a knot of panic tighten his throat.

Zilamar remained silent. A ripple of movement drifted through the waiting monks like a breeze driven wave on a still pond. Zilamar turned and addressed the figure sitting on the cushioned chair.

'My Lord Citbeag. This one is defying your wishes,' he said, pointing a thin finger at Arthur.

Arthur's heart skipped a beat and then jumped inside his chest.

'Citbeag! Citbeag is here!' he gasped.

He was surprised that a sensation of anger not fear rushed through his veins, and he wished that he could get closer to him and drive his hidden dagger into his heart. Citbeag stood up. A guard handed him his staff.

'Bring him closer to me,' said a soft childlike voice.

Zilamar pushed Arthur towards Citbeag. On his face was an olive green mask with no mouth or nose.

'Show your face! Are you afraid to show your face,' screamed Arthur, his anger fed by thoughts of his dead comrades in GuaireDun.

The watching mass murmured with anxiety. Nobody had ever shown such disrespect to Citbeag.

'My Lord Citbeag,' said Zilamar, glaring at Arthur. 'He does not know who he is addressing.'

'I know whom I am addressing,' interjected Arthur. 'This is Citbeag. murderer! pillager! thief! barbarian!'

The web mesh on Zilamer's face glowed; his eyes began to rotate in their sockets. Arthur felt his ears beginning to burn and his skin tighten on his face. He fell to the ground screaming and choking.

'Enough!' said Citbeag, raising his short-branched arm. 'He has learned his lesson.'

Zilamar averted his eyes. The pain drained from Arthur, coiled up on the ground grasping his head. He struggled to his feet, blood dripping from his nose and ears; his head drooped from exhaustion.

'Now I will show you the face of power,' said Citbeag, menacingly.

Arthur raised his pounding head and looked at Zilamar, who had a cruel grin on his lips. He turned to Citbeag. Two wet bloodshot eyes peered at him from behind the featureless mask. Citbeag placed his hands on the chin of the mask and pulled it down his face. Arthur stared in horror!

'No! It's impossible! It can't be!'

The haggard, drawn face of Meave Devereux looked down at him. He tried to speak. Words would not come. He tried to close his eyes. His eyelids would not move.

'You know this face,' said Meave in a soft voice. 'You would not harm an innocent girl would you.'

'This is …You are not Meave Devereux,' cried Arthur, not believing what he was seeing.

Meave replaced the mask on her face. Arthur trembled; his bravery was beginning to wane. Citbeag removed the mask again. Lord Colclough Devereux's face with its ruddy cheeks and orange locks looked down at him.

'Hello Arthur,' said the grinning lips of Lord Devereux. 'I need your help.'

'You are not Lord Devereux,' yelled Arthur. 'Who are you?'

Lord Devereux replaced the mask.

'I am everybody, and I am nobody,' he shrieked, 'Enough of these games. Now let us begin.'

Arthur placed his left hand inside the chest opening of his tunic and grasped his hidden dagger. The piercing sound of a single trumpet blast filled the cold air of the night. Turning, he saw, entering from a side door between the row of standing torches, ten fully armed monks, each one carrying a lance. They marched into the arena and stood below the raised platform. Zilamar stepped closer to Arthur.

'Can you reach your cell door before they impale you with their lances? If you are swift and strong you may reach it. If you are slow and weak, you will be impaled before you have gained fifteen paces. No one has ever survived this test. Perhaps you will be the first,' he hissed.

Arthur was not listening to Zilamar. He was tightening his grip on his dagger.

'You will die with me,' he screamed, plunging the dagger into Zilamar's chest.

However, Zilamar did not cry out. The blade snapped in two even pieces as it struck Zilamar's body armour beneath his white habit. He grasped Arthur's hand that held the remains of the dagger. His eyes rotated slowly, changing colour. Arthur tried to avert his gaze

'You'll never free this grip,' rasped Zilamar, tightening his grip on

Arthur's hand.

Arthur knew that Zilamar could crush every bone in his hand if he wanted to. He forced Arthur to his knees.

'You are a fool. Do you not see that you cannot win?' he snapped tightening his grip.

Arthur grasped Zilamar's closed grip and pressed the serum against his skin.

'Your time is over Zilamar,' he whispered, half smiling

Zilamar felt the soft touch of the fragment caress his hand and knew that he had been tricked.

'What have you done?' he cried, releasing his grip on Arthur's hand.

'You will see in a few moments,' answered Arthur.

Then Zilamer's eyes stopped rotating; his lips trembled. The web lines on his face deepened into thick furrows and with a squealing cry he fell to the ground, dead. The monks shuffled in their seats and stood up, aghast at what they had witnessed.

'Zilamar is dead!' they screamed. 'Kill the stranger! Kill the stranger! Let him run the lances!'

Arthur looked towards the armed monks standing below Citbeag. They stood silent, looking up at their lord and master, waiting for a command. Citbeag rose to his feet and surveyed the scene before him. A hushed quietness descended on the standing horde. He pointed his finger at Arthur.

'Your time has come. Zilamar will be avenged! When the trumpet sounds, run towards the exit. When you have reached ten paces, my guards will launch their lances!'

Arthur waited, shaking. He looked at Citbeag and then turned towards the guards holding their lances and the crowd waiting for his death. The door at the end of the arena looked far away. He figured that he might be able to avoid one or two lances. It would be impossible to avoid them all. A deafening trumpet blast rang through the arena. The crowd cheered. The guards looked up to Citbeag. Arthur tried to run. His legs would not move.

'Run!' cried Citbeag, and he laughed.

'Run!' screamed the crowd.

Arthur ran towards the door. One step. Two steps. Three steps. No lances! Four steps. Five steps. Six steps. No lances! Seven steps. Eight steps. The crowd screamed like a flock of buzzards.

'Let the lances fly,' they shouted. 'He has run far enough.'

The din was deafening. Arthur's mind blanked; he could not think. His eyes watered. He could not see. His legs felt heavy and sore. Nine steps. Ten steps. An expectant silence filled the arena. Arthur stopped running.

'*Keep ... running. Keep ... running,*' he thought. '*Don't stop -* '

A convulsing fear filled his body. His legs froze. Citbeag raise his hand. The guards stepped forward. Arthur closed his eyes and waited, preferring to die standing than be pierced like a wild boar in the forest. He forced himself to dwell on thoughts of peaceful days on the plains of GuaireDun. Citbeag lowered his arm. Arthur closed his eyes and waited for the grunts of the guards, releasing their lances and hoped he would die quickly. He did not hear any grunting guards. Opening his eyes, he saw to his astonishment, hundreds of flaming arrows descending on the arena.

'They have come!' he cried, laughing with relief.

Citbeag disappeared behind a curtain at the rear of his platform. The guards followed to protect their master. The flaming arrows landed in the arena and amongst the packed crowd of monks. Choking smoke and panicking monks filled the amphitheatre.

'This way,' boomed a voice behind Arthur, as he watched the monks running from the torrent of fire.

It was Azaromel! Arthur ran to the cell door.

'Follow me,' cried the giant. 'I have two horses waiting outside.'

Arthur did not ask any questions. He followed the giant, who led him to two black stallions. Torching arrows were now falling on the tents of the camp. Monks screamed and cursed, trying to escape the inferno.

Arthur and Azaromel galloped through the camp. Some monks attempted to stop them, but were crushed by the charging steeds. At the edge of the camp he saw his troop of warriors unleashing burning arrows into the camp.

'You must ... come with us. I owe ... you my ... life.' he panted to Azaromel, as they rode towards the soldiers.

'Aye,' said Azaromel. 'I could not watch another innocent man die so I found your troops in the pine forest, searching for you. The only time they could attack was when the arena was full. My time as a monk is over.'

The soldiers cheered, when the fleeing duo reached their ranks. They left the burning camp behind them and rode into the darkness, towards Fiordwex castle.

* CHAPTER SIX *

The Prophecy

The children of DunFaythe Castle gathered in the Great Hall, the sons
and daughters of soldiers, captains and generals. Dressed in their winter furs,
they laughed and chased whilst waiting for Lord Devereux to arrive to speak
to them. Blonde heads, brown heads, curly heads bobbled and bounced as,
they slipped and slid on the mahogany floor. Two long wooden tables
stretched side by side, the length of the Great Hall, laden with trays of spiced
bread, bowls of honey porridge, baskets of sweet currant cakes and mounds
of apples and pears. Twenty large wide rimmed jugs of sugary apple juice
waited on the table for the thirsty horde of children. Young boys challenged
each other, brandishing wooden swords and long poles with balls of fur tied
to their tips. The young ladies of DunFaythe Castle jousted with wooden
weapons, often forcing the boys to yield by knocking them to the floor with
their fur poles. Soldiers stood along the walls of the Great Hall laughing and
cheering, as the happy, noisy children chased and jumped on each other.

'There are some tough young lads out there,' said one soldier, smiling

'Aye!' replied another, grinning, 'and tougher young ladies'

Old Alesia came waddling into the Great Hall.

'Ye may eat now,' she snapped in a high pitched voice. 'His lordship will
be here soon.'

The children ran to the tables and immediately began to gorge themselves
with food. Apple juice spilled from their goblets. Porridge splattered as they
filled their bowls. Currants and crumbs fell to the floor as, the hungry, but
happy children of DunFaythe Castle filled their tummies, waiting for Lord
Devereux.

Whilst they joked and ate and drank, they did not notice the arrival of two
figures. Lord Devereux stood viewing the children, wearing a brown tunic
and wine coloured linen breeches. A green woollen cloak lined with silver
silk, draped to the floor from his broad shoulders, fastened to his chest by a
brooch with the Devereux insignia of an anchor and two crossed swords. He
smiled, as he watched the children, and it struck him that these children were
the future of DunFaythe, and they had to be protected and nourished.

Pádraig Bocht stood beside him, swaying from left to right like a high
priest venerating some ancient god, his arms folded across his chest hidden
by his green cloak wrapped around his thin frame. He did not smile and
hated being in the company of children.

As he flicked his eyes from child to child, twitching his crooked nose like a bull terrier sniffing the air for prey he wished that children could be disciplined and taught how to behave.

'It's Lord Devereux! It's Lord Devereux!' whispered the children to each other, noticing the two figures standing at the entrance of the Great Hall, their mouths full, their eyes wide with curiosity. Meave, who had a mouthful of currant cake, peered at Pádraig Bocht. Noticing his swaying body she guessed the he must be on a mission and hoped that it had nothing to do with her. Her heart missed a beat, when she realised that he was staring at her. She looked over to Ralph, sitting opposite her, smiling at their father.

'Children!' began Lord Devereux. 'I asked you all here because I have something important to say to you.'

Children who were shuffling stopped immediately. Children who were reaching for some fruit withdrew their fingers. Children who had goblets to their mouths swallowed quickly.

'You have all heard rumours of a man called Citbeag. This man thinks he can take this castle from us. But we won't let him. Will we?'

'No!' screamed the children.

'It is important from this day forward that no child leaves the castle.'

A muffled moan of sadness erupted from their ranks.

'No child will play or tend to animals or ride horses outside of the castle walls. I know you all will obey me. It's for your own safety and for the safety of the castle. Will you obey me children?'

The children had never being asked to do anything by any adult before. They were usually ordered or told to do a particular task.

'We will,' they chorused.

Lord Devereux smiled and looked at Pádraig Bocht, who was still swaying and staring at the children. All the children shifted their gaze to Pádraig Bocht. They had seen Lord Devereux many times. Pádraig Bocht however, was a rare visitor to the castle. Some said he was a druid. Others said he was the brother of Lord Devereux, who had gone insane. Lord Devereux continued,

'We will meet here again at the same time next week, and if anybody has seen or heard anything unusual, he or she will inform me.'

The children cheered.

'Are there any questions?' asked Lord Devereux in a gentle voice, hoping there would be no response.

One child put his hand up. The children turned and looked at him wishing that he would not say something silly now that Lord Devereux had asked them all to behave responsibly.

'Will we have cakes and drinks next week?' asked the young boy.

Lord Devereux grinned.

'Yes of course you will.'

The children cheered again. Lord Devereux turned and left the hall, happy in the knowledge that the children of DunFaythe would be safe, at least for a while. They continued to cheer, as he walked from the hall then quietened suddenly. Pádraig Bocht was not leaving. His bare feet plodded along the shiny wooden floor towards a group of seated children. His cloak covered his head, allowing the children only to see his blank staring green eyes, his crooked nose and pointed chin. One scared little boy whispered to his friend,

'He looks like he is dead, but he is walking.'

'Maybe he is dead, and that's why he looks so horrible,' returned his friend.

Meave shivered. She knew that he was coming to see her. As he approached the tables, the children averted their staring eyes, afraid to look at his face, afraid to look into his eyes, dreading that he would speak to any of them.

'Hello Pádraig Bocht,' said Ralph, when Pádraig Bocht reached his place at the long table.

Pádraig Bocht stopped and looked down at Ralph and knew that Ralph was not afraid. The rest of the children were shocked to hear Ralph addressing him. Meave was trembling, but was comforted by Ralph's presence.

'Tis your sister I have come to see,' snapped Pádraig Bocht, changing his gaze to Meave. 'The rest of ye may leave now,' and he swivelled in a slow circle.

The children immediately scampered out of the Great Hall and disappeared into the passageways of the castle, leaving behind them half eaten cakes, pools of spilled apple juice and upturned goblets and bowls.

'I need you to come to the lighthouse,' he said, turning to Meave. 'I spoke to your father, and he has given permission. You may bring your brother with you, if you wish.'

Meave's lips were stuck together, her hands resting on her knees tingled and shook. She noted his sooty eyebrows; the grey flecked hairs on his chin, and the wrinkles that cut deep into his forehead. The grey pallor of his skin reminded her of a corpse she had once seen. Yet despite her fear, she imagined his green eyes, staring at her, were pleading with her to come with him. He knew that she had the answers, and she could find out when they were coming and why they were coming.

'*Labhair liom a chailín*, Speak to me girl,' he said, filling a goblet of water and handing it to Meave. 'Don't be afraid. You have the knowledge, even though you are not aware of it,' his stained teeth biting down on his lower lip, as he waited for her answer. Meave guessed that if her father had given permission, then it would be all right to go with Pádraig Bocht.

'I'll come,' said Ralph. He was thinking of the lighthouse, the fire and the stairway beneath the lighthouse and Pádraig Bocht's strange drawings.

'*Ciúnas a bhuachaill*, Quiet Boy,' answered Pádraig Bocht. 'It's not you I want.'

Meave looked at Ralph who winked at her, hoping that she would say yes. She glanced up at Pádraig Bocht.

'Yes I'll come, but … Ralph must come too,' she replied, taking a mouthful of water.

Pádraig Bocht's gaping eyes softened.

'I've a coach waiting to take us to the lighthouse,' and he turned and walked toward the door of the Great Hall.

'Let's go,' said Ralph standing up and knocking over a jug of apple juice. He was looking forward to visiting the lighthouse again, and this time as a guest with his father's permission.

'You first,' returned Meave, regretting already that she had agreed to visit the lighthouse.

Meave followed Ralph and Pádraig Bocht, not knowing what knowledge she had and believing that she was too young to know anything that adults would consider important. They met several soldiers on the way, who stopped and looked at the strange procession of Pádraig Bocht, and the two children making their way towards the northern courtyard of the castle. Just as they were passing the door of a chamber, Old Alesia opened it and stepped into the corridor.

'Let no harm come to these children,' she croaked, pointing her bony finger at Pádraig Bocht,' or I will put a curse on you.'

'I'm cursed already,' answered Pádraig Bocht, without slowing his pace or looking at her. Ralph stopped and stood before the bent old woman.

'We are going to the lighthouse,' he said, shaking with excitement.

'I know where you are going,' she answered and disappeared off in the opposite direction.

'Its father's carriage,' shouted Ralph, stepping into the courtyard. Four white stallions stood before Lord Devereux's ornate carriage, flying the Devereux pennant. An escort of six soldiers mounted on horses waited for the children. Pádraig Bocht clambered into the carriage. The children sat opposite him.

'Dangerous days,' he said, glancing out the side window. 'Always travel with an escort.'

Ralph remembered the last time they had travelled to the lighthouse was on a donkey and cart. Meave remained silent. The four stallions effortlessly pulled the carriage along the cobblestones of the courtyard and down the sand track towards the lighthouse.

'They don't need a carrot to entice them to go,' said Ralph, and he laughed.

Meave smiled. She felt more at ease knowing that Ralph, always cheerful, always watching and wondering would be with her in the lighthouse. After a short bumpy journey the carriage and its escort arrived at the beach. Ralph was surprised with what he saw. There were about one hundred fully armed soldiers positioned on the beach and on the rocks below the lighthouse. A deep trench cut through the sand around the lighthouse, from Trá Bán, through the sand dunes and fields to the beach at the far side of the lighthouse. The carriage rattled, as it crossed a bridge over the trench and stopped below the rocks.

'Have to take precautions,' said Pádraig Bocht, stepping out of the carriage. 'Don't want any unwelcome visitors.'

They made their way up the stone stairway to the door of the lighthouse. A soldier opened the rusty door, and they followed Pádraig Bocht. The two children stood at the entrance of Pádraig Bocht's chamber and viewed its contents once again. The drawings were still on the wall and the shelves and presses remained cluttered with maps and documents. Ralph saw to his surprise that a door now blocked the entrance to the staircase leading to the bowels of the lighthouse. The small wooden table was replaced by a large oval one and looked, as if it had come straight from the carpenter's workrooms as it was clean and smelled of wood polish. Ralph wondered how Pádraig Bocht carried such a large table through the narrow entrance door of the lighthouse.

'I see you have got a new table,' said Ralph, trying his best to impress Pádraig Bocht.

'*Sea*! Aye!' replied Pádraig Bocht, bending down and opening a large drawer in a press, directly below an image of the full moon.

The two children sat on stools and rested their elbows on the polished wood of the oval table. Pádraig Bocht continued to remove paintings and drawings from the drawer and lay them on the floor.

'What are you looking for?' asked Ralph, trying to engage Pádraig Bocht in a conversation.

'You'll see in a moment,' muttered Pádraig Bocht.

Meave was scanning the images of the moon on the wall, dwelling for a few moments on each image. She had learned from her Greek tutor to try and look at situations as he called it 'the overview'. He told her not to treat images or drawings as individual items. It is important, she remembered him saying to see how the small pieces fit into the big picture. Closing her eyes, she tried to visualise the earth and moon as one big picture.

'Found it,' said Pádraig Bocht, and he stood up, holding a long role of parchment bound with greased cord. Meave's eyes remained closed and her chin had fallen to her chest.

'Wake up girl. This is no time to sleep!' he snapped, laying his hand on her shoulder.

Meave remained silent, sitting motionless on her stool.

'Meave is not sleeping,' said Ralph. 'She is thinking. She often closes her eyes when she is thinking about her Latin or Greek studies. I think you should leave her be.'

Pádraig thought it best to leave Meave in her sleepy trance, knowing that she had the knowledge.

Meave opened her eyes and turned to Ralph. He saw that regal look in her eyes again. They shone with confidence.

'Are you all right Meave?' he asked. 'You were thinking. You always think with your eyes closed.'

'Yes I am Ralph. I'm not afraid. I heard a voice again,'

She smiled and looked at Pádraig Bocht and then pointed to a drawing of the moon on the wall.

'That is not the moon. It is the planet Arob ... Where we came from,' she said, her cheeks glowing

'Who? When?' spluttered Ralph.

Pádraig Bocht's eyes narrowed like a snake waiting to spit venom, and he stroked his long chin with his stained fingers.

'There is no such planet,' he said, hoping she would explain it to him.

Meave stared at him with a defiant look on her face. He thought he saw her eyes swivel, as they burned into him.

'Yes there is. The voice told me it's hidden behind the moon. That's why we cannot see it. The moon has no influence over the tides. It is the planet Arob!' she said, pushing back her shoulders.

'Impossible,' said Pádraig Bocht, his long thin fingers tingling with excitement. 'It's well known that it is the cycle of the moon that causes the ebb and flow of the tide.'

Meave stood up and walked over to the drawing on the wall and pointed to the white oval shape.

'The moon is a dead planet, it has no influence,' she whispered and then put a finger on the lines connecting the planet to another oval shape, representing earth.

'Arob is a planet full of life. That is what the lines on the image are showing. We get our light and heat from the sun. The lifelines are from Arob to Tír na Leasa … some day I will return.'

Pádraig Bocht leaned against the table and ran his stained hands through his thin streaked hair, not knowing if this was good or bad news. Words and images rushed through his head – lifelines … For what? How do these people live? He walked over to the opening in the lighthouse wall and looked out at the churning sea. Maps, Symbols and Documents pounded his brain, Stories, Rumours, Sea People, Arob.

'How did the … sea people travel?' asked Ralph, choking with interest. 'Please tell me Meave.'

Meave closed her eyes again, placed her open hands on the table and raised her chin, as if she was going to smell a fresh blossom.

'The answer is here. The sea people belong to this world, just like we do. They were in this world before we were. They travelled from Arob. They are our kin,' she replied, swelling with pride.

'Yes that's it,' said Pádraig Bocht, and he placed the long role of parchment he was holding on the table and removed the chord. The parchment uncoiled and spread along the table.

'That is how they came,' he said, pointing to the image on the parchment, sketched with blue dye.

'It's like a large wheel with hundreds of spokes,' cried Ralph. 'Perhaps it spins through the sky.'

'Perhaps it does,' said Pádraig Bocht. 'I have spent years trying to understand this drawing. First I thought it was the plan of a castle, and then I guessed it might be some war machine, and now a young girl explains about the planet Arob in a few seconds. It's a sky ship! It's how they came to this planet!'

He touched her arm gently. She felt as if a large chunk of ice was pressing against her arm. Her eyes opened.

'*Cailin óg*, Young lady, You have knowledge that you are unaware of. You! Young lady will solve the prophecy for me,' he said, rolling up the parchment.

Meave looked at Ralph, who was swaying from side to side with anticipation.

'That is why ye are here,' said Pádraig Bocht, removing a large iron key from his cloak, as he walked over to a rusty iron chest on the floor of the chamber.

'Your father has given me permission to show you the prophecy. It's here.'

He opened the lock and lifted the lid of the chest. Ralph saw a folded parchment tied with a golden chord lying on three large volumes.

'*Sea*, Yes,' said Pádraig. 'You are looking at The Book of Time, The Book of Draíocht and The Book of Truth.'

He removed the parchment and closed the chest.

'Our future is written on this parchment,' he whispered, untying the golden chord and placing the parchment on the table.

'Do not touch it. It's old and delicate.'

The two children looked down at the writing on the parchment, spread out on the table. The first letter of each line of text was ornate script, written with a mixture of red and green dye. The rest of the letters were etched with black dye.

'Iseult Devereux, the daughter of the first Lord of DunFaythe wrote it. She was a prophet, a mystic and a healer. She lived for two hundred years. Her body lies in the crypt below the castle and it has never decayed,' said Pádraig Bocht, as his fingers moved across the text on the parchment.

Ralph and Meave were both afraid to read aloud the written text.

'I will read it,' said Pádraig Bocht. 'I have read it a thousand times.'

He read carefully from the ancient parchment.

> 'They will come from the sea.
> The fire will die.
> They will return to conquer.
> The time is written in the
> Language that begins at the end.
> DunFaythe depends on her.'

The two children listened to Pádraig Bocht then glanced at each other.

'*Fire will die*,' bounced around Ralph's head.

'Who will return?' he asked, almost bursting with questions.

'Don't know,' answered Pádraig Bocht. 'Maybe it's telling us Citbeag is coming, or maybe it is telling us the sea people are coming. We have to find the time.'

'The language that begins at the end,' said Meave.

They both looked at her.

'Do you know the language?" asked Ralph, expecting Meave to say that she did.

'There are hundreds of languages,' returned Pádraig Bocht. 'It's impossible to study them all.'

'The language that begins at the end,' repeated Meave, closing her eyes and touching the parchment with the tips of her fingers.

'It must be a language that you speak backwards. How can you speak a language backwards?' asked Ralph, guessing that it would be impossible to speak backwards.

'The language that begins at the end,' repeated Meave again. Her fingers began to vibrate, as if the parchment was passing on secrets to her.

Pádraig Bocht's eyes widened.

'I have spent many years searching ancient books and asking travellers from foreign lands about their languages and about the words and phrases in their languages,' he said, watching Meave's fingers dance on the parchment.

Suddenly her fingers stopped shaking. She placed her opened hands on the table.

'If you were to speak this language, you would not be speaking backwards,' she said.

'What do you mean?' asked Ralph, feeling tired and frustrated. 'Please tell us.'

'I have studied two languages. The language that begins at the end must be Latin,' answered Meave.

'Latin!' cried Ralph. 'Latin has not been spoken for a thousand years. You must be mistaken.'

Meave opened her eyes and looked up at Pádraig Bocht.

'Iseult Devereux wrote the prophecy. I wonder did she read and speak Latin?' she asked in an authoritative voice.

'How does the Latin language begin at the end?' asked Ralph, admiring how Meave could know so much about Latin.

'I have only begun to study Latin,' answered Meave and paused for a moment.

'Don't be afraid,' said Pádraig Bocht. 'Tell us what you are thinking.'

Meave was pleasantly surprised to see what she thought was a gentle smile forming on his thin lips.

'Tell us Meave,' urged Ralph, who was beaming with pride at his sister.

'If I said 'I fed the dog' and then translated into Latin it would translate directly as 'The dog I fed.' Therefore in the Latin language the sentence begins at the end,' she answered, nodding her head.

Pádraig Bocht sat down on a stool beside the children, placed his elbows on the table and rested his long chin in a cradle of his stained fingers. He closed his eyes and remained silent.

'That's unbelievable,' said Ralph. 'But it says in the prophecy the time is written in the language that begins at the end. When is the time? Is it when the lighthouse fire will die? … But where is the time written in the language that begins at the end?'

'I don't … know,' replied Meave,' and I don't care. I want to go back to the castle. I hate this lighthouse.'

She was beginning to feel unwell, her stomach ached and a rasping pain shot across her forehead. She was regretting that she had ever mentioned the Latin language. Pádraig Bocht stood up and walked over to the window overlooking the sea.

'Can we go now?' pleaded Meave, rubbing her fingers.

'Not just yet,' answered Pádraig Bocht. 'I know where the time is written. Iseult Devereux has it.'

But isn't she dead in the crypt?' exclaimed Ralph.

'*Sin ceart*. That's correct. Iseult Devereux has the Book of Freagra in a pocket of her death shroud. The book is written in Latin. Before she died she asked that it would be left with her. Tomorrow I will visit Iseult in the dark crypt and see what she has to say. I will bring you back to the castle now. Meave, you have given me invaluable information today.'

Meave was not listening to Pádraig Bocht, she still feared him. She wanted to see her cat and her friends.

* CHAPTER SEVEN*

The Lake of Fire

Pádraig Bocht paced back and forth across the polished floor of the Great Hall, his hands clasped behind his stooped shoulders, his drooping eyes frozen in a vacant stare. The early morning spring sunlight cast a long thin shadow of his frame which reached to the opposite end of the Great Hall.

'Has to be done,' he said, and he stopped pacing and looked down at Lord Devereux, sitting on a bench, his arms resting on a large wooden table.

Both men looked tired, their eyes red and sore from lack of sleep.

'We have been discussing this ... all night,' replied Lord Devereux, trying to stifle a yawn. 'Tell me again what it says.'

Pádraig Bocht removed a small leather bound volume from his tunic and opened a page of the Book of Freagra.

'The text is written in Latin. As I have told you, it was Meave who found the language.'

'Read it again,' said Lord Devereux, wishing he did not have to listen to Pádraig Bocht.

Pádraig Bocht looked down at the page for the fiftieth time.

'I will translate it,' he said, taking a deep breath and glancing at Lord Devereux. He knew every word of the text without reading it.

'Read it!,' ordered Lord Devereux, knowing that he would soon have to make a terrible decision.

Pádraig Bocht began,

> 'When she finds the language.
> It is time.
> When the little one.
> The moons will part.
> They will come for it.
> It is time.
> To return to her people.'

Pádraig Bocht waited for Lord Devereux to speak. Lord Devereux hoped that Pádraig Bocht would make a suggestion, knowing that he faced a terrible decision, and that the future of DunFaythe would be decided in the next few moments. Pádraig Bocht broke the silence.

'Iseult Devereux knew that Meave was the one who would connect the prophecy to the Book of Freagra. She also knew that Citbeag, that is the little one, who is mentioned in the prophecy, would come. The prophecy says they will come for it.'

Lord Devereux's eyes closed, his chin rested on his heaving chest. Pádraig Bocht replaced the book in his tunic.

'The book of Freagra gives the time. The time for her to return to her people is when the Book of Freagra is found. Therefore it is Meave who must return. Meave found the language therefore it is Meave who is referred to as ''she'' in the Book of Freagra,' he explained.

Lord Devereux stood up and turned his back to Pádraig Bocht, who paused for a moment, waiting for him to speak.

'Continue,' said Lord Devereux, dreading what Pádraig Bocht was going to say.

'The prophecy says that DunFaythe depends on her. She must have something to do with fulfilling the prophecy,' said Pádraig Bocht in a hushed voice.

Lord Devereux buried his drawn, lined face in his wide hands.

'You are asking me to risk my only daughter's life because of some ancient prophecy,' he moaned.

'It's the only way,' answered Pádraig Bocht, 'or Citbeag will destroy us! Enslave us!'

Lord Devereux lifted his face from his hands, turned and looked into Pádraig Bocht's eyes. He had fought many times, had seen soldiers die and heard them scream, suffering from horrible wounds. Many times he had believed that he was going to die in combat. He had been afraid before, now he was terrified. This was a different conflict that could not be won by using war strategies or with a cavalry charge. This battle was going to be long, slow and painful.

'Are you sure that this is the only way?' he pleaded, wiping his swollen bloodshot eyes.

'Yes,' whispered Pádraig Bocht. 'The only way. We have to know what they are coming for. The Book of Freagra says they will come for it.'

Lord Devereux stood up and grabbed Pádraig Bocht's shoulders.

'Do it,' he shouted and then walked the length of the Great Hall, leaving Pádraig Bocht shaking with fear.

Pádraig Bocht waited for a few moments. His body ached; a throbbing pain beat across his forehead.

He pondered for a while, sitting down where Lord Devereux had been sitting. Could he do this? What if he was wrong? What if Iseult Devereux was insane and her prophecy was the creation of a demented and sick mind?

He decided it all made good sense and then remembered Lord Devereux's pleading eyes looking at him. 'Citbeag! The language that begins at the end. Meave even identified a planet behind the moon.

"Do it!" he had said. "Do it!" He would not have given permission if he had thought that there was another way.'

He struggled to his feet, wishing that it was all over and gazed around at the vastness of the Great Hall, letting his eyes drift along the portraits of past Lord Devereux's.

'What would ye have done?' he asked, half expecting an answer.

Meave and Ralph were in the courtyard watching the locals setting up their market stalls in the castle courtyard. Meave was happy to see life returning to the castle. Winter cobwebs and winter chills were disappearing. The market came to life. New-born lambs danced and jumped amongst the vendors. The sweet scented perfumes of clusters of freshly picked multicoloured polianthes, drifted among the stalls. Bundles and bunches of daffodils, ranging from deep velvety maroon to gleaming salmon, orange to bright red with golden borders, decorated many of the market stalls and stands. Turkeys and geese, who survived the Irish feast of Nollaig, strutted around enjoying their status and their freedom.

Meave, enjoying the fresh aroma of spring flowers listened to sellers haggling and watched the buyers bartering. The noise level increased as more and more people arrived with their wares. Ralph, barefooted, was watching some fishermen filling a stall with buckets of live crabs and bunches of freshly harvested seaweed and was wondering what it would be like to have a pet crab. He never liked to eat crab-meat; it was salty and always tasted of seaweed. The surrounding high walls of the castle blocked out the chill sea breeze and Ralph could feel the warmth of the earth under his feet.

As if someone had screamed 'Silence' the bustle of the market and the banter of the crowd suddenly quietened. Meave became aware of a change of mood amongst the vendors. Lambs stopped jumping, crabs in their buckets raised their claws in anger, even the blooming flowers seemed to wilt and wane. Ralph scanned the walls of the castle. He was waiting with a repressed elation for the beginning of war.

But all he saw were the guards on the castle walls chatting and viewing the activities of the market.

Meave realised that the market crowd was looking towards the main door of the castle.

'Oh no!' she cried, her face whitened, her lips dried.

Pádraig Bocht, standing at the edge of the market, looking straight at her, was the focus of their attention. Ralph, who was counting crabs in a bucket, skipped over to Meave.

'Look!' she said, pointing at Pádraig Bocht and feeling a knot in her stomach.

Ralph followed her gaze and saw Pádraig Bocht walking towards them, his lips twitching, his fingers clenched in front of his long chin, as if he was praying.

'I ... don't like this,' whispered Meave grasping Ralph's arm.

'Don't be afraid,' replied Ralph, 'His bark is worst than his bite. I'm sure he only wants to talk to you again.'

Pádraig Bocht stopped several paces before the children.

'Put on some warm clothes. We are going to the lighthouse tonight,' he said.

Meave pinched Ralph's arm.

'Say no!' she whispered.

Ralph wasn't listening, his mind was dreaming of images of soldiers, the fire and the steps below the lighthouse.

'Why are we going?' he asked, trying not to show his excitement.

'I want to show you something,' answered Pádraig Bocht.

Meave pinched Ralph's arm again.

'Meave doesn't want to go,' said Ralph, hoping that Pádraig Bocht would insist that she went.

Pádraig Bocht looked at Meave; his pleading eyes stared through her.

'Meave doesn't want to visit the lighthouse,' continued Ralph. 'I'll go. She can remain here.'

Pádraig Bocht moved closer to the children. The bright light of the morning sun highlighted the weather worn lines between his wet eyes and the pale sickly leathery skin, stretching across his bony face.

'This will be the last time. I promise you. I will not ask you again to come to the lighthouse.'

Ralph's eyes widened with anticipation. Meave knew that he wanted to go, so if this was the last time, and if Ralph was with her, then she would go. A whispering silence wafted through the market. The animals gathered in a corner of the courtyard; turkeys, lambs and dogs all sat watching the trio. The market crowd moved to a point furthest from Pádraig Bocht, wondering what business he had with the son and daughter of Lord Devereux. They saw how young Ralph spoke to him without fear, and how he stood tall and looked straight at Pádraig Bocht.

'If this is the last time, then I will go. Promise me that this is the last time?' asked Meave, trying to sound like an adult.

'*Sea*. Yes,' replied Pádraig Bocht, hoping that maybe in another life or in another time, he would be forgiven for what he was about to do. 'The last time.'

But he was prepared to sacrifice himself for DunFaythe, feeling that he had died many years ago, and his body was moving about to fulfil the prophecy.

'Your father's carriage will collect you at midnight,' he said and then turned and walked towards the door of the castle.

The market folk looked away, as he shuffled past them. He did not see them or care about them. Meave and Ralph waited a few moments and watched him leave the courtyard. They then followed him through the castle door and silently walked to their chambers.

Whilst she waited, Meave could not eat or concentrate on her books. She put her black cat out of her chamber and paced about agitated and nervous and spent hours staring at the lighthouse from her window. The fire burned. The soldiers stood guard.

'*Why me? Why me?*' she asked herself, feeling her body tremble.

Ralph came to visit her, but she did not want to talk to him. Despite his reassuring words she was still afraid of Pádraig Bocht.

Late in the evening Old Alesia entered her chamber. Meave was surprised to see her, as she had never visited her before. Old Alesia stood at the door of the chamber, wearing a multicoloured shawl wrapped around her head and shoulders. Her flaky lined head, peered out from the folds of the shawl like the wrinkled face of new-born baby, wrapped in swaddling clothes. Her bony hands were clasped together, and her eyes like that of an infant, staring, but seeing little.

'Don't be afraid, child,' she said. 'Pádraig Bocht will not harm you.'

Meave was feeling angry and was not interested in listening to anybody talking about Pádraig Bocht. She turned her back to Old Alesia and stared out at the lighthouse. A few moments of heavy silence passed between the two of them.

'What do you know of Pádraig Bocht?' asked Meave, continuing to stare at the lighthouse.

Old Alesia opened her wrinkled fist.

'Meave!' she croaked.

Meave did not answer

'Meave!'

Meave was startled to hear Old Alesia raising her voiced. She turned from the window, and her attention was drawn to a silver brooch balancing on Old Alesia's open palm.

'What is it?' she asked, lifting Old Alesia's hand to examine it.

She did not want to hear any more mysterious stories or prophecies.

'..was your mother's,' whispered the old woman. '..has their mark on it. Take it!'

Meave did not ask who they were, or what the mark meant, as she picked up the brooch. It felt heavy for such a small item and had a circular central section surrounded by eight triangular spikes, which reminded her of drawings of the sun that she had seen in Pádraig Bocht's chamber in the lighthouse. Etched in the central section of the silver sun were two oval shapes, one larger than the other connected by two straight lines.

'Yes,' said Old Alesia, reaching out and holding Meave's arm 'You are making a connection aren't you?'

Meave could feel her cold fingers wrapping around her arm like a slithery viper. One of Old Alesia's teeth protruded over her lower lip. Meave felt nervous, yet a feeling of excitement and elation mixed with a deep uneasiness rose in her.

'Always wear this brooch around your neck. It will set you apart. Grasp it tightly and close your eyes and it will guide you,' and she tightened her snake's grip on Meave's wrist.

'What do you know of Pádraig Bocht?' repeated Meave, studying the brooch.

Old Alesia relaxed her grip.

'Pádraig Bocht ... I am his sister ... He is my brother,' and she walked towards the door

Meave stood tight-lipped. She'd never thought that Pádraig Bocht might have had a family, let alone a sister living in the castle. Old Alesia reached the door of the chamber and turned towards Meave.

'He was once a warrior. But they've made him what he is today. You can save him. Perhaps you can save us all,' and she left the chamber.

Meave grasped the brooch then closed her eyes and felt the brooch warming in her hand. A feeling of light-headed faintness fanned through her body. She reached out and leaned against the wall of her chamber. In the deep recesses of her mind a faint whispering voice spoke,

'Meave do not be afraid. I am with you ... I am with you.'

Ralph was in his chamber watching the sun crawl across the sky. He received no visit from Old Alesia. He knew that Pádraig Bocht was only interested in bringing Meave to the lighthouse and was also aware that his sister was different to other girls in the castle. He guessed that something important was going to happen soon, and he wanted to witness it. The children had arranged to meet an hour before midnight in the Great Hall.

Dressed in green woollen cloaks, thick linen tunics and breeches, they stood before a blazing fire in the Great Hall. The castle was silent, as if it knew that a momentous event was about to happen. The guards in the Great Hall, who were usually cheerful and chatty, were now solemn and erect in their stations. They watched the children warming their hands and were aware that this might be the last time that they saw the heirs of DunFaythe Castle. Meave and Ralph were oblivious to the quietness of the castle and the tension of the guards. To the surprise of the children, Lord Devereux entered the Great Hall and strode towards them. His beard had grown and now reached his broad heaving chest.

'My ... children,' he choked. 'Pádraig ... Bocht will be here soon.'

Meave was feeling much better now, as she held the brooch that Old Alesia had given her in a pocket of her cloak. Lord Devereux moved closer to the children.

'You will be a queen one day,' he said to Meave, 'and you, Ralph, will be Lord of DunFaythe Castle.'

Ralph's chest tightened with pride.

'Father,' sighed Meave. 'Are we in danger? Is DunFaythe Castle in danger? Are you in danger?'

'You saw the prophecy, Meave,' he answered, stroking his long beard with his thick fingers. 'Danger is always waiting for us. However, goodness will prevail. There are forces that will protect us. You feel that force sometimes, don't you?'

'Yes, father, I do sometimes, but I don't understand,' answered Meave.

Ralph held Meave's hand.

'You don't have to understand it. If it works and helps us, then understanding is not important. I have often tried to understand how the moon affects the tides. Despite what you think I have read many books about the moon and the tides and none of them can explain how a new moon causes a high tide.'

Meave giggled.

'I thought you never studied any texts.'

'I only study the subjects I am interested in. Someday I will understand how it all works.'

Lord Devereux listened to his son, trying not to show how proud he was of him, knowing that he would made a great Lord Devereux one day.

'Yes Ralph,' said Lord Devereux, beaming down at him. 'We can't understand all that we see and hear.'

The door of the Great Hall opened and two soldiers, dressed in black hooded cloaks, entered and approached the group, huddled in front of the fire.

'The carriage is ready, My Lord,' announced one of them.

Lord Devereux clenched his fists and struggled to hold back tears filling his eyes, as he embraced the children.

'Don't worry,' said Ralph, looking up at his father. 'We'll return soon.'

Meave thought that her father looked sad, but did not understand why he should look so unhappy. After all, they were only going to the lighthouse to look at some old manuscript or drawing. Lord Devereux removed his strong grip from the children.

'It's time. Remember! Don't be afraid,' he said in a low, reassuring voice.

They followed the soldiers to the carriage. Lord Devereux remained at the fire staring into the burning logs. A tear escaped and sizzled on the hot grate.

The children climbed into the carriage. The night felt chill, and a bright full moon looked down on them, as they made their way from the castle courtyard along the track to the beach and over the damp sands of Trá Bán, towards the lighthouse.

Ralph caught a glimpse of the lighthouse through the open window of the carriage. Its shadow spread like a dark scab on the churning, frothy sea, beneath the crimson glow of the fire.

As the carriage approached the lighthouse, silhouettes of soldiers carrying torches began to appear,

hundreds of them, always guarding, always watching. Pádraig Bocht stood at the door of the lighthouse, waiting for them, two innocent children unaware that their actions would determine the future of the Devereux line. For what he was about to do, he hoped that he would not be damned forever. Knowing that this night was the culmination of years of studying and calculating he hoped that Meave and Ralph would someday forgive him. He also believed that he could never return to the castle if Meave and Ralph did not succeed. He would be an outcast, a pariah. There would be much blood shed and destruction, but Lord Devereux would defend his castle to the last man.

The carriage came to a halt below the lighthouse rocks, and the children climbed out onto the soft sand. A funnel of soldiers holding torches lit the way to the lighthouse steps and to Pádraig Bocht. Ralph looked down the funnel, took a deep excited breath and walked between the soldiers. Meave clasped her brooch and followed Ralph. Searching the grim faces of the soldiers she guessed that they knew something that she didn't know – they wouldn't look at her and their expressions displayed a terrible sadness.

Ralph strode ahead of Meave. The torches warmed his face. His thumping heart warmed his limbs. He wanted to be a soldier some day, carry arms and look strong and fierce. They climbed the stone steps towards Pádraig Bocht. He stepped forward to greet them. The shuffling of bodies below them on the beach caused the children to turn and look. The soldiers had gathered on the beach below the rocks, holding their flaming torches aloft.

'Long live the Devereux line,' they shouted. 'Long live Meave and Ralph Devereux.'

Meave felt a tingle of pride pass through her – she was of royal stock. These were her father's soldiers. They would protect her. She raised her hand to acknowledge the soldiers. They cheered again. Ralph looked at Meave and felt again that he was standing in the presence of a queen. He took a step backwards and allowed Meave to enjoy the moment.

'Thank you for coming children,' said Pádraig Bocht. There was almost a kindness in his voice.

He wore a headband of twisted gold and a silver tunic with two purple and gold stripes across his chest. His green cloak reached to his feet, his matching deep green piercing eyes studied the children.

'Is it a special occasion?' asked Ralph, noticing Pádraig Bocht's colourful clothing. The soldiers seem to think so.'

Pádraig Bocht unexpectedly smiled down at the children.

'Yes!' he answered, trying to sound enthusiastic. 'A special occasion. Many questions will be answered tonight and over the coming days. Let's go inside.'

They followed Pádraig Bocht through the ancient door of the lighthouse. Ralph walked towards the charts on the table.

'No, this way,' said Pádraig Bocht, with a flick of his eyes. 'We are going below tonight.'

'Where?' asked Ralph, keenly.

'Beneath the lighthouse. Follow me'.

He then opened the door to the stairwell and disappeared down the stairs that Ralph had often wondered about. Meave turned to Ralph; her feet stuck to the floor.

'I can't move,' she said. 'I'm scared.'

'Hold my hand,' said Ralph, and he reached out and took Meave's hand and followed Pádraig Bocht down the stairway.

Down, down they went into the bowels of the lighthouse. Flickering torches mounted on the dripping wet walls lit the curling stairway. Pádraig Bocht never looked back. He never spoke. His cloak dragged along the wet slippery steps, as he led them down. As they stepped deeper and deeper into the heart of the lighthouse, the children became aware that the air was getting warmer. They could feel sand and the crunch of dried seaweed under their falling feet. They removed their heavy cloaks. They also noticed that the flickering shadows generated by the torches were fading, and an even light began to paint the walls. After travelling down eight hundred steps Pádraig Bocht stopped suddenly, turned around and faced the children.

'Is there an end to these steps?' asked Ralph, wiping his face.

'We need to rest,' pleaded Meave, mopping a spot of perspiration from the tip of her nose.

'We have arrived now,' panted Pádraig Bocht, standing beside an opening in the wall of the lighthouse.

An intense light filled the narrow stairwell, emanating from behind Pádraig Bocht. Ralph could feel a warm breeze blowing through the opening.

'Where ... are we?' he asked.

'What you are about to see has only been seen by your father, Old Alesia and myself,' answered Pádraig Bocht, glancing towards the opening. His eyes narrowed and his narrow thin lips trembled slightly, as he spoke.

'Follow me,' he ordered, stepping through the opening.

The two children followed and found themselves standing on a narrow ledge on the wall of an enormous underground cavern. Below them, to their astonishment was a perfectly shaped circular lake. Ralph opened his mouth to speak, but a deep gasping sound from his throat prevented him from uttering a word. Surrounding the lake was a wall of flames, reaching high into the cavern. The children could feel the scorching heat of the circular wall of fire on their faces. The roof of the cavern was decorated with giant stalactites, hanging like the teeth of a giant dinosaur.

'Where are we?' wailed Meave. 'I want to go back. The flames will burn us … I want to - '

Pádraig Bocht placed his hands reassuringly on the shoulders of the children.

'You are looking at the Lake of Fire, the entrance to Tír na Leasa,' he said. 'The flames prevent them from entering our kingdom. This is the fire that has to be kept burning.'

'But why? … How?' stammered Ralph, trying to believe what he was seeing.

'That is why we need so much wood delivered every day to the lighthouse,' continued Pádraig Bocht. 'If the Lake of Fire is extinguished, then they will come. We don't know what they are looking for. That is what we need you to find out. I come here each day to keep this fire burning.'

'What about the lighthouse fire?' asked Ralph, trying to hide his fear.

'The lighthouse fire also has to be kept burning. They can view it from the sea, and it tells them that we are still here that we are still masters of DunFaythe.

Looking into the roaring flames, Meave could feel Pádraig Bocht's fingers pressing tightly on her shoulder.

'The two of you must enter Tír na Leasa and find out what they want. Citbeag is getting close to DunFaythe, and we need to discover if the sea people sent him. They will know you Meave. You have their blood. You are of their royal line.'

Meave held the brooch tightly in her hand, remembering Old Alesia's words. "It has their mark on it."

Ralph was wondering how they were going to enter Tír na Leasa. Was there another stairwell or secret passage from the castle?

The rising heat from the lake, and Pádraig Bocht's suggestion that they should go to Tír na Leasa, was making Meave feel sick with worry.

'I want to go back to the castle now,' she cried. 'I don't like this place.'

Pádraig Bocht looked down at the children, his stomach cramped, his fingers itched.

'Time for you to go now,' he said in a low voice.

Ralph's knees were knocking.

'How do we enter Tír na Leasa?' I don't see any door or passageway or stairway,' he asked, looking into Pádraig Bocht's eyes. He thought he saw them moisten.

'How are we? -'

A gentle push was all that was needed. The two children fell forward towards the Lake of Fire. They did not scream or cry. Their minds and thoughts were blank. They felt no fear, only shock and bewilderment. They dropped from the ledge like two stones cast into a pool by a passing traveller, as they hurdled towards the lake, towards the fire, towards Tír na Leasa. The flaming lake welcomed them. Standing still for generations, it waited for something or someone to ripple its calm, deep water. The flames danced higher as the children fell.

Meave closed her eyes, as the black still expanse of water rushed towards her face. She was the first to break its placid surface. Her slim body pierced the calm blackness for a moment and she disappeared beneath its surface. She was surprised that it felt warm and pleasant. She did not panic because she knew that her body would slow down, as it hurtled into the depths of the lake. As she descended into the inky black water, she became aware of a faint shimmer of light beneath her. Her descent slowed, and she swam to the surface. She gulped for air and gasped for a rhythm in her breathing and immediately searched for Ralph.

'Ralph! Ralph!' she screamed, spitting water from her mouth and treading with her arms and legs. Pádraig Bocht remained on the ledge looking down at her.

'You're nearly there now Meave,' he cried.

'Father will hear of this,' she answered, splashing and gasping.

'You will be punished!'

Pádraig Bocht stretched his arms out in front of him and raised them above his head.

'Your father gave me permission to send you to Tír na Leasa. You must find out what they want and where it is.'

The water parted beside Meave, and Ralph's wet puffing, spluttering head appeared.

'Did you see it?' he gasped. 'Did you see it?'

'See what?' asked Meave, feeling tired from moving her arms in the water.

'There is a light at the bottom of the lake. It must be Tír na Leasa!' he cried. 'How are we going to get there? The lake is too deep. We can't swim there.'

'I don't know,' gasped Meave, pointing to Pádraig Bocht.

'What's he doing?'

Pádraig Bocht had his arms stretched above his head, his eyes closed, furrows of concentrated meditation criss-crossed his forehead.

'At least they didn't drown,' he said to himself. 'The next stage will not be easy.'

He began to chant, '*go mall, go mall, go mall.*'

They could not escape through the ring of flames. Ralph thought that the hanging stalactites had formed into the shape of a smirking grin and were about fall on them. Pádraig Bocht was not going to help them.

'What are we going to do?' cried Ralph, finding it difficult to move his tired legs through the water.

'We will drown. We can't stay floating forever.'

Meave reached over and held Ralph's hand.

'Remember what father said,' she gulped.

'What did he say?' choked Ralph, spitting out a mouthful of putrid water.

'He said that we were not to be afraid. He knew that this was going to happen. That is why he was so sad when we were leaving him.'

They both looked up again at Pádraig Bocht, still muttering, chanting and moaning. The children saw a red light shine from his eyes, like a beam of sunset through a keyhole. He raised his voice. The chant got louder, '*go mall! go mall! go mall!*'

They felt a current moving them through the lake water.

'What's happening?' cried Meave, as she felt herself being pulled by the current.

'The Lake! … Pádraig Bocht … is causing the water to move,' cried Ralph.

Pádraig Bocht continued to chant and then raised his voice, '*go mall! go mall! go tapaidh!*'

The current is getting faster,' shrieked Ralph 'He is making it go faster'.

'*go mall! go tapaidh! go tapaidh!*' roared Pádraig Bocht.

The flames jumped to the ceiling, licking the tips of the grinning dinosaur teeth. The revolving torrent dragged the children in circles, like two insects trapped in a bow of churning milk.

'Look!' cried Ralph, as they sped around the perimeter of the lake. 'There is a whirlpool forming in the middle of the lake, we are going to be sucked in, we are going to drown!'

'You're going to drown us! We are going to die!' screamed Meave.

Pádraig Bocht, transfixed in a rigid stare, with his hands outstretched, eyes and wide open was chanting, '*go tapaidh! go tapaidh! go tapaidh!*'

The children, clinging to each other, circled the lake several times.

Then the centre of the lake opened, and a whirling vortex appeared. Each time they circled the lake they got closer to the centre of the spinning vortex.

'We're going to be sucked in,' screamed Ralph.

Circle by circle, they got closer to the centre. As they reached the centre of the raging whirlpool they closed their eyes and were sucked into the blackness of the Lake of Fire.

* CHAPTER EIGHT *

Tír na Leasa

The plunging, swirling current swept the children downwards, downwards towards the dim glowing light. Ralph plummeted down through the vortex, struggling to breathe Headfirst he fell, his body twisting and jerking, as the vortex sucked him deeper into the lake. He opened his eyes. The light! He saw the light, rushing towards him. If only he could only hold his breath until he reached the light, but his lungs were beginning to ache. His eyes and neck bulged. His senses screamed; he was drowning! His lips would not stay closed. Bubbles of air dribbled from his mouth and danced in front of his eyes. He could taste the stagnant, stinking water slipping into his mouth and drip down into his stomach. Dark flashing spots appeared in front of his eyes, and he remembered Pádraig Bocht standing on the ledge. He remembered his father standing beside the fire in the Great Hall, smiling.

Meave was behind Ralph when they entered the vortex. She opened her eyes and saw him struggling in the current. The terror that had frozen her thoughts subsided, as she was pulled towards the light. A sensation of peaceful serenity flowed through her limbs, and she could not understand why she was feeling so comfortable. She could see the drowning face of Ralph struggling to stay alive. She knew what to do and had a feeling that she had been in this place before. Meave opened her mouth, and to her astonishment she realised that she was able to breathe. Bubbles of air floated about her, as she exhaled.

Ralph felt tired and sleepy. The thought that maybe he was dreaming passed through his mind. So if he closed his eyes and then opened them again, he might wake up and find himself back in the castle, and it would only have been a bad dream. He closed his eyes and tried to imagine that he was sleeping. Then opened them again, but he did not see the castle or the lighthouse. He could not believe what he saw. Meave was swimming beside him looking at him. This could not be happening. He must have fell asleep and was in the middle of a nightmare – how could Meave be swimming when he was drowning? – he was always a better swimmer than she was. Yes, he must be dreaming. Meave smiled at Ralph. He hoped that he would awaken soon, since nobody can smile under water.

He was now convinced that he was dreaming and tried to smile at Meave. His mouth filled with water. He started to cough and choke and was overcome by a shaking panic. Then Meave cupped her hands in front of her mouth, as if she was going to shout against a violent wind. A waft of clean, fresh, soothing air caressed his nostrils, and he vomited the stale water from his mouth, as the life saving breeze touched his lips. He could feel the draught fill his crushing lungs, and he was able to breathe. His senses snapped back to reality. Yes, it was Meave smiling through her cupped hand, blowing life-giving air towards him. The shaking fear lifted from his body. This was exciting! He tried to speak.

'Are we dreaming?' he gasped, not knowing what to say.

'No, we are not dreaming. We are going to Tír na Leasa. I didn't know that I could breathe or speak underwater,' she answered, continuing to feed Ralph with a draught of clean air.

'Did you hear Pádraig Bocht shouting before we were sucked into the lake?' she asked.

'Yes,' replied Ralph, trying to get used to speaking under water. 'He was chanting in Irish. I heard him screaming, ''Find out what they want - ''

'Must have something to do with Citbeag and the prophecy,' replied Meave, who was now feeling very comfortable. 'Now you must hold onto my ankles.'

Ralph grabbed her ankles. The air she exhaled formed a pocket around the two children and allowed Ralph to breathe freely, as they moved through the vortex. The pale glow in front of them changed to a dull orange shimmer and then filled with a bright red essence, as they approached. A flickering red radiance surrounded them.

'We are slowing down,' said Ralph. 'Where are we now? I can'tt see anything.'

The light increased in brightness. They could not distinguish any features or contours above or below them, only the water, brightness and silence. Meave changed direction and moved upwards.

'Where are you going?' asked Ralph, tightening his grip on Meave's ankles.

'I'm not going anywhere. The current is pulling me,' she answered, as they sped towards the light.

Ralph hung tightly to Meave's ankles.

'Look!' he shouted, as they ascended in the vortex. 'I can see an opening. It looks like a circular rock with a black hole in it.'

'I see it,' said Meave, trying to adjust her body to the flow of the current. 'I can see it … The vortex is carrying us to it.'

The children continued to hurtle upwards, towards the black circle. The closer they got the larger and wider the circle appeared.

'We're going to crash into that rock,' screamed Meave. 'The current is too strong. I can't swim out of it.'

The red radiance fused with darkness from the circle. They closed their eyes, as they entered into the blackness.

Meave broke through the darkness first. Her head appeared above the still water of a small placid rectangular pond. Ralph arrived next, spluttering and coughing. They swam about taking in their surroundings. They found themselves in a long narrow dimly lit room. The floor was covered with intricate patterns of long rectangular seashells. The walls of the room were decorated with paintings and images of DunFaythe Castle and DunFaythe Lighthouse, surrounded by images of flames and billowing smoke. Two shell shaped dishes resting on wooden poles contained a glowing substance that filled the room with a soft light.

'Let's get out of this water,' said Ralph, pulling himself on to the shell floor.

'These are sea shells!' he cried, running his hand along the contours of the uneven spines of the floor. 'I'm glad that there's no wall of flames surrounding this pond.'

Looking around the room and its drawings he stretched out his hand to help Meave from the pond and felt a cold wet grip tighten on his fingers. He jumped back from the pool, releasing his grip.

'Meave!' he shouted, looking down at her. 'Your face! It's changed! Your hair! It's changed.'

'What do you mean?' asked Meave, in a low whispering voice.

'Even your voice has changed! … Your eyes are long and narrow! … Your hair is hanging like strands of seaweed … It's sprinkled with tiny barnacles … What are those slits on your cheeks? … They look like gills.'

Meave climbed out of the pond. Ralph stepped back, amazed at Meave's transformation.

'Look at your hands. Your fingers are covered with tiny scales like those of a fish.'

Meave tried to shout at Ralph

'What's happened?' she tried to cry out loud. But only a low whisper came from her mouth. She looked down at her hands and saw no fingernails, a tiny feather like web stretched between each finger.

'Look at my fingers,' she whispered, holding out her hands.

'You are beginning to look like a fish,' said Ralph in amazement. 'And why are you whispering?'

'That's not funny. I can't … speak any louder. I can … only whisper,' she replied, looking at her fingers.

Ralph looked into Meave's wide narrow eyes.

'That's how you saved my life, how you could breathe and speak under water. You are still a girl, but you have some fish bits as well. Remember the story Pádraig Bocht told us about Maolmheasa and Farraingrá. You are like her, but she turned into one of us. I bet that if you go back to DunFaythe, you will become a person again.'

'I do hope so,' said Meave, beginning to get used to her new appearance. 'I feel I know this place.'

'I'm hungry,' replied Ralph, finally acknowledging the weakness he felt in his stomach.

'How can you be hungry?' cried Meave 'We have been sucked into a whirlpool, nearly drowned, and now we are in Tír na Leasa, and you are hungry.'

Ralph's stomach was rumbling, but he decided not to mention it again.

'Let's have a look around and see where we are. I'm sure the people here are friendly, after all they have paintings of the castle and the lighthouse on the walls,' said Ralph.

'I'm not so sure about that,' gulped Meave, seeing a figure filling an opening between the two glowing shell dishes.

'Look Ralph,' she whispered, in her new soft voice.

'What did you say Meave?' asked Ralph, examining a sketch of DunFaythe Castle on the wall.

'Look! They even have Pádraig Bocht in this painting … What did you say? I can't hear you.'

'I'm shouting,' whispered Meave. 'Look at the door! There is someone standing in the doorway!'

Ralph turned towards the doorway and saw a tall slim figure standing dressed in a tunic made of silvery fish skin. His hair was similar to Meave's except it was longer and it was pale green. There were two large gills on his cheeks, and his mouth was circular with thin lips; his narrow eyes were also similar to Meave's. He didn't seem to have any teeth and a dark vertical shadow protruded where a nose is usually found.

'He looks like … a fish,' gulped Ralph. 'He must be a sea person …he is a sea person!'

The fish man stared at the children. In his left scaly hand he held a long comb like sword.

'What will we do?' asked Ralph, moving from foot to foot.

'Stand and wait,' said Meave, and she placed her brooch around her neck.

'What have you got?' exclaimed Ralph, seeing the brooch for the first time.

Meave held the brooch in her hand and showed it to him.

'Old Alesia gave it to me. She said it belonged to mother. It has their mark on it.'

The fish man approached the children. Ralph noticed that his eyes were a deep purple and had no centre pupils. One of the gills on his cheek was exhaling while the other remained dormant. His small oval mouth was closed, and his face was covered with interlocking scales, changing colour, as they reflected the glowing light of the room. Ralph then realised that the black shadow in the centre of his face was a large irregular bone jutting out beneath his slanted eyes. The fish man stood before the children.

'He's staring at you,' said Ralph, turning to Meave.

'He's not staring at me,' answered Meave. 'He is staring at the brooch.'

The fish man opened his mouth. His lips quivered, and a low whistling whisper reached Ralph's ears.

'You are wearing the mark of royalty. Where do you come from?' touched Meave's ears.

Did he say something?' asked Ralph.

'Yes he did. He said that I am wearing the mark of royalty, and he wants to know where we came from.'

'All I heard was a whistling sound. You are able to understand his language!'

'Yes I think I can even though I never heard it before,' whispered Meave.

Ralph studied the figure standing in front of them. The creature had the shape of a person and the features of a fish; he had never seen a sword like that before.

'Say something to him,' said Ralph, nodding his head in the direction of the fish man.

'I can't speak his language,' replied Meave, looking nervously at the fish man.

'Try!' urged Ralph, clenching his fist.

'We have come from DunFaythe Castle,' said Meave.

'What did you say? I only heard a low whistle,' whispered Ralph.

The fish man stretched out his long arm and grasped the brooch with his scaly fingers.

'I think he understood me,' said Meave, touching Ralph's arm.

'You can speak the language!' gasped Ralph.

The fish man's lips quivered.

'It is a long time since we had a visitor from DunFaythe. My name is dJoucu. I am sure the Taoisi would like to meet you,' he said, in a low whistling sound

'Who are the Taoisi?' asked Meave, trying to remember if she had come across the name in her studies.

Ralph was pleasantly surprised that Meave was showing such confidence, speaking to this creature.

'They are the Council of Leasa. They will decide what happens to you. War is imminent so I would suggest that you do not prove to be troublesome,' he answered. 'Come with me now and bring your servant with you.'

'He thinks you are my servant, and he wants us to go with him,' said Meave, grinning.

Ralph felt uncomfortable in this strange place. Meave was speaking in a language that he could not understand, and he was being called a servant.

They followed the fish man through the opening in the rectangular room and along a bumpy shell floored corridor.

'It's difficult to walk on these shells,' muttered Ralph, stumbling over outcrops of seashell on the floor.

Meave and the fish man glided along effortlessly, his comb sword placed across his chest, as if he was marching in a parade.

'Where are we going?' asked Ralph, trying to catch up.

'To meet the Taoisi,' replied Meave, increasing her pace.

'I don't like this place. I wish we were back in the castle,' moaned Ralph, eyeing the cold stone walls of the passage.

'Everything will be fine. You'll see,' said Meave, feeling comfortable with her new appearance, as she strode ahead of him. 'It is usually me who is afraid of new places and things, not you.'

Ralph's feet were aching, he was hungry and tired and found it difficult to walk on the uneven shell floor. He was about to reply to Meave, when his attention was drawn to a dull light on the grey wall ahead of him, casting narrow, flickering, shadows across the corridor. He skipped quickly ahead of dJoucu and Meave to find the source of light.

'Look Meave!' he shouted, when he reached the flickering beam of light. 'The sea is in that window. It's just there!' he exclaimed, standing against the opposite wall of the corridor and looking in wonder at the sea. 'Why isn't the water coming in? Ask him Meave! Ask him why the sea is not coming into the corridor.'

dJoucu stopped and looked at Ralph's wide eyes and then glanced at the sea window. His mouth opened slightly.

'I think he is smiling,' said Meave, nodding towards dJoucu.

A low rustling sound came from his lips. Ralph could not understand. Meave listened carefully. The sound continued for several moments.

'What is he saying?' asked Ralph, feeling frustrated.

Meave replied to dJoucu by making a whistling sound through her teeth.

'He said that you should step forward and look out at Tír na Leasa. Ralph reluctantly stepped over to the sea window.

'The sea won't come in,' said Meave. 'There is a transparent skin holding it back. The skin is got from the Bsamaki fish. It is tough, like leather, but it is also transparent.'

Ralph pressed his finger against the see-through skin holding back the sea. It felt cold and wet like the tiles on the castle floors in wintertime. He then pressed his face against the skin and gazed into the ocean. His heart raced. He could not believe what he saw.

Stretching out in front of him was a long deep valley. The floor of the valley was covered in deep green sea grass and spotted with clusters of colourful ocean flowers of every colour and shape, leaning in a sea current. The cliffs of the valley were dotted with door like openings; some were emitting a blue light. Each side of the valley had three gaps in the cliffs, suggesting that there were other valleys running off it. To his amazement the valley was teeming with life. There were hundreds of sharks swimming in all directions; each one showing off its conical snout above an enormous gaping mouth filled with many razor-sharp hooked teeth. Every shark had a fish man on its back, riding it like Ralph would ride his horse. Several gigantic Orca whales went swimming past, with their skin of deep black and flawless white. Each Orca had about twenty reed baskets attached to each side of its huge body, filled with fish men. A lone fish man stood on each one's back with reins attached to its tall curved dorsal fin, guiding it through the water. A school of dolphins followed the Orca whales; each dolphin carried a small fish man.

'They must be fish children,' said Ralph, gasping in amazement.

Meave moved to the Bsamaki window and stood beside Ralph.

'This is Tír na Leasa,' she said, placing her open hand on the Bsamaki window.

'You sound as if you know this place. Have you been here before?'

He was getting used to Meave's new identity.

'No. But it all looks familiar to me. I have this feeling that I have been here before … It does not surprise me like it surprises you!'

Several times he saw fish men ride their sharks up to the openings in the cliffs, dismount and fetter them to long bone like poles.

'They must live inside the caves,' said Ralph, watching the fish men disappear into the cliffs' openings.

A constant glow from the far end of the valley produced a gentle radiance, illuminating Tír na Leasa, and reminding Ralph of the many summer sunsets he had witnessed from the DunFaythe Castle walls.

'I wonder what's causing the glow?' he asked, looking into the misty light. 'It's filling the valley.'

'I don't know,' replied Meave, but she felt a sliver of fear passed through her body. 'I think the fish man wants us to continue. Oh! By the way Ralph his name is dJoucu.'

'Wait a minute!' said Ralph, pressing his face against the cold membrane. 'What are they?'

Exiting from one of the side valleys was a train of grey melon shaped fish with huge oval eyes. The train pulled a large basket made of reeds. Thousands of glowing lights filled the basket, as the train made its way down the valley and out of sight.

'Look down there!' exclaimed Ralph, pointing to the floor of the valley.

Hundreds of fish men stood in battle formation, holding vicious comb swords and weapons that looked like crossbows with narrow pipes protruding from them. Now and again a solitary fish man would swim by and look in at Ralph and Meave.

'This is a wonderful place. I will have to find out how the fish men ride the fish. Maybe I will like Tír na Leasa after all,' he said, soaking in the wondrous scene before him.

'We must go now,' urged Meave. 'I think dJoucu is becoming impatient. He is making strange noises.'

'There is something strange going on. Are they gathering together an army? But who are they going to fight?' asked Ralph, squinting at the soldiers.

'I think that is why we are here,' she said, and she turned away from the window and followed dJoucu.

Ralph bounced along behind them, having forgotten about Pádraig Bocht, The Lake of Fire and the Vortex. This was a thrilling and mysterious world; fish men riding sharks, a world under the sea.

His head filling with ideas and questions – there is war on the land. There will be war under the sea. Why are they fighting? What are they fighting for?

A violent swishing whistle, like the sound of the wind blowing through the castle during long stormy wintry nights interrupted his racing mind. He could hear the wind, but could not feel any draught, not even a gentle breeze blowing along the corridor. The gale got louder, like a storm blowing in from the sea.

'We must be getting near the Taoisi now. Can you hear all the voices? There must be a lot of fish people up there,' said Meave

Ralph stopped walking, trying to figure how Meave could hear voices, when all he could hear was the wind blowing.

'What voices?' he asked, in an annoying whisper. 'I don't hear voices. All I hear is a storm blowing somewhere.'

'There is no storm, it is the sound of sea people talking. They sound quite agitated,' she replied, a knowing smile crossed her lips.

Then they entered what Ralph thought was a large deep bowl turned upside-down. The sides of the upside-down bowl had vertical strips of see-through Bsamaki skin which allowed a panoramic view of Tír na Leasa. Several long valleys with deep vertical cliffs intersected by shorter valleys made up the geography of this kingdom under the sea. All of the cliff faces had hundreds of dwelling holes. Fish men of varying sizes and shapes swam around the valleys: fish men on Orcas, fish men on sharks, gathering in regiments, gathering in armies, along the valleys' floors. Ralph stared out at the seascape of Tír na Leasa, trying to adjust to his new world.

The upside-down bowl was filled with many sea people, sitting around a large table made of shark skin and whalebone. Others were standing around the perimeter of the bowl chamber. They did not notice dJoucu, Meave and Ralph enter the chamber. The sound of the gale force wind increased, as the fish people talked, argued and debated. Three worried nervous old fish men and an old fish woman sitting at the table were the focus of attention of the gathering. Their long yellow seaweed hair tipped their shoulders, the scales on their withered faces dangled loosely. The webs between their fingers flopped about, as they gesticulated at each other. The rest of the gathered crowd consisted of young tall fish men with muscular frames and bright healthy scaled faces. Many of them carried comb swords. Several seated fish men stood up banged on the table and exhaled long whistling sounds from their oval mouths. With an army in DunFaythe Castle and an army in Tír na Leasa it struck Ralph that they would not be happy to see two uninvited guests

'What are they saying?' he asked, beginning to feel quite alone in this sea world.

'It is difficult to understand what they are saying' answered Meave. 'They are speaking so fast.'

A young fish man stood up. The rest of them sat down and remained silent. He opened his oval mouth and let out a high pitched gurgling sound. Another young fish man stood up, removed a scroll of parchment, bound with a silver ring from his grey whale skin tunic and threw it on the table. The gathered crowd shuffled uneasily in their seats, surprised to see the scroll thrown on the table.

'What's happening?' asked Ralph, feeling worried.

'The younger fish man is the commander of the army. He said that they might have to attack soon because time is getting short. He has the scroll of authority, and he said that many would die if they attack, but they are not sure that they will find it. He also said that the fire still burns. This means there will be many enemies protecting it,' answered Meave.

A growing uneasiness gripped Ralph, as he tried to guess who they were going to attack. Surely not DunFaythe Castle!

At that moment dJoucu let his comb sword fall to the ground making a loud thud against the shell floor. The fish men stopped talking and looked in the direction of the children.

'Who are these?' asked the young commander, pointing at Meave and Ralph

The Taosi watched and waited.

'Where did they come from?' demanded the commander.

dJoucu stepped forward and bowed, placing his closed webbed fist across his chest.

'They came through the vortex. Sire, I found them in the pool chamber,' he answered.

The young commander approached the children, watched by the fish men. Ralph trembled. Meave stood ladylike and regal.

'What is your name?' she asked the young commander, thinking that she had some status in Tír na Leasa.

'What is my name?' he snapped, enraged by such a direct question. 'You ask me, what is my name? Who are you, and why do you come to Tír na Leasa?'

He then spotted the brooch hanging around Meave's neck.

'Where did you get that brooch? It has the royal seal on it,' he asked, focusing his slanted eyes on Meave's brooch.

Meave noticed that the commander's slanted eyes were beginning to stretch along his face, as he swayed back and forth.

'There are no royal edicts passed anymore in Tír na Leasa. There is only the Taosi,' he said raising his voice.

Meave was regretting that she had spoken to the commander.

'Commander ... Sir,' she began.

'The royal family has no power anymore,' shouted the commander.

Ralph could not understand a word he was saying and did not want to ask Meave. The commander, fuming with rage raised his hands in the air and walked to one of the Bsamaki windows.

'I will ask you again,' he yelled. 'Why did you come to Tír na Leasa?'

'We were sent by Pádraig Bocht,' replied Meave, glancing at Ralph for some encouragement.

'You were sent by the Guardian of the Lighthouse,' answered the commander, as he looked down on the valley. Then turning he pointed a shaking webbed finger at the children.

'You see!' he said, looking to the seated group of fish men. 'Even Pádraig Bocht is aware that the time has come.'

'Do you know why you were sent?' he asked, facing the children and leaning forward.

Meave felt the webs between her fingers begin to flutter.

'We were sent to find out what they want,' she said, hoping that she had given the right answer.

The commander skipped back to the children, bent low and moved his face close to Meave's. The rugged protruding bone of his nose touched her cheek; his narrow eyes looked straight through her.

'What who wants?'

Ralph moved closer to Meave.

'Leave ... her... alone,' he cried. 'She is a queen. You should be bowing before her instead of frightening her.'

'Who is this?' asked the general, looking at Ralph with disgust.

'This is my brother Ralph,' answered Meave.

'Your brother! He is of humankind,' he exclaimed. 'Yet you have the sea in your blood.'

'Yes' said Meave. 'The daughters of DunFaythe have the sea in their blood,' hoping that her answer would soften the commander's mood.

The commander stared at Ralph for a moment and then turned towards the Taosi.

'What who wants?' he asked again, lowering his voice.

Meave did not answer.

'What's he saying?' asked Ralph.

'He wants to know why we came,' answered Meave.

'Tell him!'

'What will I tell him?' asked Meave, trying to think of something to say.

'Tell him we have come to find out what they want and what Citbeag wants. Tell him we came in peace,' replied Ralph in a dry edgy voice, glancing at the young commander.

'What is you brother mumbling? We do not understand his tongue,' asked the commander, glaring at Ralph.

Meave took a deep breath and was about to tell the commander, when the gathered Taosi stood up and looked towards an opening in the wall of the circular chamber. A figure dressed in a scarlet cloak stood watching the gathering. Her fish features had splashes of golden scales. A band of silver, studded with black stones adorned her head, and her eyes were almost of an oval shape. Tiny starfish speckled her dark hair. The protruding bone of her nose was shaped like the hooked beak of an eagle, and Ralph thought it could have been carved from ivory.

'Your majesty,' sighed the commander. 'You do not need to concern yourself with these matters. The Taosi will determine what happens. Please return to your quarters.'

The scarlet cloaked figure looked around the oval room.

'I am still queen of Tír na Leasa. I am still Queen Talutu!' she said, lifting her chin.

A low whistling sound passed through the gathered fish men. Queen Talutu continued, 'We still have time. There is no need for war.'

One of the old fish men raised his arm.

'Her majesty is correct. There is still time.'

The scales on the commander's face shook like leaves blowing in a summer breeze.

'You have given me the scroll of authority! You have given me the scroll of war! Look outside! Our army is preparing.'

He raised his arm and pointed to Meave.

'I'll ask you one more time, why you did you come to Tír na Leasa?'

Meave could feel the gills on her face stiffen.

'Citbeag is attacking our lands. We have to find out what he wants. He is killing our people,' she answered, with a pleading look at the commander.

The commander positioned his arms behind his back and clasped his webbed hands together. Meave saw that he was becoming less agitated.

'Citbeag! Citbeag!' he whispered to himself, walking slowly around the chamber. 'That traitor! deserter! knows what he wants and what we want.'

'It's in DunFaythe Castle,' he said in a slow reflective tone. 'Therefore we must negotiate with Pádraig Bocht or occupy DunFaythe Castle before Citbeag does. If we bring all our legions to Trá Bán, Pádraig Bocht will not fight. He'll return it to us without any blood being spilled. Then we can leave this place.'

The fish men continued to stare at the children. The commander and Queen Talutu glared at the children.

'Why are they all looking at us?' groaned Ralph, wishing he could understand their language.

'They think we know where it is,' answered Meave, her eyes downcast, not wanting to upset the commander.

'Where what is?' cried Ralph, in frustration.

'Whatever they are looking for,' answered Meave, lifting her eyes to the commander.

'I don't know what you are looking for, and I don't know where it is,' she said, almost sobbing.

The commander rubbed a webbed finger along the rugged tip of his protruding bone nose and then placed his scaly webbed hand on Meave's shoulder, his face softened again.

'You'll help us find it. You'll return to DunFaythe. But first you must rest and eat.'

'What did he ... say?' implored Ralph.

'Rest and eat,' answered Meave, a breeze of relief lightened her nervous state.

Ralph was happy that the general had mentioned food, having never spent such a long time without eating. He began to imagine roast pork dripping with chestnut sauce, surrounded by parsley stuffed onions with stewed red cabbage and apples. Queen Talutu approached the children. Ralph was so hungry that he did not notice a slight narrowing of her eyes. Meave, however, did see the change in the queen's features and felt a worrying shadow pass down her body.

'Come with me children now, and I will provide some refreshments and a place of rest for you,' said Queen Talutu, her eyes settled for a second on the commander, and then she smiled at Meave.

Meave did not move.

'What's wrong?' demanded Ralph, noticing a change in Meave's features.

'She says that she has food for us and wants us to go with her. But I don't like her. Something strange about her,' answered Meave, in a low voice.

'What are you saying children? I do not understand your language?' she asked, taking Ralph's hand and turning to Meave.

Meave remained motionless and looked at Ralph.

'We'll come with you,' said Ralph, hoping that Meave would come with him.

The queen smiled, as if she understood him.

'Come on Meave, I'm hungry,' he urged, as thoughts of food quashed any doubts he might have about the queen. 'I'm sure the queen means us no harm.'

Meave knew that Ralph was hungry and his only thoughts were of food.

'I'll come. But we must be careful,' she whispered.

The queen brought the children across the shell floor, past the staring eyes of the Taosi.

'I will call on you shortly Queen Talutu,' said the commander, as he turned to leave. 'I have some issues to discuss with the young humans.'

Queen Talutu led the children through a curtain of hanging thin octopus tentacles. They shivered when slimy wetness of the tentacles touched their arms. They then found themselves in a small oval chamber. The same glowing spheres that they had seen in the vortex chamber filled the chamber with a soft warm glow. A carpet of yellow sea moss covered the floor.

'Come,' said the queen, leading the children to a small bone table in the centre of the room. 'We will eat now and you will feel much better.'

The table was surrounded by five stools made from whalebone and topped with softly tanned dolphin skin. A green cloth covered several objects on the table.

'At last,' gasped Ralph, shaking with hunger. 'We can now eat. Hope there is some chicken or veal under those cloths.'

Meave was not hungry, she was thinking about what the commander had said and was beginning to realise that Tír na Leasa was not a safe place to be. What issues did he want to discuss?

'Eat your fill,' whistled Queen Talutu, removing the green cloth.

Ralph could not believe what he saw. He gulped and stared in horror at a large bowl filled with tiny silvery fish, swimming around in a circle, a jug of brown liquid, smelling of putrid sea-water, four flat seashells containing a slimly green substance that reminded him of frog spawn and a circular shell plate filled with pieces of what Ralph thought was dried mud.

'What's this?' he moaned, in disbelief. 'It's disgusting.'

'She expects us to eat some of that,' whispered Meave and a nauseating gurgle filled her stomach.

'What!' exclaimed Ralph. 'The fish are alive in the bowl and the jug is full of smelly sea-water. She'll poison us!'

The queen reached into the bowl and crammed her webbed fist with kicking silvery fish, opened her mouth and filled it with fish and then swallowed. The children looked on, agog with disgust. They could see the indents in her throat, as the tiny fish slid down inside her palpitating neck. Meave felt faint and sat on one of the shell stools, grabbing the table to prevent herself from falling. The queen then lifted one of the mud cakes, dipped it into the frog spawn and chewed it for several moments before swallowing it.

'Delicious!' she said, licking her fingers. 'You must have some. These are Forma fish! A delicacy in Tír na Leasa,'

She placed a finger in the bowl and touched one of the fish. The children looked away, hoping that she was not going to eat some more.

'Can't eat fish that are … uncooked and … alive,' mumbled Ralph. 'Tell her that we can't eat frog spawn either.'

'I don't think it is frog spawn, most likely to be another rare delicacy. After all she is a queen and is used to eating the best of food, even though we find it disgusting,' replied Meave, hoping that Ralph would eat some of it.

The queen sat, waiting for them to eat.

'She wants us to eat,' said Meave, trying not to look appalled by the queen's behaviour.

Ralph looked at the bowl and plates on the table. His stomach was beginning to churn.

'Tell her it's horrible, and we can't eat her food,' he moaned, not feeling hungry anymore.

'I will not! I don't want to offend her. You'll have to eat something Ralph,' ordered Meave.

He would die of starvation or be poisoned, but he knew that Meave meant what she said. The queen stood up and waited for them to eat. Ralph looked at Meave, a grimace of disgust painted on his face. She nodded her head. He picked up one of the mud cakes, closed his eyes and bit into it. It had a crusty surface with a soft centre and tasted like salty, musty cabbage. He felt sick, but forced himself to swallow a piece of it. A slow numbness filled his jaw, his eyes burned. He tried to chew another piece of mud cake.

'Ralph likes your food, Your Majesty,' said Meave, trying to force a smile.

The queen smiled, reached into the bowl and gathered another handful of fish. She then held her hand in front of Ralph's mouth and indicated to him to swallow the fish.

'Can't do this,' wailed Ralph, watching the fish struggle in her fingers.

'Do!' urged Meave, 'you must eat the fish.'

A rustle of the tentacle curtain diverted the queen's attention away from the children. The commander entered her chamber.

'I see you are eating,' he said, approaching the group. 'However, I didn't think you would like our food so I have brought you some human food.'

Ralph sighed with relief.

A servant followed behind the commander, a small fish man with a pronounced hump on his back, carrying a reed basket. The scales on his face were shrunk like dying autumn leaves, and his long orange hair reached down to his shoulders. He placed the reed basket on the table and left the chamber. Ralph nearly screamed with relief and joy, realising that he didn't have to eat the fish. Whatever was in the basket could not be any worse than eating live fish and frog spawn.

'You may eat now,' said the commander, indicating to Ralph to open the basket.

Ralph removed the lid of the basket. To his delight he found apples and pears. There were some pieces of fruit bread, two blocks of cheese and a bottle of liquid that Ralph assumed was fresh drinking water or fruit juice. When Meave saw the food she realised that she was also hungry. They ate noisily, gorging themselves like starving animals.

'I see you are hungry,' said the commander, removing a long thin red bottle from the basket.

He removed the cork and handed it to Ralph.

'Drink this. It might help you understand our world,' he said, smiling.

'What did he say?' asked Ralph, looking worried.

'He wants you to drink it,' answered Meave, trying to sound encouraging.

'I hope it's not sea water.' said Ralph, taking the bottle from the commander and raising it to his nose.

'Smells good, like honey mixed with blackberries.'

Ralph swallowed some of the liquid that tasted of peppermint and ginger. He felt a burning sensation in his throat and a hardness in his lips, bubbles of perspiration appeared on his forehead.

'It doesn't taste of honey and blackberries,' he gasped.

The commander laughed.

'We always drink the blood of a Star Crab before we venture into the deep ocean. It helps to keep our bodies warm.'

'Certainly does warm your body,' said Ralph, grinning and wiping his forehead with the back of his hand.

Then his bottom lip dropped, as if he had seen a ghost.

'Are you all right?' asked Meave. 'You look pale.'

'I can understand the commander,' he cried. 'I can understand what he is saying. This is a magic drink. Can I have some more?'

'I think you have had enough for today,' replied the commander. Let's sit down for a moment.'

Ralph quickly adjusted to the idea of being able to understand the commander. He could hear the whistle of the wind from the commander's mouth, but he could also understand what he was saying. They all sat around the bone table, Queen Talutu, the commander, Meave and Ralph.

'My name is General Nirutam,' began the commander.

The queen remained silent. She did not seem comfortable in his presence and her gaze remained downcast.

'You will both rest here tonight,' he said. 'Tomorrow I will send for you, and we will discuss Citbeag, Pádraig Bocht and the Pearl of Neamhann.'

* CHAPTER NINE *

The Lost Children

Having been assigned small chambers adjacent to Queen Talutu's living quarters, the children slept for twelve hours. Each chamber had a small cot of soft sea moss and a table, laden with fruit, cheese and a bottle of prawn juice. A vertical strip of Bsamaki skin in the walls of the chambers allowed them to have a full view of Tír na Leasa. Meave was the first to awaken and could not decide whether she should be worried or should be feeling happy to have visited Tír na Leasa. On the one hand there was an army getting ready for war and on the other hand she had a recurring feeling that she belonged to Tír na Leasa. Ralph was also awake in his chamber, thinking about the sharks.

As he munched his cheese and tasted prawn juice for the first time, he decided he that he must try and ride one of the small dolphins. Images of the fish man army and Orca whales floated through his mind. He then remembered General Nirutam and the Pearl of Neamhann – where is it? – why do they want it?

The tentacle curtain at the entrance of his chamber rustled, and dJoucu entered, wearing a cloak that Ralph thought was made of a fragile spider's web, each tiny strand painted with delicate droplets of moisture. Beneath the cloak he wore a dazzling tunic and breeches. He carried no weapons and his bright clothes and flickering web cloak gave the impression that he was radiating a brilliant light.

'dJoucu!' said Ralph. 'What are you wearing? Your clothes are glistening.'

dJoucu approached Ralph and bowed. Ralph looked up into his slanted dark eyes and saw that his facial expression showed a gentle kindness.

'I am a Knight of Leasa. I must dress accordingly, when I am going to meet General Nirutam and his officers. Hurry now! We must inform your sister of the meeting. We are going on a short journey to the general's quarters.'

'How are we travelling?' asked Ralph, agog with excitement, as many more questions formed in his head.

'You will be riding a shark,' answered dJoucu.

Ralph took a deep breath. Dreaming about riding a shark was enjoyable, but it was quite a different feeling to be told that you were actually going to mount a shark.

'I can't ride a shark. I'll drown. I can't breathe under the sea.'

'You will be able to breathe, when you wear a sea mask,' replied dJoucu, shrugging his shoulders.

'A sea mask. What's a sea mask?'

dJoucu walked towards the tentacle curtain.

'Come now. You will find out very soon.'

Ralph followed dJoucu through the curtain. They called at the chamber adjacent to Ralph's. Meave was dressed and ready.

'We're going to meet the general,' said Ralph, as Meave stepped through the curtain into the corridor. 'I'm going to wear a sea mask.'

They followed dJoucu along the shell-floored corridor and came across several fish people, who stopped and stared at them, muttering to themselves in low indistinct whistling tones. Ralph noted that the young fish people had smaller, compact scales that reflected the light of the corridor. Some had lime green seaweed hair, and others had a rusty orange colour. They also met several old fish people, strolling along the corridor, their dull grey scales hanging loose about their faces. dJoucu ignored them and kept walking.

'I guess they've never seen human people before,' said Ralph, gaping at the sea creatures.

'I'm sure they have never seen a fish girl, who is also of human form,' answered Meave.

The corridor widened, and stretching across the width of their path was a wide, drooping tentacle curtain. Groups of fish men were passing through the curtain carrying comb swords and cross bows. Others were exiting from the curtain and gathering in small clusters, as the children approached. They whistled amongst themselves and furtively pointed their webbed hands and fingers at the approaching group.

'dJoucu!' shouted one of the fish men. 'Where did these strange creatures come from? From the world above?'

'We are approaching the shark pond now,' he said to the children. 'Don't be frightened. All the sharks are used to having riders on them. You could say that they are like horses in your world.'

They passed through the tentacle curtain followed by the scrutinising eyes of the gathering fish men.

Before them lay a sight they would never have dreamed of; a sight that would conjure up the most horrible nightmares and would tingle the skin of any young boy or girl. A large indoor pond was spread out before them, frothing and churning with sharks and fish men. Hundreds of sharks were diving beneath the water or breaking the surface of the pond. Each surfacing shark had a fish man balancing on its back, holding its fin and guiding it to the bank. The sharks' wide gaping, dripping mouths looked as, if they were groping for victims. Yet the fish men patted them like humans would pat a horse. Many sharks were basking at the edge of the pond; their fins visible; their bodies sleek and still. Several times a fish man mounted a basking shark and placed his feet in stirrups attached to its body, gently tugged the shark's fin and then disappeared under the water.

Other fish men sat at the edge of the pond, their feet dangling in the water, stroking the smooth scaly skin of the sharks. Some were affectionately rubbing their wide snouts and feeding them fish from large sacks. Ralph and Meave remembered the horror stories about sailors eaten alive by sharks, told by Old Alesia. They found it difficult to believe that they were watching tame sharks that looked mean and hungry with their exposed rows of sword sharp teeth, being ridden like horses. Yet they seemed to be quite friendly and obedient.

dJoucu brought the children over to two sharks, floating lazily at the edge of the pond, their long bodies balanced beneath the surface of the pond.

'You can ride these two. They are gentle and friendly.'

Ralph was shaking. Meave was more relaxed, as she felt she knew what to do.

'Do we really have to do this?' pleaded Ralph, eyeing the sharks.

'Wait a moment,' said dJoucu and left the children standing at the edge of the pond, looking at the two vicious sharks. Ralph knelt down beside the sharks and touched one of their fins. The shark closed its drooling eyes like a kitten being stroked under its chin.

'Look Meave! These stirrups are almost the same as the stirrups we put on our horses,' and he moved his fingers gently along the fin of the shark, trying to forget how scared he was.

'I wonder what their names are?' asked Meave, as if she was talking about two playful kittens.

'Their ... names!' spluttered Ralph 'I don't care what their names are. They are sharks ... They eat people ... They might eat us!'

'We won't eat you,' the shark might have said. 'You are in our world now.'

Ralph's attention was diverted by a flurry of activity at the opposite bank of the pond. Ten sharks broke the surface of the pond. Their tall, muscular riders wore glistening suits similar to dJoucu's, with comb swords hanging in their scabbards. They rode the sharks to the bank of the pond, dismounted and marched in single file towards the tentacle curtain.

'Knights of Leasa,' said Ralph, admiring the fish men.

Fish men stepped aside, as the knights approached. dJoucu was talking to a group of fish men near the tentacle curtain. As the Knights of Leasa approached, each one stopped and bowed before him. dJoucu returned their salute, placing his webbed hand across his chest.

Ralph guessed that dJoucu was an officer of the Knights of Leasa, and he felt better believing that no one would harm them. For a moment he dreamt of riding a shark and escaping back to DunFaythe.

dJoucu returned to the awaiting children, carrying a cloth sack. He reached into the sack. Ralph gasped with surprise.

'It's a pumpkin,' he cried.

'It is a sea mask,' returned dJoucu, handing the pumpkin to Ralph. 'Our children wear them, when they are learning to breathe under the sea.

'It looks like a pumpkin, but it doesn't have the weight of a pumpkin,' said Ralph, examining the sea mask.

There were two horizontal slits in the mask and an oval mouth shaped hole. dJoucu pointed to a thin film of lace-work, filling the mouth hole of the pumpkin.

'It is a leaf of the Hewup plant which extracts fresh air from sea-water, and allows the wearer to breathe. The eye slits are filled with Bsamaki skin so you can see, when you are wearing the mask. Now you can place it on your head.'

Ralph struggled into the mask, feeling a tightness, as it melted around his head.

'You look like a monster from the Samhain festival in DunFaythe,' said Meave, grinning.

Ralph could breathe under the mask, but he could not hear any sound.

'Like a scarecrow!' she shrieked.

Ralph saw her lips move and then removed the mask.

'I can't hear any sound under the mask,' he said, looking at dJoucu.

'Yes,' said dJoucu. 'When you are in the silence of the sea your senses begin to improve. You will be able to feel the slightest change of current on your skin. You will also begin to see longer distances.'

'Just like you Meave,' said Ralph.

'Yes,' replied dJoucu, 'Meave has some of the traits of the sea people.'

He cupped his webbed hands in front of his mouth and exhaled a soft whistling sound. Suddenly the dripping, tooth filled head of a mammoth shark appeared above the surface of the pond. Immediately the children jumped and stepped back. Ralph thought that the monster could easily eat both of them with one snap of his giant jaws. The grinning teeth almost spoke to dJoucu, as it approached the children.

'This is Moonlight,' he said, and he proudly stroked the snout of the monstrous fish. 'He is a battle shark and he is trained to charge along the highest waves and resist the fiercest currents. He doesn't know what fear is.'

Moonlight moved towards dJoucu without causing a ripple on the surface of the pond. His colossal frame manoeuvred itself beside the two floating sharks. They looked like two lion cubs nestled beside the king of the jungle. dJoucu knelt down and whistled softly. Moonlight's black bulging eyes expanded. His dorsal fin flapped about, like a pet dog wagging his tail.

'What a beautiful fish,' said Meave, trying to please dJoucu.

Ralph frowned and stepped further back from the pool surprised that Meave could think such a monster was beautiful.

'Yes indeed' said dJoucu. 'We have travelled to many cities together, and we have fought several wars together.'

He slid off the bank of the pond and mounted Moonlight. Meave hopped onto one of the smaller floating sharks and settled herself behind its fin.

'C'mon Ralph. Put on your sea mask,' she said. 'It's your turn.'

'What battles? What cities?' asked Ralph. 'Are there other cities under sea?'

dJoucu rested his arm against Moonlight's fin.

'You are an inquisitive human. You would make a good sea knight,' he said, smiling.

'Certainly would, he is always asking questions,' said Meave.

Ralph mounted his shark and found it quite similar to a horse except he had a fin to hold instead of reins.

'You are beginning to look like a sea knight,' said dJoucu, admiring Ralph's upright stance on the shark.

Ralph noticed how comfortable and confident Meave looked sitting on her shark.

'You asked me about other cities. There are many cities under the sea. Tír na Leasa is a small city. Just like in the human world there are kings and lords. There are alliances and treaties, traitors and betrayals. We must move away from this world of war and death. There is suffering under the sea. There is suffering on land. We have tried for thousands of years to make peace with our sea and land neighbours. But now we have the opportunity to leave. We must not fail … Enough talk … Gently push the fin of your shark forward, and you will submerge. Pull the fin backwards and the shark will climb.'

Ralph put his sea mask over his head and tried to digest what dJoucu had been saying, as he pushed the shark's fin – wars under the sea! kings! treaties! – traitors!

The three sharks dived into the pond. dJoucu led the way. Ralph found that he could breathe quite easily under the sea mask and was pleasantly surprised that the pond water was warm. He clung to the shark's fin and was brought deeper and deeper into a circular tunnel, carved out of grey rock. As they followed dJoucu the children saw many fish men on sharks climbing towards the pond. Several times a platoon of battle sharks carrying Knights of Leasa passed them. Meave was enjoying herself, finding it easy to ride the shark. She watched other sea people on sharks, making their way downward from the pool. She noticed that they were no longer staring at her and guessed that they no longer considered her a stranger.

'Hold on tight,' shouted dJoucu, as they approached a large oval shaped opening at the end of the tunnel.

'Stay close to me. We will soon be entering the ocean, there may be strong currents.'

As the trio approached the end of the tunnel, Ralph felt a strong current blowing against his body. It felt like he was riding a horse against the wind, and he tucked his head behind the shark's fin. They passed through the opening into the city and found themselves in a melee of sharks, dolphins and fish men. They made their way through the busy valley. Once they had to stop and give way to a train of Orca whales whose huge bodies dwarfed them, as they passed. Ralph was getting used to being under water. However, he found the silence of his mask annoying. Once or twice he tried to speak to Meave, but then remembered that she could not hear him. Meave was also fascinated by the busy life of the under sea city. She turned around to see where she had come from.

'dJoucu!' she cried, pointing.

dJoucu stopped immediately, thinking that Meave had fallen or had collided with something. Ralph also stopped and looked.

'What is that?' she asked, pointing to a gigantic shape rising behind them.

A colossal pyramid shaped mountain covered in green slime rose from the seabed with many openings dotted between its base and its apex, emitting varying colours of light.

'It looks like a giant decorated tree that we have at the Festival of Nollaig!' she cried, admiring the colourful pyramid. 'I've never seen such a wondrous sight.'

'It is Dochas Mountain, where we have just come from,' said dJoucu. 'The first of our people, who came here thousands of years ago, lived in the mountain. They carved their chambers and living quarters out of the caves, formed by sea currents. Over the centuries it has become the palace of royalty. It is where the vortex brought you and where Queen Talutu has her living quarters. We must go now. We will discuss Dochas Mountain another day.'

He pushed on the fin of his battle shark. The journey continued through the bustling, teeming valley. The children observed the life of Tír na Leasa. On the seabed they saw fish people gathered around large circular tables, sorting fish, opening mussels and stretching clumps of thick leathery seaweed. It struck Ralph that maybe they were making armour for the Knights of Leasa.

Fish children chased baby dolphins, others swam among the tall stems of the colourful sea flowers, searching for crabs. Through the openings in the valley walls, filled with Bsamaki skin, the children could see sea people sitting around tables, chatting, playing with their children and preparing food. They saw large chambers where sea children were being tutored by old fish men, waving sticks of sea cane and pointing to symbols, scrawled on wide sheets of stretched whale hide, attached to the walls of the chambers.

'Just like our world,' said Meave. 'Except it's under the sea.'

Both children were aware of the light, flooding the valley from a source they could not see. Meave was admiring how dJoucu was able to manoeuvre his huge battle shark through the oncoming traffic of fish men and Orcas.

'We are nearly there,' he shouted to the children.

Ralph watching dJoucu wished he could ride a battle shark. Then without a warning the busy activity of the valley came to a stop. Fish men dispersed into the cliff openings; fish children scampered away or hid among the sea plants.

'What's happening?' wondered Meave, watching three fish children mount a dolphin and disappear behind a clump of sea grass. Then she saw them. Directly in front of dJoucu and the children was a line of five vicious battle sharks, their riders dressed in black web cloaks with dark ribbed hoods covering their heads and their comb swords drawn. dJoucu stopped and faced them.

'Who ... are they?' asked Meave, and her heart leapt.

'They are the Black Guards replied dJoucu, his hand dropping towards his comb sword.

'They are Queen Talutu's bodyguard. I don't like the look of them. They don't usually gather in such numbers. They must be looking for something or somebody. Stay close to me.'

The children edged their sharks closer to dJoucu and looked like two baby sharks cuddling close to their mother. Meave felt a tightness in her arms – Did they want her?

Ralph was bursting with questions, but no one could hear him, as he looked along the line of Black Guards and noted that three of their battle sharks had long jagged scars on their fins and bodies; the others had teeth missing from their cruel smiling mouths. He wondered would they make a run for it, then he reckoned that the battle sharks would easily catch them.

The leader of the Black Guard positioned his battle shark beside dJoucu. Ralph could see the contours of his bone nose protruding from his hood, his comb sword had several segments missing, and his battle shark had a gold chain encircling his large head.

'Queen Talutu wishes to entertain the young human female,' he said, and his slanted eyes jumped from Ralph to Meave. 'We have come to escort her to her majesty's quarters.'

dJoucu rested his arm on the fin of his battle shark. Ralph did not think that dJoucu was afraid. After all dJoucu was a Knight of Leasa.

'They will remain with me,' answered dJoucu. 'They are under the protection of the Knights of Leasa. General Nirutam has ordered them to his quarters.'

The leader of the Black Guard pointed his comb sword at dJoucu.

'The days of the Knights of Leasa, and The Taoisi are coming to an end. We will take the young humans. They have knowledge that Queen Talutu must have.'

Ralph waited for dJoucu to do something. dJoucu looked down at Meave and then at Ralph and moved his feet in his stirrup.

'You will see - '

Grasping the Black Guard's foot he lifted him off his battle shark. The Black Guard fell towards the seabed. The remaining Black Guards moved towards dJoucu and the children. dJoucu stretched out his arms, grabbed Meave and Ralph and placed them behind him on Moonlight.

'Dive for the sea bed,' he shouted, and he jumped onto a Black Guard's battle shark.

Meave and Ralph sat on Moonlight, like two timid monkeys on the back of a roaring lion. dJoucu turned the Black Guard's battle shark.

'Go to the Ardghorm grass … Be careful there are dangers among the stalks,' he cried, as he charged at the oncoming Black Guards, his head crouched low behind the battle shark's fin. Meave pushed on Moonlight's fin. She did not know where to find the Ardghorm grass and knew that, wearing his sea mask, could not hear any sound. But she was amazed that such a huge fish could respond so quickly to such a gentle touch. Ralph clung to Meave, hoping that she knew what she was doing. They dived beneath the Black Guards. One of them reached out. The children moved to their left and the Black Guard missed them. They dived towards the seabed. Ralph looked behind and saw dJoucu ram into a Black Guard and push another off his battle shark. Moonlight dived vertically. Meave clung onto his fin, as dJoucu's battle shark hurtled downwards. The seabed rushed up to meet them. Ralph remembered the horror of the vortex before Meave saved him.

'Pull the fin!' he screamed 'Pull the fin!'

Meave could not hear him, so he pushed his heels into the body of the shark. Moonlight slowed his dive and Ralph then pulled at Meave's arms. Moonlight changed direction and swam a level course. Looking behind him he saw a Black Guard following them. Above him he saw dJoucu surrounded by three Black Guards. Looking down he saw a green clump of foliage shimmering in the dull light of the valley. Meave turned around. She looked pale and frightened, pointing towards the green foliage.

The children pressed their heels tightly against Moonlight's body; the shark swam faster in the direction of the green foliage. The Black Guard continued to follow them and was gaining on them. Meave tried to figure out what they would do when they got to the Ardghorm grass and hoped that Moonlight would know where to go. Out of nowhere a Black Guard appeared beside them.

'Slow down,' he shouted 'You cannot escape.'

They entered a forest of giant grass stalks, blowing in the sea current. Moonlight carried the children into the Ardghorm grass, swerving and diving between the tall green swaying pillars, followed closely by the Black Guard. Further and further they went into the moving, lucent forest. Several times the Black Guard appeared beside them.

'You can't escape,' he roared.

'Feeling her skin tighten on her face, she sensed that there was something else moving in the Ardghorm grass

'This is a dangerous place! If you don't stop, you'll die!' screamed the Black Guard.

Ralph's arms were getting heavy, he was finding it difficult to hold onto Meave.

'There's something out there!' he shouted, pointing at a grey cloud, moving towards them through the tall grass, forgetting that Meave could not hear him. Meave was also watching the dark misty shape approach them.

'Snakes!' shouted Ralph. 'A cloud of snakes!'

The children saw thousands of snakes swimming towards them, flittering along the seabed and through the narrow gaps of the grass above them. Their upper bodies were musty brown; the underside was bright yellow. Some had their mouths open displaying their spike fangs. They were coming from all directions. Moonlight stopped swimming. Meave closed her eyes. Ralph could not move. They watched like two ants trapped on the shore waiting for the tide to swamp them. Suddenly the Black Guard moved his battle shark beside the children, picked up Meave like a child would lift a doll and placed her behind him on the shark. Ralph tried to hold on to Meave's leg, but it slipped through his fingers. He lost his balance and fell towards the seabed. As he plunged towards the ocean floor he could see Meave screaming and pointing at him, as the Black Guard carried her on his battle shark. Ralph landed gently on the soft, sandy seabed. The sea snakes began to surround him. A cloud of yellow bellied, needle fanged, slippery serpents wrapped itself around his body. Their staring blank eyes bulged with hunger. A cold darkness descended on him, blotting out the Ardghorm grass and the light of the valley. They coiled around his legs, his arms and his neck. He felt faint, as they wrapped themselves around him and began to crush him like him like a boa constrictor would crush a sheep. Suddenly a single snake wrapped itself around his ankle and began to drag him along the seabed. Then he felt the soft touch of the sea grass as, he was pulled from the ocean floor. To his immense relief the snakes released their grip and slid off his body. His head bobbled backwards, and he saw the snakes swim away! Yet there was something tied to his ankle pulling him towards the upper stems of the Ardghorm grass. He could see a reddish fish tail moving ahead of him in the water. Eventually he cleared the upper most tips of the green forest. Then he remembered Meave and hoped the Black Guards would not harm her.

He was astounded when he saw that it was a long rope, extending from an unusual looking fish that was pulling him. The fish twisted and bobbled, as it hauled him through the water; he had never seen a fish like it before, with red and mustard strips. Two wings extended from its body, giving the impression that it was flying through the water, a long beak extended from its small round head. He struggled to describe what he was seeing – was it a fish or a duck?

Mounted on its back and crouched behind the vertical fin of the flying fish was a small figure, wearing a sea mask and a fishing net like tunic, pulling him towards the light at the end of the valley. The masked figure rode the flying fish close to the valley walls, as if it was looking for a something. Ralph realised that Tír na Leasa was much bigger than he had thought at first. There were many long narrow valleys running off the Central Valley and many vee shaped valleys high up in the cliffs' walls. Several times the rider glanced back to look at Ralph, being pulled along like a hooked fish. Quite suddenly the flying fish dived towards the seabed. Ralph noticed several more flying fish with masked figures on their backs, waiting for him beside a crop of red sea flowers. He could clearly see that each rider was small in stature and carried no weapons. Ralph sank to the seabed, and the flying fish came to a stop amongst them. He stood up and removed the rope from his ankle. Each rider edged over to him and examined him closely. He gasped silently in his sea mask, when he saw that each rider had wide feet shaped like dolphin tail fins. The last rider indicated to Ralph to mount his flying fish. Ralph sat up behind the leader, and they all moved off the seabed – were these strange creatures kidnapping him? – were they going to help him? The leader pulled on the fin of his flying fish. The wings flapped gently and Ralph lifted off the seabed, followed by the rest of the flying fish. They rose in silence through the still water, like ghosts rising from a watery grave. The alternating stripes of the flying fish mirrored the light of the valley and gave them a snake like quality, as their supple bodies glided towards an opening in the valley wall. Ralph glanced behind him. All the masked figures crouched behind their fins, staring ahead, as they followed their leader.

The tunnel they entered was dark, narrow and cold. Ralph shivered, as they made their way upward towards his captor's lair. They emerged into a gloomy damp cave. Ralph saw that his captors had small, thin bodies. Under their net tunics, he could see the imprint of their thin bony frames. The masked figures silently dismounted from their flying fish, climbed on the cold damp floor of the cave and formed a line against the cave wall. Their leader beckoned to him to dismount. Ralph remained beside the lake, as the leader walked along his line of troops, inspecting them and counting them. He then turned and faced Ralph, who stood looking at the strange creatures with their sea masks, fishing net tunics and wide toeless feet. There was a shuffle of feet and movement of hands, as the creatures pointed at Ralph.

Not a word was spoken. Their leader then removed his mask. The rest of the group did likewise. Ralph closed his eyes then opened them again. He wanted to laugh; he wanted to scream. No sound or whistle would come from his throat, as he looked at each child's face, pale and thin, gaunt and hungry. Lank lifeless hair fell to their shoulders and wide undernourished eyes stared from their dark shadowed sockets. They all then bent down and removed their webbed feet.

'They are only boots,' he gasped.

They stood barefooted on the damp stony grey floor of the cave, no smiles and no cheer.

'We are the Lost Children,' said their leader. 'My name is Oisin. I have been here for two hundred years. They took us from Trá Bán because they thought we were of royal blood of the Devereux line.'

Each child was about Ralph's age. There were more girls than there were boys; all wearing the same tunics of seal skin underneath a cloak of meshed Hewup plant leaves. They began to speak,

'I am here one hundred years,' said one, a thin wisp of a girl with black matted curls and sad wide eyes. 'I want to go home,' she cried.

A tall thin boy stepped forward.

'We have not grown old in Tír na Leasa. We don't know what day it is we just count the years by watching the young dolphins growing. There is no day or night in Tír na Leasa because of the constant glow of the pearl field. Can you help us? Who are you?'

Ralph did not know where to begin his story.

'Pearl field ... No day or night ... Always young ... I am Ralph Devereux. I am the son of Lord Devereux. My sister Meave is also here ... a Black Guards took her,' he stuttered, examining the motley group of children.

Gasps of surprise passed through the group. They formed a circle around Ralph. Some cried, others cheered, many remained silent. They moved closer to Ralph, hoping that he might take them away from their endless misery. Their pale stained faces, their tight mournful lips, and their pleading wet eyes stared waiting for Ralph to tell them that he was going to take them home. Ralph was filled with pity for the children.

'How have you survived in this horrible cave for so long?' he asked, trying to adjust to the scene before him. No one answered. They all looked at each other not wanting to answer questions, waiting for him to speak again. Ralph looked into their deep saddened eyes. After a few moments of uneasy silence, a thin stick of a girl, her face stained with dust and tears, stepped forward, reached out her bony shaking arm and held his hand. Ralph looked down at her tangled black hair and wished that he could bring her back to the castle and feed her with wholesome food. He could almost see her cheekbones through the thin film of skin, covering her face. Her sunken grey eyes showed a sadness that Ralph had never seen before.

'We have been waiting for you,' she said, as a sobbing sound rose in her throat. 'We know that you have come to save us.'

Ralph was unable to answer the wretched young girl.

'The fish people don't want us. We are outcasts. When they discovered that we weren't of royal blood they banished us to the Ardghorm grass,' she sobbed.

Ralph put his arm around the frail shoulders of the young girl, afraid to hug her in case he might break some of her protruding bones.

'What do the fish men want?' he asked in a wailing voice.

'They want the Pearl of Neamhann,' answered their leader, Oisin.

Ralph remembered that the general had mentioned the Pearl of Neamhann and reckoned that the general thought that he knew where it was – that was why the Black Guards took Meave. They also want the pearl. That was why Pádraig Bocht sent them to Tír na Leasa!

His mind filled with questions of dJoucu, Citbeag, Pádraig Bocht and Queen Talutu.

'Why do they want Pearl of Neamhann?' he asked.

'Something to do with the pearl fields,' answered the young girl in a sheepish voice.

'The pearl fields!' exclaimed Ralph. 'Where are the pearl fields?'

The young girl pressed hard on Ralph's hand.

'The pearl fields are at the end of the valley. They are beyond Tír na Leasa. That is where the light comes from. That is why there is always light in Tír na Leasa.'

Ralph felt tired and hungry.

'I don't know what to do,' he said, folding his arms. 'I don't know where to begin. Must rest first … The general will help us … dJoucu will help us.'

* CHAPTER TEN*

The Tombs of Marbh

'Too dangerous. I cannot risk my family, my soldiers!' exclaimed Lord Cedric Radford, feeling the weight of his seventy years on his frail and arched shoulders, as deep furrows of pain and anguish criss-crossed his wide, skeletal forehead.

'Colclough Devereux will forgive me,' he moaned. 'I can't march to DunFaythe. Young Arthur will have to return alone.'

Arthur, sitting on a polished beech pew, remained silent, looking around at the remaining officers of Lord Cedric's army. Some were sitting on benches, others were leaning against the ancient, book filled racks of the renowned library of Fiordwex castle, books bound in goat hide, telling stories of wars and heroes, of brave kings and gentle queens. There were no heroes in the library that night. Lord Cedric sat in a cushioned chair that had often catered for many a scholar or scribe, facing his officers and could not banish the living picture of Citbeag and GuaireDun from his troubled mind. Arthur had tried to explain to Lord Cedric that they should join forces with Lord Devereux to defeat Citbeag.

'If we stand together we can defeat him,' he had said. 'If we divide our armies, they will destroy us.'

Lord Cedric was used to getting his own way and never having his commands questioned.

'We can't risk being ambushed in open country by the monks,' he had answered. 'There are too many of them.'

One of Cedric's officers, a small broad shouldered man with a full drooping moustache and a bald polished head, interrupted Arthur's thoughts.

'If we can recapture GuaireDun, I'm sure we can find their weakness. They must have a weakness.'

No one answered. No one wanted to fight or dream up a plan that might cause more deaths. Despair and defeat blanked out all of their hopes.

'There has to be a way,' continued the officer. 'There must be an answer in GuaireDun.'

Lord Cedric rose from his chair and stood looking at the gathered crowd, his legs struggling to support his swaying frame. An officer stepped forward to support him.

'Leave me be, I am not finished yet,' he snapped, raising his shaking hand to the level of his bony shoulders.

'We will meet here again tomorrow morning and decide our future plans. Now, before we adjourn. Does anybody wish to speak?'

Azaromel was standing behind Arthur, watching Lord Cedric and thinking of his children, of the pain that Citbeag had caused him and of the death and destruction that he had brought to these people. They had treated him kindly in Fiordwex. He was free to wander about the castle, and they had allowed him to eat with them, to join in their conversations and to wear their clothes. They had even given him weapons.

He wanted to help them, but he dreaded to think that they would ever find out what he was. Lord Cedric continued to stare at his officers, like an old dying bull, too proud to give up his authority.

'Tom ... orrow!' he stuttered, hoping by then he would be dead, and someone else might take on the burden 'We will talk tomorrow.'

Azaromel approached him.

'May I speak. My lord.'

Lord Cedric looked into Azaromel's soft sad eyes.

'Speak if you must.' he answered, placing his trembling hand on Azaromel's arm. 'We know you are with us.'

He then sat down again and stared at the grey stone slabs of the library floor. Azaromel faced the officers of Lord Cedric's army.

'They do have a weakness,' he said.

No one replied. Some thought that the mention of a weakness would mean more fighting and certain death. Others did not think that Citbeag could ever be defeated. Arthur was surprised to hear Azaromel speak and wondered why he had not mentioned this weakness before.

'What is this weakness?' asked the officer with the drooping moustache.

'The Deoch of Citbeag,' replied Azaromel. 'The phial of liquid that each one of them carries with them. They must take a drink of the Deoch of Citbeag daily to maintain their courage and their hatred. I have seen the Deoch of Citbeag.'

'But how can we stop their supply of this evil potion?' asked Arthur, hoping that Azaromel would have an answer.

Azaromel paused for a few moments.

'Tell us,' urged Arthur, not wanting to let the moment pass.

'There is a large cauldron in GuaireDun, brought by Citbeag, when they captured the castle. Each day a supply train leaves the castle to fill the phials of Citbeag's monks,' replied Azaromel, in a low hushed voice.

'Do you want us to attack this supply train?' asked Arthur, hoping that Azaromel would say yes.

'No,' replied Azaromel. 'They can easily send out another supply train. We have to destroy the cauldron that contains the Deoch. If we can destroy this cauldron, we can destroy Citbeag and his troops. They will not fight without their evil drink.'

Arthur noted that Lord Cedric's eyes were closing.

'We can't lay siege to GuaireDun. We do not have enough troops,' said Arthur.

'No, we cannot,' replied Azaromel, shaking his head. 'We have to get into GuaireDun and destroy it.

A shiver of emotion swelled through Arthur, knowing that whoever ventured into GuaireDun would probably never come out again.'

'This is madness' choked Lord Cedric, opening his eyes and glaring at Arthur. 'It would be like stealing the queen from a hive of bees.'

Another officer, a tall thin man with a wisp of a beard hanging from his chin stood up.

'We would never get into GuaireDun. They have patrols and guards on every lane and road. They would see us for miles coming across the plain. Thousands would die and we would not get one man inside the castle.'

A murmur of agreement rang around the library.

'It's their only weakness,' replied Azaromel in a pleading voice, as he walked towards the door of the library. 'The only way we can defeat them.'

'Just a moment!' cried Arthur. 'We can get into GuaireDun. Two or three of us might get in. They might not notice two or three extra monks moving about the castle.'

'How would you get into the castle?' asked the officer with the wispy beard.

Arthur felt a spark of hope glimmer before his eyes.

'Through the Devil's Belly!' he shouted. 'Maybe they haven't found the Devil's Belly. It's worth the risk.'

What is the Devils Belly?' asked Azaromel, stopping suddenly.

'A cavern under the castle which has an entrance from the beach,' answered Arthur.

'I never heard of it and I've explored most of GuaireDun.'

'See!' shouted Arthur. 'They don't know about the Devil's Belly. We can destroy the Deoch of Citbeag. We can destroy these monks!'

Lord Cedric raised his hand.

'I cannot ask any of my soldiers to sacrifice their lives for such a hopeless cause.'

A murmur of approving voices drifted through the gathered group, nodding agreement with Lord Cedric. Arthur was watching the image of the Devil's Belly flash before his eyes, the wide deep cavern, the steep damp steps cut into the cliff wall.

'I'll go. Will anybody come with me?'

He was answered by a shuffling silence. They looked at each other; they looked at the ceiling; they looked at the grey floor and would not engage with his pleading eyes. He was not disappointed because he knew that such a task was almost impossible. His hatred of Citbeag numbed his fears and blinded him to the task that lay before him. Yet he believed that it could be accomplished.

'Very well, I'll go alone,' he said in a low sullen voice.

Azaromel was watching Arthur and admired his innocent bravery.

'I will come with you. I may be able to pass through the gates of GuaireDun.'

'They will kill you the minute they see you!' cried Lord Cedric, moving uneasily in his chair.

'Perhaps,' answered Azaromel. 'But I also have a reason to destroy Citbeag.'

A voice from the rear of the room interrupted the exchange.

'I am also with you Arthur,' said a small thin bearded man, Captain Hewlett from the north of DunFaythe peninsula, who had travelled to many distant lands and insisted on being called Hewlett. He had watched his two brothers die during the siege of GuaireDun and like Arthur wanted his revenge.

'We cannot journey through the pine forest. We must pass through the Tombs of Marbh,' said the Captain.

'So be it,' answered Arthur and an old feeling of fear mingled with elation rose in his blood.

'We will leave at noon tomorrow,' he said, wishing he could at that moment begin his journey to GuaireDun.

He left the library without looking back, followed by Azaromel and Captain Hewlett. Each man driven by hatred only equalled by and understood by Citbeag's monks.

Arthur slept peacefully that night, being accustomed to anticipating death and not being able to remember a time, when he was not waiting to fight. Azaromel did not sleep. Citbeag's face passed before him in his waking dreams, as the long dark night dragged on. Captain Hewlett helped by several goblets of wine slept a dreamless sleep.

They left the castle without ceremony, without farewells, two soldiers hoping to find a solution to the madness that was destroying their way of life and a monk, striving to find peace by destroying his own kind. They rode their horses mercilessly through the silent countryside, each one preoccupied with his fears and dreams and imagining that his death would come soon and would be quickly forgotten. Five bright blue skies and five clear starry nights passed, as they travelled towards the Tombs of Marbh. Lonely, standing cattle watched them from fields of lush meadows. Wild boar hidden in thick gorse spied on them, as they rode through dry woodlands. Puc goats balancing on solitary peaks ignored them, as they rode through deep ravines. The screeching Crows of Cailleach announced their arrival at the Tombs of Marbh.

'What's this place?' asked Arthur in a soft tired voice.

The screeching stopped. A row of bare branched oak trees stretched before them, flecked with silent, gaping crows.

'Must be thousands of them!' exclaimed Captain Hewlett.

'Yes!' The crows might have said. 'There are thousands of us. We belong to the Tombs of Marbh. Who do you belong to? We watch over Cailleach. She watches over the tombs. Who do you watch over?'

as they ruffled their feathers and shifted their black beady eyes.

Standing before the desolate oak trees, were three identical marble buildings. Each one had an apex roof of gold leaf, shimmering in the cold spring sunlight. A stairway of polished granite led to a tall bronze door in each of the temples. Two arched windows cut into the flawless marble of their facing walls, looked down at the visitors, like empty eye sockets.

'We have been waiting for you,' they might have said.

Arthur rode towards the stairway of the central building and admired the gargoyles and animal heads carved into the steps.

'Who lives in these marble palaces?' he shouted towards the tombs, almost expecting an answer.

Captain Hewlett approached Arthur.

'The dead,' he said. Your ancestors, the great kings of history are buried here: King Cormac of Druimlinn, King Karlfort of Maudlin, Queen Anasdora of Kerrboinn and many other kings and queens are all resting in these temples.'

Arthur moved his horse along the front of the buildings, followed by the captain.

'I always thought that Cormac and Karlfort were only found in children's stories,' he said, studying The Tombs of Marbh.

'No,' replied Captain Hewlett, darting his eyes from one building to another. 'They were real people, who lived thousands of years ago. Their subjects built these monuments. Each building is identical, and each king and queen was given a similar tomb.'

'Perhaps we should pass on,' whispered Arthur. 'We can't waste time visiting the ancient dead.'

'We can't leave yet.' urged Captain Hewlett. 'We must pay our respects to the dead and to Cailleach.'

Arthur was not interested in dead kings or marble tombs.

'Who is Cailleach?' he asked, yawning. 'Can we pay our respects at a later date, if we are still alive?'

'She is the ancient keeper of the tombs, and she is as old as the tombs themselves,' replied Captain Hewlett, dismounting and grasping the reins of Arthur's horse.

'We don't have the time to pay respects to ancient kings and queens. We must continue,' insisted Arthur.

'I think you should dismount sire. If you don't pay your respects to Cailleach she will curse you. Many men have passed here without paying respects. They have lived to regret it.'

Arthur nodded sullenly. Azaromel approached.

'Better do as he says. We don't need a curse hanging over us.'

'Very well,' grunted Arthur, dismounting from his horse. 'Where is this Cailleach?'

'We must wait,' answered Captain Hewlett. 'Cailleach only comes out when the sun is setting. We must wait here until sunset.'

The crows waited and watched. They had seen visitors before, and they had seen Cailleach many times. The soldiers and the monk waited. The afternoon passed, and the crows watched. The evening passed, and the crows watched. A fuzzy orange ball of dying sun settled behind the ancient oak trees. The crows blinked and shuffled in anticipation. Azaromel peered at the burning orb in the sky.

'I think we - '

A rustle of black feathers filled the thickening evening, and the crows turned and faced the dying sun, paying their respects to this wonder of nature, opening their beaks and bursting forth a low squealing cry.

'I think she may be coming soon,' said Azaromel, watching the crows. 'They are getting restless.'

Arthur looked towards the door of the central tomb and saw beams of dull orange light filter from the arched windows. The crows increased their squealing chorus. The setting sun magnified, filling the whole western sky. Arthur wished that she would arrive soon; he was not interested in the drama that was unfolding. Droplets of sweat slipped down Azaromel's long back, when he realised that Cailleach might discover what he was.

The crows suddenly quenched their squealing chorus, turned and faced the waiting trio. A dull thud, and the sound of ancient bronze scraping on marble signalled the arrival of Cailleach. The door of the centre tomb opened, and a tall figure, its body and face wrapped with soft white linen, stood before them. Arthur was reminded of a corpse in its grave shroud, and he could see the gleam of pink flesh beneath the face wrapping.

'Is it a ghost, or is it human?' asked Captain Hewlett.

Arthur knew that he was in the presence of something that was neither ghost nor human. The figure glided down the steps. As it got closer they saw the shape of a tall young woman.

'Why are you frightened strangers?' she asked, closing on the trio and holding up one arm and with her long tapered fingers, she removed the white linen wrapping from her face.

'I am Cailleach, the Keeper of the Tombs of Marbh. Do I look like someone, who would cause you harm?'

A clump of rich hair of raven blackness, streamed in soft ripples down her linen wrapping, almost touching her sandalled feet. The trio stood speechless. Her dark penetrating blue eyes captivated Arthur. Captain Hewlett admired her unblemished, flawless skin and her noble cheekbones. Azaromel shivered and watched a slight curl develop in her thin lips. Cailleach looked at him, and he felt that behind the eyes of this perfect beauty, was the aura of death.

'Why are you afraid?' she said to Azaromel.

'It is your beauty that frightens me … O Cailleach,' he whined, falling to his knees, his voice shaking with fear.

'You are not of this world. I can see that you have brought evil with you,' she said, stepping closer to Azaromel.

Azaromel remained silent, his eyes downcast.

'Stand up Azaromel. There is no reason to be afraid,' said Arthur.

Cailleach then reached out and touched Arthur's finger. He felt a warm flush build up in his hand and travel up his arm.

'There is much to fear. Many strange events are being prepared. Your friend is afraid because I can see what he is. Now, why have you come to the

Tombs of Marbh? Speak truthfully I warn you. Have you heard of the Curse of Cailleach?' she said in an icy voice.

Her warning startled Arthur, who had never felt so uncomfortable in the presence of a woman. He wondered if this was Cailleach or perhaps one of her servants. Cailleach looked into to his eyes.

'Yes, I am Cailleach. Now tell me why you have come to my temple.'

Arthur was not able to control his shaking knees and his trembling hands. Cailleach lifted her hand and pointed her finger at him.

'You are troubled. You are not interested in the temple of your ancestors. This one,' she said, pointing at the kneeling Azaromel ... knows when he is in the presence of ancient knowledge.'

Her bright blues eyes darkened, her nose wrinkled. Though the face before Arthur was that of a young woman, it had stamped upon it a deep knowledge of grief and pain.

'We are travelling to GuaireDun,' he said. 'Perhaps Oh! Cailleach you can help us with our quest.'

Cailleach pushed her head back.. Arthur sank to his knees. Captain Hewlett knelt quickly.

'What you are looking for is in the great tower of GuaireDun,' she half whispered and placed her soft pearly hand on Arthur's head, her eyes moistened.

'Arise stranger. Come with me now, and I will show you this world,' she said, almost kindly then turned and walked up the steps and passed through the bronze door of the central temple. The three men looked at each other.

'We must not offend her,' said Azaromel, standing up. 'Cailleach has the power to destroy us.'

The others did not reply. They dared not disobey her. They rose and followed her up the steps to The Tombs of Marbh.

She led them into a vast vault whose stone walls and ceiling were etched with carved images of dead queens and kings, gaping blindly at their new visitors. Arthur felt a chill on his face, as he looked at two rows of sarcophagi, running down each side of the spacious temple. Each sarcophagus had a stone replica of its contents resting on its lid, carved kings and queens in their finery, their eyes fixed in a stony vacant ogle at the ceiling of the vault.

'Come!' said Cailleach, as she walked along the aisle, between the ancient dead, towards an object at the furthermost point of the chamber.

'There!' she said pointing at a stone casket, 'is Queen Bethesba of Gallon. Here is King Ry of Anerin, and there is King Mar of Maud who has lain there for nine hundred years.'

Arthur was shaking with emotion, almost feeling the presence of his ancestors. He believed that he was intruding that he should ask permission of the dead to stay in their temple, as he looked at the grim frozen faces of the statuesque images lying on their tombs.

'Who are you?' they might have said. 'How dare you stare at us? Remember you are in the presence of Kings and Queens. Pay your respects and leave.'

They reached a large irregular shaped rock, standing alone at the end of the aisle. Its rugged and uneven texture contrasted with the sleek lines and symmetrical shapes of the ancient tombs. Cailleach stopped at the rock.

'This is the Rock of Súil,' she said, resting her hand on its cold surface.

Arthur saw a concave indent, on the head of the rock, filled with clear water.

'Gather round! I will show you this world.'

They stood beside the rock. Cailleach paused for a moment and closed her eyes, as if she was gathering her thoughts. They waited in silence. The ancient dead might have said, 'You are waiting to view. We often view your world. Cailleach often shows us your world.'

Cailleach opened her eyes. Arthur wondered how such a beautiful young woman could spend each of her days among the dead. Suddenly a change came over her face; it began to tighten and shrink, as if a great anxiety was pressing on it. It lost its gentle softness and was replaced by a dry hard look. Cailleach's features changed colour to a dirty brown and yellow, like an old piece of withered parchment. Her long shapely white fingers retreated to stubby curled stumps and deep jagged wrinkles criss-crossed her forehead. She shrank until she could barely reach the water in the rock font. The visitors froze with horror watching her flowing raven hair change into a solid matted clump of greasy, grey matter that fell to the floor. An old shrivelled, toothless wretch stared up at them, looking helpless in the folds of her delicate gown.

'Do not be afraid,' she whined, reaching out to the font.

The transformation from a beautiful young girl to withered corpse like creature numbed their minds.

'What has ... happened ... you? Oh! Cailleach?' cried Arthur.

'Nothing has happened,' she squealed grasping both sides of the rock font with her yellow curled fingers. She then opened her clawed hands and moved them across the surface of the clear water.

'You are now looking at the real Cailleach. I must return to my true form to show you your world.'

The water darkened, bubbles popped on its surface, and it changed colour to blue to grey to black then calmed, and a red tint spread across its surface. They did not notice the water changing. They were still trying to come to terms with Cailleach's transformation, as they watched her move her claw hand across the red liquid, filling the font.

'Look now,' she whispered.

They looked into the rock font. An image formed on the water, and they saw Lord Colclough Devereux pacing about his chamber in DunFaythe Castle.

'We are doomed … We are doomed,' he kept repeating.

The image faded and Citbeag appeared, standing on the battlements of GuaireDun, watching his army prepare for war.

'Soon … Soon,' he was muttering.

Meave's face then came into view. They saw her seated in a room surrounded by strange fish like people. 'I don't know where it is,' she cried.

Pádraig Bocht's face then formed in the rock font. His lifeless staring eyes looked straight at Cailleach.

'You must help us Cailleach,' he pleaded.

The trio stepped back from the rock font.

'Why should I help you Pádraig Bocht?' replied Cailleach.

'If you do not help, we will be destroyed, and then they will come and destroy you and the Tombs of Marbh,' answered Pádraig Bocht's watery image.

Cailleach's face winced with pain, as she listened to Pádraig Bocht. She moved her wrinkled face close to the surface of the water, as if she was going to kiss the image painted on its surface.

'We have known each other for a long time Pádraig Bocht,' she croaked. 'I remember when your father brought you here to pay your respects to your dead ancestors. The crows flocked around you on that grey morning. They knew that you had a troubled destiny. They knew that you would live to carry a great burden. You were young, and you laughed, when I told you that the time would come, when you would have to send your own kind into another world.'

She paused for a few moments, and her stick of a body swayed gently back and forward. Arthur thought she was going to fall over, but she moved closer to the water.

'Have you sent the children away yet?' she whispered, as if she was talking to a scared child.

'Yes!' cried Pádraig Bocht. 'I had no choice.'

His image on the water began to fade.

'You must help … us,' he pleaded, his voice fading. 'You must help … '

The image then blurred and disappeared. The water returned to its clear cold state. Cailleach continued to stare at the water, as if Pádraig Bocht was still looking up at her. Arthur, Azaromel, and the Captain fixed their eyes on Cailleach. She raised her shrunken shrivelled head and looked at them.

'Yes … I will help … Pádraig Bocht,' she croaked.

Cailleach reached out her twig of an arm grasped Arthur with her curled fingers and raised her wizen face to his.

'You have great strength in your spirit, but you also have much hate. Your hate is blinding you,' she gasped, releasing her grip and letting her hand fall into the water font. A cloud of grey mist rose from the font and encircled the visitors. Arthur could not see Azaromel or Captain Hewlett. Cailleach's ancient face appeared before him. She beckoned him closer, moved her lips towards his ear and whispered to him. When she was finished, she bawled in a screeching voice.

'Now go! The Dead of Marbh have seen and heard enough today. They are becoming restless.'

A sleepy quietness descended on the vault. The mist cleared. They were left standing at the font. Cailleach was gone. No one spoke. Arthur walked towards the amber doors and into the night, followed by Azaromel and Captain Hewlett. The silent crows perched before a dry bright moon.

Their horses carried them through the tranquil moonlit countryside, across damp limp meadows, through gushing icy streams.

'You cannot be seen when the sun is asleep, and the moon is bright,' Cailleach had whispered. 'This will last for ten days. But my power has no influence in GuaireDun.'

Arthur didn't feel unseen, he could see his companions, and they could see him, as they rode through the night. They reached the top of a small hillock and saw the dull lights of a monks' camp below them.

'If we are unseen, then we can pass unnoticed.' suggested Azaromel, watching the flickering campfires.

When they reached the Plain of Fhaithche, stretching towards GuaireDun and the sea, they saw that it was dotted with campfires. Passing groups of monks they often heard them shout whilst looking at each other,

'Who is there?'

'Do you hear riders coming?'

They continued on their journey until they reached the grey walls and towers of GuaireDun. Torches moved along the battlements and the perimeter of the castle.

'Its well guarded,' said Arthur. 'We can assume that there are at least five monks for each torch, moving on the battlements.'

They stood beneath the cold walls of GuaireDun. The great towers with their blinking torch lit windows towered above the castle, standing defiantly against the inky starry heavens.

'If we were not unseen, we would be dead by now,' said Captain Hewlett, watching the monks and the moving torches on the castle walls.

'How do we get up to the tower, and where is this Devil's Belly?' asked Azaromel, shivering in the night air.

Arthur looked up at the moon to reassure himself that he was still unseen.

'The Devil's Belly will bring us into the castle, but then they will see us,' he said, now realising how desperate their situation was.

As he led his comrades below the east wall of the castle the thought struck him that he was leading them to their deaths. A sharp sea breeze cut into their eyes and a cold feeling of fear washed over their hearts. When they arrived at the top of the cliffs, overlooking Trá na gCarraig beach Arthur looked again for the moon. The pounding of the waves on the sand filled their ears, and the whistling sea breeze made it difficult for them to hear each other speak. Arthur gestured to the others. They dismounted and scrambled down a narrow path cut into the limestone cliffs, to Trá na gCarraig. Feeling the sea wind push them against the cliff, they struggled in the darkness. Arthur remembered a time when he had sprinted down this path to meet fishermen. Without a word to each other they hurried along the damp sand to a thicket of furze bushes and forced their way through the thorny clump.

'We must not cut or damage any of the bushes,' advised Arthur, leading them into the tunnel beneath the cliff. They must never know about this place. Remember they can see us now. We must hope that there are not too many guarding the cauldron.'

The Devil's Belly was bare and dark. A splinter of moonlight allowed them to have a shaded view of the cavern. Water dripped from the ceiling, and winding steps to the Great Hall of GuaireDun climbed up the rock face. They climbed the damp narrow stairway and reached the top step beneath a flagstone that would bring them into the Great Hall of GuaireDun. Arthur remembered closing this flagstone, when Lord Cedric ordered him to flee to DunFaythe many months before. He was glad to be back. They waited and listened for a few moments, not a word nor a sound was heard. Azaromel pushed at the flagstone. It lifted quite easily, with little scraping or scratching. Then he pushed his huge body through the opening and gently replaced the flagstone. Arthur and Captain Hewlett waited in the cold blackness of the Devil's Belly. Azaromel moved quietly through the damp silence of the Great Hall. He could hear the monks in the courtyard and on the battlements. They were not interested in guarding the chambers of GuaireDun. They were preparing to attack DunFaythe. Azaromel left the Great Hall and walked in the shadows, along deserted passageways. He reached an opening in the castle wall, giving him full a view of the busy courtyard.

As he watched under the light of a hundred torches, thousands of monks preparing for combat, he reluctantly accepted that they could never recapture this fortress.

He looked down at their painted faces, their hooded heads, and their black draping habits. Their phials of Citbeag's Deoch dangled from their belts, and he remembered, when he was one of them.

'The spoils of war are yours!' Citbeag had said 'Bring me Pádraig Bocht alive.'

Azaromel remembered the attack on GuaireDun, the dead and the dying. He remembered his sons, killed because he failed to capture Lord Cedric.

'What are you doing here?' growled a voice from the shadows. 'You should be in the courtyard.'

Azaromel turned to see two monks standing opposite him, their cowls covering their faces, the tips of their drawn swords touched his chest.

'You are the giant Azaromel,' said one of them. 'You deserted us. But now we have you. Citbeag will be happy to see you.'

'I must see Citbeag immediately I have news for him. Put away those swords. I have returned!' said Azaromel, with an urgent strain in his voice, placing his hands on his chest below the tips of their swords.

He then took a deep breath and raised his hands. They took an age to reach the swords. The swords fell to the floor, as Azaromel's thick fleshy fingers brushed them aside. He watched them fall; they seemed to be floating in the air. Then they reached the ground with a sharp steely clang. He lunged at the monks, grabbing each one by an ear, clashed their heads together and then watched them fall to the ground. Azaromel removed their habits and hid their lifeless bodies in the shadows behind a pillar. He then scanned the passageway, looked down at the courtyard and was relieved to see that the passageway was quiet, and no one in the courtyard had seen or heard him. He gathered up the monks' habits and made his way back to the Great Hall.

'What is he doing?' asked Captain Hewlett. 'Where is he? We can trust … Can't … we?'

'Of course we can,' answered Arthur, wondering what Azaromel was up to – No, Azaromel would never betray them. He remembered how Azaromel had saved him at the monk camp. Then the fall of heavy feet on stone signalled his return. Azaromel scraped the flagstone with his sword.

'He's back,' said Arthur, pushing on the heavy stone.

Azaromel grabbed it and lifted it clear of the opening.

'Put on these habits and come.'

Arthur and Captain Hewlett climbed out and looked around the Great Hall.

'Where did you get these?' asked Arthur, examining the habits.

'I borrowed them from two of my former comrades. They won't need them anymore,' replied Azaromel, grinning. 'You would make two fine monks,' and he smiled, as they put on the habits and covered their heads with the black cowls.

He then walked across the empty Great Hall to a large teak door while Arthur looked around the expanse of emptiness. As a cold moonbeam lit the grey flagstones, memories of happy days in GuaireDun flashed through Arthur's mind, memories of happy banter and music. Now a chill silence spread before him.

'We must go now,' urged Captain Hewlett, tugging on Arthur's sleeve.

Arthur's thoughts returned.

'Yes! Yes!' he said 'I was just thinking of - '

'We have no time to think about the past,' interjected captain Hewlett. 'Come now! They are all in the courtyard.'

'What's behind this door?' asked Azoramel, turning to Arthur.

'The great tower of GuaireDun,' replied Arthur walking over and placing his open palm on the door, as if he was trying to feel some memories.

Azaromel pulled on a large metal ring hanging from the door. To their surprise it opened without a creak or a scrape. They stood looking into an empty circular chamber, lit by two torches attached to the wall. A dark wooden stairway wound its way up the stone wall and into an opening in the ceiling.

'There are four chambers above us. We must examine each one,' urged Arthur, stepping into the chamber.

They ran to the stairway, swords drawn and climbed to the first chamber. The chamber was empty, but two torches again provided light. They scampered to a stairway like thieves searching for loot and reached the second chamber, finding it also empty. The great tower of GuaireDun had been an oasis of discourse and reasoning and Arthur was distracted by thoughts of the chambers filled with lords and ladies singing, reading and debating. Now it was bare and hollow like a barn emptied of its golden grain. They ran to the third stairway.

'It will be soon,' said Azaromel, almost wishing that they would not find the cauldron.

They arrived breathless into the third chamber. The three of them stopped and stared: twenty torches attached to the walls cast their heat and flickering light on a large black cauldron, positioned in the centre of the chamber. Four thick twisted legs of iron supported it. Captain Hewlett took a step forward.

'Just a moment,' said Arthur in a hushed nervous voice. 'They would not leave it unprotected … What's that wrapped around the base of the cauldron?'

'Just a rope or some decorative cloth,' answered Captain Hewlett.

'Are you sure?' asked Arthur, as a tremor of uneasiness rushed through his body. He studied the decorative cloth at the base of the cauldron for a few moments.

'They wouldn't leave the cauldron unprotected.'

Azaromel was the first to move, pressing his shoulders against the circular wall he made his way towards the opposite side of the cauldron.

'You see,' said Captain Hewlett, walking towards the cauldron. 'We can easily tip this over and spill the Deoch on the floor.'

He reached out and touched the rim of the vessel. A rustling sound like the wind caressing the leaves of an oak tree came from the cauldron.

'Look!' cried Arthur. 'The rope … It's moving!'

The rope began to uncoil itself from the cauldron.

'A serpent!' shouted Azaromel, raising his sword. Arthur's tongue stuck to the roof of his mouth. Captain Hewlett could not move his legs; terror immobilised him, and his eyes blanked as a dark brown creature with shading to yellow-white under his throat, rose up before him. It had the vertical black eyes of a viper and wide head of a cobra.

'Run! Run Hewlett!' screamed Arthur, stepping back from the serpent.

The captain froze; his legs would not run. A seaweed like mane draped along the creature's back; saliva of a dirty drab colour dripped from the corners of its open mouth, as two needle sharp fangs moved towards him. The creature's eyes began to rotate

'Run now!' yelled Arthur.

'Don't look at his eyes,' screamed Azaromel, watching in horror.

Captain Hewlett froze, as the snake's rotating eyes transfixed him. He stood looking at the creature towering above him, like a proud child looking up as his father. The snaked lunged forward and buried his fangs in his arm. He did not scream or resist, but fell cold and dead to the floor. The snake turned and focused his eyes on Arthur.

'Are you next?' it might have said. 'Do you think you can defeat Citbeag? Do you think you can empty the cauldron?' it might have whispered.

Its eyes rotated faster. Arthur remembered Zilamar in the monks' camp in the pine forest, as his gaze was sucked towards the snake's eyes. The revolving eyes of the snake seemed to drag him towards them. Shadows of orange and green crossed his vision. His arms felt heavy, his feet stuck to the floor. He wanted to lie down. He wanted to sleep. Then a gurgling gushing sound suddenly brought him to his senses. The snake's head left its body and fell at his feet. Azaromel stood before him smiling, dark yellow bile dripping from the blade of his sword. The snake's headless body lay dead before him, covering the floor like a thick woollen thread.

'Thank … you … Azaromel,' gasped Arthur. 'That is the second time you have saved me.'

He ran to the lifeless body of Captain Hewlett, knelt down and closed the captain's dead staring eyes. Then his own eyes closed and a long screaming moan of despair burst from his shattered self and echoed around the chamber.

'I will not forget you. If this madness ever ends I will look after your family. Goodbye my friend,' he whispered, brushing away a tear.

'Arthur!' hissed Azaromel, impatiently

Arthur did not reply.

'Arthur! We must destroy the Deoch of Citbeag. Help me empty this cauldron!'

They pushed hard on the cauldron, filled with a clear sparkling liquid, but it would not move.

'It looks like fresh spring water from a mountain stream,' reflected Arthur. 'We will never up end this vessel. It's too heavy.'

Azaromel looked around the chamber, stepped over the limp coils of the snake, reached down and picked up its dripping head.

'What are you doing?' asked Arthur, as Azaromel raised the snake's head.

'Stand back,' he shouted, and he threw the snake's head into the cauldron.

The liquid bubbled and steamed and then thickened like cream in a jug and changed to a grey dull colour, solidified and filled the vessel with a solid mass of grey stone. The cauldron began to crack and then shattered and broke into a thousand pieces onto the floor, covering the dead snake and the body of Captain Hewlett with a dusty grey blanket. The solidified Deoch remained on the floor, a useless rock of cold stone.

'Well done Azaromel!' cheered Arthur. 'They won't be drinking this liquid tonight. Let's leave this place now.'

'Not yet,' answered Azaromel, running to the stairway leading to the fourth chamber 'We must see what's in the fourth chamber above us. Come with me now,' feeling his blood race through his veins after killing the snake and destroying the Deoch.

Before Arthur could reply he had disappeared up the stairs. Arthur reluctantly followed him, taking each step slowly. He could not banish the dead captain from his thoughts and hesitated on the stairs to look down at his body covered in a thick coating of powdery grime. Suddenly Azaromel came running down the stairwell.

'Run!' he shouted 'Run for your life'

Arthur did not ask any questions. He turned and ran towards the second chamber. If Azaromel said run then there must be a good reason to run. They jumped and skipped through the two remaining chambers. When they reached the door, Azaromel stopped and looked behind him then pushed it open and stumbled into the Great Hall followed by Arthur, who slammed the door shut, as if he was trying to prevent a stampede of horses. Azaromel rested his back against the door, panting and gasping, his broad chest heaving like a blacksmith's bellows. Beads of sweat soaked his bald head and droplets of perspiration fell from his chin to the cold flagstones.

'Why did we run? What did you see?' asked Arthur, gulping and spiting.

Azaromel placed his sword in his scabbard and looked at Arthur, horror struck, pressing his hands under his armpits, trying to stop his body shaking.

'There are four more cauldrons on the fourth floor!' he cried. 'There are also four snakes! Two of them began to uncoil, as I stepped into the chamber.'

'Four more snakes! Four more cauldrons! We will never destroy four cauldrons. We could never kill four snakes!' moaned Arthur, resting his head against the door.

Every sinew, muscle and limb of his body cried out in despair. He wanted to lie down like a tired child and wipe away his despairing thoughts and awaken refreshed into a peaceful world.

'We must leave now Arthur,' urged Azaromel, gripping his sword.

Azaromel's voice brought him back to his world. They ran towards the opening in the floor of the Great Hall.

'There they are,' cried a voice from the shadows. 'Take them alive.'

Monks streamed into the Great Hall from two open doors, swords drawn and lances raised high.

'Run,' screamed Azaromel.

Arthur did not move. Staring blankly at the advancing monks, he drew his sword.

'I will die here and now, and then it will be over,' he cried, turning to Azaromel.

'Run Arthur!' screamed Azaromel, as he reached the opening. 'You will die.'

Arthur looked at Azaromel, smiled and turned towards the monks, his face pale, his glazed eyes almost closed. The monks stopped running.

'He wants to die,' shouted one of them.

Azaromel ran to him and picked him up like a father would pick a child, scared of a friendly pup, bundled him under his arm and slid him into the opening to the Devil's Belly. Arthur felt the damp steps beneath his knees, as he watched Azaromel climb down after him.

'Can't close it,' he said in a despairing voice, as he pushed Arthur.

'Will we fight or run?' asked Arthur, struggling down the steps.

'There are too many of them. We will fight another day. Now we must run to the beach.'

They made their way down the slippery wet stairs of the Devil's Belly. The monks poured through the opening like an army of worker ants, screaming and shouting.

'We have them now! They can't escape!' they cried.

The first monk lunged at Azaromel with his lance and was brushed aside like a buzzing bee, falling, screaming onto the floor of the cavern. They stumbled down the stairway followed by the monks. Three arrows clanged into cliff wall above their heads. When they reached the passageway to the beach, Azaromel turned and faced ten monks, gaining on him. He picked up a large rock and hurled it at the advancing monks. Five of them fell in a heap, crushed and broken. They stumbled along the stony damp passageway, their faces cooled by a cold sea breeze.

'If we can reach the beach we will become unseen,' shouted Arthur.

Two more arrows whizzed over their heads. When they reached the thorn furze bushes, Arthur stopped like a child waiting for a door to open. Azaromel kept running, picked up Arthur and ran through the prickly maze like a wild stallion running through a fiery forest, not feeling the thorns piercing his face, hands or his legs, as he held Arthur tightly under his tree trunk arm until they reached the beach. Arthur fell onto the sand and looked to the heavens. A large grey cloud covered the bright orb of the night.

'There's no moon,' he cried, punching the sand. He looked to the cliff and saw the monks struggling through the thorny furze.

'Come,' said Azaromel, running to the cliff path followed by Arthur, panting with exhaustion. 'We must reach the horses on the cliff - '

Up the cliff path they ran with the wind in their faces and the monks at their backs. Azaromel arrived first, hauling Arthur onto the grassy verge of the cliff top. Azaromel could hear the monks scrambling up the cliff path.

'Did you think you could escape?' hissed a voice from the darkness.

Arthur turned to see ten monks mounted on horses, facing him. He sank to his knees and pounded the earth. Azaromel slouched beside him.

'We will die fighting. You will join me with my ancestors this night,' cried Arthur.

The battlements filled with cheering monks.

'Bring them,' they shouted 'Citbeag wants them.'

Azaromel and Arthur stood up and faced the monks.

'We must not be taken alive,' screamed Azaromel. 'We must kill as many as we can before we die.'

The monks lowered their lances.

'They are going to charge!' cried Azaromel.

Arthur raised his sword. A dull spot of white shimmering light reflecting in the blade caught his attention. He glanced at it and refocused his attention on the horsemen. The spot of light grew brighter. Arthur raised his head to see the source of the light and saw to his joy the moon sliding from behind a cloud.

'The moon is out! We are unseen!' he choked, gulping with relief.

Azaromel did not hear him. He was crouched low waiting for the cavalry charge.

'We are unseen,' shouted Arthur and threw his arms around Azaromel's waist.

A murmur of disbelief spread through the monk cavalry.

'Where are they?' asked one. 'They have disappeared!'

'Must have jumped over,' cried another, running towards the cliff edge.

The charged to the edge of the cliff only to see monks panting and spluttering up the pathway.

'They would have died if they had jumped. They must be close. Find them!'

The two companions made there way along the edge of the cliff top to their horses. Now man and horse were unseen.

'Let's leave this place,' urged Arthur, looking back at the group of confused monks. 'We can reach DunFaythe Castle in ten days if we follow the coastline. We must warn them of Citbeag's preparations.'

As a cloud drifted across the moon they galloped along the cliff top towards DunFaythe Castle.

* CHAPTER ELEVEN *

Queen Talutu's Cold Room

Ralph delayed opening his eyes. Having slept ten times in the Lost Children's cave, he guessed that ten days had passed since his first encounter with them. Each day on awakening, he hoped that it had all had been a dream, and he would find himself back in DunFaythe Castle. However, on opening his eyes he found himself lying on his mat of Ardghorm grass in the children's cave. Thoughts of Meave, where she was and what she was doing, simmered at the back of his mind.

Raising himself up on his elbow, he looked around the cave and yawned. The rest of the children were scattered about the cave floor, sleeping on their mats. They had made flimsy tables from driftwood that they had found on the seabed. Their diet consisted of oysters, crabs and pommal fruit that grew in abundance near the pearl field. The fruit looked like a large potato and tasted like an over ripe apple.

Ralph became accustomed to life with them. He had learned to ride a flying fish. The children called them eaniascs. Oisin taught him how to spear eels and harvest oysters. The children brought him to the pearl field every day. On close examination he discovered that the pearls were much like large duck eggs, each one had a dull light shining inside it. The pearls felt cold to touch and were as heavy as a large turnip. The children had discovered that if two pearls touched each other they generated heat, so clusters of these pearls were spread around the cave to keep them warm. Each day they collected fresh pearls to keep a constant, comfortable level of heat in the cave. Oisin was also awake, collecting sea masks for their journey to the pearl field.

'What is the ... Pearl of Neamhann?' Ralph asked, trying to suppress a yawn.

'The Pearl of Neamhann' replied Oisin, in a low tense voice, 'has properties that can do wondrous and powerful things. The pearl has a dark blue band around it, and it's twice the size of an ordinary pearl. I never saw one, but we have heard from the fish people that come to the pearl field that it gives off intense heat and could burn your fingers.'

'Why do the Black Guards want such a pearl?' asked Ralph, stretching his arms above his head.

'Some say that it has other magical qualities,' replied Oisin, shaking his head and hunching his shoulders. 'They also say that there is a Pearl of Neamhann in the crypt of DunFaythe Castle.'

It was then that Ralph realised that Queen Talutu wanted Meave to get the pearl. She knew that Meave would have easy access to the lighthouse and the castle.

Ralph had also befriended an old fish man called Kcirtap, who often visited them in the cave. Kcirtap spent several hours of each day collecting pearls. His small butt of a nose was almost human and his long matted rusty hair reached to his ankles. Sometimes the gills on his cheek did not beat, and the children thought he was dying or sick.

'Only resting,' he would say.

His small thin frame was permanently arched forward, from years of carrying large reed sacks full of pearls.

'I will get it one day,' he would often whine, when he entered the cave.

The children liked Kcirtap. Many times he brought them delicious snacks of roasted sea horse legs or portions of octopus stew. One day while the children were circled around a small mound of pearls, eating a mixture of oysters and crab-meat, Kcirtap arrived into the cave.

'Still here,' he said to Ralph.

Kcirtap always looked over Ralph's shoulder, as if he was watching somebody or something behind him and never allowed his slanted green staring eyes to meet Ralph's gaze. On this day he reached out his quivering, damp webbed hand and grasped Ralph's arm.

'There is no Pearl of Neamhann in Tír na Leasa, but there is one in the castle,' he said, tightening his grip. Ralph, who was carrying two large pearls, dropped them immediately.

'How do you know? When were you … in the castle?' he gulped.

The old fish man, for the first time, looked into Ralph's eyes.

'There is a secret tunnel from the lighthouse to the castle,' answered Kcirtap.

'What tunnel? … Where is it? … How do you? … Were you in the tunnel?' blurted Ralph.

'Pádraig Bocht knows where the tunnel is,' replied Kcirtap, coolly. 'However, he thinks it is sealed. All he knows is that it was used by the keepers for centuries as an escape route from the lighthouse. He doesn't know that it is possible to use the tunnel to get to the castle. I'm sure he doesn't know about the Pearl of Neamhann.'

Kcirtap picked up one of the pearls and looked into the dull light glowing inside, like a witch looking into a crystal ball.

'The Pearl of Neamhann is in DunFaythe Castle. The tunnel leads to it,' he whispered, his eyes brightening.

Ralph remembered the time he stood on top of the lighthouse and traced with his eye what looked like an old lane or animal track that led from the castle to the lighthouse. How he had thought that was strange that a path would be used that went through trees and ditches. He now realised that he had been looking at the path of the tunnel.

'When were you in the lighthouse Kcirtap?' he asked, hoping that Kcirtap would tell him more about the pearl and Queen Talutu.

Kcirtap let his old tired body slide into a reed chair He folded his withered webbed hands beneath his chest. Ralph saw a tired shadow move across his face and thought he saw a tear twinkle in Kcirtap's eye. Kcirtap looked at Ralph with the same despairing look the young children had in their drawn eyes.

'Many years ago I was a member of a secret sect, who wanted to use the pearl to bring peace to the worlds below and above the sea. Ten of us entered the vortex to recover the Pearl of Neamhann. Five of us survived its raging current and entered the lighthouse through the Lake of Fire. Before we could reach the tunnel, the keepers of the lighthouse killed my friends. I was lucky to escape. When I returned I was banished to the Ardghorm grass and have lived here since, like these unfortunate human children ... Now! Young Ralph! It's time to recover the pearl before we are all destroyed by war!' he cried, as he struggled to his feet, his eyes lighting up.

Ralph, sitting near him tried to settle his trembling arms and legs and clear his mind of images of the vortex, Pádraig Bocht and the world of Tír na Leasa.

He remained silent, trying to grasp what Kcirtap had said. Then he remembered Meave.

'Kcirtap!' he pleaded. 'Will you help me find Meave?'

Kcirtap put his hand into the reed sack, removed a pearl and examined it closely, like a miser would examine his gold coins.

'Why should I help you?' he asked, rotating the pearl in his webbed fingers. 'There has always been enmity between your blood and my blood.'

Ralph was taken aback by Kcirtap's tone, as he had never heard him speak like this before.

'What will you do for me if I help you?' asked Kcirtap, stroking his chin with a webbed hand.

Ralph did not answer. He was trying to think of some way to convince Kcirtap to help him.

'Well!' said Kcirtap. 'Can you make it worth the effort for me to help you and your sister?'

'I will tell my father … He is Lord Devereux … He will reward you,' stammered Ralph, raising his voice.

Kcirtap's oval mouth opened wide, and he shook his old withered head; the scales on his face flapped like leaves in a breeze. Ralph did not know if he was laughing or crying.

'She will be a queen one day,' said Ralph, hoping that this would impress Kcirtap.

Kcirtap's head stopped shaking, and he stared at Ralph, his mouth hung open.

'A queen you say! A queen of what or where?' he asked, squinting his eyes.

Ralph felt that Kcirtap was becoming interested so he picked up a pearl and handed it to him.

'If we can find the Pearl of Neamhann, then we can bring peace to this world. Isn't that what you wanted to do, when you entered the vortex?'

'Yes! That is what I wanted to do,' replied Kcirtap in a soft childlike voice. 'It's what I always wanted … to do.'

'Meave can help us find the Pearl,' urged Ralph, moving closer to Kcirtap, sensing that he was softening his tone.

Kcirtap put the pearl he was holding back into the reed sack and placed the sack across his stooping shoulders.

'I will go now, but I will return shortly, and we will pay a visit to Dochas Mountain.'

'I'll be waiting for you, Kcirtap. Whether we are successful or not, my father will reward you,' said Ralph, a refreshing feeling of hope tingled his body, he nearly cried with relief and expectation.

The children finished their meagre meal. They yawned and chatted; their stained subdued faces searched for Oisin like young calves searching for their mother. When they found him they returned to dreaming of the day they would leave. Some remained on their reed beds. Others searched for something else to eat amongst the remains of the last day's meal, strewn across their rickety table, uneaten sea horse legs, morsels of crab and a small jug of eel soup. Several of them gathered around a mound of pearls to feel the dying heat before they went to replenish their supply. Oisin handed Ralph a portion of crab meat.

'There isn't much left. We will have to go fishing today. We also need to collect more pearls. The cave is getting cold again,' he said, rubbing his hands together.

Ralph admired Oisin. He was like a father to some of the younger children. He told them stories, repaired their clothes and taught them how to ride the eaniascs. Oisin always made sure that their bellies were full, and they were warm before they slept

'Have you thought about your sister?' he whispered, stepping closer to Ralph.

'I think Kcirtap is going to help me find her,' answered Ralph. 'Did you know that he once tried to find the Pearl of Neamhann?'

Oisin checked that the children were not listening.

'Kcirtap has met Queen Talutu. I have often heard him whisper her name while he slept in that chair. Several times I have seen him talking to one of the Knights of Leasa. They always show him respect by bowing to him, when they pass him on their battle sharks,' he said in low whisper.

Before Ralph could reply the children gathered around Oisin, carrying their sea masks and wearing their toeless shoes.

'We are ready, Oisin,' said a tall ragged boy.

'Are you coming with us today Ralph?' asked a young girl, rubbing her drooping eyes.

'Ralph is not coming with us today,' answered Oisin. 'He is meeting Kcirtap later. They are going on a journey to Dochas Mountain. Perhaps they will have news for us when they return.'

The children shuffled their feet and nudged each other.

'Will you take us with you?' pleaded a sad faced child. 'We want to go home.'

A knot of sadness was building up in Ralph. He felt a tear fill his eyes.

'Not today,' he said. 'But I promise you all that I will not leave Tír na Leasa without you. If I can find a way home, you all will come with me.'

A glimmer of hope lit the child's sad face. Ralph felt relieved as the tear retreated.

'Let's go now,' said Oisin, trying to sound encouraging.

In single file they silently followed Oisin to the pond, heads bowed, dragging their feet, like a line of condemned prisoners. They put on their sea masks, mounted the waiting eaniascs and disappeared beneath the pond water. Ralph remained in the silence and the fading light of the cave. Several long hours passed. He walked to the pond many times hoping that Kcirtap would appear. Eventually he settled into one of the reed chairs and fell into a deep sleep.

A cold webbed hand sliding across his face brought him back from his dreamless sleep. The old fish man's scaly face hovered in front of his tired eyes.

'It's time,' whispered Kcirtap.

Ralph was constantly being surprised that he could understand the whistling sound that came from Kcirtap's oval mouth. The drink he had received was having a lasting effect.

'Where are we going?' he asked, raising himself from the reed chair and looking around the untidy chilly cave. 'I hope the children are able to find enough food.'

'We are going where you want to go,' answered Kcirtap, and he turned and walked towards the pond, his long rusty hair, tied into a single strand, dropped down his back like a bronze coloured rope. Ralph picked up his sea mask, placed it over his head and followed.

When they reached the pond Kcirtap mounted his eaniasc. Ralph slid onto a flying fish. The eaniascs, he had discovered were fast and agile and were able to manoeuvre quite easily through the Ardghorm grass and around the long stems of sea reed, growing on the sea floor. His was called Seabird. Kcirtap led Ralph from the pond, through the tunnel of the cliff and into the valley towards Dochas Mountain. Kcirtap was careful not to be spotted by any Black Guards. They passed several fish men collecting mussels and oysters, as they followed the undulating terrain of the valley floor. Kcirtap was travelling fast and at times Ralph found it difficult to keep him in sight, as they dodged and ducked through sea reeds, up crops of jagged rock and through shoals of dolphins. Above them they viewed the busy life of Tír na Leasa. Several times he saw the vast underbellies of Orca whales pass above him, carrying large reed baskets filled with armed fish men and knew that they were still preparing for war. The dwellings in the valley walls pushed out beams of light that hung in the sea above him. Ralph was glad that he was not collecting pearls nor watching the sad children in the cave.

On they went, clinging to their eaniascs, towards the pyramid at the end of the valley. Kcirtap never looked back to see if Ralph was with him. His single strand of rusty hair trailed out behind like a tow rope from a fishing boat. At times Ralph could have grabbed it, and allowed himself to be carried along. As he followed Kcirtap he was fascinated by pillar shaped rock features on the seabed and colourful star shaped fish that passed or brushed against him. The pyramid got close; lights filtered from the rows of Bsamaki skin windows, dotting the huge edifice. Suddenly Kcirtap darted to his left, looked behind and pointed to a large shoal of sea snakes hovering on the seabed. He then rode his flying fish towards the snakes and disappeared into the slimy mass.

Ralph closed his eyes and followed Kcirtap into the slithering moving cloud of serpents and almost collided into him. Kcirtap remained motionless despite being almost completely covered by snakes, wrapping themselves around his frail body. Ralph shuddered as the snakes attached themselves to his arms and legs. Kcirtap pointed above him, then the gaping mouth of a battle shark ghosted past. The boots of the Black Guard passed before his eyes. He could almost touch the barnacles attached to the shark's body. Ralph looked at Kcirtap, who indicated to him to stay where he was. Three more battle sharks ghosted past each side of the serpent cloud; their riders dressed in black, searching the valley. Kcirtap waited until the large tails of the battle sharks faded into the light of the pearl field and then pressed his knees against the body of his eaniasc which flapped its wings and shook its body like a wet shaggy dog. The serpents seemed to know that it was time to uncoil; they slithered off Kcirtap and Ralph, and the serpent cloud moved along the valley. One scrawny long snake remained attached to Kcirtap's arm. He carefully unravelled it and gently let it float away towards the massing cloud of snakes, now quite a distance back along the sea valley.

Kcirtap brought his eaniasc alongside Ralph, reached back and coiled up his hanging length of hair. He handed Ralph the tip of the coiled hair and then wrapped the strand of hair tightly around Ralph's wrists. Kcirtap faced his eaniasc towards the pyramid. It happened so quickly, one second Ralph was sitting on his flying fish the next he was pulled off his eaniasc and dragged through the water like a trout on a hook. Kcirtap sped towards the wall of Dochas Mountain. Everything in front of Ralph was a blur, as he shot along behind Kcirtap. The sea washed against the film of Bsamaki skin of his sea mask, preventing him seeing where he was going. Several times he saw the tail of a fish or a branch of a sea tree flash in front of him. Kcirtap turned to his left and moved along the wall of the pyramid. He slowed and Ralph could almost touch the grey jagged blocks of the edifice. Kcirtap then reached the end of the mountain wall and moved to his right. Ralph was feeling nauseous and was afraid that he would vomit inside his sea mask. A sudden weakness overcame him, and his eyes closed. Kcirtap pulled him vertically up the side of the mountain. Then as suddenly as he had started Kcirtap stopped dead in the sea and Ralph came floating towards him.

Kcirtap hauled him in him like a fisherman would recover a large sea bass. Ralph's wrists throbbed, and his arms ached. He wanted to lie down and rest. He did not care about pearls or fish men, as he fell forward and sat behind Kcirtap on his flying fish, resting his head on Kcirtap's bony shoulder. Kcirtap did not object. He removed the strand of hair from Ralph's wrists and wrapped it around his body to prevent him from falling. He then pushed the dorsal fin of the flying fish forward, and they entered an opening in the wall of the mountain. Ralph did not feel the warm current against his face, as Kcirtap moved along the tunnel, for sleep came quickly to him.

Ralph awoke dizzy and confused. For a moment he thought he was back in the castle. The soft bed of seaweed felt similar to his own cot in DunFaythe Castle. Opening his eyes brought him back to reality. Kcirtap sat opposite him in a rough chair cut from whalebone. Five pearls clustered together in the centre of the room provided light. Ralph could see another seaweed bed behind Kcirtap. There were no windows in the chamber and a well-worn tentacle curtain dangled in the doorway.

'Where am I?' asked Ralph, rubbing his eyes and examining the room.

'Eat this first. You were exhausted,' said Kcirtap, handing him a bowl of eel soup and a spoon made of coral.

Ralph was glad to eat. The warm soup slipped down his throat like honey.

'I still have some friends in Dochas Mountain. You are in a chamber at the lowest level of the mountain. Few come down here. It's too close to the Dubh Pit.'

'The … Dubh … Pit,' stammered Ralph. 'What's the Dubh Pit?'

Kcirtap did not answer.

'What … is the Dubh Pit?' asked Ralph, gulping down a mouthful of soup.

Kcirtap folded his thin sea worn arms across his chest and looked at Ralph.

'Well!' said Ralph, taking another spoonful of soup. 'Please tell me.'

Kcirtap leaned forward and scratched his bone nose.

'The Dubh Pit is a vast chasm beneath Dochas Mountain. Some say that the mountain is floating in the Dubh Pit. It's filled with a substance that is similar to mud and sticks to your clothes, your skin and your hair. You can't walk or swim in this substance. Some unfortunates have fallen in and were never seen again. However, you need not concern yourself with such a place. It's time we looked for your sister.'

Ralph liked the idea of a   pit. The thought that Dochas Mountain might actually be floating on a lake or pond of black mud fascinated him. Kcirtap stroked his chin with a scrawny finger.

'Queen Talutu's chambers are at the top of the mountain. Perhaps we will pay her a visit.'

'Visit the ... The Queen!' gasped Ralph. 'But she is the one who took Meave.'

The idea struck Ralph that maybe Kcirtap was going to hand him over to the queen for a reward.

'Then ... she will have Meave and me and as prisoners,' he said, looking startled.

'We are going to try and rescue your sister; this is the only way we can succeed. We must gain access to Queen Talutu's chambers. You must trust me.'

Ralph knew he had to trust Kcirtap, this ancient sea creature.

'Before we go, do you know of Citbeag?' Ralph asked then almost regretted asking.

Kcirtap did not answer, but stared at Ralph.

'Do you know about Citbeag?' repeated Ralph, raising his voice. 'Who is he? Where is he from?'

Kcirtap eased himself off his chair and onto the seaweed cot and sat beside Ralph. He closed his eyes, a grimace of pain puckered his wide forehead; his webbed hands fell across his chest.

'Citbeag! The fiend!' he snarled. 'We were once friends. We travelled together many times, to cities beneath the sea. For a fish man he was small in stature. He had braided green hair and the dull scales on his body never reflected the light of the pearls. He was jealous of his half sister Princess Talutu. ''She has all the beauty,'' he would moan.

'He was ... your friend,' cried Ralph.

Kcirtap opened his eyes and looked at Ralph and then closed them.

'The young fish children were afraid of him, and he treated the battle sharks cruelly, often leaving them without food for days or locking them in their pens for hours. His father, King Samoths the Third, was a dreamer, who spent his days in his chambers studying the history and myths of Tír na Leasa. When Citbeag visited his father the king would often laugh and say,

''Ah Citbeag, maybe you will conquer these kingdoms for me and make me proud of you. They say that you do not have the character or the wits to become a warrior. But I don't believe that you are a coward.''

'Citbeag would moan to me as we travelled on our battle sharks, ''They think that I am a weakling. But someday all of these cities will be mine. They think that the line of Leasa will continue with Princess Talutu. They are gravely mistaken.''

'Yes! I was the only friend he had, yet he treated me as a servant. ''Kcirtap you can feed the battle sharks. Kcirtap where is my comb sword.''

'When he was twenty-three years old, he suddenly disappeared from Tír na Leasa. The army spent many moon months looking for him. Eventually, fish people believed that he had picked a fight with the wrong fish man or had fallen foul of some sea creature he was trying to snare for a pet. Tír na Leasa forgot about Citbeag. His father continued to brood about conquests and preoccupied himself with maps and imaginary war plans. Yet he believed that Citbeag would return.'

''He will return. He is too clever. He will return,'' King Samoth repeated to himself, daily.

'Princess Talutu, who never liked Citbeag and found him a constant embarrassment, when she was with her royal friends, was glad that he had disappeared. King Samoths knew his son. Citbeag did return. Five years later I met him in the Throne Room. At first I did not recognise him. His body was shrunk to the proportions of a fish boy, and his face was transposed to a pearly white pallor, his eyes retreated into his head to the size of black periwinkles. I could see that the scales on his arms had changed to long strips of decaying seaweed, and he wore a dark hooded cloak. ''Where have you been? What happened? We searched for you for months,'' I asked. ''They think you are dead.''

''I am not dead,'' Citbeag chuckled, in a rasping, throaty voice. ''I am beginning to live. I have been to the human world, and I have visited Cailleach. We made a pact. She needs the single egg of the Queen Stenzel fish to restore her to her youth.''

'He then produced a thin earthenware phial from his cloak.'

''Cailleach gave me this elixir as part of our pact. It has the power to conquer all,'' he said, laughing.

'I stood open-mouthed before him.'

'Where will you get a Stenzel ... fish? No one has seen one for centuries,' I asked.

''I'm not wasting my time searching for a fish,'' answered Citbeag.

'I know now that Cailleach never got her Stenzel fish egg. I asked him what his potion could do. He told me that when he drank it, he felt no fear of any sea creature or fish man. He said he needed to feel no fear so he could fulfil his ambitions, and he continued to drink the potion. However, Citbeag was not aware of how it was changing his appearance and his moods.'

"Cailleach told me to sip it once a day. I have sipped it once every hour. I can feel my body filling with a new spirit and fire," and his eyes sunk deeper into his head.

'Your ... body is changing,' I said. 'I can almost see the bones of your skull.'

"I don't care," he answered. "My appearance is not important."

'From that day I never spoke to him again. Citbeag and Princess Talutu became friendly, and she severed all contacts with her friends. The pair of them was seldom seen in public, spending their days in the Cold Room of Dochas Mountain. Several Knights of Leasa reported seeing Princess Talutu and Citbeag leaving the Cold Room together from time to time. They said that their bodies seemed to be connected, or joined together. A rumour began to circulate that Princess Talutu and Citbeag had become the one person. I did not believe such stories. Once I did see him scuttling along a passageway, and I noticed that his appearance was becoming more skeletal. The putrid seaweed had fallen off his limbs, and I could clearly see his bones beneath a thin layer of greyish skin.

King Samoths died shortly after Citbeag's return, Princess Talutu became Queen, and Citbeag left Tír na Leasa. It is said that they argued about the arrangements of the king's funeral, and Citbeag stormed out and has never returned. But I know that the disagreement wasn't about their father's funeral arrangements. Queen Talutu was first born, and she was claiming the throne. Citbeag argued that since he was the only male air of King Samoths, he should become king. The council of Leasa supported Princess Talutu, and Citbeag left Tír na Leasa, swearing that he would return and claim his birthright.'

'But Citbeag ...' said Ralph, as a thousand questions formed in his head.

'No questions,' replied Kcirtap, as if he was reading Ralph's mind.

Kcirtap opened his eyes and slid off the cot.

'No questions. Finish your soup,' he said, shaking his head.

Ralph gulped down the last drops of his soup. After his sleep and his soup he was feeling much better. His raw wrists were tingling, but his stomach had settled. He had forgotten about Meave during the excitement of the journey and the story of Citbeag, but now he was looking forward to seeing her and was wondering how Kcirtap was going to enter the queen's chambers.

'How will we get into the queen's chambers? I am sure there will be many guards protecting her. Aren't they searching for you? Isn't it dangerous to be walking about Dochas Mountain?'

Kcirtap yawned.

'For ... me!' he answered. 'They are not searching for me. They are looking for you! Yet I do not understand why they are searching for you, when they have captured your sister. Perhaps they want you for another reason.'

Ralph picked up his sea mask.

'You won't need that,' said Kcirtap, as he walked over to a large basket, standing beside the seaweed bed.

'We will be using this. These baskets are used to carry pearls about the mountain. The pearls that are used to provide light for the royal chambers and are replaced every day, so there is a constant movement of baskets about the mountain. There is plenty of room for you to fit inside this one; it has four casters made from hermit crab shells and can be pushed along the corridors.'

Ralph was very impressed by Kcirtap's plan. He stood up and examined the basket and saw that he could easily fit inside; the closed lid of the basket would keep him hidden.

'It's time to go. Now get into the basket, and we will go and visit our queen,' said Kcirtap, smirking.

Ralph climbed in.

'Don't make a sound,' and he covered Ralph with an old smelly Orca skin cloak.

'This should keep any prying eyes from examining the contents,' he added and then pushed the basket through the dangling worn tentacle curtain of the chamber and into a wide shell floored passageway. Ralph peered out between the gaps in the reeds of the basket. A stench of putrid fish and decaying seaweed wafted from the Orca skin cloak covering him. He could almost feel the stench dripping down his shoulders. The gaps in the reeds allowed enough fresh air into the basket to keep him conscious. The passageway rose gently, as they made their way towards Queen Talutu's chambers. Ralph wondered what he would do when he arrived, and how they were going to enter her chamber – would there be Black Guards there? – would Meave be there?

They met several old fish men pushing baskets in the opposite direction.

'Ah!' said one of them, who also had a single strand of hair trailing to his ankles. 'Kcirtap! Where have you been? We haven't seen you for some time.'

'I've have been busy,' grumbled Kcirtap, without stopping or looking in the direction of the old fish man.

They then entered a large oval area. Many old fish men were loading pearls into baskets and pushing them towards the corridor.

'Those baskets are full of dead pearls,' whispered Kcirtap. 'They are being dumped into the Dubh Pit.'

Several Knights of Leasa were supervising the filling of the baskets. A knight spotted Kcirtap, who waved and walked towards the tentacle curtain.

'Kcirtap!' boomed the voice of the knight 'Where are you going with those pearls? Do you still supply them to the queen's chambers?'

Kcirtap stopped pushing and waited for the knight to reach him.

'I was supplying pearls to the royal chambers before you were born,' he said. 'You are delaying me.'

Ralph was surprised that Kcirtap would speak to a Knight of Leasa like that.

'Yes! Indeed! You have. My apologies Kcirtap I meant no offence,' replied the knight.

Kcirtap did not answer; he pushed the basket towards the tentacle curtain. Ralph was finding it difficult to remain still in a crouched position beneath the cloak. His knees were getting numb, and the stench of the cloak brought water to his eyes. When he swallowed he could taste rotten fish slither down his throat.

'Are we getting near yet?' he choked. 'I don't think I will last much longer beneath this cloak.'

'Be quiet. I won't be long now,' answered Kcirtap, rattling the basket.

Several times they met Knights of Leasa, who placed their webbed hands on the lid of the basket and chatted to Kcirtap. Ralph puzzled over Kcirtap – who is this fish man? – how can he be so familiar with the Knights of Leasa?

Several times other basket pushers attempted to look inside Kcirtap's basket to see how many pearls he was pushing.

'How many have you today?' they would say.

'Stand back,' was Kcirtap's answer. 'These are my pearls … These are for Queen Talutu.'

They finally arrived at a large rectangular chamber. Four passageways led from the chamber. A Black Guard stood at the entrance to each aisle. Kcirtap pushed the basket towards the entrance of a corridor to the left side of the chamber. The Black Guard was about three times as tall as Kcirtap, his cloak was spattered with mud and strips of sea grass, and he held a comb sword. Ralph, peering through the basket could not see his face, but hoped that Kcirtap knew what he was doing. Kcirtap did not falter. He raised his sea worn face and looked directly into the eyes of the Black Guard.

'This is the entrance to Queen Talutu's chambers,' said the Black Guard, raising his comb sword.

'Who are you and what do you want?'

'Who am I? Who am I?' shouted Kcirtap. 'I am Queen Talutu's pearl master.'

The Black Guard hesitated for a moment.

'Well - '

'I have pearls for the queen … Now let me pass,' and he eyed the Black Guard.

The Black Guard placed his hand on the lid of the basket.

'I must examine its contents,' and he scowled, trying to regain his composure.

'As you wish,' returned Kcirtap. But these pearls have not being cleaned. The queen prefers to clean them herself.

The Black Guard lifted the lid. A waft of foul, decayed air reached his bone nose.

'It smells like the decaying corpse of an Orca,' he exclaimed, stepping back. 'What have you got in there?'

Kcirtap replaced the lid.

'Do you not know that the best pearls are found beside the Orca's graveyard? Do you not know that these pearls shine brighter and keep their illumination for two days? Queen Talutu insists on having the pearls brought to her without being touched or glossed by anybody. Her Majesty insists on having them wrapped in the skin of a dead Orca … You have a lot to learn about pearls … young soldier … Let me pass.'

The Black Guard held his webbed hand to his nose and took three steps backwards. Kcirtap stepped past him and pushed the basket through the tentacle curtain of the queen's chambers.

'We have arrived,' he said, tapping the basket.

Ralph pushed up the lid off the basket and jumped, gasping and coughing onto a black marble floor.

'Oh! You do smell,' said Kcirtap, turning away.

Ralph brushed some dead seaweed and pieces of Orca flesh from his tunic then looked around the large chamber

'Where are we now?'

'You are in … Queen Talutu's Throne Room,' replied Kcirtap, trying not to sound worried.

Ralph stood facing the length of the black marbled-floored room. The walls on each side were decorated with colourful images of planets and moons and stars, created from thousands of tiny sea barnacles. The images, he thought were similar to the ones he had seen on the wall of Pádraig Bocht's room in the lighthouse. High on a wall facing him was an image of two planets connected by lines. Below this image was the throne chair of Queen Talutu, made from polished cedar wood. The high backrest was an oak frame filled with albatross feathers, and the armrests were carved in the shape of two long arms whose hands were open to fit the queen's hand. Ralph was feeling much better, no water, no seaweed and no caves. He ran the length of the marble floor and jumped onto the throne chair.

'Look at me! Kcirtap!' he cried 'King Ralph of Tír na Leasa.'

He sat down on the throne and placed his arms along the armrests. His hands did not reach the carved wooden hands.

'The queen must have long arms,' he said, smiling. 'I'm hungry Kcirtap,' and he jumped from the throne chair, his voice echoing off the marble floor and decorated walls of the chamber.

'I'm hungry!' he repeated.

Kcirtap was not listening or looking at Ralph. He was kneeling on the floor, his head bowed, almost touching the cold marble.

'What are you doing?' asked Ralph. 'I am not a king. You don't have to bow before me.'

'He is not bowing before you. He is bowing before his queen,' said a voice from a corner of the Throne Room.

Ralph turned to see Queen Talutu standing before him. She had entered the chamber through a gold embossed tentacle curtain in a corner of the chamber that Ralph had not noticed. He stood looking at her, speechless, embarrassed and smelling of stale Orca meat. He tried to speak,

'I did not wish - '

The queen's low haughty voice silenced Ralph.

'We have been waiting for you, young human,' she said, letting her eyes drift from him to Kcirtap.

Her sparkling gown reached to her ankles, and her head-dress reminded Ralph of a wind filled sail. Ralph was not expecting such a friendly greeting. He felt the burden of embarrassment and fear lift from his thoughts.

'Kcirtap!' she said, moving towards the centre of the chamber, as her sail head dress filled like a sailing boat, tacking before the wind.

'It's good to see you again. We have missed you. You know your banishment was lifted many years ago. You could have returned to us at any time.'

'My banishment was like an illness Oh! Queen. It has taken me a long time to recover. I have cried often … I have suffered … My body has screamed for the comfort of your service. I have been in the valley too long,' he moaned, staring at the floor.

Queen Talutu moved closer to him.

'You may look at me Kcirtap,' she said, in an almost kind voice then pointed a webbed hand at Ralph.

'I am grateful that you have brought this young human to me, you will be rewarded.'

'My reward will be to serve you,' answered Kcirtap, raising his head without meeting her eyes.

Ralph, stood open-mouthed. He could not believe what he was hearing – No! Kcirtap could not be one of the queen's servants! He was only pretending to be. Why would he go to the trouble of smuggling him into the queen's chambers if he wanted to give him up to the queen?'

The queen glided over to Ralph and looked at him, as if she was examining an unusual species of bird or animal.

'Yes Ralph,' said the queen, as her eyes rotated slowly. Kcirtap has been a good friend to you.'

'A good friend,' replied Ralph, watching her eyes.

Her eyes continued to rotate. Ralph's eyelids felt heavy. His hands fell to his sides. The queen's eyes revolved faster and faster. Ralph's head slumped forward.

'I think Ralph needs some nourishment your majesty,' interjected Kcirtap, moving towards Ralph. 'He is feeling unwell.'

Her eyes stopped spinning. Ralph awoke from his half slumber.

'What happened?' he asked. 'I feel strange … As if I had been asleep … Yet I don't remember when - ' 'You nearly fainted, Ralph,' said Kcirtap, holding his arm. 'You are weak after your journey.'

The queen's face hardened, and the scales on her face fluttered.

'Ralph, you must be hungry and you need clean clothes. You and Kcirtap must join Meave and myself for a meal shortly,' and she glared at Kcirtap.

'Meave! Meave!' shouted Ralph. 'Where is she? How is she? Is she safe?'

'Of course she is safe,' replied the queen, looking again at Kcirtap. 'She has been keeping us company and telling us about DunFaythe Lighthouse and DunFaythe Castle. I am sure she will be happy to see you.'

Ralph fell to his knees confused and breathless – what had they done to her? A hazy vision of Meave's smiling angular face floated before his eyes.

'Where is Meave? What have you done to her? My father will punish you if you have harmed her,' he spluttered between sobs and tears.

'You must be patient Ralph,' whispered Kcirtap, in a reassuring voice.

'This is none of your concern,' said Queen Talutu, frowning at Kcirtap. Her face darkened, and the scales on her face lifted, as if an invisible comb was stroking them. Ralph sat on the marble floor and placed his head between his raised knees.

'Leave me alone! My father will come for me. I don't want to talk to anybody. I want my sister,' he cried, trying to remember a time, when he was in the castle, and they were all together. No such thoughts would come to his mind. Queen Talutu knelt down beside him; her aroma of stale fish made him retch and swallow. He could not decide if she was trying to be kind, or if she was gloating over him.

'I will take you to see your sister now,' she said.

Ralph didn't care if she was being kind, or if she had other motives. He wanted to visit Meave.

'Kcirtap will come also,' said Ralph, not wanting to go alone with the queen.

'As you wish,' answered the queen, standing up and scowling at Kcirtap. 'Follow me.'

They followed Queen Talutu through the gold embossed tentacle curtain. The chamber they entered had one full wall made of Bsamaki skin. The remaining walls were decorated with images of Orcas and battle sharks. Ralph guessed that he was near the top of the pyramid because the fish men on the valley floor looked like worker ants scurrying around the sand. Voices filled the air, high pitched whistling voices of young fish people, laughing, chatting and shouting. A gathering of young fish people stood around many flat-topped tables laden with dishes of crabs legs and mounds of oysters. Some of the males were drinking from deep shell vessels. Many of the young fish people were dressed in purple tunics and wore similar sail type head dresses to that of the queen. Queen Talutu stood and admired the happy boisterous scene before her.

'Here is the future of Tír na Leasa. They are the future commanders and officers of the Black Guards. Tír na Leasa will become powerful again,' she said, clasping her hands together in delight.

Ralph saw an angry look in Kcirtap's eyes.

'I thought you and the queen were friends,' he whispered.

'She has dreams and plans that could end up becoming nightmares for us all,' answered Kcirtap, tensing his frail body.

'Your Majesty,' shouted a voice from amongst the tables. 'We did not see you enter.'

A respectful silence fell on the room. All eyes watched Queen Talutu, waiting to see her mood.

'This is Ralph and Kcirtap,' she said, dangling a webbed finger in their direction. 'They will be our guests for a short while.'

'The shorter the better,' muttered Kcirtap.

'Is he human?' asked a fish boy, pointing at Ralph. 'He is ugly. Look! He has no scales on his face. His nose is stuck beneath his skin.'

Another young fish boy with long green hair and slanted silvery eyes came forward and looked at Ralph.

'Does he always smell so bad?' he asked, grinning.

Then Ralph felt a cold damp hand touch his arm.

'Hello Ralph. How are you?' said a gentle voice. He turned to see a young fish girl about his own height staring at him.

Studying her sculptured face covered with tiny scales like gossamer painted on a fallen leaf he was surprised that any of these fish people would know him. Her neat nose, and her ink dark hair made her look almost pretty.

'Hello,' said Ralph.

'Do you not know me?' she asked, half smiling.

'Ralph looked into her dark slanted eyes, thinking they might trigger some memory.

'I'm afraid not,' he said. 'Perhaps we met when I was here some time ago. I'm afraid I don't remember you.'

The crowd gathered closer to Ralph, the odour of fish hung thick in the air.

'Do you know this human?' asked one of them, pointing an open hand at Ralph.

'Have you met him before?' asked another. 'Look at his thin pale arms and his little oval eyes.'

Kcirtap was watching the queen, who was interested in this encounter between the human boy and the fish girl. The fish girl then faced the gathered crowd and looked over at Queen Talutu.

'This is my brother Ralph!' she said, raising her arm and pointing to Ralph.

The chatting stopped. The shuffling quietened. The queen waited for an answer from Ralph. The crowd waited for an answer. Kcirtap could not believe what he was hearing. Ralph could not find any words. He looked at the fish girl, hoping he might see some resemblance of Meave in her.

'But you are not human,' said a voice from the crowd.

'I have human blood and fish blood,' answered the fish girl.

You have given me the name Lamura. In my land I am known as Meave.'

'You cannot be my sister. You look ... like a fish! You smell ... like a fish!' said Ralph, aghast, taking a step backwards. 'Your hands are oily and cold.'

'Believe me Ralph,' said the fish girl, reaching out her webbed hand. 'I am Meave, and I now belong to Tír na Leasa.

Ralph remembered how Meave had begun to change when she entered the vortex, and how she had developed little gills on her cheeks and webs between her fingers. Had she now made a complete transformation? Bone nose! Scaly face! Slanted eyes! Oily, smelly hands! However, she still had her long dark hair.

'If you are Meave,' he said, still not believing. 'What is the name of your cat?'

Meave's oval mouth opened into a fish grin.

'My cat's name is Shadow,' she said, 'You once had a dog called Brutus. He ran away one night and never returned.'

Ralph now believed that he was looking at his sister.

'Children!' said Queen Talutu, with a bored look on her face. 'I'm sure that Ralph is now convinced that Lamura is his sister. Come with me now. I want to show you something that will greatly influence your future.'

They left the crowded room of chatting noisy fish children. Passing through another golden tentacle curtain brought them to a large metallic door. Droplets of water dripped down its bubbled surface, like worm trails on a morning beach.

'The first door I have seen in Tír na Leasa,' he whispered to Kcirtap.

'It's the Cold Room,' answered Kcirtap. 'I have not been here for long time.'

146

A Black Guard stood to attention beside the door. The queen nodded her head and the Black Guard pulled a roped handle. The door opened, and an icy cloud wafted towards them. Ralph shivered, and his teeth chattered, as the frosty chill touched his skin. He entered the chamber, following Queen Talutu, Meave and Kcirtap. A freezing dense mist filled the Cold Room, reminding him of frosty mornings in DunFaythe, when he had to rise early to attend a Latin tutorial. At first he could not see anybody or any thing.

'Over here!' said Queen Talutu.

Ralph walked towards the sound of her voice and found himself standing on a floor of ice. The walls and ceiling were lined with vertical strips of frozen snow. His arms and legs shivered so he placed his hands under his armpits and pressed hard on them.

'What ... is this ... place?' he asked, between the chattering of his teeth.

'We used to store precious metals and rare plants in this room,' replied Kcirtap, shaking his head. 'I don't know what it is now used for.'

'What is that?' asked Ralph, pointing to a large tubular object.

Nobody answered Ralph's question so he continued to stare at the tube, filled with a greyish pink liquid, mounted on four whalebone legs and bubbling like a cauldron on a stove. He thought he could see the outline of something floating in the liquid. Glistening frosted droplets dripping from its sides prevented him from clearly seeing inside the tube. Queen Talutu wiped a window on the frosty surface of the tube. Ralph could now clearly see a golden chalice immersed in the bubbling liquid. Tiny bubbles were escaping from the chalice and rising to the surface of the fluid. Ralph placed his open palm against the tube and felt the frosty hardness of the ice. Meave's cold webbed fingers clutched his arm, diverting his attention for a few moments.

'What's in the chalice?' he asked, glancing at Queen Talutu and guessing he would not like the answer.

He thought he saw her smile, and then her eyes fluttered like a moth in a cobweb, and the scales on her face glowed. Ralph's face drained of colour. He was sorry he had asked the question and looked again at the chalice floating in the frosted tube.

'The secret of Citbeag's success,' answered Queen Talutu, her eyes turning to Kcirtap.

'The Deoch of Citbeag.'

A raging anger filled Ralph.

'You are responsible for all the war and death,' he cried. 'You are a part of all this. Father will never forgive you,' he wailed.

He grasped Meave's arm and shook her violently, as a dark hatred rose in his soul.

'Why are you doing this? Why are you killing our people?' he screamed, turning to Queen Talutu and pushing Meave, who stumbled and nearly fell on the icy floor.

'How could you let this happen? You have betrayed us!' he shouted at her.

Kcirtap stepped between them.

'Do not despair Ralph. I am sure Queen Talutu has brought you here for a reason,' he said, trying to reassure him.

'You are a wise old fish man,' said Queen Talutu. 'Of course I have brought him here for a reason. Citbeag visits this chamber from time to time to replenish his cauldrons.'

'You are a wicked queen,' cried Ralph, sobbing.

'If I did not need you, such insolence would have brought about your death,' she rasped. 'However, there is a small task you can perform for me. If you are successful I will destroy the chalice, and Citbeag will be forced to withdraw. His army can't fight without their potion.'

'A small task!' cried Ralph. 'I will do anything to get out of this horrible place.'

'We have to return to DunFaythe,' said Meave.

Ralph felt a ripple of relief wash over him.

'To ... DunFaythe!' he stuttered 'We are ... going home!'

'Yes!' said the queen.

'You and Lamura are going to DunFaythe. We could not let Lamura go alone. No one would believe that she was the daughter of Lord Devereux. As you can see her appearance has changed somewhat since she came to visit us. Your task is a simple one. Find and bring to me the Pearl of Neamhann. When I am holding the pearl in my hand, I will destroy the Deoch of Citbeag, and we will both have what we wish.' His anger washed off him when he heard the words DunFaythe and Lord Devereux. He did not care about the Pearl of Neamhann; he just wanted to go home. Father and Pádraig Bocht would find the pearl, and then the fighting and killing would stop.

'Where is the pearl?' he asked, not daring to think that it was in DunFaythe Castle.

Queen Talutu bent down and positioned her bone nose close to Ralph's. He could smell her fishy body.

'The Pearl of Neamhann is in the dungeon of DunFaythe Castle, mounted beneath the death mask of King Polomar. For many years we have searched

148

for such a pearl in the pearl field. We have had no success. Time is running short. The Pearl of Neamhann must be returned to its home,' she said.

'I will find it,' answered Ralph, clenching his fists.

'I hope you do young human,' returned the queen. 'I must warn you. There are two tasks that must be completed before you can recover the pearl.'

'What tasks!' cried Ralph, feeling a shaking anger rise in him.

'The Pearl of Neamhann is protected by two puzzles. You will discover these shortly. Now it is time you began your journey back to your people.' and she left the Cold Room.

* CHAPTER TWELVE *

Return to DunFaythe

The light of the sky filled his view, as Ralph moved towards the surface. He clung on to the scaly body of the Black Guard while the battle shark beneath him effortlessly glided upwards. To his left Meave rode behind another Black Guard. Ralph was looking forward to feeling the sea breeze on his face, walking on solid firm earth and eating real food. He looked across at Meave and waved. She returned his gaze, but made no attempt to acknowledge his gesture.

Remembering Pádraig Bocht's story of Farraingrá he hoped that Meave would soon return to her normal self. The blinding light of a clear blue sky needled his eyes, as his head pushed above the waves. He removed his sea mask, opened his mouth and allowed the sea breeze to fill his lungs. Meave remained motionless on her shark, showing no interest in her surroundings. Ralph looked towards the beach. Blue skies with speckled clouds allowed the bright sun to warm the white sands of Trá Bán. Below the lighthouse and along the beach, wooden structures like walls or ramparts had been built. Hundreds of soldiers walked the beach and patrolled the wooden barricades, and several fishermen on the beach, busied themselves repairing their nets. Beyond the lighthouse the sight of DunFaythe Castle brought a smile to his lips. The familiar spectacle of its grey stony walls caused a longing ache to fill his stomach.

'Home! Nearly home!' he cried,

The sharks floated on the waves, threading their tails, carrying their riders towards the beach.

He glanced over at Meave again and noticed she was already beginning to look human. She, however, continued to ignore her surroundings, sitting still and aloof behind the Black Guard.

'We must be careful' said one of them, as they bobbed in the water. 'The fire is still burning.'

'Aye! The fire is still burning,' replied the other. 'He's still there.'

Ralph looked towards the black snake of smoke from the lighthouse fire, curling into the sky and felt safe again.

'When do you think they will come?' asked Pádraig Bocht, looking down at Trá Bán from a window of the lighthouse.

'Very soon,' answered Arthur, sitting on a low stool, resting his arm on Pádraig Bocht's table.

'Perhaps a week or two, no more. They were well prepared for war when we left GuaireDun. Citbeag has a plentiful supply of his potion. They will come screaming and killing. We need a miraculous event to save us.'

Pádraig Bocht returned to the table, examined his drawings and his maps, raised his chin and gazed at the images of moons and stars etched on the wall of his chamber. He then sniffed and smelled the air like a wolf before a full moon.

'Something's about to happen. I can feel it! Can you sense it?' he asked, lowering his chin.

Arthur could not feel anything. His mind was still distracted by the events at GuaireDun. He often had visions of the serpent and dreaded going to sleep at night, seeing and smelling the snake again. Every night he saw Captain Hewlett die and dreamt of the snake's head following him. Each morning a servant came to his chamber to wake him from his screaming nightmare. Pádraig Bocht sighed deeply and moved back to his window overlooking the beach.

'Will they come by sea?' he asked. 'Or from the North?'

Arthur remained silent with his thoughts. Pádraig Bocht looked out to sea again and then at the soldiers on the beach. Hundreds of men toiled under the noon sun, building wooden defences and digging deep wide pits to defend the lighthouse and the castle, hoping to stop the advance of Citbeag's army. He then became aware of a group of soldiers gathered by the foreshore. One of them shouted something to the others, who grabbed their weapons and ran to the water's edge. A captain barked an order, and the soldiers lined up along the beach facing seaward. He watched them raise their bows and prepare a volley of arrows.

'What's happening?' he asked, as he followed the line of the captain's finger, pointing out to sea. He narrowed his eyes and focused on two objects floating on the waves.

'I knew it!' he screamed. 'I knew something was about to happen,' and he ran from the chamber.

Down the lighthouse steps he stumbled, screaming and shouting, his arms waving about him, as if they had a life of their own. His long gangly legs tiptoed over the rocks, and he landed on the soft sand and slipped and fell towards the soldiers. Out to sea he could see the shape of the figures floating in the dark blue ocean.

'Hold those arrows!' he cried, running towards the soldiers, his cloak stretched out behind him like a pennant blowing in a gale.

'Stop! Hold those arrows!' he yelled, reaching the group of soldiers.

'They've come back!' he wailed, sinking to his knees in the soft sand and raising his hands above his head. 'The children have returned! Thank heavens! They are alive! We now have some hope again. The prophecy is being fulfilled!'

As the waves washed against his body and splashed against his dust stained face he emitted a slow, mournful cry, filling his mouth with phlegm. Black droplets of salty water ran down his wrinkled jutting cheekbones. He smiled with relief, looked out to sea and saw the shape of the Black Guards on their battle sharks.

'They've come to save us. Meave and Ralph have come back to save us!' he wailed, through the sea, wind and tears.

'Move away,' he screamed at the soldiers, staring at him.

They had never been as close to Pádraig Bocht and never thought that they would see him lose control of his icy behaviour. They looked at each other and looked out to sea.

'They are sea demons,' said a pale faced soldier. 'We must destroy them before they kill us.'

'Put down your weapons and stand back.! They are the children of DunFaythe!' answered Pádraig Bocht, pointing at the figures moving towards him.

'Return to your duties,' ordered a captain. 'If Pádraig Bocht says that they are the children of DunFaythe, then they are the children of DunFaythe.'

The soldiers lowered their bows and reluctantly retreated from the water's edge.

'They have moved away,' said Ralph, squinting at the beach. 'Pádraig Bocht is the only one on the shore.'

The Black Guard replaced his comb sword back into its scabbard.

'I don't want to kill any human kind today,' he said. 'I hope your Pádraig Bocht can control those soldiers. When humans are afraid they often lose control of their behaviour.'

Ralph could now clearly see the beach, and Pádraig Bocht standing in the waves, waving his arms above his head.

'I think he's waving at us,' whistled Meave. 'But I can't hear what he's shouting.'

It was the first time she had said anything since they left Tír na Leasa. She looked directly at Ralph and smiled. Ralph remained silent. He wanted to tell her that he was happy to see her return to her old self, but did not want to say anything that might upset this happy moment. He was looking forward to sleeping in his own bed, no more seaweed, no more glowing pearls. The Black Guards pulled on the fins of the battle sharks.

'What are you doing?' asked Ralph, as the sharks came to a slow stop.

'This is as far as we go,' answered one of them. 'You may introduce us to your Pádraig Bocht another day. You are safe now. Just swim towards the beach. The tide will bring you home.'

The word home echoed around Ralph's ears, and he jumped off the shark and swam towards the beach.

'Thank you,' he shouted, as a wave carried him along. 'You are not so bad after all. We'll meet again sometime.'

'Sooner than you think,' said the Black Guard, raising his fist.

Meave followed Ralph into the water.

'Tell Queen Talutu I will return shortly, when we find the pearl,' and she swam towards the beach.

The Black Guard winked at Ralph, pushed on his shark's fin and disappeared under the waves, followed by his partner. Pádraig Bocht watched the children swim towards the beach and knew that Lord Devereux would be a happy man that day.

Ralph lowered his feet and felt the sandy seabed and smiled, as the sea slipped down his body. He stepped onto the beach. Meave waded towards Pádraig Bocht. A strange feeling passed through her, then the touch of sand under her feet triggered familiar thoughts in her mind. She remembered her chamber, her cosy bed and her furry cat and felt a tightness in her arms. The scales on her hands began to crack and wither.

'Hello Pádraig Bocht,' cried Ralph, waving his hand. 'How are you today?'

'How am I today? Ralph Devereux!' answered Pádraig Bocht. 'How are you, and how is Meave?'

'We are fine,' shouted Meave, stumbling onto the beach.

'You're talking! ... You're talking,' spluttered Ralph.

'Of course I'm talking,' she said, smiling. 'We're home. I never thought I would be glad to see you Pádraig Bocht. We have a lot to tell you.'

Pádraig Bocht embraced the two children. They could smell the smoke and the seaweed from his cloak and feel his bony fingers grasping their shoulders. Meave untangled herself from his awkward embrace.

Ralph looked up into his reddened eyes.

'How ... is ... father?' he asked, heaving a deep breath.

'Your father has been very worried about you. He thought he would never see you again.'

Then Ralph noticed that Meave was looking out to sea, and it crossed his mind that maybe she wanted to return to Tír na Leasa. He could see that the gills on her face were disappearing like a healing gash, and her nose was beginning to recede. He dismissed the thought from his mind and wisp of a smile crossed his lips.

'Meave, I'll never complain about the smell of the lighthouse again. I love the sight of the lighthouse.'

Pádraig Bocht placed the tip of his finger on Meave's protruding nose.

'You certainly have the blood of the sea people. You will return to your human form shortly, once you have inhaled the dry air of the land.'

A dark shadow of concern crossed his forehead.

'Citbeag is preparing to attack us. We hope you have some news for us.'

'Citbeag!' cried Meave. 'Queen Talutu is his ally.'

Pádraig Bocht's face paled, his glazed and reddened eyes jumped in their sockets.

'So Citbeag is from Tír na Leasa. We are doomed! We can never defeat the sea people,' he moaned. 'Yet I still wonder why he wants to conquer us now. Over the centuries there have been many contacts between our kind and their kind. But we have never had much conflict.'

Meave looked up at his distraught features like a child bursting to tell some exciting news.

'You tell him, Ralph,' she said, and a shadow of a grin flitted across her face.

'Tell me what?' gulped Pádraig Bocht. 'Tell me what?'

Ralph looked out to sea and then along the beach towards the lighthouse.

'They want the Pearl of Neamhann,' said Ralph, his hands clasped behind his back.

'Something important is going to happen soon ... I think they want it now ... It's in the old dungeon.'

Pádraig Bocht guffawed loudly. The children had never seen him laugh before. His open mouth reached from his forehead to his chin, as he frothed and spluttered.

'The Pearl of Neamhann is only a myth, a fairy tale,' he cried, between the convulsions of laughter. 'King Polomar and the Pearl of Neamhann are only a fairy tale. They don't exist!'

'Oh! Yes is it does,' answered Meave. 'We have to find it. Our lives depend on it. The future of DunFaythe depends on it. The chalice - '

'What chalice?' cried Pádraig Bocht.

'There is a chalice in the Cold Room in Tír na Leasa, and it is filled with the Deoch of Citbeag. If we return with the pearl she will destroy it, and Citbeag's army will withdraw.'

'Tell him about the Lost Children,' urged Meave, glancing at Ralph.

'Children!' gasped Pádraig Bocht, almost not believing them. 'There … are children!'

'There are many children living in a cave near the pearl field. We have to rescue them,' answered Ralph.

Pádraig Bocht folded his arms across his chest and squeezed his thin body.

'Chalice … Pearl … Children!' he gulped. 'Where do we begin?'

We have to find the pearl,' answered Ralph.

'Why do they want the pearl?' pleaded Pádraig Bocht, who now believed Meave and Ralph.

'I … don't know,' replied Ralph, feeling disappointed that he could not tell Pádraig Bocht why they wanted the pearl. 'But time is getting short. I think Citbeag might want it also. Perhaps that is why he is waging war on us.'

'You have been busy, haven't you? We must discuss this with your father. We will find their pearl for them,' said Pádraig Bocht, looking towards the lighthouse and then towards the castle.

'But I am hungry,' said Ralph, feeling a rumble in his stomach, trying to remember when he had last eaten anything.

Meave giggled.

'I think we should visit father first. Let's walk to the castle. I like the feel of sand and earth under my feet.'

'If you must,' groaned Pádraig Bocht. 'We will walk to the castle.'

Soldiers digging the sea trench were surprised to see Pádraig Bocht, and the children walking from the beach to the track leading to the castle.

'Was she human? Was she from the sea?' they asked themselves.

Ralph was enjoying the simple wonders of DunFaythe. The mooing of the staring cows was like music to his ears. Two fishermen, walking towards the beach, stopped and looked, mouths open, clutching their crab baskets. They had never seen Pádraig Bocht at such close quarters or seen him walk their path before. The children reached the castle gates. Soldiers on the battlements waved to them, and Meave felt a flower of happiness blossom in her soul.

'Inform his Lordship,' shouted one of them. 'The children have returned!'

Ralph's chest heaved with pride, when he reached the weather beaten gates of the castle. For that moment he believed that Citbeag could never conquer DunFaythe. He enjoyed the familiar sound of the gates creaking and groaning like an old fisherman pulling in a large catch, as they opened.

'Father!' shouted Meave, seeing Lord Devereux appear in the gap between the opening gates, his arms outstretched, a cheerful grin spread across his ruddy face.

'You are welcome home,' he roared. 'We have been waiting, counting the days!'

Meave ran to her father and hugged him.

'It's so good to be home,' she said, burying her head into his cloak. Ralph stood and watched, happy to see Meave return to the castle and return to being Meave.

'Father!' he shouted, stretching out his arms.

Lord Devereux untangled Meave from his cloak, wrapped his giant arm around her shoulders and approached Ralph. Ralph saw that his father's hair was shorter, and his eyes were clear and bright. He had forgotten how tall and noble his father looked, as he walked towards him and hugged him.

'I'm glad to have you home,' he whispered.

Ralph could hardly breathe.

'You're squeezing the life out of me,' he squealed.

Pádraig Bocht retreated from the elated little group.

'We will talk later,' he said. 'I will come to the castle tomorrow.'

'Come in the morning, early,' replied Lord Devereux, smiling.

The children walked through the open ancient gates into the castle courtyard wrapped in Lord Devereux's cloak like two cubs protected by a lion.

'I see the market is beginning,' said Ralph, as they passed the lively stalls full of vegetables, hanging chickens, baskets of fruit, earthenware pots, saddles and a host of ironware and leather wear.

'It's good to be home,' repeated Meave, watching a young girl spread two woollen tunics across a stall made of blackthorn branches. They stopped at the open door of the castle and looked down the polished floor of the corridor leading to the Great Hall. Ralph escaped from his father's grip and ran down the passage.

'Where are you going?' shouted Meave.

Ralph lowered his body and slid along the shiny surface until he reached the door of the Great Hall.

'I've been looking forward to sliding on the polished floor,' shouted Ralph, pushing open the door and stepping into the vastness of DunFaythe Castle.

'Let's go into the Great Hall.'

Meave looked up into her father's eyes. She reminded him of a helpless kitten tangled in a sheet of linen.

'We do have to return,' she said, as a memory of Queen Talutu filled her mind.

'You have experienced so much for one so young. I am so proud of you,' he sighed, holding her hand.

'C'mon Meave,' shouted Ralph from inside the Great Hall.

'I want you both to rest. Old Alesia has been busy in the kitchen. She knew you were returning today. I need to speak to the captain of the guard and young Arthur. We will meet shortly in my chambers,' he said, hugging Meave and then returned to the courtyard, beaming with joy.

The two children looked at each other and then ran down the Great Hall, shouting and screaming. Ralph skipped around the large columns. Meave surprised herself and ran up to her father's seat at the top of the hall, jumped onto to it and screamed, 'Queen Talutu! I will find the pearl. I will find the pearl.'

Ralph stopped running and looked at Meave, standing on her father's chair. He watched a ray of sunlight from one of the high windows soak her in a warm orange glow.

'I suppose you're hungry,' croaked a voice by the fireplace.

'Old Alesia!' cried Meave, spotting her bent over a blackened hearth.

Meave jumped off her father's chair and ran over to Old Alesia.

'We have come home,' she said, not expecting Old Alesia to welcome her.

'Indeed you have. Your father was very worried about you,' answered Old Alesia, in a slow rasping voice, struggling to stand up. Ralph skipped over to help her.

'Leave me be,' she snapped. 'I was attending to these fires before you were born.'

She paused for a few moments then pressed a tooth hard against her wrinkled bottom lip.

'How are the Lost Children?' she asked, widening and focusing her hooded wet eyes on Meave.

'You may ask Ralph,' replied Meave, looking away from Old Alesia. 'I never saw the Lost Children.'

'The children! The Lost Children! Are they well?' she cried.

'They are in Tír na Leasa,' answered Ralph.

'I know!' wailed Old Alesia, rattling her basket of kindling. 'Are they alive and well?'

'They are alive, but lonely,' answered Ralph, remembering the damp cave. 'I promised I would return for them.'

Old Alesia scratched a tooth with a blackened fingernail and placed her bony hand into a pocket of her shawl.

'When you return tell them to drink this,' she said, handing Ralph a tiny glass bottle with a piece of cloth jammed into its neck.

'There are only a few drops left. Cailleach gave it to me many years ago … a precious liquid. Don't lose it!'

'Who is Cailleach?' asked Ralph, wondering if she was a childhood friend of Old Alesia's.

Old Alesia remained silent.

'It feels warm, like hot embers,' said Ralph, examining the tiny vessel.

'Tell them to drink it, and it will help them forget their loneliness,' said Old Alesia, and she picked up her basket. Ralph leaned down to help her.

'Leave me be,' she croaked. 'Come with me both of you.'

They followed her through a tapestry curtain hanging beside the fireplace and entered a small chamber.

'Oh!' gulped Ralph 'I had forgotten what real food looked and smelled like. I had forgotten how hungry I was.'

Their mouths watered, as they looked down at a table laden with roast duck, baked potatoes, apple pies, sweet cakes and jugs of orange juice.

'Eat and rest. You have much to do,' said Old Alesia and left them with their banquet.

Meave and Ralph sat at the table and began to eat.

'Did she know we were coming?' asked Ralph, dipping a slice of duck into a jug of gravy.

'Old Alesia knows many things,' replied Meave, stabbing a fork into a baked potato.

'She sure knows how to cook,' replied Ralph, giggling.

They spent the rest of the day wandering around the castle, passing time with their friends recounting the tale of Tír na Leasa.

'Can I return with you?' pleaded one of Meave's friends, thinking that a visit to Tír na Leasa would be an exciting adventure.

'I don't think so,' she answered, not wanting to mention the pearl. 'I don't really want to go myself.'

Sometime before the sun set the children went to their chambers fell into their soft beds and slept; no dreams filled their minds; no worries interrupted their sleep. Rest and peace drifted through them.

The soft light of dawn filled her chamber. Her curled black cat twitched his ear to acknowledge a new day. Meave was enjoying the warmth and comfort beneath her covers. She opened her eyes and saw her black tabby's green eyes almost smiling at her.

'You are also awake. It's not morning already.,' she said, reaching out to stroke him.

The door creaked open, and a servant came into the room, a young girl with a freckled face and a mop of red curls, carrying a small tray, bearing hot soup and freshly baked bread.

'It's time to rise, Meave,' she said. 'Your father expects you in his chamber within the hour.'

'But I've only just got into my bed,' replied Meave, a wide yawn filling her face.

'You have slept for ten hours,' said the servant girl. 'Ralph is already up talking to the guards.'

'He ... would be,' replied Meave, yawning again. 'He has to know what is happening and what everybody is doing.'

Meave dressed, ate her breakfast and hurried to her father's chamber. She was looking forward to meeting him again. After the excitement of their homecoming, she now began to think about finding the Pearl of Neamhann.

Ralph was also making his way towards his father's chamber having learned from the soldiers about Arthur's escape from GuaireDun and the serpent. He was fascinated to find that one of Citbeag's monks was living in the castle and wanted to meet him. The soldiers also told him that reinforcements were expected shortly from Arlach, a four-day march to the Northeast – Citbeag was expected to attack any day. They met outside of their father's chamber. Ralph was shaking with excitement. Meave was quiet and pensive.

'You are a girl again,' said Ralph in a teasing voice 'All your fish bits have disappeared.'

'Yes I have lost all my fish scales. Look my fingers are not webbed,' she replied holding out her hands.

'I'm glad to see you back to yourself again. I could never get used to having a fish girl as a sister,' he replied, placing his hand on the door. 'We better go inside, and see what Pádraig Bocht and father are going to do about the pearl.'

'Don't suggest anything too dangerous,' whispered Meave, touching Ralph's sleeve.

She was, however, confident of finding the pearl. Ralph pushed on the door.

'Come in children,' said their father, sitting at a table studying a withered chart.

'Did ye sleep well?' he asked, trying to add a tone of concern to his voice.

'I slept well. But I didn't get enough sleep,' answered Meave, yawning.

Pádraig Bocht, standing at Lord Devereux's shoulder engrossed in the details of the chart, ignored the children. A blazing fire warmed the room and Meave's mind drifted towards Tír na Leasa and the coldness of the chalice room. The children approached the table.

'The Pearl of Neamhann ... This is an ancient chart of the castle,' said Pádraig Bocht, without acknowledging Meave or Ralph, as he moved his fingers along worn faded lines on the chart, indicating the walls and chambers of the castle. His finger then stopped on a narrow grey square with one side completely faded.

'It's the old dungeon. There aren't any prisoners there anymore. Are you sure the queen said it was in the dungeon?' he asked, hoping that Ralph or Meave would tell him the whereabouts of the pearl.

Ralph studied the chart and spotted a tan coloured smudge in one corner.

'What's that?' he asked, placing his finger on the smudge.

'The lighthouse!' snapped Pádraig Bocht, beginning to get impatient.

Ralph moved his eyes closer to the stain on the chart.

'We need more light,' he said, squinting.

'What do you see?' asked Meave, knowing that Ralph would find something.

Ralph moved his finger from the stain towards the castle.

'There is a thin line etched from the lighthouse to the castle.'

His finger followed the faint line on the chart. Pádraig Bocht's sore green eyes watched Ralph's finger.

'I don't see a line,' he said, moving closer to the chart.

Lord Devereux strained to see the line.

'Are you sure there is a line there?' he asked, beginning to doubt Ralph a little.

'Yes there is,' cried Ralph, pressing his finger harder on the chart.

'You have the eyes of an eagle,' said Lord Devereux.

Ralph's finger trembled with anticipation, as he continued to follow the line towards the castle.

'Can you see it Meave?' he asked, swelling with pride.

Meave pressed closer to the chart.

'Yes I can,' she said, wondering what this line on the ancient parchment could mean.

The four heads studied the chart. Ralph's knees were wobbling. Lord Devereux and Pádraig Bocht watched Ralph's finger move towards the walls of the castle. Suddenly his finger stopped moving.

'What is it?' asked Pádraig Bocht, bending low towards the chart.

'The line has disappeared. It doesn't reach the castle,' said Ralph, tapping the chart with his finger in frustration. Pádraig Bocht stood up and stretched his long thin arms.

'Must be the old tunnel from the lighthouse. I had forgotten all about it. The line disappears because the tunnel must go under the old dungeon,'

The three faces looked at Pádraig Bocht.

'What … tunnel?' asked Meave, remembering her journey down the stairwell to the lake of fire.

'The trail I saw from the lighthouse, crossing the fields towards the castle!' cried Ralph. 'That's what it is!'

Pádraig Bocht walked towards the window, overlooking the courtyard and the lighthouse.

'I had forgotten about it. It hasn't been used for centuries. I've never entered it.'

Ralph looked down at the chart again.

'The line stops just before the dungeon.'

'It must go directly to the old dungeon,' answered Pádraig Bocht, looking out at the lighthouse. I remember now. The entrance is sealed in the lighthouse.'

Lord Devereux placed his large hand on the chart.

'A place we have never been was sealed centuries ago and forgotten about. It must have been sealed for a reason.'

Meave felt the old wave of fear pass through her.

'Queen Talutu did say that we would encounter some simple tasks before we could recover the pearl,' she said, looking up at Lord Devereux and Pádraig Bocht.

'Ralph, you have discovered a place I did not know existed,' said Lord Devereux, placing his arm around Ralph's shoulder.

Ralph's face shone with pride. Meave gave him a gentle nudge with her elbow.

'The pearl must be there!' continued Lord Devereux.

'Yes, that must be the resting place of the Pearl of Neamhann,' answered Pádraig Bocht, stroking his chin. 'I will bring ten soldiers with me.'

'Can we come?' blurted Meave, biting her lip after realising what she had said. Ralph was thrilled to hear Meave expressing such an interest.

'Can we please?' he pleaded.

'I think it would be better if the three of you went, without any soldiers,' answered Lord Devereux.

The children would be more helpful than ten burly soldiers would. We don't want to cause panic or rumour among the troops. Let them continue building our defences. I will order my carriage, and you can start immediately. If you are not back by dark I'll send a troop of soldiers to bring you back.'

Meave was regretting her outburst. Ralph was not afraid, he was dreaming of tunnels, secret passages and the Pearl of Neamhann.

The carriage sped through the market.

'They are going back,' said one of the stall-holders watching the carriage rumble towards the beach.

'Pádraig Bocht will be the death of those children,' answered another.

Pádraig Bocht's mind was filled with images of Citbeag smiling at GuaireDun in flames. Ralph was trying to imagine what was at the end of the tunnel. Meave didn't want to go, but she didn't want to miss out on the discovery of the pearl. They had wrapped themselves in warm woollen cloaks and wore leather boots with insets of soft rabbit skin. A soft easterly breeze chilled their faces and the smell of smoke filled their nostrils, as they approached the beach.

The carriage stopped, and Pádraig Bocht jumped out giving orders to six soldiers to follow him to the lighthouse. He also made some critical remarks about the defensives.

'They are too short,' he said, pointing at a row of sharpened poles, facing seaward. 'Make them longer and drive them deeper into the sand. A rabbit would knock them over!'

The soldiers stopped lifting and pulling wooden stakes and stared at Pádraig Bocht and the children.

'I've a bad feeling about this,' said one of them.

'He will destroy them and destroy us all,' replied another soldier, stabbing his sword into the sand. 'If Citbeag doesn't have us, he will work us to our deaths. Those children should be left in the safety of the castle.'

They made their way across the beach towards the lighthouse, followed by six soldiers. The children could taste the smell of burning tar and fish oil, being used to strengthen the timber wall. Ralph looked out to sea, half expecting to see a Black Guard riding a battle shark, but the sea remained cold and calm and devoid of visitors.

'I shouldn't have come,' whispered Meave, regretting her bravado in her father's chamber, as they climbed the steps on the lighthouse rocks. 'But I have to see what is going to happen.'

'This will be easy,' answered Ralph. 'All we have to do is follow the tunnel to the dungeon and recover the pearl. It will be as easy as swimming along the shore on a hot summer's day.'

'Hope you are right,' replied Meave, feeling a tightness in her stomach, as she climbed the steps to the door of the lighthouse.

The children entered Pádraig Bocht's chamber, followed by the six soldiers. The walls were still covered with images and drawings of the moon and planets. The table was still laden with maps and charts. The children and the soldiers stood tightly together in the small chamber.

'Remove that wooden cupboard,' ordered Pádraig Bocht, pointing at a wall of the lighthouse. 'and be careful of those books and scrolls. They are older than all of you put together.'

The soldiers lifted a wooden cupboard towards the centre of the room. A cloud of dust and particles of parchment rose to the ceiling. Ralph coughed. Meave sneezed.

'You may leave now,' ordered Pádraig Bocht.

Not wishing to linger within the confines of the lighthouse the soldiers left. The dust settled. Pádraig Bocht and the children looked at the sealed outline of an entrance in the lighthouse wall. Pádraig Bocht walked over to the wall and tapped his bony fingers on the surface of the seal.

'Not solid. Stand back! ' he grunted and drew his sword and slashed at the sealed entrance. After several thrusts, he created an opening in the flimsy material.

'Rotten wood and parchment,' he said, as his sword clanged off the stone floor and a grey cloud of centuries old stale air wafted into the room from the opening in the lighthouse wall.

'The stench of the sea people,' said Pádraig Bocht, covering his mouth with his hand.

'Can you see anything?' asked Ralph, straining his neck around Pádraig Bocht.

'Steps leading into darkness. I'll get a torch,' he replied and left the chamber.

Meave and Ralph looked at each other.

'Do you still want to go?' asked Meave, already knowing the answer.

Ralph walked to the entrance cut into the wall and peered into the inky blackness.

'Those steps must go under the lighthouse,' he said.

He took a shrivelled chestnut from his tunic and threw it into the darkness and heard it bounce and clatter down the steps.

'It goes a long way down. I'm sure it will be safe. Pádraig Bocht will know what to do … You can stay if you wish.'

Meave reluctantly moved over to the entrance, looked down the steps and felt a chill on her face.

'I have to see the pearl,' she said, and Queen Talutu's face flashed across her view.

'Follow me!' ordered Pádraig Bocht, returning to the chamber carrying a blazing torch. 'We are going to find this pearl.'

He stepped into the blackness, followed by the children. The high steps dropped steeply. Meave, holding onto Ralph's cloak, found it difficult to keep herself from falling. Down they went into the bowels of the lighthouse. The narrow passage, cut into rock by an ancient generation, curved to the left and then to the right.

'Can you see anything?' asked Meave, trying to sound courageous.

'No!' answered Pádraig Bocht. 'Will there be an end to these steps?'

Several times they felt the squelch of seaweed under their feet. Pádraig Bocht's torch light exposed images etched onto walls of the stairway. Meave stopped and examined one image.

'I saw that planet on the wall of Queen Talutu's Throne Room,' she said, touching the damp cold wall.

'We must continue,' urged Pádraig Bocht, raising his torch to examine the image on the wall.

'Should not be much further.'

After they walked down one hundred more steps, the stairway levelled out to a passageway.

'We're nearly there!' exclaimed Pádraig Bocht, turning and facing the children.

'Nearly where?' asked Meave, hoping that Ralph would reassure her with a kind reply.

'Wherever the pearl is,' snapped Pádraig Bocht, looking at Meave, as if she was an annoying child asking silly questions.

Meave was relieved to step onto level ground. Pádraig Bocht's torch-light exposed a narrow passage, disappearing into a smudgy blackness. No contours on the walls or features on the ground were apparent to give them an idea of the length of the corridor.

'Must go all the way to the castle,' said Ralph. 'The same distance from the lighthouse to the castle.'

'Of course,' said Pádraig Bocht. 'We have to walk from the lighthouse to the castle, but we are beneath the fields.'

Meave was trying to imagine what kind of people cut this tunnel into the earth – were they human or were they fish people?

'Let's continue,' grunted Pádraig Bocht, stepping into the darkness.

Pádraig Bocht's face in the torch-light, reminded Meave of a gargoyle she had seen in her history book, his nose looked longer than usual, and his eyes were yellow and rounded like two eggs spitting and frying on a hot pan.

She reckoned that the torch light was playing tricks, and Pádraig Bocht would never harm them.

They walked in silence. Occasionally one of the children stumbled on a rock or slipped on seaweed. Pádraig Bocht never stumbled or looked back. The passage began to widen.

'We must be getting close to the dungeon,' shouted Pádraig Bocht.

Meave continued to grip Ralph's cloak, struggling to keep up. Once something touched her face that felt like a soft piece of silk caressing her cheeks. She shuddered, but did not say anything, not wanting to slow down the march to the pearl. Suddenly she felt something gently stroke her forehead.

'There's something touching me!' she shrieked, stumbling forward.

Ralph stopped and looked around. Pádraig Bocht brought the torch close to her face, reached out and moved a piece of cobweb.

'Only a cobweb,' he said, raising the torch towards the ceiling of the passageway. The children froze, when they saw thick dusty layers of cobwebs, hanging from the ceiling, covered by thousands of yellow crawling spiders.

'The ceiling is alive!' howled Meave. 'I want to go back to the castle.'

'Only sea spiders. They are harmless. They have no venom. Let's move on now!' answered Pádraig Bocht.

'Will this passageway ever end?' pleaded Meave. 'I'm getting cold. I hate the darkness, and I hate spiders!'

Pádraig Bocht, ignoring her pleas, turned and continued his journey.

'We'll soon be there,' said Ralph, trying to encourage Meave. 'We've been walking for at least a half hour.'

'I suppose you are right,' answered Meave, gulping and reluctantly following Pádraig Bocht and Ralph into the darkness.

They stumbled along the passage in silence. Meave shivered beneath her cloak imagining several times that a spider was crawling down her back or along her forehead.

'Look!' shouted Pádraig Bocht, stopping suddenly.

The children squeezed passed him and saw a thin strip of dim soft light, at floor level, piercing the blackness.

'A last!' cried Meave, exhaling a sigh of relief

'There must be a door!' cried Pádraig Bocht. 'The light must be behind a door. If there is light there must be someone there. But who could be there?'

He ran towards the dim light. Meave grasped Ralph's hand.

'Don't worry we will find the pearl,' said Ralph, standing up straight and smiling at her.

Meave's grasp on Ralph's hand tightened

'I hope there are no sea people behind the door,' she said in a worried voice, stifling her tears.

'There can't be,' said Ralph, hoping to dispel her fears. 'If there were sea people there, they would have brought the pearl to Queen Talutu.'

Meave's grip loosened.

'Yes they would, wouldn't they? But who is behind the door?'

The children approached the light filtering out at floor level beneath the door. Pádraig Bocht brought his torch close to the door to reveal splashes of green dye streaked about the door's perimeter. The centre panel contained a small, carved image of two planets, one larger than the other, connected by a jagged line, engraved into the wood.

Meave could not see the images so she moved her foot to squeeze past him and felt something on the floor of the passageway.

'There is something on the floor,' she gasped, lifting her foot.

Pádraig Bocht lowered his torch. Meave pushed into Ralph, who jumped back, disturbing a cluster of spiders that fell and ran down his hair, his neck and his face.

'Get them off me!' he screamed,' brushing himself furiously. 'Get them off me!

'I have one on my arm,' wailed Meave, shaking herself.

Pádraig Bocht was not looking at Ralph and his spiders or listening to Meave, he was examining a white boned skeleton that Meave had touched.

'Be quiet both of you,' he said, bending his long thin body and examining the bones.

'They are crushed and broken as if he had been squeezed to death. Who is he? Where did he come from?' he asked, lowering his torch.

The children did not answer. They were too busy removing spiders from their cloaks, afraid to guess what had happened to the crushed wretch lying at their feet.

Pádraig Bocht fished his fingers amongst the broken bones and removed a small arm bangle. The children forgot about the spiders. His torch-light highlighted a small copper armband with vertical lines joining two snake head', carved on it.

'This is not a Devereux insignia' he said, putting the bangle in his pocket.

'How did he die?' asked Meave, still brushing spiders from her clothes.

'Something prevented him from opening the door,' said Pádraig Bocht, examining the images on the door.

He pushed on the door, but it remained solid and shut. A low scraping sound like carriage wheels on cobbles filled the passageway.

'What is … that … noise?' stammered Ralph, looking up at the ceiling.

The scraping sound increased in volume, mixed with a high pitched whistling. Meave felt something press against her shoulder and turned towards the wall expecting to see another cobweb filled with spiders.

'The wall is moving!'

Ralph felt a pressure against his shoulder.

'The walls are moving,' he cried. 'The passageway is getting narrower.'

The pitch of the whistling sound increased. Their ears ached. The passage walls pressed towards them.

'Open the door,' screamed Ralph, 'we will be crushed.'

Pádraig Bocht pushed on the door.

'Won't budge. Now we know how the unfortunate met his end. He was crushed to death,' he said, as the walls pressed closer.

'We are going to die. Open the door!' wailed Ralph, pressing his open hands against the damp wall. 'We will never get the pearl.'

Meave closed her eyes, remembering what Old Alesia had said to her.

'Grasp it tightly and it will guide you'

Holding Old Alesia's brooch in her hand she squeezed it until her fingers ached.

'We don't have time to return to the castle,' gasped Pádraig Bocht, struggling against the squashing wall. 'When I am … crushed my body may leave some space for you to … escape,' he said, as the walls crushed on his chest.

'Push the images of the moon and the planet on the door at the same time with the flat of your hands,' screamed Meave.

'What do you mean?' gasped Ralph.

'I can't reach them,' squealed Pádraig Bocht. 'I cannot move.'

Meave squeezed past Pádraig Bocht, reached up to the door and pushed against the images of the moon and earth with her open hands. She felt the panels in the door move. The whistling and scraping sound stopped. The walls stopped moving. The door opened.

Meave squeezed through the narrow opening, followed by Pádraig Bocht and Ralph. They stumbled into a large bare chamber. A layer of still, stagnant water covered the floor.

'It's freezing!' said Meave, shuddering and grating her teeth, as the icy water touched her ankles.

'How did you know what to do?' asked Ralph, grasping Meave's arm.

'Old Alesia,' answered Meave. 'She told me what to do.'

'Old Alesia,' growled Pádraig Bocht, looking about the chamber. 'She has many secrets in her wrinkled head.'

A dull light glowing on one of the stone walls of the chamber distracted Ralph.

'Look there,' he said. 'There is the light. It's shining through a window. Maybe the pearl is there.'

He ran over to the source of the light, followed by Meave and Pádraig Bocht.

'There is something glowing in there,' he shouted, pressing his nose against the window. 'We have found it! Bsamaki skin! We will never break it.'

'What is Bsamaki skin?' asked Pádraig Bocht, trying not to show surprise that the children would know what the window was made of.

'The sea people use it,' answered Meave.

The three faces peered though the window. A glowing sphere mounted on a tall column of granite dazzled their eyes.

'Is that the Pearl of Neamhann?' whispered Meave, trying not to show her excitement. 'Have we found it?'

'I think it is,' answered Pádraig Bocht, pushing his hand against the window 'But how do we recover it?'

'Look above the pearl … on the wall,' said Ralph, pointing a shaking finger. King Polamar's blank expressionless face gaped at them, his narrow eyes, his protruding nose, and his gill sockets cast in stone paled above the glowing orb.

'He was a fish man,' gasped Meave, staring at the death mask.

'He is a dead fish man,' spat Pádraig Bocht.

As they looked through the Bsamaki skin window at the lustrous pearl, their eyes adjusted to the low light of the chamber. Meave turned away from the window and examined the dreary room.

'There is something in that corner,' she cried, jerking Ralph's cloak.

Ralph and Pádraig Bocht turned around to look.

'A table,' said Pádraig Bocht in an icy voice.

'There is something on it,' squealed Ralph, hoping Pádraig would go over and examine it.

'There is also something on the floor beside the table,' shouted Meave, her throat dry with excitement.

They followed Pádraig Bocht towards the table, their feet sloshing in the chilly water. Pádraig Bocht was hoping to find something that would allow them to recover the pearl. Meave was wishing that she could return to the castle. Ralph was thinking of ways to break the Bsamaki window.

'There's a skeleton on the floor,' cried Meave, stepping back when they reached the table.

The low light of the pearl washed over the bare carcass.

'At least this one is not crushed,' said Pádraig Bocht, examining the pile of bones. 'He must have survived the passageway and died here. I wonder what killed him?'

'I don't care what killed him. This is a horrible place. I want to go home,' pleaded Meave.

'We can't go now,' answered Ralph. 'We must recover the pearl.'

Pádraig Bocht bent down and examined the skeleton.

'Look!' said Ralph. 'There is a chess game on the table. And look! There are markings on the wall.'

Pádraig Bocht and Meave first looked at the table and then at the wall. The cast iron table stood waist high, carved on its surface were sixty-four black and white squares of a chessboard. Aligned opposite each other like two opposing armies were the chess pieces. On one side of the board stood sixteen frosted white, perfectly sculpted statues. The queen wore a tiny tiara; the king wore a tiny crown.

'They look like little people!' exclaimed Ralph, examining the chessboard. 'The king even has a tiny sword in his hand,'

Standing opposite the frosted white chess pieces were sixteen rose red figures.

'Look at the red pieces,' said Meave, as she lowered her eyes closer to the board and saw that the king of the red army was an exquisitely carved fish man.

'They are sea people. I can see the gills on his face. The pawns are tiny black guards riding battle sharks,' she exclaimed, picking up a red pawn and scrutinising it. She examined his tiny comb sword and his belt of coral, delicately carved in ivory.

'This is unbelievable!' exclaimed Pádraig Bocht. 'It's comparing the conflict between human and sea people to a game of chess,'

'Where is the queen of the sea people?' asked Ralph, looking about him. 'It's not on the board.'

'I see no ... queen,' answered Pádraig Bocht, examining the chess set.

'There is the queen. The skeleton is holding it in his bony fingers,' exclaimed Meave, spotting the chess piece lodged between the skeleton's fingers

Six wide eyes looked down at the skeleton. Pádraig Bocht bent down and reached towards the rose red chess piece.

'Don't touch it,' gasped Meave. 'Maybe that is what killed him.'

Pádraig Bocht ignored her and removed the chess piece from the skeleton's grasp. It was the red queen, perfectly chiselled out of ivory. He could see quiet clearly the folds in her gown, her gills on her cheeks and the tiny straps on her sandals.

'See ... There is an arrow painted on the wall,' gulped Ralph, pointing towards the wall, his thoughts bursting with ideas – the pearl! – the chess set! – the skeleton!

'It's pointing to an image of the red queen.'

The children could clearly see a sketch of the red queen cut into the stone of the chamber wall.

'That is why he removed the queen,' said Pádraig Bocht. 'He thought the arrow pointing to the sketch of the red queen suggested that he should remove it, probably his last action on this earth.'

'What shall we do?' asked Meave, in a hushed nervous voice. 'We can't stay here forever. We must do something. We will never break the Bsamaki window.'

Pádraig Bocht replaced the queen in her position on the chessboard and studied the chess pieces.

'There's something wrong here,' he said, his eyes darting around the chessboard.

Meave felt a movement at her feet.

'The water is moving,' she squealed. 'What did you do?'

'I only replaced the queen,' answered Pádraig Bocht. 'The chess pieces are not in their correct positions.'

'It's rising up my leg,' gasped Meave.

'The queen has something to do with the rising water,' cried Ralph. 'That is why the skeleton had it in his hand.'

'I think he drowned,' replied Pádraig Bocht, feeling the water rise up his leg. 'We have to find the secret of the queen.'

'It's over my knees now,' cried Ralph. 'and getting colder.'

Pádraig Bocht continued to examine the chessboard.

'I see it now,' he said. 'The white queen is opposite the red king. The two queens should be opposite each other.'

'Move them,' urged Meave.

Pádraig Bocht repositioned the white queen.

'There … is still something wrong,' he said in a frustrating voice, biting his bottom lip.

'Why is the arrow pointing towards the red queen?' he asked, glancing at the image of the red queen etched on the wall, hoping that Meave or Ralph might know.

'I don't know,' squealed Meave. 'We will soon have to swim and the water will cover the chessboard.

'Should the red queen face in the direction of the arrow?' asked Ralph, wading through the water to the far side of the chessboard. 'We must turn the chessboard,' and he grabbed the corner of the table and pushed.

'Won't move,' he gasped, pushing harder.

'Do something now!' screamed Meave, watching the water begin to dribble onto the table.

Pádraig Bocht grabbed the edge of the table again and pushed. It didn't move. The water trickled over the pawns, toppling them over.

'One more time,' hissed Pádraig Bocht, lifting his foot and pushing hard on the table with the sole of his boot. The table moved two degrees.

'It's moving!' he cried, pushing again with his foot.

The table rotated and turned one hundred and eighty degrees, knocking the chess pieces into the rising water.

'If the pieces were still on the board, the red queen would now be looking in the direction of the arrow on the wall. We've done it.'

The water started to recede.

'Well … done,' squealed Meave, shivering 'But how do we get out of here?'

A high pitched ticking sound came from the direction of the Bsamaki window. They turned to see the window open.

'It's opening!' cried Ralph. 'The window is opening!'

The children looked towards the window and then turned to Pádraig Bocht, who was rubbing his chin with his fingers.

'Let's get it.' he said, and he waded through the water towards the open Bsamaki window.

* CHAPTER THIRTEEN *

Arthur and Azaromel

Azaromel pushed his large ivory head into an earthenware basin; the rush of cold water against his leathery skin almost refreshed him. He lifted his dripping face and looked around his bare chamber. His bed of goatskins, his maple table and his wrought iron stool contrasted with his memories of former days, when he had many luxuries. Azaromel dragged himself towards the narrow vertical slit in the wall of his chamber, giving him a view of the lighthouse and the castle grounds. The high sun in the sky hurt his eyes, as he looked at the soldiers labouring on the beach. Whilst flexing his thick fingers he came to the conclusion that he had waited too long.

He bent down and opened a wooden chest, lain untouched and unopened from the day he had first arrived in DunFaythe Castle. He hesitated for a moment, his eyes focusing on his monk's habit, folded neatly and washed of its grime and blood. A painful picture of GuaireDun, screaming, dying men and choking dense smoke washed through his mind. He withdrew his hand, stood up and glanced out again at the lighthouse and knew it had to be done. He then removed his tunic, picked up the monk's habit and covered his bulky, scarred body with the black woollen tent of a garment. Reaching into a pocket he removed a small sachet, inserted his bulbous forefinger and then painted each cheek with two vertical, wide, coal black stripes.

In another pocket he discovered his phial of Citbeag's Deoch, removed it, dangled it between his thumb and forefinger and raised it to his mouth.

He replaced it in the folds of his habit and whispered to himself,

'Maybe later.'

Reaching down again to the chest, he grabbed his broad sword, removed it from its scabbard and ran his thumb along the stained flat blade. He remembered the blood he had spilled, the screams he had heard and the men he had killed then pushed those thoughts from his mind. For now he could only be occupied with the task he had to complete. He glanced again through the window then left his chamber and walked down the steps towards the Great Hall.

'Where are you going Azaromel?' asked a young soldier. 'You are painted for combat!'

He ignored the question and continued walking until he met a group of soldiers standing near the castle door.

'He hasn't worn that habit since he arrived here,' said one.

'Must be doing his Lordship's business,' returned another, examining Azaromel's monk's habit.

'Are you leaving us Azaromel?'

Azaromel stopped before the group, looked down and caught the eye of a fresh-faced youth, bent under the weight of body armour.

'You know nothing of war. You are just a child,' he said to the young soldier. 'I am going to the lighthouse. I will be away for a while.'

The young soldier peered up at the rocky painted face of the monk and noticed droplets of moisture dripping down the fleshy grooves of Azaromel's cheeks and was glad that he was on his side in the war.

The he wondered was Azaromel afraid, but then decided, No, a giant could never be afraid..

The hills and hollows of bone, protruding from Azaromel's forehead reminded him of images of demons he had seen in books in the library, when he was on guard duty. Yet the giant's eyes were soft and bright.

'I wish you well Azaromel, whatever your mission is,' said the soldier.

Azaromel looked into the eyes of each of the watching soldiers, opened his lips to utter some words, but then changed his mind and left the castle.

The soldiers on the beach stopped and gaped, as he passed through their ranks. A high wall of timber and stone now ran the length of the beach. A deep pit, cut into the beach in front of the wall on its seaside and several paces beyond the high tide mark, was filled with dry gorse bushes and sprinkled with animal fat. Burning torches were placed at intervals of twenty paces along the wall, to ignite the pit at a moments warning. The soldiers were now building ramparts on the wall. From their positions they would easily see any threat that might appear on the horizon. They had watched Azaromel digging the pit, carrying two or three logs at a time under his arms to reinforce the wall, felling bushes and cutting tree trunks. Many times he had refused food or water whilst digging the pit. They felt safe when he was amongst them and knew that their work had a purpose. But now he was dressed for war.

On reaching the end of the beach Azaromel skipped over the rocks and disappeared into the lighthouse.

Arthur raised his head from the cradle of his fingers, as his chamber door opened.

'Azaromel!' he cried. 'Why are you dressed like that? Have you decided to return to them?'

Arthur stood up from his cot, stretched his arms above his head and yawned. Streaks of silvery grey were flecked amongst his jet-black locks.

Bulges of fleshy skin hung beneath his eyes. His once fresh and flawless face was scarred with stains of dried wine and grime

'Come with me now, Arthur!' urged Azaromel. 'You have spent enough time thinking about yourself and the past. The past cannot be changed, and you need to restore some life to your body and soul. You are beginning to look like Old Alesia, and you are wasting your life away in your loneliness and self-pity. Time for you to return to the world of man. Come with me! We are going to visit a queen!'

'What ... queen?' stammered Arthur, rubbing his swollen eyes with his fingers. 'Where is the queen? There is no queen!'

'You'll see,' answered Azaromel, grabbing Arthur and pulling him towards the door of his chamber.

'I'm coming! I'm coming,' he puffed. 'I hope you know what you are doing.'

'So do I!'

They descended the stone steps from the door of the lighthouse and landed on the soft sand. Soldiers on the wall watched, as Azaromel, followed by Arthur, strode along the beach beside the gorse pit. The hot sun, and the glittering sea dazzled Arthur's eyes, his head racked with pain and his bones ached from days sitting in the lighthouse, brooding and dreaming. Two weeks of self-pity and wine had left his body weak and shaking. However, he did agree that it was time to return to the world of man.

They reached the end of the beach wall and stood at the edge of the gorse pit. Azaromel looked out to sea.

'What are we doing here?' moaned Arthur, sinking to his knees in the soft sand.

Azaromel lifted his arms above his head, took a deep breath and closed his eyes. Arthur remained motionless watching the monk, as the waves flowed around his knees. He saw the blood drain from the monk's face and watched, as the muscles in his neck swelled and took the shape of an ivy rope wrapped around an oak tree. Then Azaromel opened his mouth and bared his yellow tombstone teeth to the sky. A whining gurgle came from his throat and then a moan followed by a scream that softened to a low whistle. The whistling sound increased in pitch until it sounded like a flock of blackbirds calling to their mates. Arthur covered his ears with his hands and continued to stare at Azaromel whose face was now changing from a deathly grey to blood red, as the shrilling whistle poured from his throat. Needles of pain shot through Arthur's ears.

'Stop! Stop!' he screamed, curling up on the beach like a baby, crying and shaking. 'My ears! My ears!'

'What are you doing?' he cried between panting gasps.

Azaromel lowered his hands and pointed out to sea.

'I am calling my battle shark,' he said with a slight scowl. 'We are going to Tír na Leasa. We are going to meet Queen Talutu!'

Arthur struggled to his feet. A wave broke over him and nearly pushed him into the gorse pit.

'Battle sharks! Queen Talutu, Tír na Leasa,' he shouted. 'You have been drinking too much wine!'

'Look there!' said Azaromel, pointing to the sea.

Arthur did not want to look out to sea. He wanted to return to his lonely chamber in the lighthouse. Forcing himself to look, he saw the dorsal fin of a shark cutting through the waves, towards him.

'There are no sharks in these waters. I must be dreaming ... Azaromel.'

Azaromel smiled down at Arthur.

'You, my friend, and I are going to Tír na Leasa,' he said and reached down and picked up Arthur.

'Settle yourself on my back,' he said, as he waded into the waves towards the shark.

Arthur did not bother to ask any more questions, hoping that soon he would wake up from his nightmare.

'You will have to trust me,' said Azaromel.

He placed Arthur on the shark's back and then climbed on behind him. Arthur felt the wet scaly skin and saw the wide maddened eyes of the shark, as he held on tight to the dorsal fin, speechless and shocked.

Hanging from the shark's wet body, were two reed baskets. Azaromel removed his broad sword from its scabbard and threw it into the sea.

'I won't need you anymore,' he said, reaching into a reed basket and pulling out a comb sword.

'I have missed you,' he whispered, examining the razor sharp teeth of the weapon.

He reached into the other basket and pulled out a sea mask.

'Put this on,' he said to Arthur, who was still finding it difficult to believe that he was sitting on a shark.

'Is this really happening?' asked Arthur, examining the mask.

'Only the beginning,' replied Azaromel, stroking the fin of the shark.

Arthur took the mask and placed it over his head. He watched, as Azaromel squeezed the shark with his tree trunk legs and saw the shark's tail move in sweeping wipe and carried them through the waves. Arthur held tightly to the dorsal fin, he felt sure that Azaromel would never let him fall into the sea. Without warning Azaromel reached forward and pushed on the dorsal fin. Immediately, the shark dived beneath the waves. Arthur, to his surprise, adjusted quickly to the undersea world. He was terror-stricken when he saw fish people riding sharks and dolphins, and he heaved and screamed inside his sea mask, as the shark dived faster and faster towards a dark stain on the seabed.

He was carried into a wide dark cavern. Down they went, silent and smooth into the warm water of the chasm. To his surprise, the walls of the cavern were lit with glowing pearls hanging in reed baskets on its glassy surface. A dull light in the distance above his head attracted his attention. The battle shark changed its direction with a single flip of its tail and ascended towards the light, surfacing into a large lake.

Arthur saw many sea people walking about the edge of the lake and many battle sharks basking in the warm still water. He took off his sea mask. Azaromel guided the shark to the shore and jumped off. Arthur struggled off the shark and stood looking at the scene before him. Silence descended on the lake cavern. Arthur stood dumbfounded staring at the sea creatures. Some of them pointed their fingers; others shook their scaly heads and made strange whistling sounds. Even the basking sharks stared at him. A Black Guard approached Azaromel, who had his back turned to Arthur. The knight placed his clenched fist across his chest.

'You have returned Commander!' said the Black Guard, crossing his chest with his closed fist.

Arthur only heard a low whistle. He also heard Azaromel reply in a high pitched sound to the Black Guard.

'Good to be back,' replied Azaromel.

'What's going on?' asked Arthur, realising that all the fish men were eyeing him.

As he reached out to grasp Azaromel's habit, the monk faced him. But Arthur did not see a monk. He did not see Azaromel. He saw the grotesque scaly face, the wide gills and the protruding bone of a fish man. Arthur wanted to vomit – he wanted to scream.

'You're one of them. You've betrayed me!' he cried feeling his legs go limp, and he collapsed to the floor of the cavern.

A spurt of whistling notes came from Azaromel's mouth. Arthur looked into the black slanted eyes of the giant fish man and felt himself being helped to his feet by two Black Guards.

'What will you do with him Commander?' asked one of the fish men, glancing at Azaromel.

Arthur heard the whistling sound again.

'I haven't decided,' answered Azaromel 'Queen Talutu will be very interested to meet him since he has much knowledge of DunFaythe castle. Bring him to Queen Talutu's quarters.'

Azaromel left the cavern followed by the two Black Guards, supporting Arthur, along the uneven shell floors of the passageways. Arthur hoped that he was dreaming and wished that he would awaken and find himself back in his chamber of the lighthouse. Azaromel did not speak to him, as he walked towards Queen Talutu's chambers.

After being helped down several pearl lit passageways, Arthur felt himself passing through a tentacle curtain, bringing him to the ante-room of Queen Talutu's living quarters. A Black Guard raised his clenched webbed fist to his chest.

'Commander!' he said.' Queen Talutu has been asking about you.'

Azaromel walked past the guard through another tentacle curtain and into Queen Talutu's chambers and motioned to the Black Guards to place Arthur on a chair made of polished whalebone. The ornate room was filled with a large oval table covered with stretched dolphin skin, surrounded by high-backed whalebone chairs. Pearls hidden behind Bsamaki skin windows filled the room with a lazy soft light. Azaromel whistled towards Arthur, sitting motionless in the chair.

'This is her War Room. We will soon be meeting Queen Talutu.'

Arthur sat motionless and speechless, listening to the whistling sound. His sense of betrayal and disappointment was nourishing his old feeling of hatred and anger. He promised himself that this time he would not run away – this time he would destroy some of them. A movement at the far end of the room interrupted his thoughts. Queen Talutu glided in like a leopard after a successful kill, wearing a silver cloak speckled with glistening gold suns. Her seaweed hair hung about her face like ivy draping down an old plum tree and the scales on her face reflected the dull light of the pearls in the Bsamaki windows. A soft whistle poured from her oval mouth. Azaromel stood up sharply and motioned Arthur do to likewise.

'You have returned Commander,' she said in a sarcastic tone.

Arthur studied her face and thought she looked like a witch. He guessed she might be related to Cailleach. Then Azaromel and Queen Talutu began to exchange whistling sounds,

'I have returned to serve you,' said Azaromel.

'What news of Citbeag?' asked Queen Talutu, hunching her shoulders slightly.

'We are almost ready to finish with the humans. There is only DunFaythe Castle between the pearl and us,' answered Azaromel

Queen Talutu moved closer, her slanted black eyes examined him.

'It's not necessary to attack DunFaythe just yet. The pearl is on its way to me. However, if Citbeag wants the castle, he may have it. I will have the pearl, and I will control its power ... I am not interested in ruling over a world of barbarians ... The sea world is my domain. With the pearl I will conquer all of the cities of the sea and of course, the planet Arob.'

She paused for a moment, placing a thin scaly finger to her oval mouth, as if she was trying to decide what to do.

'Perhaps I will use the inhabitants of DunFaythe as my slaves,' she said, smirking.

'How is the pearl returning?' asked Azaromel, hoping she would tell him her plans 'Citbeag is going to attack soon, and I see you are preparing for war. Are you going to attack DunFaythe Castle?'

The queen moved her bone nose close to Azaromel's

'A lot of changes have taken place since you left,' she hissed. 'You have many questions Commander. No! I am not going to attack DunFaythe Castle. Citbeag will complete that task for me. My arrogant half brother will be angry, when he discovers the pearl is not in DunFaythe. When he discovers that I have the pearl. But I will be ready for him and his army of killer monks. The power of the pearl will destroy them all! You Azaromel! You have a choice to make. You can spend your life confined like General Nirutam, or you can join me and be part of my kingdom.'

Azaromel took a step backwards and glanced at Arthur, who was watching both their faces, trying to understand the tone of the conversation.

'Where is the general?' he asked, trying to sound, as if he was unaware of recent happenings 'Where are the Knights of Leasa? I did not see any of them when I arrived.'

'The general is confined, and the Knights of Leasa have been disbanded. They have now joined the Black Guards and are part of my army,' replied Queen Talutu, eyeing Azaromel suspiciously.

Citbeag's faceless face hung in Azaromel's thoughts like a sickness eating through his mind. He could see the anger bursting from Arthur's eyes and was glad that he had returned to his old self.

'What is she saying?' asked Arthur, clenching his teeth.

'Tell this human not to interject, when a queen is speaking,' snapped Queen Talutu in a haughty regal voice, refusing to look at Arthur.

Azaromel raised his finger to his mouth. Arthur did not speak again.

'I am with you, my queen. We must prepare for Citbeag's coming. His troops are combat hardened. Ours have little experience of the horrors of war.'

'Yes,' answered Queen Talutu. 'But we will have the Pearl of Neamhann. We cannot be defeated. Citbeag does not know the full power of the pearl.'

'What is the secret power of the pearl?' asked Azaromel, hoping the queen would reveal some of its secrets. The scales on her face fluttered, she raised her bone nose like a wolf sniffing for a kill and then pointed a webbed finger at him.

'I assume you will be disposing of this human. He is of no use to me. Why did you bring him here?'

'This human is familiar with the layout of DunFaythe Castle. I thought he might be of use to us. I thought you were going to join with Citbeag to attack DunFaythe castle,' answered Azaromel.

She lowered her nose and glared at Azaromel.

'Why should I attack DunFaythe Castle and risk losing my army, as Citbeag is going to do it for me?'

She then turned her attention to Arthur.

'He must never return to DunFaythe. Dispose of him!'

She then removed a small shell bottle from her cape and placed it on the whale skin table.

'Let him drink this He will then understand our tongue. Get whatever information you need and then feed him to the battle sharks. I will summon you shortly. I hope for your sake that you will join us. Events will happen quickly when the human children return with the pearl.'

She turned and glided towards a tentacle curtain, watched by Azaromel and Arthur. Then stopped suddenly and faced him.

'Perhaps I will visit Pádraig Bocht. I have not decided yet.'

She then disappeared through the tentacle curtain. Azaromel slouched back into a whale bone chair, picked up the small bottle and handed it to Arthur, indicating to him to drink the milky liquid. Arthur did not question Azaromel. He put the bottle to his lips and emptied it down his throat.

'What have I drunk?' he asked, tasting a sweet and bitter liquid. 'Have you poisoned me?'

Azaromel whistled softly.

'I can understand you,' exclaimed Arthur. 'You say that you have not betrayed me. Yet these fish people treat you as an army general. You have brought me to a place I thought only existed in children's stories or the ramblings of old demented women. Who was that you were talking to?'

Azaromel dragged his chair closer to Arthur's.

'Queen Talutu, the sovereign of Tír na Leasa. She wants me to feed you to the … sharks. I brought you here to help me. Citbeag is Queen Talutu's half brother. He wants to destroy DunFaythe Castle and recover the Pearl of Neamhann. Queen Talutu has sent the children to find the pearl. She will then destroy Citbeag and maybe DunFaythe Castle. We have to stop them. Too many have died because of this wretched pearl.'

'Where is this damned pearl?' asked Arthur, now realising that everybody was looking for it.

'Somewhere in DunFaythe Castle, and it has powers that are not of this world. Whoever has the pearl can be become the ruler of all,' answered Azaromel

Arthur stood up and stretched his arms above his head.

'So that is why Citbeag wants the pearl. We have been fighting and dying because of the greed of a queen and her evil half brother.'

'Yes … that's why you've been killing, why … your kinsmen have been dying,' replied Azaromel, rubbing his wide forehead with the back of his webbed hand.

Arthur sat down again in a whale bone chair, put his head in his hands, placed them on his knees and rocked from side to side like a scolded child.

'What can we do? It's impossible … Too many of them,' he moaned.

'Capture the queen and bring her to DunFaythe, or we have to kill her,' answered Azaromel, 'But first I have to find a reason to keep you alive.'

Arthur continued to sway back and forth in the chair, his head buried in the palm of his hands.

'You will be my servant,' said Azaromel, placing his hand on Arthur's shoulder. 'It's the only way I can keep you alive. Together we can defeat this queen and return Tír na Leasa to the Council of Leasa.'

'Your servant!' growled Arthur. 'Yes … I suppose being your servant should help me to stay alive.

Whatever you say. Whatever it takes to rid us of this Queen Talutu and her half brother.'

'Come - ' said Azaromel walking toward the tentacle curtain 'General Nirutam is still alive and may be able to help us. I was once a Knight of Leasa before Citbeag kidnapped my family and forced me to do his evil work. He murdered my wife, three-year-old son and my ten-year-old son. Queen Talutu refused to intervene. She said that an example had to be made to the army, to teach them that no disobedience would be tolerated. So you see. I have a lot of scores to settle. Revenge will be mine! Let's find the general.'

'Who are the Knights of Leasa?' asked Arthur following him through the tentacle curtain.

Azaromel strode walk down the shell-floored passageway.

'The Knights of Leasa are the guardians of Tír na Leasa. They have protected this world for a thousand years. General Nirutam is the Knight Commander. You now know why I returned.'

Arthur stopped walking and held out his hand to Azaromel. Azaromel grasped it. Arthur could feel the wet scales between his fingers.

'Together we will fight. Together we will win or die,' he said.

Azaromel's oval mouth enlarged into a circular shape. Arthur guessed that he was smiling.

'We must hurry now,' said Azaromel, gently pushing Arthur. 'The queen will summon me soon. I will agree to join her, and she will then give me duties to fulfil, probably as commander of a legion of Black Guards. We will now visit General Nirutam.'

They passed down through the passageways of Dochas Mountain.

'I hope there are no serpents here,' said Arthur, as they went deeper into the mountain.

'No serpents,' replied Azaromel, increasing his pace. 'We are getting near the Dubh Pit. 'I assume the general is confined in the cells near the Dubh Pit.'

The passageway levelled out. Arthur saw that there were several chambers on each side of the passage. Each chamber had a Black Guard standing beside its tentacle curtain. At the end of the passageway there was one chamber with two Black Guards standing outside of it.

'This one,' said Azaromel, nodding towards a chamber.

The two knights clenched their fists to their chests, as Azaromel approached. They entered a small oval shaped cell. A figure lay on a cot of dried seaweed, its arm covering its head. Arthur and Azaromel stood over the still body.

'Azaromel,' said a weak voice from beneath the folded arms. 'You have been away a long time. I know you are with us. You would not have come if you were part of her plans.'

The figure lowered his scaly arms to reveal the pus-covered face of General Nirutam. His once flowing orange locks were matted and pressed against his head like moss on a sun-baked rock.

'General!' exclaimed Azaromel. 'What have they done to you?'

'She wanted me to lead her army. She promised the army untold riches. I refused,' croaked the general,

raising himself up from the cot and clutching Azaromel's arm.

'She has crushed the Knights of Leasa and forced them to fight for her. You have to act now. The planet Arob will be visible in three days,' he mumbled, slumping back down on his cot. 'This is our last chance … our last hope. I hoped to bring our army to Trá Bán to negotiate with … Pádraig Bocht. I hoped that he … would have been reasonable and given me … the pearl.' he said, slurring his words and closing his eyes. 'There … would have … been peace forever.'

'You must rest … general,' choked Azaromel. 'We will get you out of this place.'

The general opened his eyes; daggers of pain crossed his face.

'Too late for me now. Queen Talutu and Citbeag want to use the power of the pearl for conquest. The human children, who came here are going to retrieve the pearl for her, and she has promised them that she will destroy Citbeag's chalice. They are gravely mistaken,' he said, raising his voice in one last painful effort and forcing himself up again on his elbow

Arthur could see that the general had two deep wounds in his chest.

'I … do not have much time left,' whispered General Nirutam, grimacing with pain. 'These wounds are too deep. My life is dripping away.'

Azaromel bent closer to him and examined the gashes in his chest.

'I will summon a physician immediately. There is always time.'

'No!' whispered the general. 'Listen to me…before I go. Find the ancient one…Kcirtap. He knows the power of the pearl. He will know … what to do. But first … you must seize the … pearl when the human children bring it to Queen Talutu.'

He fell back exhausted, his breathing slowed to a silent gasp; the two gills on the side of his face closed like the sleepy eyes of a tiger.

'General!' shouted Azaromel.

General Nirutam held Azaromel's arm.

'The…future of Tír na Leasa is with…you,' and his grip loosened. His arm fell limp to the floor. The tiger's eyes closed and were still. Azaromel raised his head and poured out a long mournful whistle from his throat. Then fell to his knees.

'He was my wife's brother. They will all be avenged,' he cried.

Arthur's mind was sharp and clear, like a newly forged sword. His body was energised. Anger and hatred filled his heart.

'Let us find this Kcirtap. Let us put a stop to all of this killing,' he said in an almost inaudible voice.

* CHAPTER FOURTEEN *

The Pearl of Neamhann

Lord Devereux stood on the wooden ramparts of the sea wall. The lighthouse smoke mixed with the dry dust of the crackling gorse in the pit below him itched his nostril, and a salted sea breeze moistened his eyes and crusted his lips. The early morning eastern sun caused damp bubbles to grow on his face; his dishevelled hair and tousled beard blew about his craggy face like an old lion, as he surveyed the scene about him. Fully armoured soldiers grasping broadswords and spears lined the sea wall from the lighthouse to the end of Trá Bán. Behind them, with filled bows, stood a silent line of archers. They breathed deep and were silent. No one wanted to ask – when are they coming? Their waiting eyes watched the green, blue rolling sea. Lord Devereux, squeezing his sword handle until his fingers throbbed, asked himself how it had come to this.

'The future depends on two children. My children!' he said to a captain, a young man of twenty-two years with sallow skin and dark eyes, standing beside him.

'We are ready for them,' replied the young captain, trying to reassure himself.

'We think we are,' whispered Lord Devereux, lowering his gaze and focusing on the three figures standing at the water's edge, the Guardian of DunFaythe Lighthouse and his own two children.

The had been waiting and watching the receding tide for more than one hour. Meave felt the reed strap of the leather pouch carrying the pearl weigh on her shoulder. She placed her hand on the pouch; a low heat tingled her fingers, and she remembered climbing through the Bsamaki window in the dungeon below the castle. She remembered looking up at Kink Polamar's death mask, a slithery smile formed on his lips. King Polomar might have said, 'You have found the pearl. What will you do with it?'

Meave remembered removing the pearl from the granite column. It glowed like a small sun at dawn and felt as light as a slice of fresh honeycomb. She remembered staring into its misty glow and seeing swirling planets and streaking stars wrapped around a cobweb covered image of DunFaythe Castle. She saw the frosted faces of Lord Devereux and Queen Talutu float across the castle walls like shadows of a storm cloud. She tried to decipher what she was seeing, but the image faded, the pearl increased in weight, and the dull light reduced to that of a single candle in an expanse of darkness.

'Bring it here,' demanded Pádraig Bocht, reaching out for the pearl.

Pádraig Bocht's voice focused her mind. She returned to the window and handed him the pearl.

'I didn't think it would have been so large,' he said, examining the oval shaped object.

'Queen Talutu will be happy to see it,' said Ralph, wishing he could hold the pearl. 'Now she will destroy the chalice.'

Meave did not reply. She had an uneasy feeling in her stomach.

Meave remembered Pádraig Bocht carrying the pearl back to the castle wrapped in a goatskin and placing it on the table in the Great Hall. Lord Devereux and the children stood looking down at the pulsing pearl.

'They have been searching for this for a thousand years. Shall we give it to them?' asked Pádraig Bocht, leaning against the table and looking expectantly at Meave.

'Can we trust your Queen Talutu?' he asked in an almost threatening voice, stepping closer to Meave.

Ralph and Lord Devereux turned to Meave. She wanted to give the correct answer and say, of course we can trust Queen Talutu.

I ... don't ... know,' she stammered.

Lord Devereux placed his open hand on the pearl.

'We have to make a decision, here and now. We cannot delay because we don't know the power of this wretched sphere. Perhaps we should return it.'

Pádraig Bocht reached into a pocket of his green cape and produced a small bronze box. He removed the lid and picked up a pinch of red dust with his fingers.

'I will ask Cailleach,' he said, sprinkling some dust on the table.

The red granules spread across the burnished surface, forming an uneven diamond shape. He then lowered his nose to the edge of the table.

'Cailleach!' he whispered and blew a sharp breath over the diamond shaped dust.

'Cailleach! Cailleach! You were once one of us. Talk to me!' he said, raising his voice.

The dust on the table began to thicken and solidify; spatterings of bubbles appeared on the stain and splashed and spit like water thrown on a plate of hot animal fat.

'Cailleach we are waiting for you,' said Pádraig Bocht in a cold whisper.

The diamond smudge lifted from the table like an apple tart rising in a hot oven. Two circular eye shapes appeared on its crusty skin and a slit of a mouth traced itself below the eyes.

'What do you want of me?' croaked the muddy mouth.

Ralph stood flabbergasted, watching the mouth shape into a smirking smile, and he wondered who

Cailleach was. It struck him that he was watching real magic. Pádraig Bocht moved his face closer to the carved mouth, his eyeballs almost touching the tip of his crooked nose.

'We have the Pearl of Neamhann. Shall we return it? Oh! Cailleach, or shall we keep it?' he asked.

The mouth rose from the table and darkened.

'The pearl belongs to Leasa,' it said in a high pitched voice. 'Return it immediately or suffer horrendous misfortune.'

Pádraig Bocht stood back from the table and glanced over at Lord Devereux whose face was grey and drooped. He edged back to the table.

'Can we trust Queen Talutu?' he pleaded, like a child wanting permission to stroke a vicious dog, knowing that he would not be allowed.

'The world of nature will deal with Queen Talutu. Return the pearl I tell you or be damned!' shrieked the mouth.

The mouth then receded to the shape on the table. The solidified stain cracked and returned to dust. Pádraig Bocht stroked his long chin with a stained fingernail then ran his fingers through the sprinkled granules on the table.

'Cailleach has spoken. We must obey her judgement and return the pearl,' he said, rubbing the dust from his hands.

Meave and Ralph had mixed feelings about returning to Tír na Leasa. Meave knew that she behaved strangely when she was there, yet she also knew that the chalice had to be destroyed. Ralph also wanted to see the chalice emptied of its poison, but he dreaded meeting Queen Talutu again.

'So be it,' said Lord Devereux, lifting the pearl from the table and placing into a leather pouch.

'It will be tomorrow.'

The children had a troubled, sleepless night. Meave dreamt of flashing pearls dancing about her room and being chased by battle sharks. Ralph kept seeing the Lost Children of DunFaythe walking towards the Lake of Fire. They were both glad to see the dawn end their long night.

Standing on the shore next to Meave was Ralph, who looked back at the wooden wall lined with silent grim soldiers. He raised his arm and saw his father high up on the ramparts, return the gesture.

Ralph glanced at Meave.

'Are you feeling well?' he asked. 'You look like you are day dreaming.'

'I was thinking about the pearl ... Who is Cailleach?'

'I don't know. She must be a witch or an oracle. Pádraig Bocht never mentioned her name before, but he didn't hesitate to obey her command.'

'Yes,' whispered Meave. 'There is a lot about Pádraig Bocht that is mysterious and secretive.'

'Very mysterious,' said Ralph, grinning. 'I sometimes think that Pádraig Bocht does not know himself, about himself.'

The children giggled. Ralph was happy to see Meave tittering about Pádraig Bocht. But he knew that she would soon change into a fish girl, who never smiled.

'I won't leave you there,' he said, taking her hand.

Meave wasn't listening she was looking out at the blue ocean. Ralph dreaded feeling alone, being the only human in Tír na Leasa.

'There ... is ... something ... in ... the ... water,' came a cry from the wall. All eyes scanned the frothy rolling waves.

'Stand firm and await orders,' bellowed a captain on the sea wall, lifting a torch and raising it above his head.

'Prepare to light the pit,' he ordered.

Pádraig Bocht watched the shape of two figures moving through the waves, towards the beach.

'There are only two of them,' he said, somewhat surprised. 'We expected their army!'

Ralph took a step into the tide.

'Black Guards riding battle sharks,' he said, turning to Meave.

Meave, who was gripping the strap of the pearl pouch, was already beginning to feel a change coming over her mind and body. The two Black Guards halted their battle sharks close to the beach.

'They are ugly creatures,' snarled Pádraig Bocht.

'They are not ugly. They are people of the sea. They think we are ugly,' snapped Meave, surprised with herself that she felt insulted by Pádraig Bocht's comment.

One of the Black Guards, a large fish man with dark green seaweed hair draping down his shoulders, his black cloak flapping behind him like a wide bunting, raised a comb sword above his head. Ralph noticed that there was a slight bend in his comb sword, and his bone nose had a large chunk missing from the tip of it. Behind him waiting on another battle shark was a second Black Guard. Ralph, shivering from the chill sea breeze, realised that they had sent battle hardened knights. The Black Guard opened his oval mouth wide and made a loud whistling sound.

'What is he doing?' asked Pádraig, finding it hard to believe what he was seeing.

'He is speaking,' answered Ralph. 'He says that they are coming in peace this time. We may wade out to him, and they will take us to Tír na Leasa.

Meave turned and looked up at the soldiers on the sea wall and saw her father staring at her.

'I'll see you soon,' she said under her breath.

'Let's go now,' urged Ralph, stepping into the sea and hoping that the sooner he travelled to Tír na Leasa the sooner he would return. Meave followed him into the waves. The Black Guard emitted another burst of whistling.

'What … is he saying now?' asked Pádraig Bocht, frustrated by his inability to understand what the Black Guards were saying.

Ralph kept wading through the waves.

'What did he say?' cried Pádraig Bocht, stamping his feet in the waves.

Ralph hesitated for a moment and faced Pádraig Bocht.

'He said Queen Talutu would visit you soon. He said your name. He knows who you are.'

Pádraig Bocht suddenly felt cold. The sea water flapping at his feet numbed his toes; the tips of his fingers began to turn pale blue, and he shivered. The sea breeze on his face felt like an ice storm blowing in mid winter. Tiny frosty specks appeared on his bushy eyebrows and the tip of his long chin, and he fell to his knees, squeezing his hands under his armpits, remembering his mother holding him and wanting to be a child again.

'Tell Queen Talutu … that I will be waiting for her. Tell … her that the world of nature will not let her conquer this … land!' he shrieked.

Ralph could not hear Pádraig Bocht, as they climbed onto the battle sharks. When they turned towards the shore to wave goodbye, they saw him kneeling in the sea, waves washing about him. Ralph thought he was praying. Then the battle sharks dived and brought them to Tír na Leasa.

As they journeyed to Tír na Leasa the children did not look at or speak to each other. Ralph knew that once Meave had entered the sea, she would change into someone that he did not like. The battle sharks emerged into a pond, reserved for Queen Talutu. As the battle sharks brought them to the edge of the pond Ralph removed his sea mask and surveyed his surroundings. Drapes of gold coloured sea leaves dropped from the low ceiling of the pond cave, covering the rock walls. The floor of the cavern was covered with irregular shaped tiles of crushed silver coral. Several Black Guards waited for them to reach the steps, cut into the stone perimeter of the pond. Ralph watched Meave climbing the steps and saw that she had changed into a fish girl, her hair a long mane down her neck.

'What do we do now?' asked Ralph, as he followed her up the steps.

'We will return what belongs to her majesty,' answered Meave, in a low whistling sound. 'She will be waiting for us.'

Ralph reached out to take the pouch, hanging from her shoulder.

'Do not touch the pearl,' she snapped, glaring at Ralph.

Ralph did not argue.

'What about the chalice?' he asked, hoping that Meave would change her mood.

'The chalice is the property of Queen Talutu. I doubt that she will destroy such a remarkable potion. She may drink the Deoch herself someday.'

A shaking anger rose in Ralph. He grabbed Meave by the shoulders and shook her, almost knocking her into the pond.

'You witch,' he cried. 'You are not my sister. Queen Talutu promised - '

Two Black Guards stepped forward and restrained Ralph.

'She promised!' he shouted, as Meave walked away from him.

'Bring him with us,' she said and followed the Black Guard through a tentacle curtain in the golden drapes covering the rock wall.

The Black Guard led the children along several shell-floored passageways, lit with dim pearls, until they reached the tentacle curtain for Queen Talutu's Throne Room. Ralph did not speak or look at Meave. He was feeling lonely and afraid, trying to imagine what Queen Talutu was going to do with the Pearl of Neamhann. Before they passed through the curtain Meave stopped walking, turned to Ralph, bringing her bone nose close to his cheek.

'Before we enter, remember that you will be in the presence of a queen,' she said in a high regal voice and lowered her eyes.

She passed through the curtain, followed by an angry Ralph and the Black Guard.

'Welcome! Welcome!' screamed Queen Talutu, sitting on her throne. 'You have brought it to me. At last! You are a true daughter of Leasa ...

Now I am the possessor of the Pearl of Neamhann ... It's back in Tír na Leasa ... It ... is ... mine!'

Ralph remembered the last time he stood in her Throne Room. He remembered sitting on her throne and watching Kcirtap prostrate himself in front of the queen. As he looked to his left and right, scanning the faces of hundreds of fish men, watching him he wondered where Kcirtap was. Their white tunics and red cloaks reached to the floor of the chamber, and their seaweed hair was tied back with coloured strands of sea grass. The scales on their faces were decorated with yellow and orange dye, reminding Ralph of clowns he had seen at the summer Sun Festival in DunFaythe. A whistling sound passed amongst the sea clowns like a soft wind through a creaking door.

Queen Talutu stood up from her throne, wearing a long yellow-buttoned cape, reaching from her thin neck to the shell floor. Glittering in her seaweed hair were flecks of seashells. The scales on her face ruffled, and the gills on her cheeks opened and closed rapidly. Ralph looked into her slanted eyes, but she ignored him and focused on the pouch that Meave was carrying. He looked around at the images and paintings etched on the walls of the Throne Room and tried to figure out how the pearl was connected to planets and stars and why she wanted it. Queen Talutu moved towards the children. She seemed to be floating just above the shell floor.

'You have done well Lamura,' she said, approaching Meave 'You will be rewarded.'

'We obeyed your command Oh! Queen,' replied Meave, handing the pouch to Queen Talutu.

The queen took the pouch in both her webbed hands, opened it, removed the pulsing orb and examined it. Meave peered at Ralph. Still shaking with anger he ignored her. The queen continued to examine the pulsing pearl, as the gathered fish people whistled amongst themselves.

'What about the chalice?' asked Ralph.

Queen Talutu took no notice of him. She rotated the pearl in her hands and then raised it above her head. A screeching high-pitched whistle filled the room. The crowd clapped their hands and stamped the floor.

'I have the power in my hands,' screeched the queen. 'At last my destiny can be fulfilled. I now have Tír na Leasa and DunFaythe Castle in my hands.'

Ralph tugged on Meave's sleeve. She looked at him, her slanted eyes widened.

'What do you want?'

'What about the chalice?' asked Ralph, raising his voice.

'Do not bother me,' replied the queen, lowering the pearl and flicking her wrist in a dismissive gesture.

'You promised … us - ' stammered Ralph.

The crowd stopped clapping and cheering. Queen Talutu stared angrily at Ralph, her eyes started to rotate and then stopped, as if she had changed her mind.

'I do not have to fulfil a promise to you, human!' she snapped.

A feeling of sadness rose in Meave, but she could not understand why she was feeling pity for the young human boy. She saw a tear fill Ralph's eye and saw his chin drop and his eyes close.

Queen Talutu then turned her back on Ralph and walked slowly towards the throne. The crowd cheered. Meave clapped her scaly webbed hands. Ralph opened his eyes and clearly saw three images of the pearl embroidered on the queen's yellow cape. One had a faint light in its centre and another had a wide brighter light that filled the pearl. The third and larger image, made of pink periwinkles, showed the pearl pulsing brightly. The queen reached the throne, turned and faced the cheering crowd.

'Is it time?' they shouted 'Is it time?'

Meave could feel the scales on her face flutter with excitement. Ralph was wondering what was going to happen. The crowd dropped to their knees. Meave dropped to her knees. The Black Guard standing behind Ralph pushed him, and he fell to his knees.

'Is it time?' repeated the crowd.

'Yes! The time is now!' screamed Queen Talutu, holding the pearl out in front of her face.

The sails of her head dress shimmered and her eyes rotated slowly. The whistling of the crowd increased in pitch, as Queen Talutu released the pearl from her webbed fingers. Ralph expected it to crash to the floor and break into a thousand pieces. He was hoping it would fall and smash, and then the wretched pearl would be gone forever. The pearl did not fall. Instead it remained stationary, hanging in the air, as if suspended by invisible threads. A whispering murmur passed through the crowd watching the floating globe. Queen Talutu moved to the centre of the Throne Room and faced the floating, pulsing pearl.

'Show us the power of the pearl. Oh Queen!' cried one of them.

'Show us your power. Oh Queen!' shouted another.

Queen Talutu stretched out her arm and with a pointed web finger, beckoned the pearl to come to her. To their astonishment the pearl began to float towards her. The fish people pressed forward. Meave moved closer. Ralph stood up and took a step backwards, away from the captivated throng. The Black Guard, mesmerised by the queen and the pearl, did not see Ralph retreating towards the tentacle curtain.

'Stand back!' shouted Queen Talutu.

The scales on her face were shaking and rustling like the broad leaves of a chestnut tree during a winter's storm. The crowd retreated. Ralph took another step back towards the tentacle curtain. The pearl began to rise and pulse out light quicker and quicker until the pulses merged with each other and fused into a blinding beam of light, hanging in the air above Queen Talutu. The crowd waited. Meave waited. Ralph waited. The queen then raised her head and looked up at the shining star suspended above her, opened her mouth and blew a whisper of breath towards the hanging pearl. The pearl rose vertically towards the ceiling of the chamber. Its bright pulse changed to a cold white light. The lights in the Bsamaki windows extinguished. The crowd gasped. Ralph took another step towards the tentacle curtain. He wanted to run, but he also wanted to see what was going to happen. A lone star high up in the ceiling like the North Star on a dark winter's night now lighted the chamber. Many of the fish people averted their eyes from the frosty brightness.

Realising that they had forgotten about him, he turned and hurried towards the tentacle curtain then stopped and looked back at the pearl. Queen Talutu continued to look into the light of the shining star. The radiant brightness narrowed into a single silver column and focused on her, like a finger of starlight pushing through a slit in a window curtain. The chamber was shrouded in total darkness except for the narrow shaft of light, pouring on the queen, who turned in a full circle under it. Ralph saw her fade into the light and appear again, as she rotated, like a ghost dressed in a white shroud. He could not make out any features on her face. Yet her slanted eyes emitted a dull orange hue like the embers of a dying coal fire.

'You will now see the power of the Pearl of Neamhann,' she cried, basking in the pearl light.

Queen Talutu stepped out of the light. Ralph wanted to run, but he also wanted to stay and watch, as she raised her arms and pointed her finger at the shining star. A bolt of orange light suddenly burst from the pearl. Another bolt hit the floor and then another, until a pillar of fire reached from the star to the floor of the chamber. The crowd retreated, feeling the intense heat and the smell of sulphurous fumes of the vertical furnace, dancing on the floor.

'You will be burned Oh Queen,' shouted a young fish girl. 'Move away now!'

'The Pearl of Neamhann will not harm me,' she cried, walking with her arms stretched out in front of her, towards the roaring pillar of fire. The column of roaring flames moved towards her like a twisting firey tornado.

'You will be destroyed,' gasped another fish man. 'Move back!.'

Ralph hoped that she would not move and wished that the burning tornado would gobble her into its firey belly and burn her to a cinder. The tornado did not gobble her. It moved though her body. She did not burn, but bathed herself with the fire. Ralph could not believe what he was seeing, as she stood in the middle of the pillar of roaring heat and did not burn. Queen Talutu held the flames in her hands. They wrapped around her like an orange serpent. She opened her mouth and drank the burning essence, her face glowed, her eyes darkened. The crowd stood watching and wondering how their queen could survive such intense violent heat. She looked up directly into the source of the flames and the fire danced down her limbs like soft spray of a summer mist.

'I can feel its power,' she screamed, as the flames poured onto her face. 'I can feel the power of everlasting life soaking into me. I will never die.'

Ralph could feel the heat pressing against his face, reminding him of the lighthouse fire.

'Never die! So that's the power of the pearl,' he gasped, as he took another step away from the burning pillar. Meave stood numbed by what she saw; she could not take her eyes off the queen. Yet she felt no affinity with this creature, even though she was not able to disobey her commands. She watched, as the flames poured over the queen's face and body.

Queen Talutu stepped out of the pouring furnace. The pillar of flame changed colour from a burning orange pumice to moonlight white; the intense heat softened and faded away. Queen Talutu moved her hand through the pillar of moonlight, descending from the pearl. The needle of light extinguished like a door closing on a bright starry night. A dark inky blackness descended on the chamber. Ralph stepped back through the tentacle curtain.

'Don't fret,' said the queen, raising her arms like a high priestess. 'I will re-light the Bsamaki windows'.

Before she had finished speaking the crowd cheered, as light returned to the chamber. The pearl still hovered above the queen. She pointed her finger at the sphere, and it floated down to her. She held it in her hand. The crowd moved closer to her.

'You are now queen of the land and sea,' said one of them.

'Yes,' answered the queen.

'Your eyes, Oh! Majesty,' said another fish man. 'They have - '

'The power of everlasting life,' replied the queen, as her slanted eyes changed shade to a light sunset red. 'What Citbeag has been searching for … what he always wanted. He failed! However, he will now turn his attention to Tír na Leasa, when he has discovered that the pearl is not in DunFaythe Castle. But I am going to DunFaythe Castle. I am going to visit Pádraig Bocht. He and his ancestors have kept the pearl from us for centuries. It is time for revenge! Time to destroy Pádraig Bocht and his lighthouse!'

Ralph found himself alone in the passageway. He had to find a place to hide and then escape and warn his father and Pádraig Bocht. He stumbled and fell along the passageway. This time he was not interested in looking out of the Bsamaki skin windows to view Tír na Leasa or wonder at battle sharks or dolphins. His chest heaved. His throat felt raw. An intense whistling sound, increasing in volume burst from the Throne Room, behind him. He didn't slow down; he knew they were looking for him.

'We will find him. He can't escape!' they cried, pouring into the passageway.

He ran faster. His chest tightened. His heart pounded.

'Must hide,' he gasped, stumbling into a small circular room with six passages extending like the spokes of a cartwheel. Like a fox escaping from a pack of hounds, instinct took him down the narrowest corridor cut into rock.

'Must hide,' he puffed, as instinct also brought him through the first tentacle curtain that he came upon.

Standing in the darkness of a small chamber he felt soft, sodden seaweed under his feet, and his nose tingled with the familiar salty smell of the sea. The hounds went running past.

'He can't have gone far,' they shouted. Queen Talutu wants him confined. He must not escape.'

Ralph took a deep breath hoping they would not hear his heart pounding, as he waited behind the tentacle curtain until their whistling had dissipated into Dochas Mountain. A cold silence followed their disappearance.

A deep aching loneliness welled up in his body. How could he escape from this world? Maybe he could find a shark pool and escape to DunFaythe. He wished he could talk to his father. He knew Meave would not help him. Thoughts of Meave triggered a confused anger in him – was she ever his sister? – maybe she was never his sister. He dismissed that idea from his mind as his eyes adjusted to the darkness. Suddenly feeling that he was not alone, a cloud of numbing fear closed on him. His senses told him that he was being watched. To his surprise a low light broke the darkness; his shaking legs would not turn his body. He clenched his fists and waited.

'So you are Lord Devereux's heir,' said a voice.

A thundering sound exploded in his ears. For a moment he thought he was imagining that he heard words being spoken – no one speaks words in Tír na Leasa – but he felt relieved to hear a human voice.

'You may turn around Ralph Devereux.'

Ralph turned to see Arthur sitting on a large pile of sea masks and wondered if he was seeing a vision or maybe Queen Talutu had bewitched him. He rubbed his eye – yes, it was Arthur Furston. He had seen him with his father and Pádraig Bocht in the castle. Standing beside Arthur, dressed in the tunic and cape of the Black Guards was a giant fish man.

'This is Azaromel,' said Arthur, jumping off the pile of sea masks. 'Where is your sister?'

'Azaromel!' cried Ralph 'I thought Azaromel was a monk, who was loyal to my father … and do not speak of my sister. She has betrayed me. She has been bewitched by Queen Talutu … she is now a fish girl. Queen Talutu has the pearl … she will attack DunFaythe … Meave is with her'

Azaromel placed his hand gently on Ralph's shoulder.

'We must recover the pearl. Without the pearl the queen has no power,' he whistled.

'She will live forever … cannot die,' answered Ralph, his voice choking with despair.

'Queen Talutu may live forever,' said Azaromel. 'But she needs the pearl to fulfil her greedy ambitions. She needs the pearl to conquer DunFaythe and the other cities under the sea. We don't know the real power of the pearl. But if she has stood under the furnace of light, then she can control its power.'

Ralph sat on the pile of sea masks and placed his head on his knees. A heavy wave of tiredness washed over him. He grasped his hair with his fingers and pulled hard.

'I want to go home!' he shouted. 'Father will know what to do. I don't know who to believe or trust anymore.'

He lifted his tear stained face and looked up at Arthur, who saw the pleading eyes of a tired young boy.

'Ralph, you have come a long way. Don't give up now. You are a very brave young man.'

Ralph heard Arthur speaking, but he was not listening. He did not care about courage, all he wanted to do was sleep and forget about Tír na Leasa and Queen Talutu.

'I … am tired,' he whispered, yawning and rubbing his eyes.

Arthur sat down beside him, placing his arm around him, trying to comfort him.

'We need your help,' he said. 'We know about Queen Talutu's plans. We know that she bewitched your sister.'

He paused for a few moments then turned to Azaromel, who nodded his scaly head in agreement.

'Have you heard of an ancient fish man named Kcirtap?' continued Arthur. 'We need to find him urgently. We think he has knowledge of the power of the pearl.'

'Kcirtap!' said Ralph, surprised. 'I had forgotten about him.'

'You know him!' cried Arthur.

'Yes, I know him. He brought me to Dochas Mountain … to meet Queen Talutu. He often visits the cave of the Lost Children of DunFaythe.'

Arthur stood up. A fresh breeze of hope blew through his senses. He could not find words to describe his admiration for the young boy sitting below him.

'I'll show you where you can find him, if you help me save the Lost Children,' cried Ralph.

'Are there human children living in a cave in Tír na Leasa?' asked Arthur, looking at Azaromel and trying to take in what Ralph had said.

'There are,' answered Ralph. 'They have been there hundreds of years, but they have not grown old!'

Arthur did not question Ralph. He was prepared to believe anything the boy told him.

'We'll do everything we can to save these children and return them to DunFaythe,' said Arthur.

Arthur's words refreshed Ralph like a tonic of black-currant juice mixed with honey. He stood up, his eyes bright, his strength restored.

'I promised Oisin I would return,' he said, walking over to the tentacle curtain.

'Can we go now,' he urged, as he separated the tentacles.

'Just a moment,' replied Azaromel. 'Close the curtain I can hear them coming.'

A low whistling breeze was heard moving towards the corridor. Azaromel covered the lighting pearl with his cloak. They moved back into the darkness of the chamber. The windy sound got louder and stopped at the closed tentacle curtain. Ralph tried not to move. Arthur was almost hoping they would enter the chamber so he could engage with these fish men in a hand to hand fight.

'Queen Talutu will be angry,' cried a voice in the passageway. 'Queen Talutu wants the young human confined. He knows too much about her plans.'

What's behind this curtain?' asked another.

'Only a store for sea masks,' answered the first voice.

The curtain separated and the light of the passage filled the chamber.

'Perhaps the young human was here and is now heading for a shark pond. We must guard all the exits from Dochas Mountain,' said a large fish man filling the entrance.

He then closed the curtain without searching the chamber. The muttering whistle continued down the passageway. Darkness returned to the chamber.

Three heads popped up from behind the pile of sea masks.

'They are looking for us everywhere. I can't escape,' moaned Ralph, as memories of the Lost Children filled his senses.

'Can you take us to the children's cave,' asked Azaromel, as he removed the pearl from his cloak and light returned to the chamber.

'I know where the cave is. But … how can we get there?' replied Ralph, feeling glad that he had a giant like Azaromel on his side.

'On battle sharks,' answered Azaromel. 'Have you forgotten that I am a commander of the Black Guards? I was getting Arthur a new sea mask when you ran into the storeroom.'

'But the fish men are … everywhere, looking for me,' stammered Ralph. 'Perhaps you should go and leave me here.'

'We'll not leave you,' said Arthur, glancing at Ralph. 'Your father would never forgive me if I returned without you.'

'Enough talk!' said Azaromel, looking impatiently at the tentacle curtain, 'There is a shark pond at the summit of Dochas Mountain, used only for emergency evacuations. We should be able to escape from there. Come now! I will show you. It's the only way we can find Kcirtap. Bring a sea mask with you.'

Arthur and Ralph picked up a sea mask from the pile in the chamber and followed Azaromel through the tentacle curtain into the passageway.

'You'll be my prisoners,' he said, removing his comb sword.

The passageway was silent and empty of fish men.

'Take the next corridor on the left and then the one to the right,' ordered Azaromel. 'If we meet any Black Guards I will deal with them.'

They arrived at a large rusty metal door covered in bubbles of dripping sea water.

Azaromel wrapped his thick webbed fingers around a rusty handle and pulled hard. The door scraped along the shell floor, as it opened, and a cold breeze of sea air cooled their cheeks. Ralph walked through the doorway and found himself in a narrow cylindrical chamber that reminded him of the towers in DunFaythe Castle. They stood on a circular slab of rough uneven stone.

'What happens now?' asked Ralph, casting his eyes around the chamber.

'You will see very soon,' replied Azaromel, looking up towards the ceiling of the circular cell. Ralph and Arthur followed his gaze to a similar circular stone slab directly above their heads.

'We are going to the summit of Dochas Mountain,' said Azaromel, as he bent down and grabbed a reed handle, embedded in the slab beneath his feet.

'Are ye ready?' he asked, winking at Ralph.

'I am,' replied Arthur, breathing deeply.

His mind was blank, and he did not want to think of what might happen, but knew that Azaromel would look after him, as he always did.

'Are you ready Ralph?' asked Azaromel, gripping a reed handle.

'We are,' answered Ralph, with a slight shudder in his voice, wondering what was going to happen. He was not afraid for he was not alone this time.

'Let's go now,' said Azaromel, pulling on the reed handle.

A thumping sound like horses stampeding in the distance filled the chamber. Sea-water began to seep into the cell and climb up their legs and chests.

'Put on your sea masks,' ordered Azaromel.

The rising water covered their heads and reached the ceiling. Azaromel pressed his hands down on their shoulders to stop them from floating to the ceiling. When the water reached the ceiling Azaromel reached down again and pulled on the reed handle a second time. To their surprise the circular slab rose in the water.

'We will be crushed,' shouted Arthur from inside his mask, as their heads neared the ceiling. Nobody could hear him.

The speed of the rising slab increased. Ralph could feel the weight of the water on his sea mask, as they approached the circular ceiling slab. Just as he was thinking that he was going to crush his head against the ceiling rock, the slab opened vertically and the three of them went gushing into a water filled vent, cut into the rock of Dochas Mountain. Up they went like three ladybirds huddled together on a wind blown leaf. A flash of light dancing on Ralph's fingers told him that they were near the summit of Dochas Mountain. The light increased and illuminated them clearly on the rising stone slab. They raced towards the light, and then with out any warning they broke the surface of a small pond. Several clusters of pearls provided a dim cold light in the bleak and bare cave. Ralph and Arthur swam to the bank and removed their sea masks. Azaromel remained in the water opened his oval mouth and poured out a high pitched whistle.

'What's he doing?' asked Ralph, pressing his hands against his ears.

'Calling his battle shark,' replied Arthur, feeling glad that this time he was not surprised by Azaromel's actions. After several moments of watching and waiting, Arthur and Ralph saw the still, stagnant waters of the pond froth and bubble. Two dorsal fins surfaced, followed by the charcoal coloured blunt noses of two battle sharks. Ralph and Arthur put on their sea masks and swam to the centre of the pond. Ralph climbed onto one of the sharks followed by Arthur. Azaromel climbed onto the other. Arthur still found it difficult to believe that he was mounting such a vicious sea monster. The sharks dived and brought them beneath the surface of the pond and through a sea tunnel that emerged into the valley of Tír na Leasa. Ralph felt a strong sea current against his sea mask, as he pushed the shark's fin forward. Arthur, sitting behind him, hoped that Ralph could control such a vicious monster and prayed that Ralph knew where he was going. The sharks plummeted towards the ocean floor. A passing dolphin would have seen two small bodies emerge from the colossus of Dochas Mountain like two acorns falling from a giant oak tree. Arthur closed his eyes as the sandy surface raced towards him. Ralph bent low over the shark found it more exciting than riding his father's black stallion. The shark seemed to be more sensitive to his commands than his father's horse.

When they reached the end of their dive, Ralph realised that the valley was deserted, no fish men, no Orcas, no dolphins. He pulled on the dorsal fin and his shark slowed to swim along the ocean floor. Ralph also saw that there were no lights in the openings in the cliffs of the valley, and no fish children played amongst the sea plants. The dull light of the pearl field in the distance exposed a deserted valley of varying green foliage fluttering and waving in the sea current. He turned and looked back at Azaromel, who waved his arm in acknowledgement. Arthur felt more comfortable now that they were travelling at a steady pace. Ralph saw the Ardghorm grass rising in the distance and remembered the snakes, the Lost Children and Meave.

Remembering her smiling face before she became a fish girl he began to believe that she didn't want to be a fish girl, which made him more determined to bring her home. Then children's sad faces crossed his mind, and he hoped that they were still in the cave and that Kcirtap was with them.

The Ardghorm grass got closer, as they neared the children's cave. Ralph pulled on his battle shark's dorsal fin and led them over the green forest. Looking down on the canopy of waving stalks he saw shoals of snakes sliding between the moving trunks of the forest. Just beyond the shimmering forest he spotted the entrance to the children's cave cut into a cliff face and guided the battle sharks into the dark narrow tunnel and emerged from the stagnant pond into the children's gloomy cavern. The trio dismounted from the battle sharks and climbed onto the bank.

'How could children live in such a place?' asked Arthur, looking around at the dripping cold rocks of the cave.

Ralph removed his sea mask.

'This way,' he said, pointing to a passage cut into the rock. 'I hope they are still alive.'

The tunnel brought them to the children's living area.

'The day will come, when you will return to DunFaythe. The day will come, when you will walk again on Trá Bán,' said Kcirtap in a shaky voice, standing in the middle of a circle of bedraggled children. Their thin stick arms protruded from their seal skin tunics like the bare branches of a winter Hawthorne tree. They looked up at him, eating and drinking his words, wishing and hoping his speech would translate into reality. He seemed to have grown older, and his forward stoop was more pronounced. Ralph thought that he was going to topple over at any moment. He spotted Oisin in the group, his face was much thinner, and his hair caked with dry sand, reached to his shoulders. Ralph scanned the cave and saw oyster shells and crab shells, the remains of a frugal meal, scattered amongst their sleeping mats.

'Do not despair,' continued Kcirtap. 'I will always be with you.'

Ralph opened his mouth, but no words would come. He turned to Arthur, standing beside him.

'These … are your children?' asked Arthur, shaking his head in pity.

'Yes these - '

'Ralph!' cried the young girl with the matted curls 'You have come back to us.'

All the children turned and looked at their visitors. Then the young girl jumped up, ran over to Ralph and hugged him.

'I knew you would come. I knew you would come,' she cried, burying her head in his chest.

The rest of the children remained in the circle around Kcirtap, too tired and too weak to move.

'Kcirtap!' exclaimed Azaromel. 'We need your help. We need your knowledge of the pearl.'

Kcirtap stepped from the circle of children and shuffled towards Ralph. Ralph, his arm around the young girl, saw that Kcirtap was finding it difficult to walk and was gasping and wheezing, as he made his way towards them.

'Azaromel!' he coughed. 'Are you with us or are you with her?'

Azaromel took a step towards him.

'I am with you Kcirtap. I have always been with you,' he answered, bowing his head.

'You have the pearl?' he panted, as he reached the group.

'No,' answered Azaromel. 'Queen Talutu has the pearl, General Nirutam told us before he died that you knew how to use the pearl.'

'He is dead!' cried Kcirtap, almost falling.

'Yes, the brave general is dead,' answered Azaromel. 'He would not be a part of her greed … they killed him.'

'He was our only hope,' wheezed Kcirtap, clutching his chest, and he fell to his knees and stared at the rocky floor of the cave. Ralph untangled himself from the young girl and moved towards him.

'Leave me be,' he coughed. 'Only old age. I have not long left. But I want to be laid with my ancestors on Arob.'

'Kcirtap!' pleaded Azaromel. 'Can you use the force of the pearl? Do you know how to harness its power? Will you help us?'

'I … do,' he panted, as he struggled to his feet and raised his shaking head. 'The pearl will return us to Arob. We will have the chance to return … in three days time.'

'How can we travel to Arob?' asked Azaromel.

Ralph stood listening to Kcirtap. He knew that Arob was a planet, but he was flabbergasted to hear that they were talking about travelling to another planet. He remained silent, not wanting to interrupt the discussion.

'If you can recover the pearl I will show you how it can bring us to our home planet,' answered Kcirtap. 'First the pearl has to be brought to the Dubh Pit, when Arob is aligned with the full moon … then you will see the force of the Pearl of Neamhann.'

'Will you help us recover the pearl?' asked Arthur, trying to figure out who this Kcirtap was.

'Has she stood under the pillar of fire?' croaked Kcirtap, swaying on his feet.

'She has,' answered Ralph, holding his arm to prevent him falling. 'I saw her standing under it. Queen Talutu now has the gift of everlasting life.'

'Not a … gift,' sneered Kcirtap, almost grinning 'A curse! She does not realise what she has done.'

Arthur was watching the circle of children.

'What about the children? Will I remain with them?' he asked. He had decided that he was not going to leave the children to fend for themselves anymore.

'We must bring them with us,' pleaded Ralph. 'Look at them. They will not endure this wretched place much longer … they are weak and starving.'

The children listened to every word, their black sunken eyes, their stained faces, their shrunken bodies, cried out, 'Take us with you! Take us with you!'

Oisin struggled to his feet, his thin chicken legs, covered with scratches and sores, could barely support his body.

'If you don't take us with you, we will surely die here,' he pleaded.

'We do not have to discuss this,' said Azaromel, walking towards the cave entrance. 'We will take the children with us. Whatever chance they have with us they have no hope in this woeful place.'

The children did not whimper, cry or shout. They remained silent. The young girl with the matted hair tugged at Azaromel's sleeve. 'Thank you!' she cried, as tears slipped down her face. 'Thank you!'

* CHAPTER FIFTEEN *

Queen Talutu's Visit

Pádraig Bocht lingered on the lighthouse rocks. He pondered about visiting Lord Devereux and then considered inspecting the sea wall. Raising his head, he looked up at the roaring lighthouse fire and remembered the words of the prophecy,

'They will come from the sea. The fire will die,' he muttered to himself.

A constant blurred effigy of the pearl filled his thoughts. It was there when he slept, when he awoke, and when he walked or talked or ate. A drape of fluffy grey clouds rested on the towers of DunFaythe Castle. The sea was flat and silent like a placid river, not a single wave broke on Trá Bán, not a whisper of a breeze ruffled his hooded cloak. The grey head of a surfacing seal broke the still water and sent circles rippling towards the silent beach.

'You are watching the sea,' the seal might have said. 'We are also watching. It will be soon.'

Pádraig Bocht showed no interest in the seal; he was looking at the horizon where the glassy sea kissed heavy clouds. Guards on the sea wall stood listless and bored.

He stepped off the rocks onto the soft sand of the beach. He suspected that the sea wall was a useless monument to his fears and a waste of hard labour. The guards became aware of the solitary figure, his arms hanging limp beside his long gaunt body, his head bobbling about, pacing the beach, searching for something that might tell him that it was about to happen.

'Too quiet. Where are the seagulls? Where are the fishermen?' he whispered to himself, as he scanned the horizon again. Then it dawned on him that Ralph and Meave had been gone for two days, and the queen said she would come to visit him. He rubbed his eyes with the back of his bony hand and felt the raw smell of sea weed irritate his nostrils, as his blood shot sunken eyes scrutinised the deserted beach.

He reassured himself by believing that the guards would warn him, and then he felt a tickle of dampness on his stretched, sculpted cheek. Looking to the horizon he saw a grey shadow of a mist beginning to rise from the sea and could not see where the tranquil sea met the hanging clouds

'She is coming,' he choked, looking towards the sea wall, clenching his fists, trying to deny the lapping fear that was filling him.

'What do you see?' he shouted to the soldiers standing on the sea wall, rubbing his forehead with his stained fingers.

'Can't see anything,' they yelled. 'No ship would sail in that fog!'

His eyes returned to the sea. He froze; his mouth locked open.

'What do you see?' he demanded, closing his eyes and opening them again.

'The fog is too dense,' they replied. 'No men will sail today.'

'It's not a man … not human,' he whined, watching a dim light move towards him through the fog.

'Do you see the light?' he screamed, pointing out to sea.

'There's no light,' answered a soldier.

'There's a light … There's a light!' he spluttered. 'In the mist … Do you not see it?'

The solders gathered in groups on the sea wall battlements, peering into the mist.

'There is no light, only a dark mist,' one of them shouted.

Pádraig Bocht continued to watch the light approaching the beach, as the cold mist washed against his face and a raw chill seeped through his bones. A single grey shape became visible, contoured against the darkening muggy curtain. He turned to the sea wall. He could not see it. The mist had crept behind him, blocking his view of the lighthouse and the expanse of Trá Bán.

'She's coming. How can we fight what we cannot see?' he wailed, running towards the lighthouse.

Reaching out for the rocks, he crept and groped his way until he fell against the cold lighthouse door. He looked out to sea again and to his horror saw that the shape had changed course and was moving towards him.

Ralph stood at the bow of the battle ark behind Queen Talutu and Meave. In the water ahead of him he could see, through the mist, the dorsal fins of twenty battle sharks, pulling the ark towards Trá Bán. The ark reminded him of a Viking ship he had seen in his history book. However, this ark had a large horizontal platform placed between the bow and the stern, filled with Black Guards.

'We do not need to bring the fleet,' Queen Talutu had said. 'One battle ark will suffice. We have the pearl. They will not cause us any problems.'

Behind Ralph stood Kcirtap, Arthur and Azaromel. The Lost Children were huddled together at the stern of the platform, behind the Black Guards. As the battle ark approached the shore, Ralph could see the flickering light of the lighthouse waft through the mist. The dense fog prevented him from seeing Trá Bán, the sea wall or DunFaythe Castle. He shuddered when he remembered Queen Talutu standing on the bow of the battle ark under a clear blue sky. First she summoned white fluffy clouds to gather. Then she darkened the clouds and commanded them to lower themselves and called on a mist to rise from the sea.

He remembered thinking that Queen Talutu could control nature, and that his father and Pádraig Bocht would never defeat her.

He looked back at Azaromel and Kcirtap, two silent ghosts shrouded in a grey sodden blanket of fog. Azaromel acknowledged his stare with a slight movement of his huge head. Kcirtap, leaning on a carved rib of an Orca, ignored him and continued to stare at the deck of the ark.

Arthur was deep in thought. He tried to reason why Kcirtap had betrayed them. Glancing over at Kcirtap he remembered travelling back to Dochas Mountain from the children's cave with Kcirtap, Azaromel, the Lost Children and Ralph. He remembered the children riding their eaniascs in a single file behind the two battle sharks and entering Dochas Mountain and emerging into the pond at the summit of the mountain. Kcirtap struggled off his eaniasc and climbed onto the bank of the cavern.

'Remain here I will get some knights that are loyal to us,' he said, as he shuffled away and disappeared through a lank tentacle curtain in the wall of the cave.

'Do you trust him?' asked Arthur, helping the children climb off their eaniascs and onto the cave floor.

He was surprised how light their thin bodies were, as he lifted them out of the pond.

'I … trust him,' said Ralph, feeling a slight doubt rise in him. 'He hates the queen, and he wants the pearl.'

'I don't know. Yet, General Nirutam considered him a friend,' said Azaromel, looking around the dimly lit cave.

Arthur remembered the Lost Children huddling around Oisin.

'Where are we?' asked one of them.

Nobody answered.

'Are we going home soon?' whined the young girl with the matted hair.

'Yes!' answered Arthur looking into her sad wide eyes. 'Yes! we are going home, but not just yet.'

Azaromel removed his comb sword from its scabbard and walked towards the tentacle curtain.

'I don't like this. He has been gone a while,' he whispered, placing his hand on the tentacle curtain. 'We must leave this pond now before they find us. Come with me, I know a place where the children can hide. We must - '

Two Black Guards pushed through the curtain. One of them struck Azaromel on the chest with the flat side of his comb sword, knocking him to the ground. The children screamed. Arthur grabbed his sword handle. The other Black Guard thrust the sharp tooth extending from his comb sword, close to Arthur's throat. Arthur released his sword. Ralph froze.

'They'll kill us,' cried one of the children.

'Be quiet,' shouted a Black Guard, stamping his foot on Azaromel's chest.

'Nobody is going to be killed.'

The children stopped screaming, and Ralph felt the blood return to his legs.

'Did you really think that you could escape?' said the Black Guard, his eyes wandering from child to child.

The tentacle curtain rustled, as four more Black Guards entered the cavern followed by Kcirtap.

'Kcirtap,' cried Oisin. 'Why have you betrayed us?

Kcirtap hobbled up to Oisin and placed his withered webbed hand on his cheek.

'I have not betrayed you, young human. I have come to take you home. But first I must deliver these enemies of Leasa to Queen Talutu,' and he glanced at Azaromel, still pinned to the floor of the cave, under the boot of the Black Guard.

'You have betrayed me. You have betrayed General Nirutam,' cried Azaromel, struggling beneath the Black Guard's boot.

Kcirtap remained silent, glared at Ralph and then glanced at the Black Guard, holding his comb sword to Arthur's throat. The frayed scales on his weathered face quivered, as he lifted his hand and pointed a shaking finger at Ralph.

Ralph wanted to scream, but no words would come to his lips. His dry tongue filled his mouth. Kcirtap lowered his hand and looked at the children, shaking with fear.

'We will clothe and feed these children. They and their descendants will rule DunFaythe and its neighbours for Queen Talutu. They will become Black Guards and conquer more lands for their queen,' he said, ignoring Ralph.

Oisin emerged from the group of children.

'Are we going home? All we want to do is go home,' he pleaded, putting his arm around one of the children.

'Yes,' whispered Kcirtap, his hand shaking uncontrollably, as he turned to one of the Black Guards and nodded his head. 'You are going home.'

The Black Guard passed through the curtain and returned carrying two large reed sacks.

'There is food in one sack and clean clothes in the other,' said Kcirtap, gently nudging one of the children towards the sacks.

Arthur was trying to fathom Kcirtap. On the one hand he considered him an enemy, yet he was feeding these wretched children. Kcirtap reached into a reed sack and removed a green woollen tunic and handed it to one of the children.

'Put on these garments and eat your fill. You must be presentable when you meet your queen.'

The children dived and plunged into the food like starving vultures tearing a freshly killed goat. Cakes of fruit bread, grilled salmon, vessels of black-currant juice and apples and pears filled their hands. Warm linen trousers and cloaks of sheep's wool appeared on their thin sunken bodies, as they adorned themselves. Ralph nearly cried with joy to see them smiling and eating.

'I had forgotten what chicken tasted like,' cried one of them, biting into the tender meat.

'This fits perfectly,' cried another young girl, wrapping a pale green cloak around her emaciated frame.

'Pity about the colour,' cried another, tittering

Ralph, Azaromel and Arthur watched the children feeding themselves. The happy, chatting children provided a sharp contrast to their grim surroundings. They sat on the rocky floor of the cavern and for several moments they forgot about their miserable lonely lives. Kcirtap broke the happy moment by pointing his finger at Azaromel, the comb sword still at his throat.

'You have betrayed your people,' he cried, his long mane of seaweed hair rose like the tail of an angry dog. 'You have brought this stranger to our land, and you have fought against Citbeag, the queen's half brother,' he hissed, pointing his finger at Arthur. Arthur could feel the sharp point of a comb sword touching his throat.

'I'm not afraid of you,' cried Arthur in a dry hoarse voice. 'I have killed your monks. I have fought your serpents. I have seen the result of your greed. I have seen many of my comrades killed by Citbeag's savage troops.'

Kcirtap lowered his hand. A torrent of despairing anger rose in Arthur.

'You can kill me,' he screamed. 'But you will never defeat us!'

Kcirtap leaned forward, supporting himself with his bone stick.

'No!' he cried, stamping his foot. 'You are not afraid of me. But soon you will be afraid.'

Then paused for a moment, as if he was gathering his thoughts.

'Let us go and meet her majesty,' he continued, gesturing to one of the Black Guards.

'We have completed our task. Queen Talutu will be well pleased.'

Meave, standing beside Queen Talutu at the bow of the battle ark, could clearly see the outline of the lighthouse through the mist. The sight of the lighthouse flames triggered a confused uneasiness in her head. A surge of happiness burst through her veins, followed by a sense of anger and betrayal, when she remembered sitting on a soft couch of dried sea moss in Queen Talutu's living quarters. The queen was sitting opposite her in a large ornate whalebone chair padded with the deep white velvet skin of a thousand moonfishes. Images of generations of queens stared at her from the walls of the oval chamber; small lifeless faces with blank black eyes and varying colours of seaweed hair, looked down at her. A small pearl positioned behind a seashell cast a cold light on each of the faces. Their frozen open oval mouths gave them the demeanour of howling ghosts. Queen Talutu was examining a chart of the lands of DunFaythe, stretched across a table; its surface made of crushed mussel shells.

'You see,' said the queen, as she moved her open webbed hand across the map. 'Lord Devereux has vast estates. We will take DunFaythe Castle first. If Citbeag does not join us and accept me as his queen we will destroy him and his army.'

Meave remembered feeling honoured and excited that the queen should invite her to her quarters and then confide her plans to her. But then a thought had entered her mind like a tiny thorn sticking in a finger that can be ignored for a while, but eventually it has to be dealt with.

'Your majesty,' she said then immediately regretted addressing the queen.

Queen Talutu lifted her gaze and wrinkled her forehead.

'What ... about ... the chalice?' asked Meave, feeling confused about asking about the chalice.

The queen opened her oval mouth. Meave then looked at the wide mouthed images on the wall behind the queen. Queen Talutu's face paled to the pastel colour of a death mask, and the queen images behind her seemed to be staring directly at her, as if they were proud of their descendant.

'The chalice remains where it is,' answered Queen Talutu. 'I may need to use its contents some day. Do not mention it again. You may tell the young human that the chalice belongs to Leasa.'

Ralph's smiling face passed before Meave's eyes.

'Will I - '

A tentacle curtain rustled, and a Black Guard stepped into the chamber.

'Your Majesty. We have captured them. Kcirtap led them to us.'

'Have you got Azaromel?' cried the queen, standing up.

'Yes,' answered the Black Guard. 'We have the traitor Azaromel.'

Azaromel was also watching the lighthouse, as the battle ark approached the shore. He had come to the conclusion that his ancestors should never have come to this world, and that there would never be peace between fishman and human. He looked down at Kcirtap and saw that his hand was vibrating and wondered if he was nervous, and did he realise what his betrayal would mean? Kcirtap raised his head like a waking cat and looked at Azaromel through his half closed slanted eyes.

'Why did you do it?' asked Azaromel, trying to control the anger rising in him.

Kcirtap continued to stare. The scales on his face hung loose and lifeless like the dry autumnal leaves of a maple tree, as he grasped his rib stick tightly and then looked away. Azaromel wanted to pick him up and throw him into the sea. But he knew that such an action would mean certain death for him. Instead he looked towards the shore and saw the outline of the sea wall. He was surprised and disappointed to see that the gorse pit below the sea wall was not blazing. Closing his eyes, he allowed his thoughts to wander back to the cavern at the summit of Dochas Mountain. He remembered Kcirtap, and the Black Guards coming through the tentacle curtain. He remembered being separated from Ralph and the children and being thrown into a cell near the Dubh Pit. After waiting several hours in his small cell, he was dragged before Queen Talutu, who was sitting on a high-backed chair, carved from limestone. Beside her stood two Black Guards leaning on their exposed comb swords. Behind him stood four more Black Guards, their lances pointing at his back. The queen wore a white robe which spread on the floor in front of her feet like a white stain of spilled milk.

'You are in the Hall of Judgement,' she said, her half closed slanted eyes rotated, emitting a dull orange glow. He knew that her eyes were displaying the mark of the pearl. Then he looked around the narrow hall to see the faces of past judges of Leasa carved into the walls; bland, grey, lifeless, features cut into the rock, staring at each other from opposite walls.

'Do not … look at those faces,' rasped Queen Talutu, choking with rage, as the scales on her face lifted. 'You do not deserve to be in the presence of such honourable judges!' she cried. 'Come closer to me.'

One of the Black Guards pushed him forward. The idea struck him that he could reach out and easily strangle her, but then he would be immediately killed. The queen reached out and grasped a crosier with a silver skull mounted on its tip, balanced against her stone chair.

'Why did you betray us?' she asked, gripping the arms of her throne, trying to suppress her fury.

Azaromel could feel her rotating, glowing eyes looking into his mind, and the cold faced judges watching him.

'Why did you betray Citbeag? You were one of his most loyal commanders,' she demanded.

Azaromel remained silent, thinking he saw one of the judges' eyes close in despair.

'Answer her majesty,' said one of the Black Guards, slapping him across his back with a flat side of his comb sword.

Azaromel fell to his knees.

'Azaromel!' screamed Queen Talutu, stepping closer, her eyes glowing brighter, 'Why am I passing judgement on you? Did you think that you could defeat us?' pointing her crosier at Azaromel and resting the skull on his shoulder.

'Did you not know that it is our destiny to rule the land and the sea?' she said, pressing the skull against his cheek. 'Did you not know that Kcirtap was my father's brother? Answer me!'

Azaromel took the skull in his hand and looked up at Queen Talutu. Her rotating eyes glared at him, her thin grey lips formed circles on her face like wrag worms on a beach at low tide.

'I did not betray you. You have betrayed Leasa. You have betrayed our ancestors. The pearl is only to be used to return us to Arob, not to conquer other lands, not to attain everlasting life or be used to satisfy your greed,' whispered Azaromel.

Queen Talutu's nose receded into her face, she closed her eyes and swayed back and forth, her cloak moved across the floor and touched Azaromel's knees.

'You will come to DunFaythe with me,' she hissed, opening her eyes and pointing her shaking webbed hand at him.

'In the presence of these noble judges, I tell you, you will die in the Great Hall of DunFaythe Castle. You will burn, and you will be forgotten,' she said, pointing a finger at the carved faces on the wall and pulling the crosier from Azaromel's hand.

'You have my judgement,' and looked at one of the Black Guards.

'Take him away,' she ordered

Realising that Queen Talutu was coming, Pádraig Bocht collapsed to his knees on the lighthouse rocks. He closed his eyes, wishing he could return to the days when he was young and strong, when he was a commander in Lord Devereux's army. The days before he read those cursed books. He had only discovered three of them. If only he had found the Book of Deireadh.

'Stay on your knees Pádraig Bocht,' screeched a voice from the mist. 'I have come to visit you. I have come to show you what real power is.'

The mist brushed against his face like a moist cloth.

'I have brought Lord Colclough Devereux's children with me,' said the voice. I have also brought the traitor Azaromel, his servant and the wise Kcirtap. Come down and join us. We have much to discuss'

He could not understand where his soldiers were, or why they had not lit the gorse pit or raised an alarm beacon. Pádraig Bocht felt himself being pulled towards the beach like a rabbit mesmerised before a blazing fire and found himself standing before Queen Talutu. Her eyes rotated, and he could feel them penetrating into his soul. He tried to avert his gaze.

'Why have you come to DunFaythe?' he asked, trying not to show his shaking fear.

Ralph and Meave stood behind the queen. To their right Kcirtap waited, staring at the wet sand. Four Black Guards guarded Azaromel and Arthur. The Lost Children wandered about the beach, trying to understand what had happened, trying to believe that they had returned home.

'I have come to claim your kingdom,' she yelled.

'Look!' and she pointed to a leather satchel hanging from her shoulder 'I have the pearl … I have the Pearl of Neamhann. My ancestors have searched for it for generations. Now I have my destiny in my hands!'

Pádraig Bocht looked towards the beach wall, hoping to see soldiers lighting the gorse pit. Queen Talutu took a step forward and placed her face close to his. A spark of pain flashed across his forehead.

'Your soldiers cannot see us,' she cried. 'We are unseen!'

Padraig Bocht remembered Arthur telling him about Cailleach giving him the gift to be unseen – was she also from the sea?

'Who are you?' he asked, trying to delay a few moments.

'Who am I?' sneered Queen Talutu, her eyes rotating faster. 'I am Queen Talutu of Tír na Leasa, and shortly I will be Queen Talutu of DunFaythe. It is time you paid homage to your queen.'

He felt his knees weaken, and he slumped on the beach.

'Yes Pádraig Bocht. You are now kneeling before your queen. Soon Lord Colclough Devereux will pay me homage,' she cried, raising her arm and exhaling a rolling laugh.

An arc of light like a falling star on a spring night left the tips of her fingers and soared into the sky. The sea mist disappeared. Soldiers on the sea wall looked out to sea, wondering how the mist could disappear so quickly.

'Stand up lighthouse keeper,' said Queen Talutu, an orange glow flickered behind her rotating eyes. 'We are going to visit your master.'

Pádraig Bocht hauled himself to his feet.

'But before we enter DunFaythe Castle, let me show you what power means.'

She raised her webbed hands above her head a second time and pointed her webbed fingers at the lighthouse. The tips of her fingers began to glow and then sparkle; she opened her oval mouth and closed her slanted eyes. A loud sizzling sound, like that of a hot cinder dropping into cold water, rose in her throat. Pádraig Bocht felt a warm breeze touch his face. Wisps of sooty smoke emerged from her fingers. Then a jagged bolt of lightning shot into the clear sky and wound its way to the lighthouse fire. A loud boom was then followed by a sharp crack. The lighthouse fire cauldron exploded into a thousand pieces of granite and coal and spraying sparks, as the lighting bolt found its target. The Lost Children cowered on the beach, avoiding the storm of red embers and stones passing over their heads. Pádraig Bocht stood rigid and watched the lighthouse crumble into the sea.

'They will come from the sea. The fire will die,' echoed through his head.

The sea oozed and frothed, taking the lighthouse into its bosom. A thick layer of black dust rose into the sky and drifted towards DunFaythe Castle, carried by a gentle sea breeze. Confused and frightened soldiers on the sea wall grabbed their weapons and ran towards the beach. Queen Talutu lowered her hands and looked at Pádraig Bocht.

'Now keeper, your lighthouse has gone to the sea. DunFaythe Castle will be next,' she said, smirking, and she brushed past Pádraig Bocht.

Twenty grunting soldiers ran towards the remains of the lighthouse.

'Kill her!' screamed Pádraig Bocht. 'Kill her!'

Queen Talutu looked back.

'Remember you are unseen, lighthouse keeper. They can't see you. Let us go and meet your master,' and allowed a suppressed laugh to escape from her oval mouth.

They followed Queen Talutu up the path from the beach towards DunFaythe Castle. A seagull on its way out to sea glanced down at the beach.

'What have you done? Queen Talutu,' he might have said. 'What do you want? We all have what we need. What do you need?'

Hundreds of armed soldiers poured out of the castle and surged towards the beach.

'What's happened?' they cried. 'What has he done to the lighthouse? Those children, where did they come from?'

They ran panting past the unseen group, walking towards the castle.

'This is only the beginning of your troubles,' said Queen Talutu, smirking.

As they entered the castle courtyard Pádraig Bocht saw soldiers mounting the castle battlements and turrets.

'They are wasting their time,' he moaned. 'We are all doomed.'

Several captains ran from the open castle door into the courtyard, shouting orders and barking commands at a troop of cavalry.

'They have opened the door for us,' shouted Queen Talutu. 'Let us meet Colclough Devereux.'

The Black Guards pushed Azaromel and Arthur through the doorway, down the corridor and into the Great Hall. Ralph and Meave followed them. Ralph noticed that Meave was beginning to change back to her human form, and the scales on her face were shrinking, and her eyes were starting to widen into an oval shape.

'Will she kill us all?' whispered Ralph, pressing close to Meave. He saw a confused, despairing look in her eyes.

'The queen will not kill me ... I don't know ... Father will ... Her majesty's wishes ... Pádraig Bocht will help,' she stuttered.

A tear filled her eye. Ralph was saddened to see her crying, but he was glad to see her begin to return to her old self.

'I know you are confused. Father will know what to do,' he replied, hoping that his father would escape from the castle.

'Is father ... Is queen Talutu?' she choked, shivering. 'I don't know what I am saying ... I feel as if I am two people,'

Ralph put his arm around her shoulder.

'You are two people, but you will soon be one person. You will soon be Meave Devereux again.'

They walked behind the Black Guards, entering the Great Hall, and saw Lord Devereux sitting at the oak table addressing his adviser Hugh LaMitchel and his army commander General Fredrick Sinnolt.

'We will fight to the end. They will not defeat us,' he said, adjusting his sword belt. 'If Pádraig Bocht is dead we will fight now and remember him later. My children are still in Tír na Leasa. We must enter through the Lake of Fire and recover the pearl.'

Hugh LaMitchel raised his hand. Lord Devereux nodded his head.

'They say there are many passageways and tunnels beneath the lighthouse, perhaps we can find them,' replied Hugh LaMitchel.

Lord Devereux eyed General Fredrick Sinnolt

'Arm every able man in the castle. Have troops of cavalry search for Pádraig Bocht's body before the sea claims him.' He paused for a moment. 'We must be strong! We must not despair. Many will die for the few who will survive.'

His two senior commanders left the Great Hall without replying. As he walked through the doors of the Great Hall, unaware of Queen Talutu, General Fredrick Sinnolt remembered the day Arthur arrived with his news of Citbeag. Hugh LaMitchel was silent with fear, knowing that there was no advice he could give to Lord Devereux that would help him save DunFaythe Castle.

Lord Devereux in full armour stretched out his long thick arms and looked towards the door. Ralph expected him to say, 'Ralph you're home,' but he turned towards the blazing fire and stared into its flames.

Meave ran to her father. 'Father! Father! We are home!' she cried, grasping his arm.

Lord Devereux did not feel Meave clutching his arm or hear her shouting, so she sat on the tiled floor beside the fire and sobbed.

Queen Talutu moved towards the centre of the Great Hall.

'So this is the lord, who thought he could defeat Leasa. This is the lord, who dared to think that he could defeat me,' she said, raising her voice.

'He … will defeat you,' replied Azaromel, trying to figure out a way to kill her.

'Ah Azaromel! You have spoken,' she said, sneering at him.

Ralph looked at Meave sitting by the fire and remembered that it was not so long ago that he had sat by that fire with Meave on stormy nights, listening to Old Alesia telling stories of ghosts and ghouls that haunted

DunFaythe Castle. Queen Talutu raised her arm and pointed a webbed finger at Lord Devereux, closed her eyes and opened her mouth wide.

'Do not kill him yet,' cried Kcirtap. 'Reveal yourself. Let him see and hear the power of Leasa.'

The queen lowered her arm and looked down at Kcirtap, standing beside the giant Azaromel.

'Yes! I shall reveal myself before I destroy him and the traitor Azaromel. He shall see his children before he dies. He shall see the Queen of DunFaythe before he dies.'

Azaromel reached out and grabbed Kcirtap's throat with his giant fingers and lifted him from the tiled floor.

'I'll kill you now. Do you wish to humiliate his Lordship before he dies?' he said, squeezing Kcirtap's neck.

Kcirtap's eyes closed, as Azaromel's fingers tightened. His wizened face began to shrink; the scales on his face fell limp.

'Release him! Or I will destroy these human children,' cried Queen Talutu, pointing her webbed finger at Meave.

'Release him Azaromel,' pleaded Arthur. 'She will kill Meave!'

'You would not kill me ... Oh! Majesty,' sobbed Meave 'We are ... of the same blood.'

Azaromel released Kcirtap, who dropped to the floor.

Kcirtap struggled to his feet and fell back on his knees.

'Show them the power of the pearl Oh! Queen,' he croaked, caressing his throat.

Meave stood up from the fire and approached Queen Talutu.

'You would not destroy me Oh! Queen,' she repeated.

'You are not of our blood. Your blood is tainted with human weaknesses. We needed you to recover the pearl. Don't you ever think that you could become one of us. Don't you ever think that you have any affinity with Tír na Leasa,' replied Queen Talutu, in a sneering and dismissive voice, looking down at the half human, half fish girl.

'Who ... am I?' pleaded Meave. 'What have you done to me? I don't want to be a fish girl.'

'You are a weak human,' replied Queen Talutu, raising her chin and lowering her eyes.

'Meave is my sister,' cried Ralph, as a wave of pity for Meave rolled through him. 'She will be Queen of DunFaythe one day.'

'I might have some use for her some day,' said Queen Talutu, 'as a messenger between my dominions on the land and under the sea. Yes! She would be useful. She does have some talents that may prove beneficial to us. Return to your father, human!'

Meave looked at her father, staring into the flames, unaware of what was happening around him, and then sat on the cold floor beside the fireplace, rolling her body back and forth. Ralph ran to Meave.

'You will be queen,' he said, trying to reassure her. ' ... Queen of DunFaythe.'

Meave raised her head, and Ralph saw that she had returned to her human form. She had no scales on her face, and her nose had returned to its human length. He remembered, as he held her hand that Meave was conscious of her long thin nose, but he was happy to see this nose replace the uneven bone of her fishy face.

'You are coming back to us,' he said, touching her arm. 'Look ... You are almost human again.'

Meave gripped his hand tightly.

'I never want to see or hear of Leasa again,' she sobbed, feeling her face with her fingers.

Lord Devereux moved away from the fire and examined several charts, spread across the oak table.

'Reveal yourself Oh Queen!' screamed Kcirtap, 'and let us be done with these creatures. You have the pearl! You have the castle! We are victorious!'

Arthur stood in silence trying to decide whether he should tackle the queen or die trying. Azaromel struggled to free himself from the Black Guards.

'Remember Kcirtap,' he pleaded. 'Remember you are from a line of royalty! Remember your ancestors, who were philosophers and teachers.'

Kcirtap stoked his bruised neck with his finger and pointed a shaking arm at Azaromel.

'My ancestors wasted generations talking and debating about the morality of conquest. Queen Talutu is fulfilling our destiny. We are superior beings. We have known that for a thousand years. When these humans were living in mud huts, we were building pyramids in the East and the West of this planet. Queen Talutu ... is a true and noble queen ... a warrior queen!' he cried stamping his feet and gasping with anger.

Azaromel could see that Queen Talutu's fingers were glowing, and an orange halo encircled her face.

'Kcirtap, I will make you my adviser. You are truly a wise old sage,' she said.

'A great honour Oh Queen to serve in any capacity,' replied Kcirtap, bowing his head.

Pádraig Bocht shuffled over to the long table, sat on a wooden chair, pressed his elbows into his knees and rested his chin in his hands.

'What do you want Oh Queen?' he cried, thinking he saw her features soften and hoping that she would be merciful 'What will it take to save Lord Devereux and DunFaythe Castle?'

'You have kept the pearl from us for generations,' she screamed, gliding towards him.

'We did not know that the pearl was in the castle,' pleaded Pádraig Bocht.

'If we had -'

'Do not listen to him,' shouted Kcirtap. 'He is trying to bargain with you. He is - '

Queen Talutu raised her arm.

'You will be my slaves, your children will be my slaves. You will sign a pact that will bond the next ten generations to me as slaves. Then I will spare his life,' she said in a cruel, jeering voice.

Pádraig Bocht closed his eyes and moaned. Azaromel freed himself from the Black Guards and rushed towards the queen. Arthur seeing his chance followed Azaromel.

'We will never be your slaves!' he cried, lunging at her.

Six of the Black Guards immediately tackled them. Arthur and Azaromel collapsed like felled trees at the queen's feet. Two of the Black Guards raised their comb swords and looked at Queen Talutu, who nodded her scaly head. The Black Guards took deep breaths, tightened their grip on their comb sword, knowing that one swipe would take Azaromel's and Arthur's heads clean off their shoulders.

'Wait a moment Oh Queen!,' said Kcirtap, raising his bone cane. 'Let them see the power of the pearl before they die. Let them know the awesome power that they are trying to fight against.'

Pádraig Bocht went down on his knees and prostrated himself in front of the queen.

'We will be your slaves. Do not destroy the Devereux line. Do not kill his lordship or his family. We did not understand the power of the pearl. If we had known such a power was in our midst we would have returned it to you and acknowledged you as our queen,' he said, staring at the wooden floor of the Great Hall.

Ralph could not believe what he was hearing.

How could Pádraig Bocht surrender so easily? There had to be a way to defeat this monster. Meave sobbed by the fire. Pádraig Bocht lay face down on the floor before Queen Talutu. Azaromel and Arthur were pinned to the ground waiting the order for his execution. Lord Devereux continued to study his charts, unaware that his life was being debated, unaware that his enemy was only a few paces from him. Ralph glanced at Kcirtap. He had thought that Kcirtap was a kind old fish man, who had looked after the Lost Children and wanted to destroy Queen Talutu. It was all a lie. He had been deceived. Instead, he was the queen's loyal subject.

Queen Talutu placed her foot on Pádraig Bocht's prostrate head.

'You are weak, human. It is time your master was able to see his queen,' she hissed.

The Black Guards waited for their order to strike. Queen Talutu reached into the satchel, dangling from her shoulder and removed the pearl. She held it in her hand and watched the slow pulse of the pearl bounce a shadow across the room. She then rubbed it delicately like a witch would caress a crystal ball. Ralph felt a tingling sensation pass through his body. Lord Devereux turned from his charts.

'What is? ... Who is? ... How did?' he stammered, reaching for his sword, when he saw the gathered group standing before him.

'Do not bother with your sword, Devereux,' said Queen Talutu. 'You will not need your weapon anymore,' and she exhaled a squeaking laugh that reverberated around the Great Hall.

'Father!' shouted Meave and ran and embraced him.

'They want to kill you and make slaves of us,' she said, burying her face in his cloak.

Lord Devereux's eyes moved form Queen Talutu to Pádraig Bocht to Azaromel and Arthur and finally to Ralph, pausing for a few moments, trying to make sense of what he was seeing.

'You may kill me now,' he said, pushing back his shoulders. 'My army will fight to the last man. Future generations will destroy you. You will never make slaves of us.'

Ralph felt proud that his father was standing against her.

Queen Talutu laughed, and then caressed the pearl.

'Your lighthouse keeper,' she said, pointing to Pádraig Bocht on the floor, 'will be happy to be our slaves.'

Lord Devereux felt an anger rise in his chest.

'Whatever - '

'With your permission,' said Kcirtap, bowing low. 'Surely, Oh Queen it is time to show them what the pearl can do, what you can do.'

Queen Talutu cradled the pearl in her hands like a mother would hold a new-born baby; her eyes moistened.

'I will show them your power,' she whispered, removing her foot from Pádraig Bocht.

'Before I destroy Colclough Devereux, he first must see your power. I will then destroy him and enslave his people,' she screamed.

'Yes my Queen,' replied Kcirtap swaying back and forth, supporting himself with his rib stick.

Queen Talutu removed her hands from the pearl. All eyes watched the pulsing orb, as it floated in front of them then rising until it reached the bubbly ornate ceiling of the Great Hall. Darkness descended on the room. The pearl stopped pulsing, and a silver pillar of light beamed down from it. Queen Talutu stretched out her arms to embrace the shining column, as it moved towards her, as if she was pulling it with an unseen rope. She then stepped into the light and looked up directly at the pearl and almost disappeared into the translucent whiteness. The beam of light changed colour to a light warm orange. Ralph could feel the warmth on his face, as the pillar of light turned into a pillar of flames.

'Are you watching, Colclough Devereux?' screamed Queen Talutu, as the flame wrapped around her arms and washed her face with its firey substance.

'Do you see?' she shouted, watching the flames dance down her body. 'You are looking at the source of everlasting life. You are looking at the source of infinite power.'

Lord Devereux stood speechless. Meave squeezed his arm. Kcirtap raised his arms above his head.

'It is time? Oh Queen. It is time?' he chuckled, and he did a little dance about the floor. Ralph thought that Kcirtap was going insane. Quite suddenly a change came over Queen Talutu's face. Her defiant look disappeared and was replaced by a howling scream. The scales on her face started to melt and drip from her squirming face like blobs of hot molten fat. Her cloak began to burn.

'Kcirtap! Kcirtap!' she screamed, clawing at the sides of the column, finding that she was imprisoned in the scorching furnace. The pearl was keeping her for itself. 'What is happening? I am burning! ... The pearl! ... I am burning!'

Flames and sparks burned along her arms and down her legs. She opened her mouth and emitted a mournful scream, 'Kcirtap! ... Help me Kcirtap! ... Why? ... Why?' she howled.

Kcirtap move towards the flaming pillar.

'Why! Why!' he cried, laughing and jumping up and down waving his rib stick above his head. 'Because your greed and arrogance has no bounds. Did you not know that you could only stand under the pearl once? To stand under the pearl a second time shows that you are not worthy of its power, and therefore you must die ... That is why I urged you to show them the power of the pearl,' he said, giggling like a child, who had received an unexpected present. 'The only way I could destroy you, before you destroyed us all ... I could not kill you ... You were invincible ... Only the pearl could destroy you! ... Only your greed could destroy you!'

'Kcirtap!' she screamed. You have betrayed me'

'I have not betrayed you,' answered Kcirtap, tapping his rib stick on the timbers of the Great Hall. 'You have betrayed Leasa.'

'Kcirtap ... Kcirtap ... Kcir...' she wailed.

The flames engulfed her body like a twig of kindling thrown into a coal fire, and she began to shrivel and shrink and then crumpled to the base of the furnace. Queen Talutu raised a charred finger in a gesture of defiance. A muffled scream rang around the Great Hall, and she melted into a pile of hot ashes. All that remained was a smouldering heap of smoking bones.

The blazing column softened to a beam of light and then retreated into the pearl. The pearl descended from the ceiling and rested beside the smoking remains of Queen Talutu. No one spoke. No one moved. All stood and wondered about what they had witnessed.

'It is ... done,' cried Kcirtap, falling to his knees before the smouldering pile on the floor. 'Now we must wait for Citbeag.'

A company of soldiers, hearing the roar of the pearl furnace and the screams of Queen Talutu, burst into the Great Hall. The Black Guards, stunned by the demise of their queen, threw their weapons to the floor.

'Take them away,' cried Pádraig Bocht, as he dragged himself to his feet, trying to regain his composure.

* CHAPTER SIXTEEN *

Citbeag's Revenge

A white seagull circled DunFaythe Castle.

'What have you done?' he might have said. 'Where is the lighthouse?'

Ralph watched the white seagull from the rocks, swoop low over the ruins of the lighthouse. The warmth of the early morning summer bathed his face. He found it difficult to believe that he was actually at home, and Queen Talutu was dead. At any minute he expected to see an Orca or battle shark surface through the waves.

Lord Devereux, walking along the battlements, noticed the seagull. He was certain that Citbeag would come for the pearl and seek revenge for the death of his half sister. The seagull distracted Pádraig Bocht, as it fluttered into the courtyard, its screeching lament burrowed into his wavering spirit. He looked up from the ancient manuscript he was reading.

Kcirtap, watching the sea from his tower window, saw the seagull land in the courtyard. He knew that he had to return to Tír na Leasa. Arob would be visible in twelve hours. But he had agreed to stay and help them defeat Citbeag. He was convinced that Citbeag would attack soon.

Arthur stood on the battlements above the castle gate waiting for Citbeag. He had been there since Queen Talutu was burned in the pillar of fire. He would not eat; he wanted to lead the attack on Citbeag's monks. The serpent still haunted his soul. He did not see the seagull.

Azaromel walked along the beach, trying to dream up a plan to defeat Citbeag and was sure he would attack from the sea. Feeling the early sun water his eyes, his tired legs struggled to carry him across the soft sand.

Meave sat beside a blazing fire in the Great Hall, watching the pearl. Kcirtap had placed it in a wooden trunk, and four soldiers stood guard. Through cracks in the wooden trunk she could see the pulses of the pearl pushing daggers of light across the floor. She promised herself that she would never return to Tír na Leasa and did not care what happened to the pearl. She could smell the charred bones of Queen Talutu lying in a low pile beside the wooden trunk. She was trying to make sense of the events of the previous evening, as she replayed in her mind what had happened. Thoughts and images came to her in flashing spasms – the pillar of fire! – the burning queen! – Kcirtap dancing! – Pádraig Bocht lying on the floor! She had fallen exhausted into her cot, her mind numbed. She slept for twelve hours. Her first thought on awakening was to rush down to the Great Hall to see if the queen was really dead. She asked about Ralph and was told by one of the guards that he had arrived in the Great Hall at first light and was now down at the ruins of the lighthouse.

The door of the Great Hall opened. Meave raised her head and saw Pádraig Bocht, silhouetted against the dry light of the morning, approaching her. He paused for a moment, glanced at Queen Talutu's charred bones then knelt down beside her. She could see heavy veins beneath his pale skin and folds of wrinkly skin hanging from his sunken flat eyes; a coating of grey, musty red and orange hairs covered his chin. He smelt of smoke, and she felt a crushing tiredness pass through her, when it crossed her mind that he might ask her to go with him.

'Citbeag won't attack us now that we have the pearl and Kcirtap is with us,' said Pádraig Bocht. He felt a surge of hope rise in him. Yet a nervous worry that he could not explain, tugged at his senses. She saw a glimmer of relief in his eyes, but noticed that he had aged, and his body had shrunk, and his reeking breath forced her to avert her gaze.

'Kcirtap will have to leave us soon. He needs the pearl to return to Arob,' she said. 'And he'll return to Leasa soon and bring the pearl with him.'

Pádraig Bocht stood up and looked at the trunk.

'How will he travel to the planet?' he asked, remembering how Meave had solved the prophecy.

'I don't know,' answered Meave. 'Ralph might know. The fish people came from Arob thousands of years ago. They built the pyramids of Egypt and other pyramids that we don't know about … Dochas Mountain is a pyramid.'

'Do you know when he is leaving?' asked Pádraig Bocht, rubbing his bristled chin with his fingers.

'When the planet Arob is visible in the sky. It is only visible every five hundred years. Such an event cannot be missed,' answered Meave.

'I will talk to Kcirtap,' muttered Pádraig Bocht and slouched away towards the door of the Great Hall. 'Hello Pádraig Bocht,' said Ralph, entering the Great Hall.

'Ralph!' answered Pádraig Bocht, as he passed through the doorway.

'He sounds a bit cheerful,' said Ralph, approaching Meave, surprised that Pádraig Bocht had acknowledged him.

'He thinks that he can convince Kcirtap to stay with us,' she replied, watching Pádraig Bocht leave the Great Hall.

'Don't be sad,' said Ralph, trying to sound cheerful. 'Queen Talutu is gone, and we are home, and you are human again. We have the pearl, and we will never have to return to Leasa again.'

Meave stood up and approached the pearl trunk half expecting it to burst out and rise to the ceiling.

'Kcirtap will be leaving with the pearl soon, and Citbeag is still out there, waiting for revenge. He must know that Queen Talutu has been destroyed,' she said, her bottom lip trembling, looking down at the trunk containing the pulsing pearl.

Ralph skipped towards the trunk and watched pulses of light escape and bathe Meave's tired face.

'Maybe he will return to Leasa. Anyway we have the power of the pearl. He will not dare attack us yet,' he said, again trying to cheer her.

Meave looked into Ralph's eyes and was happy to see the fire of his optimism flicker again.

'When Kcirtap returns to Leasa with the pearl we will be ... alone and ... defenceless, won't ... we?' she asked, pressing her hands into her armpits

Ralph could see tiny lines stretch across her forehead and noticed that her eyes had changed to a dull grey colour.

'Father and Pádraig Bocht will be prepared for any attack,' he answered. 'Remember we are at home now. Let's forget about Citbeag and war.'

'It's not easy to forget,' she said, sighing.

'Have you seen the lighthouse?' asked Ralph, trying to change the conversation. 'There's nothing left except a pile of ancient stones and a stench of rotten seaweed.'

'No, I have not been outside today. Let's go outside now and walk the beach like we used before all this happened,' knowing that Ralph was trying his best to cheer her up.

Ralph was delighted to hear Meave expressing an interest in walking.

'We'll go now?'

The two children left the castle and passed through the courtyard to the beach path; no market, no stalls, no shouting vendors, only soldiers, spears and arrows. They saw Pádraig Bocht and Lord Devereux standing on the battlements with Arthur.

'You see,' said Ralph. 'Father and Pádraig Bocht are planning to defeat Citbeag.'

As they strolled along the beach path Meave enjoyed the warmth of the sun on her face and examined her cheeks and hands several times, making sure that she had no gills or fish features.

'You are human again,' said Ralph, watching her pull her nose and stroke her face.

'It's not a nice feeling being fishy,' she replied eyeing the lapping waves breaking on the beach.

Lord Devereux watching his children from the battlements above the castle gate stroll towards the beach, ran his bulbous fingers through his thick mane of hair.

'He's leaving tomorrow or the next day and will be bringing the pearl with him,' he said, turning to Arthur and Pádraig Bocht, standing beside Lord Devereux, who also had their eyes fixed on the children.

'Citbeag needs the pearl and he also will want to avenge his half sister's death, despite any enmity there was between them,' said Arthur.

'*Sea*. Aye!' answered Pádraig Bocht. 'We have a choice. We can allow Kcirtap to leave with the pearl, and then we'll be at the mercy of Citbeag's hordes, or we can force Kcirtap to remain here and then he will have to use the pearl to defend the castle.'

Lord Devereux remained silent for a few moments, remembering that it was Kcirtap, who destroyed Queen Talutu and saved the castle.

'We owe him our allegiance,' he said 'We can't force him to stay. He wants to return to his ancestral homeland.'

Arthur, still watching the ocean, leaned against the chiselled stone of the rampart.

'No surrender! No surrender!' he insisted.

The serpent still floated, smiling before his eyes.

Pádraig Bocht watched the tide rise on the ruins of his lighthouse. He knew that Lord Devereux would not betray Kcirtap.

'Let me talk to Kcirtap,' he said, swallowing deeply. 'Perhaps I can convince him to remain with us a little longer.'

'There has been enough talk. Destroy the pearl and throw Talutu's bones into the sea,' answered Arthur.

Lord Devereux ignored his comments walked towards a stairwell to the courtyard, hesitated, looked back at Pádraig Bocht and saw how shrivelled and undernourished his appearance had become.

'Eat some wholesome food, you are beginning to look like a living skeleton.'

Pádraig Bocht looked down at his bony fingers and remembered a day when he was strong and handsome. Now, he did not care how he looked; he believed that he was a walking dead man and food would not make any difference to his appearance.

'I will find Kcirtap.'

He waited until Lord Devereux had reached the courtyard and then descended the stone stairway. Dragging himself through the courtyard he struggled against a sharp pain in his chest and a panting, wheezing sound grating in his throat.

'Must be near the end of my time,' he mumbled, walking past groups of soldiers, sharpening their swords and blacksmiths arriving with bundles of lances reinforced with metal tips. He struggled through a narrow door of a tower and then puffed his way up a curling stairway until he reached Kcirtap's cell.

'I have been waiting for you,' said Kcirtap, examining a chart made of crushed sea petals, as Pádraig Bocht pushed open the heavy wooden door. Kcirtap placed his finger on the image of a planet and then followed a gold shaded line that brought him to a symbol that looked like the sun rising over a dark blue sea.

'When the sun goes to sleep tonight, Arob will be in the heavens, and I must leave your land and take the pearl with me,' he said, turning to Pádraig Bocht.

Pádraig Bocht dragged himself over to the table, examined the chart and let his thumb fall on the sun symbol.

'If you leave with the pearl Citbeag will destroy us,' he pleaded, bending over the chart .

'You have suffered much for this land,' said Kcirtap, raising his head from the chart and looking into Pádraig Bocht's dying eyes.

Kcirtap was beginning to lose his fish features; the scales were fading from his face.

'I have,' replied Pádraig Bocht, a blank expression crossed his cramped face. 'But it will soon be over, and I can die in peace.'

Kcirtap lifted a small vessel from the table and handed it to Pádraig Bocht.

'Drink,' he said 'It will numb some of the pain.'

'What is it?' asked Pádraig Bocht, examining the spotted green fluid in the vessel.

'Drink,' answered Kcirtap.

Pádraig Bocht felt the sweet honey taste spread though his body, as he gulped the liquid. For a moment he forgot about the heavy weight of pain, crushing him.

'Drink it every hour,' said Kcirtap. 'It should alleviate your aching body.'

'I'm grateful for your concern,' gasped Pádraig Bocht, as a finger of soreness crossed his chest, reminding him of his weakness, 'but I must beg you to remain with us.'

Kcirtap moved away from the table and looked out at the bright sea through a long vertical window cut into the stone wall of his cell.

'Citbeag will be here before the sun sets this day. He craves the pearl and wants to conquer DunFaythe and Leasa and maybe our ancestral home on Arob. If I leave now he will destroy DunFaythe Castle. But if I remain we will have a chance of defeating him together,' said Kcirtap, staring at the sea.

Pádraig Bocht was glad to hear him say that he might remain in the castle with the pearl and was hoping that Kcirtap would use the power of the pearl to defeat Citbeag. Kcirtap turned to Pádraig Bocht.

'You are a courageous and loyal human. I know that you have made decisions and taken actions that you might have regretted. You have read the three books and sacrificed yourself for your kinsmen.

'I had no choice. I am the Guardian of the Lighthouse … my duty … my destiny,' replied Pádraig Bocht and a grating cough rose in his throat.

'There is a fourth book,' said Kcirtap, 'The Book of Deireadh … If it is read completely in one day it will restore you to yourself,'

'Where … is this book?' demanded Pádraig, raising his voice, in desperation. 'I have searched for it, but I have failed to find it.'

'It's in the three books that you have read,' answered Kcirtap, like a teacher revealing an answer to a difficult problem.

'But I have read the three books. That is why I am such a miserable wretch.'

'Yes you have,' said Kcirtap, trying to encourage him 'but you must read them again and this time only read every tenth page of each book within four hours,'

'That's impossible,' croaked Pádraig Bocht, clutching his rib cage. 'Took me three weeks to read each book.'

'If every tenth page is removed from each book and placed in a single volume you will see that the amount of script on each page is quite small, and it is possible to read such a volume within four hours. You do not have time to read the Book of Deireadh now. First we must prepare for Citbeag's arrival. Then if we survive you will have a chance to restore yourself.'

Pádraig Bocht felt a glimmer of hope lighten the mountain of despair bearing down on him.

'If it is possible I will attempt this reading. But I cannot attempt such a task until Citbeag is defeated. Surely you can use the power of the pearl to defeat him.'

Kcirtap leaned against the table and closed his eyes.

'I can't use the pearl!' he cried. 'If I stand beneath the pearl I will be burned alive.'

Pádraig Bocht fell back against the cold wall of the cell. A low lamenting moan escaped from his throat.

'I thought you were of the royal line,' he cried. 'I thought you were the Guardian of the Pearl.'

Kcirtap opened his eyes and turned to Pádraig Bocht with an anguished look.

'I am the Guardian of the Pearl as you say. But I cannot stand beneath the pearl. I cannot use its power.'

'We are doomed!' cried Pádraig Bocht. 'He will destroy DunFaythe! He will destroy us all!'

A slow creeping tiredness crawled over his body. He felt a thousand years old.

'All a terrible waste … What can I do? … How can I tell them we are doomed?' he sobbed.

'I do see a flicker of hope,' answered Kcirtap.

Pádraig Bocht saw the word 'hope' before his eyes, like a man lost in a snow blizzard sees a flicker of a warm light in the distance. He tried to repeat the word 'hope'. His lips would not move; his aching body cried out for sleep.

'Say that … again,' he mumbled. 'Say that word again.'

Kcirtap reached towards Pádraig Bocht and handed him the vessel.

'Drink more!'

Pádraig Bocht felt the sweet liquid lighten the weight of his thoughts.

'Tell … me about … hope,' he gasped, gripping the vessel with both hands.

Kcirtap paused for a moment.

'You must rest. Lie on this cot for a while.'

Pádraig Bocht lay on the cot and placed his hands across his chest, draping his hood across his forehead, like a waked corpse waiting for burial. Kcirtap dragged a small reed chair to the side of the cot and sat down facing him.

'Tell me about hope,' groaned Pádraig Bocht.

Kcirtap joined the fingers of his webbed hand together like a high priest praying.

'There is one amongst us, who may stand beneath the pearl and soak in its power. There is one amongst us, who is a direct descendent of the Queen's of Leasa - '

'No!' screamed Pádraig Bocht, jumping from the cot and standing over Kcirtap, swaying on his feet.

'No! We can't! We can't ask her to stand under the pearl. I have pushed her into the Lake of Fire. I have brought her through the chambers beneath the lighthouse. I forced her to return to Leasa with the pearl. I cannot ask anymore of her. She has suffered enough … She is just a young girl.'

Without speaking another word he left the chamber.

Kcirtap stood up and examined the chart on the table, moved to the window and looked down again at the ruins of the lighthouse.

'Citbeag will brush them aside,' he thought, staring at hundreds of soldiers lined along the sea wall.

Two figures standing on the ruins of the lighthouse attracted his attention. He narrowed his eyes and saw Ralph and Meave.

'We should return to the castle,' suggested Meave, as a familiar inkling of fear rose in her. 'We've been here too long.'

Ralph was enjoying his freedom.

'Soldiers surround us! We could not be in a safer place. The soldiers are ready for combat,' he replied, pointing towards the sea wall.

He sat on one of the scorched rocks that once was part of the lighthouse wall and looked along the beach. Then he felt a tug on the fishing line he was holding.

'I have one,' he cried, pulling a large crab from the sea.

'Let it go.' said Meave. 'I have seen enough sea creatures.'

Ralph released the fishing line and allowed the crab to fall back into the sea.

'He will have a nice meal today,' he said, chuckling. 'There were four pieces of chicken on that line.'

He looked out to sea and tried to imagine what was happening in Tir na Leasa – were they waiting for her to return? – did they know she was dead?

'Shall we walk along the beach and see what the soldiers are doing?' he asked, hoping that Meave might forget her troubles, if he could divert her attention.

Meave was not listening. She was watching a solitary hunched figure stumble down the path from the castle.

'Is ... that ... Pádraig Bocht?' she asked, her voice shaking.

Ralph turned towards the castle.

'It is. He's probably coming to inspect the ruins of his lighthouse,' he replied, trying to stop Meave fretting.

Meave felt a coldness pass through her body.

'Where are you going?' asked Ralph, as she scampered off the rocks and jumped onto the soft sand of Trá Bán.

'I am going to see what he wants. I don't think he is coming to view the lighthouse,' she called back.

Ralph turned to the sea again and fastened some pieces of raw chicken to a fishing line. A shiver passed through his body. He turned to look towards the castle and saw Meave and Pádraig Bocht walking up the path from the beach, deep in conversation. He guessed that Pádraig Bocht wanted her to look at some old chart or obscure writing in an old book.

The afternoon passed pleasantly for Ralph, who was enjoying being by himself by the sea and was able to forget about Citbeag and Tír na Leasa, whilst he caught many crabs with his fish line. He kept them in a shallow rock pool, brown scary crabs, small starry crabs and large flat-backed crabs. The soldiers continued to patrol the sea wall and the battlements of the castle. Ralph reached into the rock pool several times and grabbed a crab by its claw. He then brought the crabs down to the beach, lined them up and let them race to the incoming tide. The soldiers cheered, when they saw ten crabs racing to their freedom into the waves. A large crowd gathered around Ralph, as he fished for crabs and deposited them in the rock pool. The soldiers wagered on which crab would win each race to the sea.

'The long legged one,' shouted one soldier.

'No!' cried another, 'the flat backed crab with the barnacles on its claws.'

The crabs scuttled sideways and backways. Some ran away from the sea, others tried to return to the rock pool, many found their freedom in the frothy waves. Ralph giggled when a large clawed crab pinched a soldier, as he tried to direct it towards the incoming tide.

'Doesn't want his freedom,' cried the soldier. 'Wants to race again.'

'Back to your duties,' boomed a voice.

It was Azaromel.

'Do you not realise that we are at war? I will have you all whipped for leaving your posts!' he roared.

The soldiers dispersed and returned to the sea wall.

'We were only racing crabs,' said Ralph, straining his neck to look into the eyes of the giant Azaromel.

'I know,' replied Azaromel, touching his chin, as if he was deep in thought, 'but we cannot be complacent, even for a few moments.'

Azaromel was fully armed; he held a broadsword in his left hand, a bow was strapped across his chest. He carried a short sword in his belt. He stuck the broadsword into the sand and leaned on it. The sword bent and quivered under his weight. Ralph took a step backwards thinking the sword was going to snap. Azaromel pressed down harder on the sword and looked out to sea. Ralph watched the bending sword while studied the sleeping sea.

'I think you should return to the safety of the castle,' he said, looking out to sea.

'Your sword!' cried Ralph.

Azaromel did not answer him. He continued to look out to sea. The bend of the sword increased like the string of a bow being pulled by an archer.

'Azaromel' cried Ralph, running behind the giant, expecting the sword to snap into two pieces.

Azaromel leaned towards the sea. Ralph peered at the bent sword using Azaromel's huge body to protect him and then saw a mist was rising from the sea.

'Azoramel ... I - ' he stuttered.

Azaromel suddenly lifted the broad sword from the sand, spun around and picked up Ralph up like a sack of potatoes and ran from the beach towards the castle.

'What's happening?' screeched Ralph, struggling to stay in Azaromel's grip.

'They are coming,' panted Azaromel. 'Coming from the sea.'

He stopped running when he reached the side of the sea wall.

'Go now!' he shouted, dumping Ralph in the sand 'Run to the castle!'

Ralph struggled to his feet and watched the soldiers, shouting and running on the sea wall. Then he felt a sudden warm draught of hot air beat against his face, as the gorse pit burst into flames. A spurting orange inferno shot into the cloudless sky, and he could hear the crackling and spitting of the dry gorse bushes as, the fire consumed them.

'What are you waiting for?' asked Azaromel, pointing towards the castle. 'Go now!'

'Where is Meave?' asked Ralph, ignoring his orders.

'She is with Pádraig Bocht. Go to the castle, or I will have two guards bring you there,' ordered Azaromel, and he turned and looked out to sea.

Ralph stood his ground and watched the flames rise above the sea wall, and he smelt the sweet burning whiff of blazing gorse.

'What did he want with her?' he asked, feeling the smoke sorely watering his eyes.

'I don't know,' shouted Azaromel, pushing Ralph in the direction of the castle. 'They will soon be here,' he said, climbing a stairwell of the sea wall.

Ralph ran up the path to the castle. The battlements were filled with archers ready to unleash a shower of arrows.

'Hurry!' shouted two soldiers, closing the castle gates. Ralph felt a sharp pain in his side and gasped for breath, as he collapsed on the ground after sprinting through the castle gates, moaning and creaking, as they slammed shut. Looking around the courtyard, he saw the chaos of an army preparing for an assault. Soldiers sweating under armour; soldiers' faces white with fear; captains trying to encourage and calm the ranks, as they gathered in the courtyard or filed to their positions on the castle walls.

'What about Azaromel on the sea wall?' he cried, watching the soldiers seal the castle gates.

'He's on his own now. He is the first line of defence,' said a soldier, struggling up a stone stairwell with his burden of arrows.

A soft grey mist descended on the sea wall. Dark storm clouds shaded the bright sky.

'Stand and be ready,' shouted Azoramel at the line of grim faced soldiers. 'He will not pass through the fire.'

A deep silence fell on the ranks of soldiers. Each one knew that he was there to fight to the last man and would not be returning to the castle. A gush of cold sea air brushed against Azoramel's face, and he felt drops of rain patter on his body armour. The smoke from the gorse fire billowed around the sea wall stinging the eyes of the soldiers.

'Hold your positions,' shouted Azaromel. 'This is only the beginning.'

The storm clouds emptied a torrent of rain on the sea wall. A wind arose and blew into their faces forcing them to seek shelter behind the wooden battlements. Azaromel stood firm, as the soldiers cowered. He knew that the deluge of rain pouring down on the burning pit would extinguish the fire. For several minutes the rain fell on the sea wall, the beach and the gorse fire. Then quite suddenly it stopped. The clouds dispersed and the wind died to a gentle breeze. The soldiers stood in amazed silence. Gaping down at the pit they saw a smouldering black hole, filled with sodden charred gorse branches.

'What's happening?' asked one wet soldier, standing beside Azaromel.

'The work of Citbeag,' answered Azaromel.' He has just shown us that he has power that we will never understand. He can control the elements.'

What do we do now?' asked the soldier, white with fear.

'We wait,' said Azaromel, knowing that worse was to come.

Soldiers watched the sea, others turned and looked in the direction of DunFaythe Castle and many gazed into the sky.

'Where will he come from?' one asked,

'From the sea,' answered Azaromel, remembering his wife and children.

A white seagull flew over the sea wall. 'You are all waiting. Look! What you have done to this land?' he might have asked.

Azaromel noticed the white seagull swooping low along the shore, and he saw it fly towards the incoming tide, hover for a few moments, as if it was thinking about going out to sea and then glide directly towards the castle. He knew Citbeag was coming – even the sea birds were trying to escape.

'Did you hear it?' cried a soldier. 'Sounds like thunder.'

A rolling droning sound touched their ears.

'Not thunder,' answered another. 'There is not a cloud in the sky.'

'What is it?' one cried, looking towards the castle.

'Where is it coming from?' asked another, feeling his tongue tighten in his mouth.

They felt a slight vibration in the sea wall that tingled their toes and then spread up their legs.

'The wall is moving,' cried one.

'Look!' cried another. 'The tide is going out.'

They saw the sea retreating, leaving behind a large expanse of wet glistening sand. The droning sound increased. The wall shook and then swayed back and forth. Soldiers clung on to the wooden stakes, supporting the wall. The sea began to churn and bubble and spit.

'The sea is rising,' screamed a soldier. 'What's that on the horizon?'

A grey churning wall of water rose on the horizon.

'It can't be a wave,' answered another, 'There is no wind,'

Azaromel stood and watched the sea rising on the horizon.

'It is a wave,' he cried, 'and it's coming towards us.'

'Run to the castle or drown in Citbeag's wave,' he screamed.

The soldiers did not look to the sea again. They clambered and jumped down from the sea wall and ran towards the castle. Azaromel remained on the wall and watched the crest of the mountainous wave as tall as the castle, rolling towards him. The droning wave roared like a thousand charging bulls, as it approached the beach. Soldiers screamed and cried, as they tried to escape to the castle. The giant wave fell on the beach, bounced and gushed, as it hit the soft sand. The crest of the wave rose into the sky and for a moment, a precipice of frothing, fizzing water stood before the sea wall. Then the roaring sea cliff collapsed and a sheet of angry sea covered the sea wall and lifted it high, like a surging rapid would carry a floating twig. Soldiers were carried like leaves on the wave; some tried to swim, others held onto their shields, many were dragged along and battered against the trees and hedges dotting the landscape.

Lord Devereux watched the destruction of his sea wall and his soldiers from the walls of the castle. He saw them being swept towards the castle, poles and timbers of the sea wall gushed along in the torrent of ocean. Soldiers struggled to find a piece of debris to cling to, and Lord Devereux was certain that the wave with its load of timbers and drowning soldiers was going to swamp the castle.

'We can't escape,' he cried, his face wide with horror 'We will all drown.'

The deafening flood approached the castle. Soldiers on the wall panicked, jumped into the courtyard or tried to open the castle gate.

'It's over,' moaned Pádraig Bocht, leaning against the castle wall, watching the mountain of sea cascade toward him. 'Meave cannot help us now. Citbeag wants to kill us all. His thirst for revenge is going to destroy us.'

'It's stopping,' cried the soldiers, in disbelief watching the wave slow down and stop its charge about twenty paces from the castle. Lord Devereux almost laughed with relief. The wall of water stood stationary in front of the castle, as if it was pressing against a gigantic Bsamaki skin window. It looked like a giant blue drape with folds of speckled froth, topped with a border of sea foam, a watery drape waiting to cover the castle. Pádraig Bocht strained his neck to look up at the crest of the wave, almost directly above his head.

'What now?' he whispered.

Arthur with his sword in his hand, stood mesmerised by the wave. The thought that there were serpents in the water forced him to retreat from the wall. The soldiers stood speechless, gaping at the wondrous, but terrifying sight before them. Then they saw a movement at the base of the standing wave. A black oval shape appeared in the wave, close to the ground, increasing in size until it was more than the height of two men. The shape burrowed into the wall of water and cut a passage into the standing wave.

'What's happening now?' asked Lord Devereux, trying to understand what he was seeing.

The soldiers on the castle walls could clearly see that the earthen floor of the passageway was dry, not a trace or stain of water remained.

'A tunnel into the sea,' gasped one of them.

The soldiers waited. Lord Devereux waited. Kcirtap, who had just arrived on the battlements, waited and watched. Without warning a large figure dressed in a monk's habit, his face covered with a cowl, emerged from the tunnel. Behind him and pointing lances at his back were six more monks. They pushed the large figure to the ground and removed his cowl.

'It's ... Azaromel,' cried Lord Devereux.

Arthur on hearing Azaromel's name conjured up the courage to return to the battlements.

'You will not die alone, Azaromel,' he shouted to his old friend

They could see bruises and scratches on his face and neck. His hands were tied behind his back. One of the monks drew his sword and placed the sharp edge of the blade on Azaromel's neck. The other five monks stood around him and faced the wave tunnel.

'What are they doing?' asked Pádraig Bocht, watching the monks.

'They are waiting for their master,' answered Kcirtap, knowing that his old friend, now his enemy was about to appear.

A glowing white light filled the opening of the tunnel.

'He's making a grand entrance,' shouted Kcirtap, shaking with anticipation.

Fifty more monks filed from the tunnel, each carrying a lance and formed a corridor from the tunnel to the kneeling Azaromel.

'A public execution!' cried Kcirtap. 'He intends to kill Azaromel, and we can do nothing about it.'

The light at the mouth of the tunnel increased in intensity and changed from white to blue and finally to blood red. A small figure appeared carrying a silver skull and wearing a monk's habit, the cowl pulled back high on his forehead. Kcirtap looked at the face of the figure, and to his astonishment he saw his own face staring at him. Lord Devereux expected to see the stained face of a monk, but instead he saw his own ruddy image staring back at him. Arthur howled in despair, when he saw the serpent's laughing face staring at him. The soldiers screamed and shouted. Each one saw his own face, when he looked into the eyes of the figure carrying the silver skull. Pádraig Bocht saw his own wretched dying image, his sunken grey eyes, his yellow protruding teeth and his dry flaky skin peeling from his hooked nose.

'Citbeag is with us,' said Kcirtap, looking at his own face staring back at him.

Ralph came scampering up the stairwell and stood rooted, his legs would not move.

'It's like … like Tír na Leasa … the sea is everywhere!' he stammered.

'Who is that?' he asked pointing a trembling finger at Citbeag 'Why has he no face? Why has he no nose or mouth? How can a person have a head with only eyes?'

'What … do you see?' choked Pádraig Bocht. 'Do you not see your own face, when you look at him?'

'No, I see a skull with two eye sockets.'

'So that is what he is,' said Pádraig Bocht, decisively, as if he had solved a great mystery. 'A living skeleton.'

'Azaromel! … What are they doing?' asked Ralph, pointing at Azaromel.

'Azaromel … will die, and they will take the pearl. They might … destroy DunFaythe,' sighed Pádraig Bocht, pressing his bare knuckles against the battlements and wishing he could think of something that could prevent the inevitable.

Ralph saw his father and Kcirtap in deep conversation.

'Where is Meave?' he asked, looking down on the courtyard.

'She will be here soon,' replied Pádraig Bocht, watching Citbeag raise the silver skull above his head.

'I have come for the Pearl of Neamhann,' whined Citbeag, as he rotated the silver skull.

Lord Devereux raised his hand and four hundred archers positioned along the castle wall, filled their bows with iron tipped arrows. He lowered his hand. Like a whistling wind the arrows left their bows and streamed towards Citbeag. He did not move or retreat, but lowered his head like a prisoner awaiting execution. Lord Devereux waited for him to fall. Citbeag did not fall. The arrows went through his body. He did not cry or scream. The arrows formed a circular cluster in the earth behind him. Lord Devereux stared in bewilderment. Silence descended on the baffled ranks of soldiers on the castle wall.

'This cannot happen,' cried Lord Devereux. 'He is a demon! We cannot harm him.'

Citbeag raised his head and looked up at Lord Devereux, who saw his own face looking at him. A cruel trembling smile formed on his lips.

'I will ask you one more time,' he croaked. 'Bring me the pearl.'

'Kcirtap! Kcirtap!' hissed Lord Devereux's face from beneath the cowl. 'You are standing with my enemies. You have betrayed me like you betrayed my half sister.'

Kcirtap looked down from the battlements at the face staring at him, and saw Queen Talutu's scaly face gloating at him.

'Kcirtap, why did you let me burn?' she cried. 'Why did you?'

Queen Talutu's face faded, and the shadow of a skull filled the cowl.

'Her spirit is in him,' gasped Kcirtap, supporting himself against the castle wall.

'Queen Talutu is dying fast, but he has some of her power.'

'We are one,' cried the voice of Citbeag.

Queen Talutu's face appeared again like a mist filtering through a curtain.

'Destroy them!' she screamed.

The skull face appeared again.

'She's in his body, but she's dying,' cried Kcirtap, pointing at Citbeag.

Lord Devereux raised his arm, and two hundred lances left the arms of his soldiers. They pierced Citbeag's body and embedded themselves in the ground behind him. Lord Devereux stood looking at himself; standing dressed in a monk's cowl and saw himself raise the silver skull. An orange fireball jumped from its mouth and hit one of the towers of the castle.

'I should have destroyed you, when I had the chance,' screamed the voice of Queen Talutu.

The tower shook for a moment and then collapsed in a cloud of dust and rubble. A second fireball left the skull and dropped on the battlements to the left of Lord Devereux, Kcirtap, Ralph, Arthur and Pádraig Bocht, like a giant cinder falling from a coal fire. The wall creaked and groaned, and then three hundred soldiers screamed and roared, as they fell amongst the stones of the crashing wall. A third fiery ball crashed into the castle wall to their right. Five hundred soldiers were crushed, as it demolished the wall into a cloud of burning bricks and choking sulphur. A fourth ball of sulphurous fire crashed into the castle gate and burned it to black cinders. They were left standing on the battlements above the gate of DunFaythe Castle. To their left and right lay the crushed and mangled bodies of his soldiers, scattered amongst the ruins of his castle walls.

'I will give you the pearl,' he screamed.

'I am waiting,' hissed Citbeag.

'Kcirtap, bring the pearl to him,' ordered Lord Devereux.

Kcirtap stood firm.

'If we give it to him, he will destroy us,' he answered.

'Bring it to him,' cried Lord Devereux, looking down at his own face wrapped in Citbeag's cowl.

Kcirtap scampered down the stairwell, scuttled along the courtyard and entered the castle. Ralph stood beside his father trembling and wondering where Meave was. Pádraig Bocht stood watching Citbeag. His chest heaved; he could not control his twitching bottom lip.

'There she is!' shouted Ralph, pointing to the castle door.

Meave glided into the courtyard, holding the pearl out in front of her. She wore a white linen gown that trailed behind her and the veil on her head filled like a sail, as she crossed the courtyard, followed by Kcirtap.

'Meave is carrying the pearl!' cried Ralph.

She made her way toward the castle gate, her eyes staring into the distance and her dark sprinkled with glistening sea shells. She did not look at the piles of scorched granite on each side of her that once made up the castle walls. As she neared the castle gate Lord Devereux screamed, 'Meave! Meave! What are you doing? You will be killed! He will kill you! '

Meave did not hear Lord Devereux's pleas or look up at him, as she passed through the smouldering gateway.

'Kcirtap!' shouted Lord Devereux. 'What have you done?'

Kcirtap looked up at Lord Devereux for a moment and then continued to follow behind Meave, as she approached Citbeag. The monks formed a line behind him, their lances pointing towards the gateway. Azaromel, still on his knees, raised his head.

'Meave! You should not be here. This is no place for you,' he pleaded.

Meave did not reply. Azaromel saw her eyes close and watched her extend her arms and offer the pearl to Citbeag.

'Come and take your pearl,' she said, opening her eyes.

She looked at Citbeag and saw a grey toothless skull in a monk's cowl. Citbeag moved towards her.

'But I warn you. The pearl is not for you,' she said.

Meave saw Citbeag's skull face open its mouth. A screeching laugh swirled around her.

'Kill her! Kill!' screeched the voice of Queen Talutu, as her face re-appeared and then was replaced by Citbeag's skull.

'I am of the royal line of Leasa,' said Citbeag, pointing his finger at Meave 'It is my destiny, my birth right.'

'If it is your destiny, take it!' she replied, taking a step closer to Citbeag.

Citbeag hesitated for a moment.

'Who are you?' he asked, in high pitched voice 'Who are you to tell me to take the pearl?'

Meave lowered her arms and placed the pulsing pearl on the earth at her feet and stepped back.

'Take it! Take it!' moaned the distant voice of Queen Talutu.

'Seize her, and let us end this farce,' squeaked Citbeag.

Five of the monks ran towards Meave. She raised her arm and opened her hand. They saw a blue spot in the shape of a seashell. They then felt a force lift them from the ground and throw them screaming into the sea cliff frothing behind them. Meave closed her hand.

'Who are you?' demanded Citbeag 'You are but a weak human.'

Meave opened her hand again. Citbeag saw the rest of his guard lifted and thrown into the depths of the sea cliff. Meave saw the blank sockets in his skull face fill with tiny circulating serpents, and she felt a stinging pain across her forehead.

'Close your eyes,' screamed Ralph, from the castle walls.

Meave turned and looked up at Ralph, standing beside his father on the battlements above the castle gates, smiled and turned back to look at Citbeag.

'Burn her! Burn her!' whined the almost inaudible voice of Queen Talutu.

The serpents in Citbeag's eyes rotated faster. Meave felt weak and hot, her chin fell to her chest.

'You will see who is master,' hissed Citbeag, raising his arms above his head.

Meave fell to her knees. She looked at the pearl in front of her and saw Ralph's smiling face. She saw Pádraig Bocht's pained image appear beside Ralph's and the Lost Children crying out to her.

'You will be my servant,' squealed Citbeag, as his fingers began to glow.

The serpents twirled and danced, moving towards her. Azaromel raised his head.

'Use your power, Oh Queen,' he whispered. 'You have the power.'

Meave heard the word 'queen'. She remembered Tír na Leasa and Ralph's words; 'You are Queen Meave.'

She remembered the last line of the prophecy: 'DunFaythe depends on her.'

Opening her eyes, she saw the pearl change colour. A sea green filtered through it, and she felt a warmth fill her body.

'Do it now,' urged Azaromel, raising himself with one arm.

Meave opened her mouth, and Citbeag felt a light breeze touch his bones. 'What is this?' he laughed. 'Are you blowing me kisses?'

He did not speak again. He did not move again. The serpents vanished. The light breeze blew about his bony body. He screamed when he felt his feet and body slowly turn to stone. He tried to raise his arm, but it froze solid and remained stationary, pointing at her and pleading with her like the crooked branch of a hawthorn tree. The sockets of his skull face filled with sand and solidified. Citbeag stood rigid and silent like an ancient statue. The cliff of sea behind him cracked and groaned, as it turned into rock. Meave raised her arms, and the rock face shattered and crumbled with a roar into a dust cloud which settled on the earth before the castle like an early morning mist.

Meave could see the sea again. She looked down at Azaromel and then turned and looked up at the castle battlements. She could not speak. She looked again at the rock statue of Citbeag, pointing his crooked arm at her. A tingle of warmth rose from her feet. She fell to the ground like a withered flower. The pearl stopped pulsing.

The white seagull dropped beside her and rested his graceful wing across her sleeping eyes. 'There will be peace now Oh Queen,' he might have said.

* CHAPTER SEVENTEEN*

Queen Meave

Meave awoke at midnight. She looked around to see where she was, trying to figure what had happened.

She could still see the frozen rock statue of Citbeag pointing a twisted angry arm at her – was it a dream? She remembered seeing Azaromel smiling. Then she remembered being picked up and being carried towards the castle. Before she fell into a deep sleep she heard the deafening cheer of soldiers chanting her name and Ralph's words echoing around her mind, 'You are a queen Meave.'

Above her she saw the familiar ornate ceiling of the Great Hall. Warm shadows flicked about the walls, and the soft heat of a coal fire warmed her face. Four guards stood near her; she felt warm and safe. Ralph was lying on a sheepskin on the floor beside her cot close to the fire. He saw her open her eyes.

'You did it,' he whispered.

'Did what?' she asked, staring at the shadows and then raising herself up on an elbow and looking down at Ralph.

'You stood under the pearl,' he said, his eyes filling.

'I don't remember much of what happened. Pádraig Bocht told me that I was his last flicker of hope. I remember seeing the pearl rising and floating above my head. The last thing I remember was sitting beside the fire, my fingertips were numb. Kcirtap then came through the door and asked me to bring the pearl to the castle gate. I didn't know, then that I possessed the power of the pearl. When I was speaking to Citbeag I felt that I was someone else. I felt as if I was watching myself, speaking, and the pearl was telling me what to do.'

'You have saved us all,' cried Ralph, standing up and stretching his arms above his head.

'Is it over now?' she asked, remembering Queen Talutu and Citbeag.

'Yes I think it is,' answered Ralph. 'But we will have to rebuild the castle walls. Citbeag nearly destroyed the castle.'

'So it did happen,' said Meave, yawning, not yet fully convinced that she had not dreamt it all.

'Yes, it did happen,' answered Ralph. 'Citbeag turned to stone. You turned him into a stone statue! He is still standing outside of the castle gate pointing his bony fingers at us.'

Meave lay back in the cot, a peaceful tiredness wafted through her body.

'Where is Kcirtap?' she asked, rubbing her eyes.

'He's gone. He has taken the pearl back to Leasa. A battle ark rose from the ocean and took him away. Before he left he told us to look to the heavens one hour after midnight'.

Kcirtap stood in front of Queen Talutu's throne holding the pearl in his hand and looking around at the assembled fish men. They chatted, nodded their heads and looked at each other. All of them wore white shark skin tunics and ankle length sea moss breeches. The Council of Leasa stood in the front row waiting for Kcirtap to speak, the elders of the city behind them. The officers of the Knights of Leasa were placed at the rear of the assembled throng.

'We have it at last,' he cried, raising the pulsing pearl above his head. 'I have spent one hundred and fifty years looking for this pearl.'

Silence fell on the expectant audience. He struggled to hold the pearl whilst they admired and wondered at the pulsing light.

'We can return to Arob now,' he cried.

'Are they gone?' asked an old fish man, his unkempt withered seaweed hair hung to his shoulders.

'Yes,' answered Kcirtap, lowering the pearl and placing it at his feet, as tears filled his narrow eyes. 'Queen Talutu was burned and Citbeag was turned to stone.'

He paused for a few moments trying to take in the enormity of the occasion.

'It's difficult to believe that we are rid of both of them,' one of them then cried.

'The young human girl destroyed him. She is of our blood,' he continued, remembering Meave.

'How was Queen Talutu destroyed?' asked a voice from the crowd.

'Her greed destroyed her. She stood under the pearl a second time, and it consumed her,' answered Kcirtap, smirking.

A loud whistling cheer rose from the gathered fish men.

'Silence please,' urged Kcirtap. 'We don't have much time. Arob will be visible soon.'

'Will the young human return with us as queen?' asked another voice.

'No,' answered Kcirtap. 'Meave will remain with her human family. I think it is time that the royal line of Leasa ceased to govern Leasa.'

The fish men applauded and stamped their feet.

'I think it is time that the Council of Leasa ruled Leasa,' whispered Kcirtap, snuffling.

Let's go outside,' suggested Ralph, wishing to see Meave smile again. 'Father is waiting for us.'

'Yes I think we will,' replied Meave, jumping off her cot and walking towards the door of the Great Hall.

'They are all waiting for you,' said Ralph, skipping after her.

'There are others also waiting for you Ralph,' croaked a voice from the shadows.

Ralph turned to see Old Alesia.

'Come with me now both of you,' she said, waving her bony stick of an arm.

The children did not hesitate. They followed Old Alesia through a narrow door and into a darkened chamber.

'Why are we here?' asked Ralph 'There are no torches - '

A torch flamed, and a cheering chorus bounced and echoed about the chamber.

The children smiled and laughed, happy bright faces, glowing in the torch light.

'The Lost Children!' cried Ralph.

'We are home!' shouted Oisin.

Ralph searched the beaming faces for the source of the voice. His gaze settled on a handsome, fair-haired youth, wearing a white linen tunic and leather breeches.

'You are not the same Oisin from Leasa,' he cried, and he put his hand into the pocket of his breeches, laughing, as tears welled in his eyes.

'Old Alesia's potion ... I forgot to give it to you,' he sniffled, taking out the small bottle.

'I gave it to them ... I found a second bottle,' said Old Alesia, displaying the phial in her crooked fist.

The children gathered around Ralph and Meave. The young girl, who had pleaded with Ralph in Tír na Leasa, held his hand.

'You said you would come back for us, and you did,' she said, grinning and pulling him towards a long table stocked with roast ducks, freshly baked bread, apple pies and tankards of lemon juice.

'We will never forget your kindness. We are not the Lost Children anymore. Come and eat with us. We have a lot to talk about.'

He forgot about his father and Citbeag's statue, as the savouring aroma of the waiting meal induced in him a pleasant dizziness.

'Yes! Let's eat. Let's eat real food,' he said, grinning and took a few steps towards the table then hesitated and looked at Meave, who smiled and shook her head.

'On second thoughts perhaps we can eat later, and then we can have a long chat about Tír na Leasa and the pearl. Father is waiting for us,' he said.

He looked again at the group of children and then nodded to Old Alesia, who for the first time smiled, showing a single tooth standing in the centre of a dark gummy mouth.

They left Old Alesia and the children and entered the Great Hall, passed down the corridor and stepped through the castle door. Meave hesitated, when she entered the courtyard. Before her stood two lines of soldiers forming a guard of honour, leading to the scorched castle gate, each holding a torch. All heads turned and smiled, when they saw her. In perfect unison they dropped to their knees and bowed their heads.

'What are they doing?' asked Meave, surprised by the soldiers' actions.

Ralph gave her a gentle nudge, and she walked slowly down the passage of kneeling soldiers. She stopped for a moment and looked down at one of the soldiers, who raised his head and then his torch.

'Your Majesty,' he said. 'You are our queen.'

'Queen Meave!' shouted a soldier to her left.

'Queen Meave!' shouted another.

A chorus of, 'Queen Meave! Queen Meave!' rose into the starry moonlight night.

Ralph gave her another gentle nudge. Meave walked down the corridor of torches, looking into the eyes of each soldier and wondering was she really a queen – she didn't feel like a queen.

On reaching the end of the guard of honour she turned and faced the soldiers. Without realising what she was doing she raised her arm. The soldiers stood up and gathered before her.

'Say something to them,' whispered Ralph.

'I thank you for your allegiance,' she said, without thinking.

The soldiers cheered and raised their torches. She then turned and looked at the battlements above the arch of the castle gate. She saw her father, Azaromel and Arthur smiling. Her father beckoned her to come and join him. Meave climbed the stone stairwell to the battlements, feeling a dizzy excitement pass through her body.

Kcirtap, gripping the pulsing pearl, scampered down the passageways of Dochas Mountain.

'Are you sure, you know what you are doing?' asked the old fish man with withered dry seaweed hair, struggling to keep pace with Kcirtap

'I'm not sure what I am doing,' panted Kcirtap. 'But I am confident the pearl will succeed.'

Down they went; they panted and coughed; they stopped and rested and leaned on each other.

'Don't ask any more questions,' gasped Kcirtap. 'When the Dubh Pit receives the pearl, Dochas Mountain will return to Arob.'

The old fish man opened his mouth to speak. Kcirtap pushed him ahead of him.

'No more questions,' he snapped, impatiently 'No questions!'

'It … can't be far now,' croaked the old fish man, holding his chest with a webbed hand. 'I can smell the putrid pit.'

They struggled around one last corner and then stopped and looked at the still silent lake of black liquid, stretched out before them.

'What is - '

'No questions,' answered Kcirtap, hoping his plan would succeed, as he placed the pearl at the edge of the pit, pushed it gently and watched it roll away from him and bobble over the rocky floor. They heard a soft plopping sound, as it dropped into the murky blackness.

'It's done?' gasped the old fish man, in a breathless wheezy voice.

'It … is,' answered Kcirtap. 'Now let us return to the Throne Room. They are waiting for us.'

They were about to turn and leave, when the surface of the pit began to change colour from deep black to soft grey and then to bright orange. As they stared at the pit transforming itself they did not know whether they should be excited or terrified. Kcirtap could hear a sizzling sound rise from the bosom of the orange liquid, bubbles popped on its surface and spit out droplets of burning orange treacle. One landed beside Kcirtap's foot and hissed, as it touched the cold stone carving a crevice in the cavern floor. The bubbling increased, and Kcirtap felt a hot draught of air brush his face.

'Time we left,' he shouted and ran back up the corridor, followed by the old fish man.

Ralph walked behind Meave, as she glided up the stairwell to the battlements. To his left and right he could clearly see under the flat white moon, the rubble and debris of the castle walls. Meave reached the battlements and was greeted by the outstretched arms of her father.

'You are a queen,' he said, hugging her. 'And you Ralph are the brother of a queen.'

Ralph puzzled over what the brother of a queen was called – was it duke or baron?

'You have both saved us,' continued his father. 'We owe our lives to you both.'

'Father,' gasped Meave, 'you are crushing me.'

Ralph grinned, as Lord Devereux released his grip of Meave, who stepped back and looked up into her father's eyes.

She then saw it to the left of his smiling face.

'Look there it is,' she cried pointing to the moon. 'There is the planet Arob. Kcirtap said it would appear!'

Everybody turned and looked to the sky. They could see a brilliant crystal hanging in the blackness beside the wide whiteness of the moon. Ralph looked at his father then Meave and was about to say something when the movement of soldiers down in the courtyard attracted his attention. The cluster of torches parted and a figure walked from the castle door towards the battlements. Ralph could not see its face. The soldiers gathered around the figure, as he approached the stairwell.

'Who is that?' asked Ralph, watching the figure cross the courtyard.

Lord Devereux turned from gazing at the new planet and put his arm around Ralph's shoulder.

'Come and meet your new queen,' he shouted to the figure, ascending the stairwell.

When he reached the top of the stairwell, Ralph noticed that the figure was wearing the full armour and breastplate of a knight, his emerald green cloak reached to his ankles and his long flaxen hair was tied back with a strip of soft leather. As the stranger stepped onto the battlements, a flicker of a smile formed on his lips. Meave looked into his kind green eyes and felt there was something familiar about this stranger. The thin nose and slightly protruding chin reminded her of someone. The tall knight knelt before her.

'You are our queen now. Meave!' he said and bowed his head.

She wondered how he knew her.

'You may rise, stranger. Have we met before?' she asked, looking towards her smiling father.

'You have met this knight many times,' he said, with a glimmer in his eyes. 'Arise Pádraig Bocht. But we will never call you Pádraig Bocht again. Pádraig Bocht is gone forever.'

'Pádraig ... Bocht,' stammered Meave. 'How?'

'I read the Book of Deireadh,' said the knight rising from his knees. 'Kcirtap told me what to do. I am now restored to who I was.'

Ralph moved closer and touched his arm.

'It is difficult to believe that you are Pádraig Bocht,' he said, noticing that there was no smell of fish from the knight.

'That is not Pádraig Bocht,' said Lord Devereux, grinning. 'He was Pádraig Bocht. But that time is over.'

'Who are you?' asked Ralph, looking up at the knight.

'Ask my queen,' answered the knight, in a deep quiet voice.

Meave looked into his green eyes and then looked at the new planet.

'You will be known as Pádraig Dochas,' she said, trying to add a regal tone to her voice. 'You are the one who suffered most, and you were the one, who was prepared to live in misery to find the secrets of the books.'

Pádraig Dochas smiled and looked out at the moonlit sea.

'Is it time?' he asked, smiling, and he remembered, when he was wretched Pádraig Bocht.

'Time for what?' asked Ralph, thinking that he might have missed out on something.

'It is - '

They all heard the whistling sound, and saw the apex of Dochas Mountain rise silently from the sea like a basking shark. There was no wind or tremor as it ascended, breaking the waves without a ripple. They saw the flickering lights of Dochas Mountain, as a giant pyramid grew from the placid and silent sea and rose into the sky like a dark cloud specked with diamonds. No one spoke; they all watched the mind stopping sight. It climbed higher and higher into the cloudless night. Within seconds it had faded into a spot of brightness, and then it disappeared.

Azaromel, standing beside Arthur, listening and watching, moved towards Meave.

'Kcirtap has brought them back to their ... homeland,' he said in a quiet sad voice, and he knelt before her. 'But now I have a new homeland and a new queen.'

Meave placed her hand on the expanse of his bald head.

'You do not have to kneel before me Azaromel,' she said.

'Is it over now?' asked Azaromel, rising to his feet and looking at Arthur.

Arthur grasped his sword and gazed down at the ruins of the lighthouse.

Yes it's over. I don't see the serpent anymore. It died with Citbeag and Talutu. We will easily recapture GuaireDun. When they discover that their master is dead, and the chalice is gone back to Arob they will have no heart to fight. Yes! Azaromel, my friend, it is over- '

Arthur then faced Pádraig Dochas.

Pádraig Dochas turned his gaze to Meave.

'What now? Oh! Queen.'

Meave looked to Ralph, who was still staring into the sky.

'Well, Ralph,' she asked, knowing that was one question he could not answer.

Ralph glanced at his father and then Meave.

'I think we will have to rebuild the lighthouse,' said Ralph, smiling.

'I guess we will,' answered Meave, feeling a tightness in her eyes.

'And you will be the Guardian of DunFaythe Lighthouse!'

www.ingramcontent.com/pod-product-compliance
Lightning Source LLC
Chambersburg PA
CBHW020652030726
47498CB00002B/475